Praise for Ted Dekker and Erin Healy Novels

"A perfect 10 packed with romance, politics, scandals, and non-stop suspense."

—Laura Wilkinson, Olympic gold medalist
and world champion diver

". . . no less fast-moving than the Christy Award–winning author's solo prose, but also more gripping as it plunges into the life of a woman with frayed and painful family relationships . . ."

—*Publishers Weekly*

"Dekker and Healy form a powerful team in crafting redemptive suspense. *Kiss* is emotionally absorbing and mentally intriguing—don't miss it."

—Lisa T. Bergren, author of *The Blessed*

"The human brain could actually be the real final frontier—we know so little about it and yet it drives the world as we know it. So when authors like Erin and Ted bravely explore these mysterious regions, going into complex places like memory and soul and relationships, I become hooked. The creativity of this suspenseful story is sure to hook other readers as well. Very memorable!"

—Melody Carlson, author of *Finding Alice*
and *The Other Side of Darkness*

"Dekker and Healy prove a winning team in this intriguing, imaginative thriller."

—James Scott Bell,
best-selling author of *Try Darkness*

Burn

Burn

TED DEKkER
& ERIN HEALY

THOMAS NELSON
Since 1798

NASHVILLE DALLAS MEXICO CITY RIO DE JANEIRO

© 2010 by Ted Dekker and Erin Healy

Published in Nashville, Tennessee. Thomas Nelson is a registered trademark of Thomas Nelson, Inc.

Published in association with Thomas Nelson and Creative Trust, Inc., 5141 Virginia Way, Suite 320, Brentwood, TN 37027.

Thomas Nelson, Inc., books may be purchased in bulk for educational, business, fund-raising, or sales promotional use. For information, please e-mail SpecialMarkets@ThomasNelson.com.

Scripture quotations taken from the King James Version and from the HOLY BIBLE: NEW INTERNATIONAL VERSION®. © 1973, 1978, 1984 by International Bible Society. Used by permission of Zondervan. All rights reserved.

Publisher's Note: This novel is a work of fiction. Names, characters, places, and incidents are either products of the author's imagination or used fictitiously. All characters are fictional, and any similarity to people living or dead is purely coincidental.

Library of Congress Cataloging-in-Publication Data

Dekker, Ted, 1962–
  Burn / Ted Dekker and Erin Healy.
    p. cm.
  ISBN 978-1-59554-471-1
  1. Romanies—Fiction. 2. New Mexico—Fiction. I. Healy, Erin M. II. Title.
  PS3554.E43B87 2010
  813'.54—dc22

2009041504

Printed in the United States of America
09 10 11 12 WC 7 6 5 4 3 2 1

"*The part of us that has to be burned away is something
like the deadwood on the bush; it has to go,
to be burned in the terrible fire of reality, until there
is nothing left but . . . what we are meant to be.*"

— MADELEINE L'ENGLE

PART I

Ignition

1

Salazar Sanso raised his binoculars and looked out over the edge of the steep drop into the rosy New Mexican desert. Through the lenses, he scanned the modest-sized Gypsy camp that hugged the base of the mesa. A brisk river separated it from twenty-five tents, which were a combination of sturdy canvas and tall wood-stilt frames. Surrounding them were several trucks and a few SUVs, larger tented structures that Sanso assumed were facilities for school and medicine and whatnot, and a large meetinghouse, which perhaps had once been a rancher's barn.

Children played a game of kickball outside the camp, within shouting distance. A group of men smoked near the entrance of the meetinghouse. Few women in sight. Most of the community—a hundred, hundred twenty-five by his estimation—were tending their carnival booths in Albuquerque for the weekend.

"Tell me what I'm looking for," Sanso said to the woman standing next to him. A hot breeze played with his hair and stroked his close-cropped beard. The wind's uncharacteristic humidity predicted an approaching thunderstorm. In the west, crowding clouds positioned themselves between the camp and the fading afternoon sun.

"She's fairer skinned than the rest, and taller." Callista held out a grainy picture of a young woman in blue jeans. Sanso lowered the binoculars and took it. Long hair the color of New Mexico's red rocks dunked in water, dark eyes, tan skin, heart-shaped face. She was walking with another woman who wore a long skirt, arms linked, heads inclined toward each other. "They say she is the daughter of a *gají*."

"A non-Gypsy woman? But Jason Mikkado is the leader of this group."

"Which is why they tolerate her. She's his only surviving child after all. But he has difficulty . . . controlling her. If he weren't the *rom baro*, I think they'd have cast her out by now. They call her *Rom Ameriko* behind his back."

"But not hers?" Sanso smiled at the characterization. An Americanized Gypsy. Someone who could be counted among neither the Gypsies nor the outsiders, the *gajé*. It was a biting insult.

"She doesn't really care what anyone thinks of her."

"Good. She's younger than I expected."

"Seventeen. But don't be fooled."

Sanso winked at Callista. "Are you saying you and she are cut from the same cloth?"

"When I was seventeen I was worth cashmere. She's all denim. But she knows cashmere when she sees it. She aspires to cashmere. She and I could be . . . friends. Of a sort."

Sanso returned to his study of the camp and noticed a rusty sedan approaching from about a mile off, kicking up pink desert dust under the gathering gray sky. "Will she cooperate?"

"If I've judged her correctly." Callista paused. "She's more like you."

He wouldn't stoop to asking how much more. Did the girl merely share his love of fine food? Or did she possess his need to trample the barriers set up by family and culture, barriers that prevented one from reaching his full potential? When he was seventeen he turned his back on his wealthy South American family so he could become the lord of his own kingdom. His father and brothers wouldn't have allowed him to be anything more than a servant.

"You say that like it's a bad thing," he said.

"For her, it could be."

That was the truth, if she shared even half of his yearnings. "The exchange is still set for Tuesday?"

"Yes. One million dollars. We confirmed this morning."

"What do they suspect?"

Callista placed her hands on her hips. "They suspect that we suspect nothing."

The sedan, a dump of a Chevy, was speeding. Three hundred yards outside the camp, the car left the narrow dirt highway it had been traveling and made a beeline for the meetinghouse. The front driver's-side tire looked low.

The car kept up its pace through the perimeter and came to a skidding stop in front of the smoking men. The door opened and the driver stepped out, slamming the door.

Sanso homed in on the frowning face. Here was the denim girl, an outsider born on the inside, where he needed her.

Janeal Mikkado was wearing jeans. And flip-flops. Footwear the old-timers would disapprove of. Sanso already loved this child.

Her excuse for shoes flapped their way past the group of men. The eldest in the bunch averted their eyes. Sanso had always found this Gypsy quirk amusing: Everything above the waist was considered pure and good. A woman could bare her chest and no one would blink. But everything below the waist was considered dirty, impure, taboo. A true Gypsy woman should cover it up.

The youngest man in the gathering leered and leaned in toward Janeal, saying something that likely only she could hear. Quick as a striking rattlesnake, she jabbed him below his rib cage without breaking stride and proceeded into the meetinghouse. The man doubled over, holding his stomach, trying to laugh it off.

Yes, this girl was going to work out fine.

2

Janeal Mikkado stormed into the meetinghouse. From the outside, the building looked like little more than what it once had been: a large old barn, abandoned decades ago by an eccentric rancher who died without heirs. Janeal's great-grandfather had purchased the remote property, too arid for successful ranching, at auction for ten thousand dollars. The Gypsy *kumpania* led by Jason Mikkado returned to it every spring and stayed through the summer, doing business with the people of Albuquerque and entertaining narrow-minded tourists who thought Gypsies had no identity or culture outside of fortune-telling and magic tricks.

For this, Janeal hated the outsiders, the naive *gajé*. And yet she also loved the outside world, the promise of freedom and choice and opportunity. She toyed daily, hourly, with the idea of leaving this place.

If not for her father, she would leave right now, leave him behind with her boyfriend, Robert, and best friend, Katie, who said they were as curious about the world as she was but, when pressed, showed only feigned interest in it. They mocked her fascination as nothing more than a girl's childish fantasy, though they were never intentionally cruel.

Her father didn't know of the hopes she harbored, nor of the bitterness she sometimes indulged in; it soothed the loneliness of her most adventuresome self. Confiding these thoughts to him would be the same as turning her back on him after all he'd suffered. Of all the people she knew, he was the only one she truly loved. In the deepest, most honest sense of the word *love*, she understood it was something she couldn't define or identify outside of her relationship with him.

Not even the love she bore for Robert Lukin came close.

No, she hadn't found the courage to leave yet. It wasn't like she could go off and come home for holidays, as she heard the *gajé* her age did. Leaving the *kumpanía* would be synonymous with rejecting it—and everyone in it. Then they, too, would be free to reject her. Finally. Janeal didn't have any misunderstanding as to what the people of this community really thought of her.

Not that she needed it, but that gave her one more reason to hate them. They wouldn't allow her to belong if she'd wanted to.

Someday she would leave. Someday, when she knew she could endure not being welcome here ever again, when she knew her father would be able to endure it too.

Inside the building, Janeal hesitated at the sight of Mrs. Marković, who had appeared yesterday as the *kumpanía* prepared for the annual festival and asked for their hospitality for the weekend. She was ninety-eight, she said, though one of the elders said he'd seen her walk into camp straight out of the desert and didn't believe she was a day over seventy. At Jason's encouragement, she stayed with a young family at the edge of camp but spent the hottest hours of the day in the cool of this building. From the squat oak rocker by the front window, she gazed down the corridor between tents and observed everyone's comings and goings.

The woman's brown paper-skinned hands lay folded atop her gold-and-fuchsia-colored skirt. She wore her waist-length gray hair in front of her shoulders and hadn't stopped smiling since she arrived, showing off strangely healthy teeth.

But when Janeal caught her eye this afternoon, Mrs. Marković offered only a curt nod. A slight, short nod that seemed to yank the tablecloth off Janeal's thoughts, exposing them. Startled, Janeal shut down that part of her mind.

She turned right and took the stairs to the game room two at a time. If she was lucky, Robert would be finished with his work already, and she could download her frustrations on him while she had his complete attention.

Unlike the outside of the structure, which her father said was best left dilapidated to avoid attracting troublemakers while the *kumpanía* wintered in California, the interior had been renovated and built out into a practical, attractive community space that included a social area, a conference room, a kitchen, and her father's business offices. On the north side of the building, Jason Mikkado had added private living quarters.

Upstairs, he had transformed the old loft into a game room, which now ran all the way from the front of the barn to the back. The roof on each side sloped.

Janeal stopped climbing the stairs when her eyes broke the plane of the floor. She scanned quickly.

Against the left wall, on the floor that provided a ceiling for the kitchen and dining room, stood three old arcade games rigged to be played without coins or tokens.

Spread across the middle of the room were a pool table, a foosball table, and a Ping-Pong table. Café chairs surrounding chess and checker tables filled the rest of the floor.

The rectangular Tiffany lamp suspended over the pool table filled the room with a dull red ambiance.

No Robert. Janeal sighed and turned on the ball of her foot to go back downstairs. She placed her hand on the wrought-iron banister and felt a shock of electricity zing up her arm.

She flinched, let go, and heard the air crack behind her right ear all at the same time. She closed her eyes too, though she didn't register this until she opened them.

Her shadow stretched out in front of her and spilled down the green-carpeted stairs, swaying like a ghost clinging to her ankles, rocked by a strange red glow. Janeal turned around.

The Tiffany lamp was swinging gently.

She stared at the fixture for several seconds, trying to guess what could have set it in motion. No idea. Its arc shortened on each return until finally it was almost still again.

Without touching the handrail, Janeal went back downstairs, rubbing the palm of her hand. It still tingled.

She passed Mrs. Marković without looking at the old woman, though Janeal sensed the stranger's eyes on her. Janeal jogged through the gathering room, taking long strides directly through the rear doors and down a hall to her father's office. She burst in.

Her boyfriend jumped in his seat at her entrance and knocked over a Styrofoam cup of coffee at his right hand. "Man, Janeal. I wish you'd quit doing that."

"I do it often enough that you ought to be used to it by now." She grinned to take the bite out of her words and snatched tissues out of a box. Dabbing at the desk, she thought she shouldn't have said that. "I didn't mean to come barreling in."

"Of course you didn't mean to." Robert took a deep breath and righted the cup. "You barrel through everything without meaning to because that's what you do. You're a tornado."

She wondered why she bothered to rein in what she said when Robert wouldn't keep tabs on his own words. She scowled at him and took a step toward the door. He reached out and touched her arm.

"I'm sorry. That's not the best metaphor for what your family's been through," he said, not entirely apologetic. "I get that. But it's the best one I can think of for you." She crossed her arms. "Take it as a compliment."

She tried to read affection into his tone.

"Good thing there wasn't much left." She gestured to the empty cup.

"Good thing. Here, let me have that." He reached for the limp, wet tissues and she grabbed his hand, pulled him close for a kiss. He neither protested nor lingered.

Robert released her lips and leaned around her to toss the tissues in the trash. Janeal released his fingers and focused on her feet.

"So what lit a blaze under you today?"

She collected her thoughts. "Katie."

Robert laughed at her. Of course he would laugh. In Robert's eyes, Katie could do no wrong.

"What could Katie have done to annoy anyone?"

"Nothing. That's just it. Katie never ruffles anyone's feathers."

"You're looking pretty crazed."

"I'm not crazed, Robert."

He took her hands, reigniting her attraction to him. "So tell me what Katie *didn't* do that has you so upset."

Janeal sighed and supposed that one of the reasons she couldn't resist Robert was because he had this strange power to defuse her when she wanted to be inflamed. That and maybe because he loved her even though everyone else in the *kumpania* told him he shouldn't.

She was caught off guard by the possibility that his love for her was nothing more than his own rebellion against the *kumpania*. That could explain his wavering behavior of late.

She set the disturbing idea aside without completely rejecting it and leaned against her father's desk. Robert surrounded her feet with his and waited for her to explain.

He was her height but twice as broad. His brown skin made hers look alabaster white, though she had plenty of color in it. Robert's coarse black hair fell sloppily across his forehead and covered his brows. He had full lips and a square face—a handsome, true Romany.

"You should have seen the line outside her booth at the carnival."

"Yeah? She did well, then? She was nervous this morning about going."

"Nervous. You'd have thought she came out of the womb telling fortunes."

"So she's a natural." His smile seemed unnecessarily pleased.

"She's a fraud, Robert! Everything we do at these events is a fraud."

Robert dropped her hands and stepped back. "We've been over this. It's not fraud. It's entertainment. The *gajé* are always willing to part with their money for a little cultural fun. It's how we stay alive."

"Our *culture* is not about fortune-telling. It's about music and art and story—the *gajé* will pay for that too!"

"Not as much." Robert started stacking the papers he had been bent over when she had come in. He was nineteen and had been put in charge of managing the *kumpania*'s accounts—a tremendous statement of her father's faith in Robert's maturity and skill. "And since when did you think highly of our 'culture'?"

Janeal frowned. "Katie always said she would never stoop to this."

"There is no stooping going on here. Katie is pretty and has the voice of a siren. She's a model woman." Janeal hated it when Robert talked about Katie that way, even though she admired Katie's beauty herself. But he didn't have to make a point of things. "Not a person in this *kumpania* has ever had a bad word to say about her. Unlike . . ."

Unlike her. At least he had the presence of mind to stop himself. He tapped the edge of the papers to straighten them.

"She's doing her part to bring in funds for the group," Robert finished.

"She doesn't have to do it so well," muttered Janeal.

Robert straightened and caught Janeal's eye. "You hate it all anyway. Why do you care whether Katie tells a few fortunes for fun?"

"Because it reinforces what the *gajé* think of us. That we're cons. Swindlers. Vipers."

"Listen to you! You don't think any better of your own people. You're talking out both sides of your mouth, Janeal."

"I might like 'my people' more if they didn't reinforce their own stereotypes with this kind of behavior."

"If your food booth made as much money as that fortune-telling booth did, I don't think you'd be so upset."

Warmth flared in Janeal's cheeks. "That's not true."

"You know I'm right."

"You are so wrong."

Janeal turned toward the door, uncomfortable with the direction of the conversation. All Janeal wanted was a little sympathy, a little commiseration.

"I got a tattoo today," she muttered, not sure why she would bother to tell him at this point. Earlier, she thought he might have found it alluringly risqué.

Robert's eyebrows shot up. "You must have really been upset to do that."

"Would you stop with that already?"

"Let's see it, then."

She turned her leg sideways and hiked up the hem of her jeans. Above her left anklebone, right where her slender calf started to curve, was a tattoo of a flaming sun. Robert whistled his surprise and bent to touch it. She snatched her leg away.

"Your dad's not ever going to see that, right?"

"Not if you don't tell him," she whispered, dropping her hem.

Robert straightened.

"Maybe you should stop going to these things if they bother you so much. Don't attend the carnival. There's plenty of work to be done here at the camp."

"If I don't go, who will cook the *sármi*?"

Janeal's stuffed cabbage leaves were known even in other *kumpanías*. Her work in the kitchen was the source of the only praise she ever received from her people.

Robert leaned against the doorframe and crossed his arms. She tried to read his expression, but when she thought she saw annoyance there, she looked away. This conversation had not turned out the way she planned. He cleared his throat.

"Did you bring some back for me today?"

Janeal walked away, not sure if she was more disgusted with herself or with him. "Tomorrow," she said. Tomorrow she would probably have leftovers. Katie's booth had attracted three times as many patrons today, and five times the cash.

3

After the carnival troupe returned and supper had been served, Janeal kissed her father at the dining room table and went outside, leaving Jason with the advisers and close companions who usually took meals with their leader. The day had been profitable, and there was plenty of happy discussion to cover her quick exit.

She walked every evening atop the lowest mesa, which only took about fifteen minutes to climb. Often Robert or Katie or both of them came with her. Not tonight, though. Tonight she slipped out before either of them could ask her about going. Tonight she needed to work some things out in her own mind about Robert and Katie and her own future with this little traveling family.

A few short yards from the kitchen's rear door, Janeal took her favorite passage across the narrow river. She'd traversed the series of fifteen umbrella-size boulders so many times over the years that she could leap them in the dark without getting wet. On the other side, she leaned her body into the angle of the steep slope and started to climb. The air and the earth shared the scent of fresh rain, which had passed through before nightfall like a politician, quickly and with only enough substance to be convincing.

She did not want to stay put in this cycle of Gypsy life, spending summers in New Mexico and winters in California. She despised their way of earning a living, hustling the *gajé* for whatever money they would part with or settling for blue-collar work. This attitude made her an alien in her own community but wasn't enough to win the favor of outsiders, who scorned her because she was Rom.

Part Rom. She was fair enough that the average person wouldn't guess it, but when she went to the carnival, guilt by association was all the average person needed to convict her. And she resented what the others murmured about her mother, who was indeed a wife Jason had taken from among the non-Gypsies. But Rosa Mikkado's mind if not her body was Rom through and through. She had died fifteen years ago with Janeal's other siblings when a tornado ripped through their Kansas community.

Janeal's foot slipped on a skittering layer of loose rock, so she dropped to her hands until the earth stopped sliding, then resumed her climb.

Did she fit anywhere?

At the top of the mesa, she dropped to her bottom and swung her legs over the edge, looking down on her summer home. Interior lanterns had turned some of the tents into evening fireflies. A few families were building campfires outside. Someone had turned up a radio. With the weekend festivals at an end, tomorrow the camp would rest and play.

Maybe she'd sneak out. Drive to Santa Fe. If her little beater could get her there and her father wouldn't find out.

She heard a sound behind her. Footsteps on gravel. Had Robert come up another way, looking for her? He knew better than to follow if she was in one of her "moods," as he called these times. She resented that too—even her contemplative nature could be held against her in this place. She twisted her waist to see.

"Robert?"

Two people she did not recognize approached her. A woman, she thought, and a man. The sunset had faded, and one held up a flashlight directly into her face. She threw up an arm to shield her eyes.

"Janeal Mikkado?"

"Who's asking?"

"A friend of your father's."

A friend of her father's would come to the camp to inquire about her. Any other approach would be inappropriate. Even the *gajé* knew this.

"I doubt it," she said. She scrabbled to her knees, debating whether she ought to bolt. Curiosity and something else she couldn't name held her in place. The palm of her hand tingled where she had zapped it on the stairway banister.

The flashlight beam dropped, and the man laughed.

"You were right about her," he said, speaking to the woman but looking at Janeal. He handed the light to his companion and stuck his hands into the pockets of his dark slacks. In four long strides he put himself at the edge of the dark mesa but kept enough distance from Janeal to hold off any inkling that he meant her harm.

It was the first time she'd ever encountered a stranger up here, let alone one who knew her name.

From what she could see in the poor light, the man was younger than her father but much older than she. He was nicely dressed in belted slacks and a button-front shirt. Long-sleeved, even though it was summer. Moonlight reflected off his shoes. A neatly trimmed black beard matched his neatly trimmed wavy black hair. It had been slicked back off his forehead and touched the tops of his shoulders. She smelled a sharp-edged spice and wondered if he styled his locks with clove oil. She wanted to touch his hair.

The desire startled her.

He was slender, handsome. Beautiful. In fact, more stunning than Robert— more delicate than rugged, more intellectual, she assumed. More powerful, or capable of commanding at the very least. She realized she was staring.

Something glinted in his earlobes. Diamonds. She'd seen plenty of those. Most of the men in her *kumpanía* wore such jewels to the carnivals, joking they were safest there among *gajé* who assumed the Gypsies were poor and their jewelry fake.

"Do you love your father?" The man's voice shocked Janeal out of her musings.

"What?"

"Do you love your father?"

The question was so unexpected that the easy answer escaped her. "What does that—"

"Maybe nothing. Maybe everything."

Janeal's own breath sounded like wind in a tunnel to her. "Of course I love him."

"Does your father love you?"

Janeal frowned, mystified.

"I guess you'd have to ask him."

"No. No, I don't. Children know when they are recipients of their fathers' love. Are you?"

"I—yes. What is this?"

"A verification of—"

"Who are you?" she asked. "And why are you here?"

He turned his eyes to hers for the first time, and she could not hold his gaze. She didn't believe he was angry at her, but his eyes were like spotlights that exposed her.

Exposed what? She had nothing to hide.

"I am Salazar Sanso. And I am here because I want you to save your father's life."

Alarm caused Janeal's breath to quicken. "His life isn't in danger," she said, feigning confidence.

He took his hands out of his pockets and wove together his fingers. "I wasn't sure you'd be willing to do this thing if you did not feel he loves you."

"What thing?"

Sanso gestured and Janeal's eyes followed the line of his arm, which pointed to a shadowy hulk of a car.

"Will you allow me to show you?"

She turned back to him. She should have been terrified. That's what she thought at the moment she realized she was only anxious, and perhaps curious, which sent a small thrill of excitement through her chest. But it didn't eclipse her caution. She wasn't a fool; she was a young woman in the dusky desert with a man of unknown intentions.

"What do you need to show me that can't be discussed here?"

"That I am trustworthy."

She had not expected that. A reply evaded her.

"If you come with me, and I return you unharmed in two hours, you will doubt me less than if I preach to you and then leave you to question my spontaneous visit."

The strength of her desire to go with him surprised her, but she said, "Or I could go with you and never be heard from again."

"You are safe, and I am telling you the truth: your father's life is in danger, and unless you save him from his enemies, he will be dead by Wednesday morning. Come. Let me show you. I will not harm the one person in the world who can help him."

Maybe she was a fool after all. More than that, though, she was a daughter who would step between her father and death without having to think about it.

And perhaps if she was forced to tell the truth, she would acknowledge she was a daughter who would be willing to leave her father after all.

He extended his hand out to her, beckoning, palm turned up with the smooth skin of a man who'd never known manual labor.

Janeal slipped her fingers into his.

4

The car smelled of new leather—like the pristine tack room of a horse breeder's estate; like a life that took luxury for granted. Janeal ran her fingertips over the surface of the backseat. She wondered what color it was, and if her father had sat here at some time.

"I think it's a stupid idea to take her back," the blonde had muttered to Sanso as she tied the cloth behind Janeal's head. "You don't know what she'll do."

"She'll save her father, Callista."

Callista yanked the blindfold into a tight knot that snagged Janeal's hair hard enough to make her exclaim.

"Don't punish me for your argument with him," Janeal snapped. "I don't have to go with you."

Sanso silenced her with a gentle hand on the small of her back and steered her away from Callista. That scent of cloves was stronger than her threat to stay put.

Even so, Janeal chose not to speak again until they reached their destination.

Her silence might have been her undoing, though, because Sanso and Callista seemed content enough to live with it, which gave her far more time than she needed to contemplate how much danger she might have put herself in. By the time the car stopped and doors started opening, she felt uncertain of everything.

Callista helped her out of the car. Janeal allowed herself to be led and shuffled across a paved area. She heard the sound of a door opening, then the woman pulled her into an enclosed space.

"Stop here," Callista said, then stripped the blindfold off without untying it, taking pleasure, Janeal believed, in ripping that tiny strand of caught hair out of her scalp.

They stood in a dark hallway. Behind Callista, a red Exit sign glowed over a metal door with a crash bar. Ahead, linoleum lined the floor and led to another door. Sanso was passing through it.

Callista, fair-skinned and maybe in her forties, dressed as if she wished she were still in her teens. In the marginally better light of the hall, Janeal recognized her as a woman who had visited her booth during the carnival and bought several helpings of *sármi* throughout the weekend. Once she had stopped to chat. Janeal tried but could not remember what they talked about.

"I know you from the festival."

"I go to a lot of festivals."

Callista turned her back on Janeal and walked toward the opposite door. Janeal followed.

Passing through the next door, Janeal found herself in a dim room that smelled of fish and cigarettes. It might have been an office, except there was no desk. Full bookcases lined three of the four walls, leaving gaps only for the door she had entered and a door on the opposite side of the room. Above the shelves, close to the ceiling, three small windows in two of the walls allowed moonlight in.

In the center of the floor, a green velvet sectional in the shape of a C surrounded a coffee table and took up much of the space. A flat-screen TV dominated the fourth wall of the room. Three reading lamps placed at intervals behind the sofa cast off yellow light in the shape of cones.

In one corner, a candlelit café table held a plate full of food. Sanso was sitting at it.

"Hungry?" he asked Janeal.

She shook her head.

"Sit, then, and give me a minute."

Janeal sat gingerly at the mouth of the C. Callista left the room.

Sanso did not speak as he ate—fish and rice, she guessed from the aroma—in large mouthfuls, chasing each bite with a gulp of wine. His silverware clattered against his plate, but even that was not loud enough to cover the sound of Janeal's own breathing, which she found distracting and somehow more unnerving than not knowing where she was or precisely why she was here. That he would put off telling her only caused her irritation to mix like a bad science experiment with the other emotions in her belly.

She studied his wide mouth as he ate and willed her body to be quiet enough to hear him chew.

Had her father missed her yet? Probably not. She frequently walked two hours or more with Robert and Katie at this time of night. Considering her outburst today, the two might not miss her until tomorrow morning.

The sound of his chair scraping against the floor brought Janeal's mind back into the room.

Sanso wiped his mouth, picked up his wine, and rounded the sofa. Excitement charged Janeal's blood again. She wondered for a moment if the thrill would burst its container and morph from controlled fear into the most horrifying kind of danger. Involuntarily, she glanced toward the door Callista had exited and wished she would return.

As if prompted, the door opened and the woman walked in holding a glass. She leaned across the sofa and set the glass full of amber liquid on the coffee table in front of Janeal, then walked to the corner and took the seat Sanso had vacated. Janeal picked up the glass and sniffed. Apple juice. As if she were two years old! She set it down again.

"See," Sanso said, approaching one of the bookcases, "the reason I questioned your father's love for you is because he loves money too. Perhaps more than you."

Finding all words inadequate, Janeal glared at him.

"There is no question that he loves the money more than he loves *me*," he said. "We've done business in the past, good business that you would not have been privy to. But I think Jason no longer appreciates my business. Someone else has paid him better."

The insight sounded a dissonant chord in Janeal's brain. "You led me to believe that you and my father are . . ."

"What? Friends? That term is not quite accurate." Sanso picked up a framed photograph off one of the shelves and turned toward Janeal.

"Friendly competition, then?" Janeal tried.

Sanso chuckled. "No, not friendly. Not friendly at all. It's his life or mine now, and I have him in my crosshairs."

Janeal looked down at the floor, both needing him to explain and not wanting him to. She had misunderstood the man. Terribly, terribly misunderstood him.

He sat opposite her on the C-shaped sofa. Their feet nearly touched each other's.

She was shaking. She picked up Sanso's glass of wine, sitting there by that disgusting juice, and splashed the contents of it across his crisp white shirt. She gasped and stood, stunned by the idiocy of her reflexes. What had she done?

She tried to recover. "My father has no enemies."

"Oh, but he does, and I am among his worst." Sanso, unfazed, reached up to take her hand and pulled her back down onto the sofa opposite him.

Janeal's stomach soured. Sanso did not even appear to be angry with her, which she would have preferred to this . . . this eerie paternal calm. She grabbed the glass of juice and took a long drink. She hated apple juice, the sticky too-too sweetness of it. She wished Callista had brought strong coffee. Or, better, that she had swallowed that wine instead of tossing it away.

"This is a sick joke," she said, regretting her lame choice of words.

"I never joke, Janeal Mikkado. But don't be afraid of me. You're not in any danger." He motioned around the room. "Do you see any weapons? Any threat to your well-being? Has anyone intimidated you?"

Janeal shook her head without taking her eyes off him.

"This is because you're safe here," he said. "Safe with me." He smiled enough to make his mustache lopsided, which, rather than make her feel safe, gave her the impression he would as quickly run a knife through her. He extended the framed picture under her nose.

Four men slung their arms around each other's shoulders like brothers. From the left: Sanso, her father, and two of the *kumpania*'s elders, one of whom had died unexpectedly last summer. Food poisoning, they thought. Jason wore an earring Janeal had given him for his birthday only two years ago.

Sanso leaned forward and lifted her chin with his knuckles. "Look at me so I can be sure you understand, girl."

She kept her eyes averted. *You don't have ahold of me, BOY.*

He extended his fingers and pinched her jaw until she winced. "Look."

She met his eyes, trembling.

"Your father has accepted one million dollars from the DEA to set me up for a sting operation that will go down Tuesday morning. One million dollars now has become the value of your father's life. And you have until Monday midnight to bring me this ransom."

One day.

"My father doesn't have that kind of money," she whispered. Not in cash, anyway. The Gypsies had plenty of assets, invested in the community and shared as its members had need. But cash was not their preferred exchange. If he had such a sum, he would have told her. He would have *alerted* her. Like he did the time he held those uncut stones for two weeks on behalf of the *rom baro* in—

"He does have it, and you are going to find it. And then you are going to tell me where it is, and I will come retrieve it. Because if you don't, your father will die, and likely you will die, and I don't care how many more in your precious little *kumpanía* die with you." He spat the name of their group.

One million dollars. One *million* dollars. Shocking herself, Janeal realized that her first thought was not for her father's safety, but for what she could do with one million dollars if she found it before Sanso did.

"You're lying to me," she challenged. "My father has never done business with dealers. There is no money."

He released her jaw. Sanso was already sitting down. "A romantic notion for the only surviving child to have of her precious father. It won't be too much longer before you learn the truth of the human condition, Janeal."

If her father had that kind of money, he would run with it, relocate the family, take them to a new place where neither the DEA nor this Sanso would ever find them. Wouldn't he? The *kumpanía* as a whole barely broke a hundred thousand each summer, all of them working together. Would her father have so much money hidden somewhere, stashed away without telling anyone, not even her? He told her everything.

She dropped her eyes and stared at the picture until Sanso removed it and placed it on the coffee table. "I think I would know if there were drugs in the *kumpanía*."

"There aren't. Your *kumpanía* is only a way station. You're a bunch of traffickers, you Gypsies. Plenty you never see goes on in those festival booths while you're cooking your cabbage rolls. Why do you think the DEA went to Jason for help? It's death by my hand or imprisonment by theirs. That's the stew he cooked himself up in."

"If my father had so much money, he wouldn't hang around here with it."

"He is waiting for the other half, which he will get when he betrays me like the Judas that he is."

Two million dollars. What she and her father could do . . .

"Wouldn't it be less hassle for you to hold me for ransom?"

Sanso clucked his tongue and shook his head.

"And bring the DEA and a dozen other agencies right to my front door? No, I'm a patient man, and I believe that in due time you will agree that giving up the money is in your best interest, and the simplest thing for everyone."

Moonlight caught Sanso's eyes, reflecting off them like a midnight pond. Janeal's breathing quickened the way it did when Robert looked at her too long.

Her involuntary comparison between the man she loved and this, this . . . stunningly beautiful criminal intrigued some far corner of her brain.

"I have seen your restlessness among your own people," Sanso whispered. The word *restlessness* came out like a serpent's temptation. "There are shackles holding you to them that I can break." He moved off his seat and turned to sit next to her. Without touching her, he spoke into her ear, his breath ruffling the strands of her hair. "It's not beneath me to share generously with a beautiful young woman. I can show you the world you want to see."

Janeal's palms broke out in a chilly sweat. "You're revolting." But she couldn't muster the will to mean it. In this moment, when someone's life rather than hers was in danger, she found him fascinating, and she sensed in his relaxed posture that he knew this. She stole a glance at Callista, who sat in the corner. The blonde's expression was smug—apparently she was pleased with the course the conversation was taking. Janeal leaned away from Sanso to take another drink of juice, and to think. Four seconds were all she needed.

"A million dollars must be pocket change to someone like you," she said, holding on to her glass. "Hardly worth this kind of a headache." There was some detail in this fact that she must pay attention to, if she could define it.

"In simple dollars it is. But I'm a man of principle. My reasons for demanding this money have less to do with its actual value than its . . . symbolic value."

Symbolic?

Sanso withdrew a handkerchief from his pocket and started dabbing at the wine on his shirt.

"The money belongs to me. The DEA stole this money from me last year in partnership with a traitor like your father," he continued, "and I intend to reclaim it. It's rightfully mine, and I don't tolerate thieves who intrude on my sweat equity. One can place no price on a man's reputation."

"You can't place a price on my father's life."

"But I have. It's very simple: You give me a million dollars. I'll give you your father's life."

Janeal did not believe a word of it—not that the money was his, not that he would spare her father's life for it, not that the true stakes weren't far, far higher than what Sanso represented to her. For the first time that evening, true fear struck her at the center of her heart, stabbing fear that her father might not trust her, that he might not tell her everything, that he might not include her in the whole truth of his life.

Janeal stood, trying to break something that she could only describe as a gravitational pull toward this horrible man who dealt in lives and lies so casually. She walked within the circumference of the sofa to the opposite side of the coffee table.

"I'll find the money, and we'll leave this place so fast you won't find us."

Sanso wrapped his fist around the wadded kerchief and examined his fingernails. "I have passports in every country in North and South America, plus several others. I am not a person you want following you."

Janeal felt dizzy. She allowed her shoulders to sink back into a cushion. This would be okay. She had to look resigned.

There had to be a way to foil this man, if only she could think it through. Think it through with her father, who would explain everything. Together with what she knew now, they could find a way to keep the money and protect each other.

"I don't believe there is any money," she repeated, not sure why she continued to sing the same note.

"You also believe that I might be right, which is enough to compel you to look. And when you find it, you'll take it, hide it, and call me to tell me where it is. I'll give you a number before you go. Like I said, I am trustworthy."

"It'll be hard to find something that doesn't exist."

"I promise you a tenth of what doesn't exist that you'll test me on this. And then you will change your mind."

Janeal was not quite sure what he meant. A tenth of the money? Her mind was fuzzy. Change her mind? "About what?" she said aloud. She felt Sanso's palm heavy on the top of her head, playing with the strands of her hair. He had moved?

"About me, child. I think you will come with me before this is over."

"I want to be able to . . ." What was the word? "What if I need to . . ." She put her hand over her eyes. "You want me to call you?"

"Yes, child, you will be able to call me."

Janeal fell asleep against her will.

5

Someone was shaking her roughly.

"Janeal? Janeal, are you okay?"

She registered a few facts slowly, scientifically, as if they were not in any way connected to her. A sharp rock was digging into her hip. Her right arm was pinned awkwardly underneath her. She smelled dust lining the inside of her nose.

"Janeal." More shaking. She held up her free hand, and the person made a sound that sounded like relief.

"Get her to sit up," another voice said. Someone grabbed her uplifted hand and pulled. She allowed her eyes to open a slit and squinted into the sun. Beneath her, the river flowed noisily westward.

"Oh."

"How on earth did you fall asleep up here?"

Janeal's mind made a slow connection between voice and name. Katie. Katie's shoulder-length mass of black curls was barely restrained by a wide headband, the headband she donned when she was in a hurry and didn't have time to tame her hair. Katie reached up and brushed off Janeal's cheek. She heard pebbles fall.

"Those rocks might as well have been a feather bed," the other voice said. Robert's voice. He sat down on the other side of her and picked gravel off her arm. Janeal covered her eyes with her hands.

"Ugh." She felt sluggish and hazy.

Robert was punching a number into a cell phone. She leaned against him, eyes closed, and he put an arm around her shoulders while he waited for an answer. Katie patted her back.

"Found her," he said. "She fell asleep on the mesa." He listened, then laughed. "Yeah, she is. We'll come down with her in a bit. Okay." He closed the phone.

"She is what?" Janeal asked.

"She's a cowgirl," Katie said, "sleeping under the stars instead of her own bed. She's a night snake, hunting for lizards at all hours."

Janeal felt silent laughter shaking Robert's body. "She's a true individualist," he said, "looking for new ways to raise her father's blood pressure."

Katie giggled.

Janeal straightened and frowned at Robert. "Oh stop. My father wouldn't have said any of that." She caught him rolling his eyes at Katie and slapped his arm. "Knock it off." How many jokes would these two share at her expense? She suspected that they shared more than that—a flirtatious touch, a significant gaze. The trio's mutual friendship didn't usually anger her, but this morning, Janeal found these two irritating.

"Okay," Robert conceded. "He wouldn't have said that."

"So he said I'm what?"

"Trouble. He said you're trouble."

"Or maybe he said you're *in* trouble," Katie mused. She tapped her heels on the downward slope of the mesa.

"She's never *in* trouble with him," Robert said.

"Right. So. You *are* trouble, Janeal. Not exactly earth-shattering news."

Robert made another crack but Janeal didn't hear it. She was looking at the palm of her hand, on which were written ten numbers, trying to remember what these numbers were and why she thought they had something to do with the word *trouble*.

One million dollars.

Janeal closed her palm into a fist, fully awake. The others seemed not to have noticed her hand. They were too engrossed in each other's wittiness.

"What would you do if you found a million dollars?" she asked, interrupting something Robert was saying.

Robert looked across Janeal at Katie. "Is she on the same planet with us?" he asked.

"Seriously, guys. If you had a million dollars, what would you do with it?" Or a hundred thousand, for that matter. *I'll bet you a tenth of it that you'll change your mind . . .*

"I'd put it in the *kumpania*'s general fund," Katie said, leaning back on the palms of her hands.

"No, you wouldn't," Janeal challenged. "A *million* dollars. You could travel. Start a new life somewhere. Take a few friends with you. Launch a real business of your own instead of having to con a bunch of—"

"If Katie said she'd put it in the general fund, that's what she'd do." Robert shot Janeal a warning glance that wounded her. She tried to remember the last time he'd taken her side on anything.

"Why do you think I wouldn't?" Katie said. The unflappable Katie. Janeal thought she would be more interesting if she'd *react* now and then, get back in Janeal's face, get emotional. Fight her for Robert if that was what she wanted.

Was that what Katie wanted? Janeal asked the question seriously for the first time. Katie was talking to her but looking at Robert. "Jason is a good *rom baro*, Janeal. I'd trust him to do what's right with the money."

"It was just a question. There was a time when you would have come up with a more imaginative answer."

Robert intervened again. "I'd set up an emergency medical fund for the kids."

Why was he always doing that, coming to Katie's defense?

Janeal shook her head. "You two are such do-gooders. If you had a million dollars of cash in your hands, I'd bet you half of it that you'd think twice."

"Maybe," Robert acknowledged. "I wouldn't mind going to Egypt."

"Egypt?" both girls asked at once.

"And South Africa."

If this was the extent of their thinking, maybe she wouldn't tell them about Sanso's claim at all. Definitely not until she found the money.

"I'd go to Greece," said Janeal. "And then I'd buy one of those new Mercedes, and I'd drive it to New York City."

"From Greece?" Robert razzed her. Janeal pretended not to hear.

"I'd get a downtown loft and a job at an international political magazine. I'd work my way up and buy books and visit every museum and spend Friday nights at jazz clubs. I'd entertain on Sunday afternoons and cook five-course meals for my friends and colleagues."

Neither one of them responded for a minute.

"And you'd set aside some money for your father," Katie said.

Janeal sighed. Katie had changed in the last few months—become stunted in her thinking or maybe too much of a conformist. Janeal had the fleeting thought that Katie was holding Robert back too. Why had she asked these two to do a little dreaming with her?

Perhaps to avoid the larger questions at hand: What did her father plan to do with the money Sanso claimed he had? Or with the money the DEA supposedly promised him? Would he survive to be able to put it to use? And was there a way for her to save both him and the cash?

Robert stood and brushed off his pants, then reached down to help Janeal stand, then Katie.

What was the truth she knew so far? One, she believed that Sanso would kill her father if the money slipped away. Two, there was something about that money that Sanso needed that had nothing to do with its face value.

Janeal wondered if she could get her father not to follow through with his promise to the DEA. They'd give Sanso his money, then act surprised when Sanso didn't show up for the sting. Of course, the DEA would want its money back, and how would her father repay them?

There might be a way to give Sanso the money then lead the DEA to him after the fact. Of course, she didn't know where Sanso was, and he'd said he wouldn't be the one to come claim his cash tomorrow night. But if she could do it, her father might end up with two million dollars: the bait as well as the second half of his deal.

If there was a second half.

If anything Sanso told her was true.

And if her betrayal of Sanso went badly, she'd never forgive herself for her father's death.

The trio made their way down the slope toward the camp. Many of her neighbors slept in this Monday morning, tired after the rigorous carnival work of the weekend. She imagined that somewhere in that camp—in a tent, in a car, in a hole in the ground—was a million dollars, banded and stacked and ready for a drug swap, and she wondered how hard it would be to find.

Janeal sneaked another look at the numbers on her palm. Ten numbers. A bank account? What would she do with a bank account number, not knowing which bank?

A phone number.

Yes, child, you will be able to call me.

She shoved her hand into her pocket as they made their way down the mesa slope in skidding steps. She could match his nerve. She would.

Robert and Katie went down in front of Janeal. He held Katie's hand to help her balance. She was smooth in a fortune-teller's booth but a klutz on a hike. Even so, Katie never turned down an invitation to join them, a fact that irked Janeal now that Katie and Robert had reached a level spot and turned to wait for her.

Robert did not let go of Katie's hand. A flame of jealousy licked at Janeal's mind, and she welcomed it. Emotions, at least, were something worth experiencing in this desert place where relationships were dry.

"What if someone told you the money was already hidden in that camp down there, and all you had to do to keep it was find it?" Janeal asked.

"What money?" Katie asked.

"Her million dollars," Robert supplied, setting his lips in a line.

"I'd start looking!" Katie said.

"But would you keep it to yourself? Would you tell everyone to start looking? Settle for a cut?" She caught up with the pair and moved past them, catching up Robert's free hand as she went by, yanking him away from Katie. "How far would you go?"

"I'd keep it simple," Katie said, following slowly. "Tell the *rom baro*. Let him decide."

"That's a no-brainer, Janeal." Robert dug in to wait for Katie and tried to shake his hand free of his girlfriend's. Janeal hung on.

It would be a no-brainer if this were a situation where her father could make an objective decision. Janeal was undecided on whether to ask her father about Sanso's story. He might deny it, or say it was true and send Janeal away until the danger had passed. There was no way for her to ask about it, after all, without divulging that Sanso had seized her. Besides, she wasn't convinced yet that the money existed, although she could come up with no other explanation for Sanso's behavior.

"What if the money involved the *gajé*," she persisted, "and they wanted the money too?"

"Is it theirs?" Robert asked.

"Yes and no."

Robert shook his head, and his smile turned impatient. Janeal decided to release him. "Then tell Jason and the *gajé*'s police. We don't break their laws."

"Never?" Janeal raised her eyebrows.

"*I* would never. Not in this little scenario of yours. Enough said."

"Their laws don't apply to us."

"That's what you'd like to think."

"What if finding the money might mean someone could die?"

Katie gasped. "That's terrible."

"But at the same time, finding the money might mean you could save a life? What would you do then?"

"You're not making any sense," Robert said.

"I still think Jason would know what to do," Katie insisted.

"Not if he had a conflict of interest," Janeal said. "Then the decision is for the three of us to make. The whole burden of the scenario rests on our heads."

"Sheesh, Janeal. What were you doing up there all night? Dreaming up a novel?"

Katie tilted her head slightly. "It's kind of an interesting idea though, Robert, don't you think?"

The gaze Robert bestowed on Katie was not lost on Janeal. For half a second his frustration was replaced by appreciation. He was glad Katie was here. Glad that her generous manner was bigger than his petty annoyance. Glad that he wasn't alone with Janeal.

"To pass the time, maybe." The hand he placed on his hip told Janeal he agreed only for the sake of ending the conversation. "If I had the time and wasn't spending it looking for my wandering girlfriend."

His accusation stabbed Janeal. She believed he hadn't meant to wound her, that she'd caused him unnecessary worry and he was only tired. It was wrong of her to pepper them with so many questions but not tell the whole story.

"You're right, I'm sorry. You two were great to come after me. I didn't mean to worry anyone." A flash of regret crossed Robert's face, as she expected it would. She started back down the hill and sent rocks skittering to the bottom.

"You haven't said what you would do, Janeal," Katie said.

"I haven't decided what to do," Janeal said. The words were in the air before she recognized her slip. She put her head down and hurried to reach home before they could ask her to explain. Not that they would have known what to ask.

6

At one o'clock that afternoon, Robert found Janeal crawling around in the back of her father's Lexus SUV. She had tipped back the collapsible passenger seats to examine the hideaway compartments underneath. After four hours of looking for the money, she was evenly divided over whether Sanso was full of hot air or whether her father would be dead within hours.

"Looking for some bundles of cash?" he asked.

Janeal's heart caught in her throat. "Lug wrench," she muttered when she saw that the wells were empty. "I have a flat." That much was true. She had thought she might go to the carnival site to see if the money was stored in any of the trailers there . . . until she discovered that one of her balding tires had lost too much air to take her.

Robert opened a compartment in the side panel, pulled out the wrench, and handed it to her.

"You want to explain all that strange talk this morning?" he asked.

"You want to explain what's going on with you and Katie?" she retorted.

Judging by his slackened jaw, Robert was stunned. "What are you talking about? The three of us have been friends for years. Nothing's changed."

"Something's changed, Robert. And I know it's not me."

Robert hesitated for one second longer than he should have before saying, "That's not true."

"Do you like her?"

"Of course I like her. She's—"

"You know what I mean."

"I'm not going to answer that, Janeal. How long have I loved you, bull-headed ways and all?" The proclamation seemed forced.

Long enough to become fed up?

Janeal climbed out of the SUV and replaced the carpeting over the wheel well. She wasn't sure what she needed from Robert right now, in this singular moment when she couldn't decide which path to take and the clock was ticking the daylight hours away.

Maybe she needed him to believe her. To believe *in* her. Even in her bull-headed ways. Would that make a difference? She wasn't sure but decided to take a gamble.

"Last night a man and woman visited me on the mesa."

Robert's eyes twinkled. "Another novel rattling around in your mind?"

"They took me to . . . I don't know. It was an office or something. The man says there is money hidden in this camp, money Dad has secured in a deal with the U.S. government."

Robert crossed his arms and leaned against the rear bumper.

She tried to gauge his expression but couldn't. "He wants me to find it for him. If I don't, he'll kill my father."

Robert nodded.

"Don't patronize me," she snapped. "Either believe me or don't."

"Did he hurt you?"

Janeal shook her head and Robert exhaled.

"Why did you stay on the mesa last night?"

"I didn't—I think they drugged me. I don't remember."

"You seemed clearheaded enough when we found you."

Skepticism made his eyebrows uneven. Clear and obvious disbelief.

Robert scratched at the hairline over his right ear. "This wouldn't have anything to do with your being upset over Katie's fortune-telling debut yesterday, would it?"

"Robert! You think this is some demented cry for attention? I would never . . . I can't believe you would think . . ."

"I don't know what to think," Robert said. "No, wait. I do. I think you should stick to your hypothetical questions." He straightened and closed the rear door of the vehicle before starting to walk away. "And cut Katie some slack. You're jealous of her."

"It appears I have reason to be."

"Keep this up and you will."

Janeal blinked. Robert stalked off. They'd had their share of arguments, but never like this. She should follow him, she thought, but couldn't. The issue of the money, of her father's life, needed her more urgent attention. When she was finished, she'd put her mind to finding a way to pull Robert back to her. There wasn't room for three in this romance anymore.

Or maybe she'd take the money and run. Leave the two lovebirds to their righteous selves.

By four that afternoon, Janeal started to panic. She had searched every possible hiding place, and short of the money being buried in a sack somewhere in the hundreds of square miles of desert, she was out of ideas. All but one.

Janeal grabbed the lug wrench she had taken from her father's car and headed out to her dilapidated Chevy. She would swap her flat out for a spare and go see if the money was in the carnival trailers. If not, she'd go straight to her father and tell him everything, give him time to muster the other men in camp against whatever this lunatic Sanso had planned. And then she would call Sanso and tell him what to do with his threats.

The trunk of her car was cluttered with all kinds of junk. She hadn't cleaned it out in . . . maybe never, not since her father had given her the wreck when she was fifteen. Emergency kits, an extra pair of hiking boots and flip-flops, blankets, a phone book, three boxes of cooking utensils and supplies, and a suitcase half full of spare shirts and jeans. She would have to unload at least a third of it to pull away the carpeting that covered the spare-tire well.

A few minutes later, with her junk in the dirt around her rear bumper, she lifted the corner of the panel.

And saw, rather than a tire, bundle upon bundle of hundred-dollar bills. In spite of the fact that she had been looking for this very thing, the actual sighting of it confused her for a minute. What was it doing here, in her car?

She snatched up a stack and flipped through it, did a quick mental calculation of how many more belly-banded wads of cash had been layered under the flooring of her wide trunk, mentally tallied up the zeros. Easily a million.

The texture of the money in her hands, smooth, stiff, ever so slightly slippery with newness, blocked out her sense of anything else going on around her.

The things she could do with this much money—or a couple little bundles—overwhelmed her with possibilities. Freedom and adventure and discovery.

Sanso had made some kind of offer to her regarding this money. She would get a cut, wasn't that it? A cut if she joined him?

Join a man who was her father's enemy. No, the thought of that was beneath her. Besides, who would notice a missing bundle? Or two?

What would happen to her father if she drove away with the whole take, never looked back?

He would die twice, figuratively and literally, and her life would be full of freedom and self-hate. She discarded the option in two seconds.

Without devoting too much time to processing her decisions, Janeal settled on a plan: She would take some of this money and call Sanso to let him know where the rest of it was, right here in her disabled car. After she called Sanso, she could confide in her father, get him to call his contact at the DEA, and they could set up a little sting of their own. Advance the plan by a day.

If Janeal had been one to wear skirts, she'd have plenty of hiding places in the yards of fabric for two or three stacks of bills. Slipping even one into the form-fitting curves of her jeans was more of a challenge, though. She eventually decided on tucking one into her rear waistband and covering it with her shirt. When it was dark she would come back for more. Not too much. A few more that neither Sanso nor the DEA would miss right away. And when they did, what could they do if they suspected her of taking it, anyway?

She'd use one to show her father that she was telling the truth—that Sanso had told her everything and she'd found the money. She would decide what to do with the rest, her own little cut, later.

Janeal covered up the money and began to return items to the trunk.

"Janeal!"

Her surprise at the sound of her name was so great that she jerked up and smacked her head on the trunk. She yelped and covered the spot with her hand. Through watery eyes she peered around the side of the car and saw her father rushing toward her.

Jason Mikkado's brown skin had been weathered by fifty summers in the dry desert sun. The deepest lines framed the corners of his mouth and eyes, laugh lines that couldn't be erased in spite of family tragedy. His hair was still as black and thick as a twenty-year-old's, and his chocolate brown eyes were clear and bright. But today they were tinted with worry, though he was grinning.

Her pulse sped up like she was a child caught with her hand in a forbidden candy dish. "Dad," she said, rubbing her head.

"What are you doing?"

She looked down at the three boxes of kitchen supplies sitting at her feet in the red dirt. "I'm, uh . . ." Her eyes alighted on the lug wrench she'd tossed into the trunk. "Changing a flat." Thank goodness she didn't have to lie about that. She could not lie to her father.

The bills at her waistband caused the base of her spine to itch. There were a dozen reasons why she should tell her father everything, right this moment. Janeal opened her mouth, then hesitated. She could tell him after she'd come back for more of it, couldn't she?

"Why don't you let me do that for you?" Jason said, picking up the wrench.

"I can change a tire. You're busy."

Her father's laughter warmed her and calmed her racing heart. "You've never changed a tire in your life."

She smiled back at him, assessing the worry in his eyes. He didn't want her to find the money.

He didn't trust her.

Janeal's heart sagged. "It can't be that hard," she said.

He tipped his head to one side. "True. For you, nothing is too hard, is it?"

"Only because I take after you."

"You're far more like my better half," Jason said. "Your mother was willing to try almost anything, fortunately for me." He took the wrench from Janeal. "Otherwise she wouldn't have married me and borne me such beautiful children. But, like you, she was most skilled in the kitchen. So why don't you go help Veronica with the meal and I'll take care of this for you?"

Her feet stayed rooted to the dusty ground. He was shooing her off, hiding the truth, forcing open a gap between them. "Okay. Sure I can't help? If I get stuck out in the desert alone one of these days—"

Jason Mikkado gave a hearty laugh that mocked her fear. "You'd talk a pack of Gila monsters into giving you a tow, no doubt."

"Okay then, you win." She leaned against the car, not wanting to go, hoping she could find the courage to ask him what he'd been caught up in. "Good weekend at the carnival."

Her father started slowly unloading the items she had returned to the trunk. "One of our best so far. It should continue to pick up as the summer wears on, though. We might have a great year."

"I heard Katie did well, first day in the tent."

Jason looked up at her as if trying to discern the true nature of her compliment. And maybe she *was* wishing for something from her father that she couldn't get from Robert, some sense that Katie wasn't about to overtake her in every way that mattered to Janeal—in relationship with Robert, in value to the *kumpania,* in talent and beauty . . .

For heaven's sake. She could embrace her jealousy of Katie if she wanted to, but standing here in the presence of her father, she was confronted by her own self-centeredness.

Was it so wrong of her, though, to want these things: the undivided love of a good man, the trust of a father, affirmation, adventure?

A cut of a million dollars? Janeal looked at her feet. She needed time to think this through. An hour maybe.

Janeal didn't have an hour. She made a quick decision. She'd call Sanso and tell him where the cash was. That would keep him appeased and her father alive. Then she'd tell her father the rest. If she told him now, he'd never let her make the call to Sanso. Later, though, she'd need his help to get the DEA here in time.

"Yes," her father finally said. "Katie did well. She'll be a favorite."

Janeal nodded and made as if to go. "It's not surprising. Katie, you know."

Her father straightened and waggled the wrench toward her in a scolding fashion. "No, not surprising. But Janeal, you must remember."

She turned back toward him.

"Cards and crystal balls never satisfy like a good meal." He winked at her. Then he waved the wrench at the flip-flops on her feet. "Now go change your shoes before you set one foot in that kitchen, or the elders will go to bed hungry and wake up grouchy."

7

Janeal did not carry a cell phone, though she had frequently wished for one. It was a connection to the world at large that she had not convinced her father she needed. She thought at times that he saw the phone as a threat to her, a device that would cut her last dangling threads of connection to the *kumpanía*. To him. And maybe it would.

Robert's phone had cost him a hundred fifty dollars. Well, she'd be able to buy one now without her father knowing.

Instead of changing her shoes as instructed, she went into the meeting-house through the front door, intending to use the phone in the back hall. Mrs. Marković's chair by the front widow was empty.

Anyone in the *kumpanía* was allowed to use the phone, though hardly anyone ever did. There were few reasons to call anyone outside the camp.

Janeal tapped in the number written on her palm.

A woman answered the phone in a low voice. "What?"

Janeal lost track of what she meant to say. Had she expected Sanso to answer? She looked down the hall and whispered, "I . . . This is Janeal Mikkado?" She was irked with herself for having said it like a question.

"Just a minute."

She thought she waited for several minutes—half worried Sanso would turn out to be a joke after all, half worried she would be interrupted by someone who wanted to use the phone.

"Janeal, yes." Sanso sounded as much like a snake as his name suggested he was. "You have something for me?"

"It's in my car. Under the carpeting of the trunk."

"Good. Good. And your father doesn't know you found it?"

Not yet, jerk. "No."

"Because you understand that if he has staged your car as a trap, I won't be there to fall into it. In fact, I won't be there at all. I send lackeys I can deny knowing. Lackeys who are happiest when I let them loose to do damage when things don't go my way."

Janeal immediately questioned the plan she had set into motion. If the DEA could not secure Sanso tonight, what might the man levy as a consequence for her betrayal? Maybe she should let him take the money, try to defend herself to the authorities tomorrow. But her father—what would happen to him if that money vanished?

"And if any of the money is missing, even one bill, I will know."

"Look, I didn't stop to count it, you know?"

Sanso chuckled. "If you had, you might have a better sense of how much I would be willing to give to you. And there is more, Janeal Mikkado. Much more you would be entitled to if you choose the life I offer you."

Janeal gripped the phone and reconsidered. Maybe going with Sanso would give her the solution she needed. She could go with him and the money, leave a note for her father explaining all that had happened, promise to keep in touch and lead the DEA to Sanso at her first opportunity. They'd work with her father under those circumstances, wouldn't they?

"The car's unlocked," she said.

"You have thought about my offer?"

His *stranglehold* was more like it. She would give him the money and run away with him in exchange for her father's life. Her father would live, but if anything went wrong, she would never be welcome among the family again.

"I . . . I can't leave. It's not like our people come and go as they please, you understand?"

"I wasn't thinking you would go back, Janeal, not once you got a taste of what I have to offer you. Something tells me you wouldn't want to."

"My father—if I did that . . ."

"Think of his survival as your reward."

Janeal's stomach turned over. She wanted that reward. She also wanted that money.

She hung up before she gave him an answer she'd regret.

Turning, she bumped into Mrs. Marković. Janeal gasped. The old woman's legs were as stable as oak tree trunks and as firmly rooted. How long had she been standing there? Janeal might have apologized, but the woman must have eavesdropped, and that was the worse offense.

Janeal took a step to move around the woman's wide body. The agile Mrs. Marković matched her move.

"Excuse me," Janeal said.

Mrs. Marković leaned forward, her neck craned slightly to place her tiny round nose almost directly under Janeal's.

"I see you, Children." The woman's breath smelled of fresh mint.

Janeal's lips parted. Children? She was not a child. She looked past Mrs. Marković up the hall. It was empty.

"Please let me pass," Janeal said.

Mrs. Marković shook her head. "Not both of you, no. You two should not be free to roam in this place. I see you."

Janeal took another step, and Mrs. Marković continued to block Janeal's path.

"There is only one of me, Mrs. Marković. I promise to be the only one to leave. Okay?"

"Nobody can make such a promise. Especially not you, Children."

Janeal huffed. She forced her way between the woman and the wall, and Mrs. Marković's arm snaked out to grab her wrist.

Electricity shot up Janeal's arm, as it had in the game room, only this raced, zoomed up her nerves and through the muscles of her neck straight into her head with a thunderous *crack!* of breaking bones. Janeal's head ignited with the most intense headache she had ever experienced. It radiated from the center of her brain like a starburst, pounding on the inside of her skull like a million miners with picks.

Only Mrs. Marković's firm grip kept her from sinking to the floor.

"Daughters, you are full of deceit," Mrs. Marković said without any condemnation. She raised her hand to Janeal's shrieking head, then placed her other palm on Janeal's hair and stroked it maternally. "Do not lie to yourselves. There are two chambers in every heart, one for Judas and one for John."

Janeal shivered though she was not cold. She wanted to escape this insane talk. Gliding over Janeal's smooth hair, Mrs. Marković's whispering fingers pushed the pain away. "One must be pumped out, or you will both die."

Janeal's head ached too much to sort meaning from babble. She leaned against the wall until the pain abated completely, and when she finally opened her eyes, Mrs. Marković was gone.

8

In spite of her father's instructions, Janeal did not help Veronica with the meal that night, nor did she put on acceptable shoes. Instead, she skipped dinner entirely, because it took her nearly three hours to write the letter that she would need to leave behind for Jason, the letter explaining what she had chosen to do, and why. Though she had waited patiently to pull him aside and speak with him face-to-face, the elders had not left his company since arriving for the evening meal, and she didn't dare mention Sanso or the money in front of them.

"We can talk at any time of the night," he told her when she asked to speak with him privately, resting a hand on her arm. "But these men need my attention now so they can get back to their families."

But the clock ticked on, and she knew she'd be lucky to see Jason before the weekly Monday night poker games ended. If he was able to participate tonight. Sometimes he got so busy he couldn't make it to those.

Uncertain as to when Sanso's "lackeys" would show up, Janeal knew she couldn't wait any longer to be ready.

She decided: she would go with Sanso tonight. To save her father, she'd leave him.

A small voice in the back of her mind told her she was only doing what she really wanted to do. She had found her excuse to leave the camp and could claim her escape would help her father rather than hurt him. She could finally justify her own desires without admitting another truth: that she wanted Sanso's money, that she was attracted to his bad-boy persona, that she—

Janeal silenced the voice.

Though most of the carnival trailers stayed in Albuquerque through the week, the kitchen trailer came back for cleaning each weekend and was parked behind the garages where they had access to running water and room to make a mess without offending anyone. The large structure stored her father's rarely used Lexus, the equipment the *kumpanía* needed to make auto and machine repairs, and gasoline in drums for other vehicles.

She and the other cooks often let the trailer sit for a day or two before rolling up their sleeves and scrubbing the thing down.

Tonight, though, Janeal cleaned off one of the greasy prep counters, decided that her creepy encounter with Mrs. Marković was only an unfortunate sign of the old woman's imminent slide into dementia, then wrote her way through three drafts of inadequate explanations for why she had gone off with Sanso before finally settling on one that made sense.

Whatever the short-term fallout with the DEA might be, they at least wouldn't kill Jason Mikkado. Nor would Salazar Sanso. She believed this, she wrote to her father, or else she would not have gone.

The pull of the money and a life outside the *kumpanía* was an afterthought that she didn't mention.

She became so engrossed in the explanation that she didn't notice she was losing daylight until the rear door of the trailer flew open and a high-beam flashlight cut through the rank interior.

"What are you doing in here?" Robert stepped in, accompanied by Katie.

Janeal scrambled to pull her letter together and fold it. She crammed the papers into her back pocket. She had to get back to the community house, where she and her father kept their rooms.

Robert noticed her gestures—his eyes went to her pocket, the broken pencil, the wads of discarded paper on the floor—but he didn't say anything.

"You keep disappearing," Katie said. "Are you okay?"

"I'm fine," Janeal muttered, frowning at Robert. She wasn't willing to confide in him again after the way he responded to her this afternoon. "I needed some space."

"Or a darn good hiding place from *gajé* bandits," Robert said. "But I don't think the perimeter of camp is your best bet."

Janeal turned to throw a comeback in his face but held her tongue when she saw he was not teasing her. She looked at Katie. She was not poking fun either. Had Robert told her the story? Did they believe her?

Did she care?

"What time is it?" she asked.

Robert looked at his watch. "It's after ten."

"Don't you have anything better to do? Poker game with the men?"

"Most of them went to watch a tournament in Rio Rancho. Didn't want to go."

She wished he had. The stack of bills she had taken earlier in the afternoon was in her room now. Five thousand dollars. She'd get it when she went back to leave the note for Dad.

Robert was looking at her, perplexed. He leaned against the counter, crowding her. "Katie and I want to hear more about what happened to you last night."

The direct request made Janeal slightly angry. Hadn't she told him enough? What else did he want to know?

"I was out of line this afternoon," Robert said.

"No, you weren't," Janeal said, though she thought he had been.

"Oh, he was," Katie inserted. "He told me what he said. He was an absolute dork."

Janeal cleared her throat, worried that Robert might have also mentioned her accusations about the two of them. She was considering clearing the air when Robert jumped back in, maybe to prevent Janeal from opening another can of worms.

"Did you find the money?" Robert asked.

"I did."

Katie put a hand over her mouth. Robert seemed surprised.

"Where is it?"

Janeal frowned at him. "Now you want to know."

"Look, I'm trying to apologize."

She picked up the wads of paper on the floor and threw them into a soup pot. She pulled a box of matches out of a drawer next to the stove and lit one, then tossed it into the pot.

"How much is there?" he asked.

"A million."

"A million!" Katie echoed. "All those what-ifs you asked us this morning— he told you there was that much? Why didn't you say anything?"

"I said plenty." Amusement poked a hole in Janeal's irritation.

Katie was shaking her head. She put her hand on Robert's arm and leaned toward him. "If this *gajé* has threatened the *rom baro*'s life—"

"He won't be able to do anything to my father."

"How do you know that?" Katie asked.

"I've taken care of everything."

"What do you mean? Tell us what happened."

The discarded drafts of Janeal's letters burned out within seconds. Janeal didn't have the time to explain everything to them, and even if she did, she didn't know if she wanted to. She squeezed past them in the close space and tried to reach the door.

"Janeal," Katie pleaded. "Please don't go. Tell us what we can do to help."

"Nothing."

"Where are you going?"

"She's going to go put gas in her car and drive away to New York now." Robert's remark was not a question, and Janeal saw something between fear and accusation pulling down the corners of his mouth. "Or was it Greece?"

"Of course she wouldn't. She loves her father too much to do that to him, don't you, Janeal?"

Janeal's eyes were still locked on Robert's. Could he have guessed she'd leave him? Did he want her to?

"She's going to give that money right to whoever wants it so that her father will be fine, we'll be fine, the whole *kumpanía* will be just fine. Isn't that right?"

Janeal lowered her eyes. "It's a little more complicated than that."

"How complicated?" Robert challenged. When Janeal tried to exit, he stepped out and gripped her wrist. "Why don't you explain it to us?"

Katie stepped between them and touched Robert's hand, silently urging him to let Janeal go. He did.

From the rear door of the trailer, Janeal couldn't see or hear anything that was out of order in the camp. If she was lucky, Sanso's people wouldn't show up until after midnight. She could spend those hours alone, pacing in her room, or . . .

Janeal looked at her friends. Robert still seemed angry, but Katie—she had paled and looked at Janeal with such concern that Janeal decided to explain her dilemma. In two short minutes she gave them the condensed version.

Katie didn't believe the possibility that anyone in the *kumpania* had ever done that sort of appalling business with Sanso; Robert did not voice an opinion on the matter. Janeal interpreted his silence as knowledge. She explained her fear of what the government might do to her father when he produced neither Sanso nor the money at their command; she was in greater fear, though, of what would happen to her father if Sanso did not get his way.

"I'm going to go with him," she said, barely loud enough for them to hear. She didn't look at either one of her friends.

"You can't," Katie whispered. "Janeal, what if he kills you?"

"I don't think he will," she said.

Disgust wrinkled Robert's face. "Why not? Because you've already talked it through with him? Made your little plans?"

Janeal turned on him. "I'm doing what I need to to save Dad's life!"

"How does going with that animal help your father?" Robert asked. "This is what you want, Janeal, and it has nothing to do with your father, or with *us*, or with anyone else in this community."

"This man will kill him; don't you get that? If you think I've got some selfish idea in mind—"

"Now why would I think that, Janeal? What did he promise you in exchange for turning the money over to him? A cut? A fancy car? His *bed*?"

Janeal put her hand on her stomach as if he had punched her. She could not decide if she was more hurt that Robert thought so badly of her or that he seemed to be driving her away.

She kept her response under control. "If I go with him, I could lead the DEA to Sanso myself when the time is right. They can recover their money, and the *kumpania* will get its pardon. That would be worth it, don't you think? And the *kumpania* might let me return. I might even come back a hero. Certainly Dad—"

"You don't know what that man might do to you," Katie repeated.

"I can handle him." She said it with more confidence than she felt.

Robert turned on the flashlight and pushed her aside to jump out the back of the trailer first.

"What are you doing?"

"I think the *rom baro* ought to have a say in what you decide, considering that your friends don't."

Janeal's temper flared. "You can't go to him! You *know* he won't let me do this."

"Exactly! And doesn't that matter to you?" Robert shot back. Katie finally stood, looking distressed and reluctant to put herself in the middle of this standoff.

"You'll get him killed! Doesn't it matter to you that he stay alive? If Sanso doesn't get that money—"

"Don't be naive, Janeal. This is a DEA problem. Let them own it. You don't have to. Neither does your dad."

"They have him on drug trafficking charges!"

"According to Sanso."

"Well, why else would the DEA have pinpointed my father for the job? And why would he have agreed to go along with their plan?"

"For the money? I don't know, Janeal, but I do know that this isn't something you need to shoulder alone. Let the government protect their own."

"They *will*. Don't you get it? Don't you have any idea how Sanso might have found out about the sting in the first place? They *will* protect their own, and my father—your *rom baro*—is not one of them!"

Katie surrounded Janeal with a hug. She squeezed, her brows aligning to express her worry. Instead of accepting the sympathy of her friend, though, Janeal felt herself tipping over the edge of a cliff. She decided to let herself fall.

No one understood her, not even these two, who had so gradually been shutting her out of their circle that she hadn't noticed until today. It no longer mattered to her that they didn't understand, that they didn't need her.

Janeal pulled out of her embrace and shot a withering look at Katie.

And Robert! If he really did intend to inform her father of what she had done, of what she now planned to do, she had better get to the meetinghouse ahead of him. She jumped out of the trailer and broke into a jog.

"Janeal, wait."

She did not want to. She heard Robert's foot grind the dirt as he pivoted to follow her. She ignored his attempts to reason with her and Katie's pleas that she slow down. Instead, she turned her mind to how Robert might head her off once they got within sprinting distance of the meetinghouse. She would probably have to let him go straight to her father.

She, on the other hand, would go straight to her car keys. She'd pull out of camp and call Sanso from Albuquerque, have him meet her there.

As she anticipated, Robert sped toward the meetinghouse like a tattling little boy. For the first time, Janeal felt disgust toward her boyfriend. Katie could have him if she wanted. Janeal headed to the garage. She would need a few gallons of gas. Katie wavered, then followed Janeal.

"What are you doing?"

"What does it look like?" she said as she snatched a red canister off the shelf.

"Where will you go?"

"Nowhere that matters to anyone here." She punched open the side door with the heel of her hand and headed for the meetinghouse kitchen. She kept her keys on a hook by the door. A mere hundred yards and the propane tank that heated their water supply was all that stood between her and her escape.

"Janeal, please." Katie grabbed hold of the crook of Janeal's elbow.

"What?" Janeal yanked her arm away.

The two faced each other in the darkness. Janeal registered the sounds of men shouting some distance away. She told herself it must be an argument over a card game in one of the far tents.

Katie dropped her eyes. "You'll go, and he will have no spirit to lead us, Janeal. He'll withdraw and leave the decisions to someone like Rajendra, and then—"

"My father is not a weakling. And if I don't go, he'll *die*." Or be carted off to prison by the very government that had tried to provide him with a pardon. And then what? Then the *kumpanía* would be without a leader and she would be without a father and he would be without a family—and how was that better than what she was planning to do right now? "What will it take for you to hear me?"

Janeal rushed to the kitchen door, which Robert had left wide open. Inside, gas can in her left hand, Janeal snatched her keys off the hooks, dropped them into the pocket of her jeans, and turned to leave. The whole maneuver took her only three steps. Through the frame of the kitchen entry, she saw Katie still standing in the barren open space between the garage and the meetinghouse. She was looking away from Janeal, though, toward the shouting. The noise gave her pause. Hadn't Robert said the men had gone to a poker tournament?

She didn't especially care.

Janeal smelled smoke. The odor smelled chemical rather than woody, and she wondered briefly what would cause—

The sound of feet pounding in a dead run sounded from down the hall. Among the voices of men shouting, a woman screamed.

The door between the kitchen and the dining room swung open with such force that it hit the wall and bounced off. Robert slapped back at it as he headed for Janeal without breaking stride.

"Get out," he yelled at her.

Janeal didn't move.

"Go!" He reached her in the same instant and shoved her through the doorway so that she stumbled over the wide concrete step. She dropped the full gas can with a heavy thunk and it tottered, then ended upright. He grabbed her by the arm and nearly yanked it out of its socket.

"What are you—"

"Katie!" Robert was flinging his arm up to wave in her direction. "Katie, *move*!" She noticed him then and took a step in his direction.

"I mean *run*!"

Janeal had adjusted her feet to match Robert's pace finally, and they raced toward Katie. "What happened?"

Robert put his head down and lengthened his stride. "Your friend's people beat me to the punch."

9

From the backseat of his speeding silver Mercedes, Salazar Sanso glowered at Callista, in the driver's seat. He should not have had to make this trip out to Jason Mikkado's camp. His men should have been able to deliver the money into his hands by now. But Janeal was a fool.

A beautiful, wild-hearted fool.

What had she done with his cash? The anticipation of his finding out was the only bright side of this turn of events.

"They swear the bills aren't in her car," Callista said for the umpteenth time.

"She moved it," he said.

"Why would she do that and risk your ire?"

"Because she thinks she's smarter than she is."

"She's smart."

"Just enough to be simultaneously stupid." He spit the words.

Callista's eyes flickered up to meet his in the rearview mirror, but she didn't say anything.

They were less than a mile from the Rom camp. His men should have had plenty of opportunity to get it under control by the time he arrived. "Have they found her yet?" he asked.

"She might be a few hundred miles away by now."

"She's not."

Fortunately for Callista, she did not ask how he knew this. He had little patience for questions tonight.

"The camp is intact," she said. "We've killed ten men, corralled most of the rest, the women and brats."

"How many?"

"About seventy people."

"There's at least a hundred and twenty living there."

"Most of the men are in town."

"Lucky for us."

"Until they get back."

"Set up an ambush."

"Salazar, it can't be worth it."

"Don't tell me what's worth it, woman. You know what's at stake here. I want everything that I need, or I want everything reduced to ash."

Callista stepped on the gas.

Sanso looked at his watch. "Kill anyone who tries to leave. How many of our own have we lost so far?"

"Three."

"We can afford three. At least their blood's not on my hands."

Callista didn't say what he wanted her to, that he had a wicked and warped sense of humor. Instead, she said, "No one seems to know where Janeal is, and Jason either doesn't know or won't say. They're waiting for you to tell them what's next."

Sanso withdrew a small pistol from the interior pocket of his jacket, checked the chamber, and sniffed the barrel.

"If Janeal Mikkado is as smart as you think she is, she understands by now that the only way to save her father's life and prevent him from going to jail is to come with me. And the only way she will come with me is if she brings the money with her."

"You're wasting unnecessary attention on the girl. She didn't pan out. We'll go to plan B."

"But I *want* the girl, my dear. There's no reason for me not to have her." This time he held Callista's mirrored gaze. Envy was becoming on her.

"Why do you always want the ones who don't think you rule the stars?"

"Don't be jealous."

"Burn the camp. Burn the cash. Be done with it."

A cell phone rang on the seat next to Callista.

"Why don't we both get our way tonight?" Sanso said. "Tell them to search the camp and then torch it. One tent at a time, until we find the money or burn her out."

Callista flipped open the phone to answer the caller, saying to Sanso, "I think she's gone already. You'll have to use the father to bring her back."

"No. She's still there because she thinks she loves him. She won't leave. But if I learned anything from the girl last night, it's that her love for the money is stronger than her love for precious Daddy. She doesn't know this about herself yet, but that will work in my favor, won't it?"

10

"Where is my father?" Janeal demanded of Robert. The trio crouched behind the garage. Robert tried to catch his breath.

"I didn't . . . see him."

"Then what sent you after us like there were scorpions in your shoes?" she demanded.

Robert craned his head low around the corner of the building. The shouting had intensified.

A gun fired and Katie flinched. "I need to find my parents," she whispered. Janeal tightened her hold on her friend.

"Robert," Janeal said.

He ignored her, so she poked him in the backside with her shoe.

"Answer me."

"Rajendra," Robert said without turning around. Two more shots went off. What was going on out there?

"Rajendra *what*?" Janeal demanded. The fear that she was about to face responsibility for something horribly, horribly wrong agitated her.

Robert snapped around and got in Janeal's face. "Rajendra *dead*, Janeal. Rajendra on the steps of the meetinghouse bleeding from his mouth. You need more details?"

Janeal recoiled and Katie started to cry. Robert swore.

"He's got two kids," Katie murmured.

Janeal let go of Katie and started to stand. "I need to get to Dad."

Robert tugged her back to the ground. "You stay here. I'll go find him, let him know you're okay. Your folks too, Katie."

"I can take care of finding my father," Janeal said.

The smoke had increased now, but the shouting and screaming seemed to have diminished.

"Stay put, Janeal."

"Don't bother, Robert. You'll leave and I'll do what I want."

Robert rubbed his eyes with his thumb and forefinger and sighed. "Yes, you will, won't you?" He dropped his hand and scooted closer to Janeal, took her hands in his. "Just this one time, would you do what I want?" He leaned in and she thought he was going to kiss her, firm and confident, the way that made it impossible for her to stay stubborn. He seemed to rethink this, though, and held back.

Janeal tried to withdraw her hands, but his grip pinched her knuckles. "Please. Stay here with Katie until I get back." Of course. This was about Katie, not her.

She frowned.

"Don't leave Katie alone. She needs you."

She nodded and Robert took off. *Whatever.*

Pushing herself off the wall of the garage, she stood and held out a hand to Katie. "We have to go to my car. I have the keys."

"What's in your car?"

"The money. If we're lucky." She tugged on Katie, who rose like a limp doll.

"Somehow I don't think money or luck will be of any good to us tonight." Katie's expression had flattened into blank disbelief.

"So what?" Janeal said, pulling her around the building away from the direction in which Robert had gone. "I don't think you're such a reliable fortune-teller, myself."

At the opposite end of the camp, three tents were completely engulfed in smoke and flame. One of them was the tent Katie shared with her parents and two younger brothers. Robert didn't see them anywhere.

About fifty yards from where he stood behind the medical building, several women and children were piling into a small pickup truck while men called out to each other from the tents. One carried a bucket of water toward a tent that had not ignited yet. Robert heard a gunshot. The man collapsed, the bucket spilled, and the thirsty dust drank up the water.

Robert smelled a stink unlike any he had ever smelled before, a scorched rotting that rose above the chemical burn. Flesh, he registered without thinking too hard. Human flesh.

All this, over *money*?

He covered his nose and mouth with his shirt. He had to find the *rom baro*. Had to find his own family. He could not see their tent from where he stood, but there wasn't any smoke from that direction.

Stragglers tried to jump into the crowded truck as it pulled by, until someone started shooting at it. A woman fell out of the back in a heap, and a girl started screaming. The truck accelerated as gunfire persisted. One of the shots caught a tire and sent the truck sideways into a burning tent. The passengers scattered, tripping over themselves and trying to help each other before the flames licked the gas tank.

Robert rushed to the woman, not sure whether he'd be shot himself before he reached her. But no one seemed to notice him. Flames licked at the canvas sides of a fourth tent, and the chaos set into motion by their invisible enemy was a complete distraction to everyone else. She lay facedown, her long hair a blanket over her head and shoulders. He grasped her by the armpits and dragged her under the medical building's rear porch. She would be protected here, at least until this building went up in flames too.

A lantern dangling from a rod by the screen door sent light through the splintering slats of the crude porch and shone down on them in stripes.

He turned the woman over. She'd lost a boot. Her skirt had torn at the knees where he'd dragged her. Blood stained her blouse under her ribs, still oozing, but she was breathing. Slow, shallow breaths, but Robert could see her chest rise and fall like gentle lake water.

His eyes went to her face.

"Mrs. Golubovich?"

Her eyes were closed, and she did not seem to hear Robert speaking to her. She lived with his parents, an adopted grandmother whose own family had excommunicated her from their *kumpanía* over a business transaction she entered into with the *gajé*. Jason Mikkado had felt her relatives' judgment was overly severe.

Robert checked for a pulse and had trouble getting one. "Mrs. Golubovich, I'll try to find the doctor." After pulling a pocketknife from his pants, he flipped it open and cut a generous portion of fabric off the hem of her blouse. Using it as gauze, he applied it to her ribs to try to stop the flow of blood. He lifted her hand from her side and placed it over the improvised dressing, applying pressure. "Can you hold this down?"

Her lips moved as if she was talking in her sleep, but no sounds came out. The muscles in her hand did not respond.

"Hold this down." He helped her for a minute. "Did my parents get out?" He could only hope they had. Several more shots rang out on the opposite side of camp. "Were they with you on the truck?"

Mrs. Golubovich's lips stopped moving.

"Do you know where they are?"

Shouts, voices of men Robert didn't recognize, were moving in his direction. The sound of a slow-moving car, engine purring, tires crushing pebbles, reached Robert's ears. He peered out from under the porch but saw nothing on this side of the structure. The smell of smoke had intensified, and now Robert could hear loud crackling, fire's teeth devouring a crunchy feast nearby.

"Stay here."

Robert removed his hand from her side, and the old woman's arm slipped back to the ground. Robert tried to prop it up, anything to hold the blood at bay, but she did not respond. Her chest had stopped moving.

The blood had stopped flowing.

Blast this. Blast this all. Who would engineer this kind of a slaughter over money that was still to be had? Who was this monster Sanso that Janeal had become entangled with? Why didn't the man ask for the money? Anyone here would willingly give it to him.

The first explanation that came to him gave way to no other: Janeal had done something stupid. So stupid that this time they all would pay a price much higher than the usual cultural embarrassment.

If they survived this, he'd be finished with her.

Robert left the broken lighting of the underporch and slipped out into the safer shadows. Sidling along the rear of the building, he reached the corner and tried to assess the situation. He peered out toward the center of the camp.

Over his head, a window shattered and rained glass down into his hair. He ducked and felt tiny shards cut into the back of his neck and hands. Someone was ransacking the medical center. He tried to shake the glass off without getting any near his eyes.

For a moment he was afraid to open them. But the sound of Jason Mikkado's voice made the threat of the glass insignificant. Robert looked. Tiny diamond flecks littered the desert dirt around his feet.

In the center of the camp, in front of the schoolhouse, the *rom baro* stood like a blockade with crossed arms in front of a shiny sedan. It was impossible to see the color in this night lit only by fires. The rear door of the car opened, and a tall man with dark hair and a glistening leather jacket emerged.

The men examined each other for a moment.

"Our exchange wasn't scheduled until tomorrow," Jason said.

"I had reason to come early," said the man.

Robert noted that the gunfire had stopped, though the sounds of the ransacking above him continued.

"What is the meaning of this violence, Sanso? I have your money; I trust you have my product. If there were a problem that warranted such drastic measures, we should have been able to discuss it."

"There is little you and I will be discussing from now on, Jason. Where is your daughter?"

Robert thought it a bad sign that the *rom baro's* eyes flickered away from Sanso as if the question came as a complete surprise. His tone did not change with his answer, though. "Safely out of your reach. She has nothing to do with this."

"Do you really think so? Your daughter has been known to create troubles no other person has the imagination to invent. I must see your daughter."

"No."

"Yes. Because here's the thing: either she has my money—and you can see that I don't trust her to deliver it to me without a clear understanding of what's at stake—or you both have my money, in which case I will not be inclined to deal with you individually."

"I have your money, Sanso, and if you come with me, I'll give it to you now. But end this massacre. My people haven't done anything to offend you."

Sanso laughed. "How is it that leaders are so blind to their own families? Your daughter has deceived you, Jason."

"I'll take you to the money now before you burn it without realizing what you are doing."

"I've *been* to the money and it's *gone!*" Sanso withdrew a knife from his hip and hurled it to the ground, where it embedded itself in Jason's shoe. The *rom baro* yelled and dropped to grab at the knife. Sanso kicked him in the chin, and Jason fell backward, knocking his head on the ground. Sanso jerked the knife out of the shoe himself.

He gestured to two men standing by the car, who lifted Jason to his feet and pointed him in the direction of the meetinghouse. "Now," Sanso said to Jason, "let's go find your devil daughter."

11

Janeal didn't have to get close to her car to see that the money couldn't possibly still be in it. All four doors of the old rusty beast stood open, plus the trunk, the contents of which were spread out behind the car, including the carpet that had covered the spare-tire well.

"He's taken it," she said.

Katie stood beside her, looking at the car without seeming to register what the strange sight meant.

Janeal thought of the bundle of bills tucked up in her bedroom. Five thousand dollars. Coffee change in the context of a million. Sanso couldn't have been so mad over so little.

Janeal approached the car. Someone had busted out three of the windows and cracked the windshield. The first-aid kit was scattered. The contents of her suitcase had been strewn around the rocks. She thought someone must have driven a car over one of the boxes of cooking supplies. The other box lay on its side, utensils and recipe cards spilled out and tossed by the breeze.

Where was the third box?

A thought caught in Janeal's mind at the same time that Katie left the car, running toward the fires.

"Where are you going?" Janeal screamed. She chased Katie, snatching up her empty suitcase on the way. It flapped open and she tried to hold it closed while she ran.

"I have to find my parents. Caleb and Jeremy must be—"

"Robert's looking for them." Janeal reached her and grabbed her hand, pulling Katie up short. "Stay with me. I'm going to the house."

A puff of hot wind caught Katie's curly mass of hair and tossed it across her face. She didn't brush it away. In the distance, the crack of an imploding structure caused Janeal to envision a tent collapsing into glowing embers and coals.

"I don't know why this money is so important to you, Janeal."

"It's not about the mon—"

"You're going to the house to find the money."

"I don't know if it's there!"

"Why look?"

"Because . . . you don't get it, Katie. I don't have time to explain."

Katie shook her head. "When you find it, maybe then you can help the rest of us save lives. If you care." Katie tugged away from Janeal, then bolted.

The suitcase felt heavy in Janeal's hand. The handle cut against her finger joints. Katie would never understand, couldn't understand what was really at stake here. Janeal had no more time to try to convince her.

She ran to the community house.

What happened, Janeal had realized in a flash of missing that third supply box, was that her father had taken the cash when he changed her tire. Now, as *rom baro*, if he hadn't gone to Rio Rancho with the other men to watch the poker tournament, he would be out in the camp, either trying to minimize the damage from the fires that had been set or—more likely, if Sanso's fury was rooted in the missing money—trying to negotiate with his enemy.

In either case, he wouldn't be at the meetinghouse.

While her father and Sanso were occupied, Janeal would go to the community center and find the cash. If she could get to it before Sanso did, she still might be able to help her father, ransom him with it. Jason couldn't have had much time to hide it carefully, and she knew his favorite spots in the little structural addition that was their home. It wouldn't take her long to search. With common sense and a little bit of luck, she could still save him, even if the community was already lost.

That much she was no longer responsible for, and she found it to be a relief. She had done everything Sanso demanded. She couldn't have prevented her father from moving that money.

Janeal raced back into the kitchen and turned back at the door when she saw the gasoline can she had dropped earlier. After a moment's thought, she picked it up and took it into the house with her. She might need it, she thought as she exited the kitchen and turned down the hall that led to her father's rooms.

Sanso would probably burn everything. She would outthink him. She would douse the meetinghouse in fuel, tell him the money was inside, and threaten to send it up in flames if he didn't release her dad.

She hoped to find the money herself first.

Someone shouted her name. Outside, down in the direction of the medical office. She froze. The meetinghouse was silent. Her name came again, faint but close enough for her to believe that the voice was one she knew.

Knew and feared.

12

Robert ran in a crouched position. The camp wasn't so sprawling that it would take him long to get back to the garage. The bigger problem was that now Sanso's men were looking for people like him, hiding, their attention diverted from killing and burning.

By Robert's estimation, Sanso had no fewer than forty armed men with him, and they'd parked their cars at the perimeter of the camp. Though the *kumpanía* numbered more than a hundred, nearly two-thirds of the group was comprised of women and children. And as a whole, the community was less organized and less generously armed—more peacefully minded, in other words—than this group of criminal *gajé*.

"Janeal!" someone shouted. Sanso, Robert thought. "Janeal Mikkado! You have something that belongs to me. So I have taken something that belongs to you!"

A gunshot spit pebbles at Robert's leg and then snagged the thick sole of his work boot, causing his ankle and knee to wrench out from under him. He fell and rolled and felt glass shards still caught in his hair bite his skull.

His momentum was cut short when his spine connected with the support beam of a tent. The wind left him, and it took him several seconds to get it back. When he did, pain shot through his left leg and ankle.

"Janeal Mikkado, bring me what I want so your father can live!"

Robert quickly examined his shoe, wondering if he'd been hit. A small-caliber bullet had embedded itself in the rubber sole, hot enough to melt the materials and prevent Robert from extracting it for a closer look.

Robert crouched again, teeth clenched against the pain, and scooted across the tent's wooden floor to the opposite side, which gave him a view down the corridor to the meetinghouse. The silhouettes of two gunmen moved back and forth in front of the stairs, pausing when they saw Sanso approach, guiding the limping *rom baro*.

"Jason!" Robert's eyes darted in the direction of the voice. It belonged to a man running out into the open space toward his leader, waving his arms and crying. Robert recognized him immediately as Katie's father. "Jason, what is happening? My Crystal, my boys, my Katie!"

Jason stumbled and Sanso did not try to prevent him from falling. Katie's father groaned and reached for Jason as a gunshot cracked the night in two. The man crumpled.

Robert gasped.

A woman screamed, then shouted, "Father!"

Katie.

Katie rushed out in the flickering light toward the still form. Jason pushed himself to his knees and reached out toward her as if begging her to stop and turn away.

Robert was sure Katie didn't register anything but the horror of what had happened. He scrambled out of his hiding place to stop her and was standing upright in the breezeway between two tents before he realized what he had done.

"Katie, don't!" he yelled. One of the dark figures in front of the meeting-house raised his gun.

"No!" Robert shouted, one word appropriate for everyone at the same time.

Katie collapsed over her father, draping his back like a blanket.

The man aiming his gun didn't fire, and Robert realized in a moment that Sanso's raised hand held him off.

The drug dealer leaned over the sobbing girl and gripped her long hair in a fist. Robert took a step forward involuntarily. Sanso forced Katie's face to tilt up at him. Her eyes were squeezed shut, and her mouth was open in a wail.

Sanso smacked her across the temple. "Shut up now so I can get a good look at you."

Katie closed her mouth but did not open her eyes. She continued to cry loudly enough for Robert to hear her.

"Yes, I thought I recognized you," Sanso said. "In a photo. With your friend Janeal. A good friend?"

Katie's shoulders were shaking.

"A good friend, according to my sources. Maybe you can be of help to me. Stand up now. Stand up."

Sanso lifted Katie by the hair still clenched in his fist. She put her hands on the spot and covered his knuckles as she rose to her knees, then her wobbling ankles. Not once did she open her eyes.

"Yes," Sanso said. He let her hair go as if throwing it away. She bowed under the force of his thrust and went down on one knee. "Yes, help your *rom baro* rise and walk, since he is too weak to do it himself. Then you will help me."

Robert rushed to the nearest tent, shielding himself behind the short flight of steps. Katie slipped a hand under Jason's arm as if to help him stand, but Robert could see she had no strength. Jason pushed himself up with his free hand.

Robert would follow as closely as possible, assist when he wasn't so exposed or—

A *crack* sounded at the base of his skull, and he felt a piece of glass go deep into the skin behind his right ear, driven in by some blunt object.

The world tipped, and he found himself capable of just one thought.

Where was Janeal?

13

In her bedroom at the far end of the added wing, without turning on any lights, Janeal threw the five-thousand-dollar bundle she'd taken earlier into the suitcase. It landed next to a change of clothes and a picture of her parents and dead siblings, three sisters, taken before she was born. She stood in the center of the small space on a pink rag rug, imagining the room in daylight, and tried to think of anything else she could possibly want to take with her. She had seconds to decide.

Her eyes lit on a small packet of seeds that sat in the beam of moonlight reaching in through the window. Katie had given these to her for her fifteenth birthday. Sweet peas, too fragile for this desert's summer climate. Janeal had meant to plant them at their California base during the winter, but early frosts two years in a row had discouraged her. That and the idea that she might some-day have a heartier, more permanent place for them to bloom. This, after all, was why Katie had given them to her.

"To plant in that place you daydream about," the card had said.

She picked up the packet and threw it into the case next to the bundle of bills. She closed the case again and set it in the hall. Then she turned over the gas can and emptied about a quarter of it onto her bed, the rug, the desk by the door. She tossed a splash into her closet for good measure.

Moving into her father's room, she checked the places where he usually kept his valuables. He didn't have many, because he wore most of his treasured posses-sions: his wedding ring, his engraved tenth-anniversary watch, a tattoo across his back bearing the names of "his girls." But in the loose floorboard under his bed she found a bowie knife with an ivory handle given to him by his brother, who was now *rom baro* of a *kumpanía* in Canada. In the opaque light fixture she found the keys to the Lexus. In the safe behind the painting of a California vineyard she found his journal, her mother's wedding ring, and a small bag of uncut stones she had not seen before.

Janeal took all these items, planning to find a way to put them back in her father's safekeeping after the house burned and she was on her way with Sanso.

The hidden compartment built into the bookcase-style headboard was empty.

No money.

Janeal ran to the suitcase and heaved her armful of items into it, all but her mother's diamond-studded band, which she slipped onto her own finger. It was safer on her hand than in a container that might or might not survive this night.

She hastily repeated the process with the gasoline in her father's room. She'd been in the house maybe three minutes now, and she'd broken out in a sweat. There was only one other place for her to look.

Her confidence waned as she ran into the bathroom. By the dim glow of the night-light, she opened the medicine cabinet and swept the contents into the sink. A box of matches rattled as it fell onto the top of the pile. She retrieved it and shoved it into the pocket of her jeans. She pried the glass shelves out of their brackets and in her flustered state dropped one. It crashed against the sink and shattered across the floor.

She removed the last shelf then pried out the back panel, breaking two fingernails in the process.

A cascade of bundled bills spilled into the sink.

"Janeal Mikkado!"

The voice that had called to her from outside minutes earlier now traveled down the hall. It could be coming from any part of the house.

"Janeal Mikkado, I'm looking for my money!"

Janeal crammed the bills into the suitcase, tossing out the change of clothes when she saw that it wasn't all going to fit.

Doors in the house started crashing open, bouncing off the doorstops or walls as someone kicked them in.

By the time she scrambled for the last bundle, she was hyperventilating and hardly thinking. He could not come back here so soon. She could not let him see the bathroom and know that she already had the cash.

She closed the case and grabbed the gas can, trailing it behind her as she ran for her bedroom at the end of the hall.

. . . rushed into the room, threw open the window over her desk, climbed onto it, kicked out the screen

. . . heaved the weighty suitcase onto her desk, scraped it over the surface, shoved it to the ground

. . . tumbled out and landed on her backside next to the case, breathing hard.

Apart from the licking tongues of flame in the distance and the occasional far-off shouts, the night was still.

While she lay on the ground, she reached into her pants and fetched the matches, withdrew one, and struck it against the sandy paper on the side of the box.

The wood stick snapped in half.

She lit another one on the fifth strike and made sure it was burning before she tossed it into her room.

Nothing.

The third match would not light.

Tears of anger and frustration escaped against her will.

Standing, she withdrew three matches from the box and struck them together, then leaned in through the ripped screen and hurled them onto the gasoline-soaked throw rug.

It blazed like the red New Mexican sun.

"Janeal Mikkado! You hold your father's life in your hands!"

Janeal stared at the red sun and stopped breathing. He had her father. Her father was in the house. Her father would take Sanso to—

Someone was crying, sobbing uncontrollably. Not her father.

What had she done?

The free flames ran out her bedroom door and down the hall.

Janeal dashed away from the window, the bouncing suitcase biting at her heels, toward the mesa she had so often climbed with her friends. At the base, a pile of rocks that had slid down the face created a short wall. She threw the case behind the pile, then ran back toward the meetinghouse. Already flames had eaten their way through the roof of the living quarters. She raced around the wing and aimed for the kitchen door.

The room had filled with smoke. She ran through, bent over double, holding the collar of her shirt over her mouth. Her eyes burned from tears and heat. She emerged in the dining room. To the left, through the French doors, she could see flames and smoke consuming the hallway and bedrooms. Smoky fingers curled up from under the door. The glass panels were starting to sag in front of the heat.

She moved right, into the hall that led past her father's office and out to the large meeting room.

No sign of anyone. The lights were out here too. Only the fires outside cast a flickering illumination into the large room.

"Dad!" she yelled. "Dad, where are you? *Dad!*"

To the left of the main entrance, the flight of stairs followed the wall and then turned at the corner, leading up into the open-floor game room. To the right, Mrs. Marković sat in her chair, looking out the window.

"Mrs. Marković! You need to go now!" Janeal rushed to her side. "You need to get out."

The old woman turned her head to look at Janeal and smiled this time.

"Please go!" Janeal pleaded.

"You go," Mrs. Marković said, flipping her wrist in a backhanded way toward the stairs. "Both of you. You decide now."

"Who are you talking to?"

Janeal gasped and spun toward the new voice. Salazar Sanso stood on the stairs in the corner landing, leaning against the wall, arms crossed. His face was in shadow. She recovered quickly and turned back to help Mrs. Marković out of her chair. It was empty. Where had—

"You look empty-handed, Janeal." Sanso looked down on her like a hawk about to swoop for a mouse. She caught her breath, tried to change mental gears. Where was Mrs. Marković?

"Why are you doing this?" she demanded. "I did everything you asked! I left the money exactly where I said—"

"You're a fool to betray me."

"I wouldn't . . . I didn't . . . I meant to go with you. Please."

Sanso descended the steps slowly. Behind her, in the dining room maybe, Janeal heard glass explode. She wondered if the fire had hit the wiring of the light fixture over the wide walnut table.

"You were more reluctant last time we spoke," he said. "It's better that you be direct with me. It prevents"—he gestured to the burning tents outside the front window—"misunderstandings."

"Let's be clear then," Janeal said, wondering if she sounded as frightened as she felt. "When I know my father won't be harmed, I'll leave with you."

Sanso stood in front of her now and reached out to tip her chin up toward him. He spoke to her like a lover, whispering low and tender, but the words were all wrong. "Yes, let's be clear. A good number of your little tribe here are already dead. I blame your sloppy communication skills. And if you don't produce the money before this shack burns down, the rest of you will die too."

He let go of her chin and ran a finger down the buttons of her blouse, then let his hands drop. "Except maybe you," he whispered. "I haven't completely decided about you yet." He lowered his face toward hers. "I expect we have two or three minutes to decide."

Janeal's entire body shook when Sanso kissed her, touching her only with his lips as if to test her sincerity. A simple step backward would separate them. A simple step backward might also end her father's life. And hers. Not entirely unwilling, she kissed him back. After a few seconds, he broke contact.

"Now then, that's promising," he whispered. "You can communicate when you like, I see." He turned back to the stairs and began to ascend, stopping on the fourth step to look over his shoulder and say, "I'm pretty good at convincing others myself. Let's go see who plays best at this game."

Upstairs? He was crazy to stay in the building. No doubt that was part of his plan. Janeal looked back toward the wing that was burning. If the fire had moved into the office hallway, she could see no sign of it yet. Still, the man was insane to go up in this burning tinderbox when the front door was two yards out of her reach. She looked at the door. How easy it would be to run out . . .

"Your father is waiting," Sanso said as he turned the corner of the stairs.

"I don't know where the money is," she blurted. Sanso kept walking. His feet hit the steps in a steady rhythm. "Someone found it, moved it—maybe they were watching me."

"Don't say too much more," he said as his head disappeared into the upper room. "You're not so convincing when you lie."

Janeal raced up the steps to the game room. She could smell smoke in the air. The table games separated her from a door on the opposite side of the room that led to an exterior flight of stairs. Next to the door, vinyl-covered bar stools surrounded a green-felt poker table.

The beam of a low-hanging café lamp illuminated her father, perched on one of the stools.

"Dad."

She took several steps toward him before she noticed another figure sitting on a bar stool against the back wall. Katie! Her head was haloed by the dartboard that hung behind her, and her wrists and ankles were bound to the stool's metal rungs. Her eyes were closed, and her face looked puffy, accentuated by the poor lighting in the room. Was she conscious?

"Katie?"

Her friend's eyes opened to slits.

An invisible cold hand reached out of the darkness and touched Janeal directly over her heart, all five fingers grazing her like feathers yet with the power of a force field.

"That's as far as you get to go." Sanso stepped into the boundaries of the red pool table light, loading a gun. "Let's work quickly now, shall we? Here's how the rules of this game will go: I ask a question, you answer. If you give me the wrong answer, I get a point. When I get two points, I win. But you need only one right answer in order to win. And by that I mean you get to come away with me, and I will promise to take care of your loved ones here."

Janeal gripped the edge of the pool table for balance. She nodded her understanding.

"First question. Where is the money, Janeal?"

Janeal's knees weakened.

"I set fire to this house in hopes of smoking out the thief," she said. Her father's eyes rose to meet hers, and they were filled with a fear she had never seen in them before. She tried to communicate with her eyes that he shouldn't be afraid, but how exactly could one do that and keep up a believable pretense? "If they hid it here, they would come running for it, give away the location—"

A gunshot rang out, hammering out the sound of Janeal's words.

Jason crumpled on the poker table.

"Wrong answer."

Janeal started screaming.

14

The problem with women, Sanso thought as he turned his back on Jason Mikkado's body, was that they devoted too much precious thinking time to foolish fantasies. In particular, they thought they were smarter than men like him, which was ridiculous, because no woman he'd met had ever understood the practical matters at stake in a situation like this.

He had hoped this Gypsy daughter would turn out to be an exception to the rule. An exception who might have bested his darling Callista, who was a sharp little tack, if not a genius.

Instead, Janeal was blubbering and howling on the floor now, all because of her own stupidity. After this episode he would have to rethink his theory about younger people being more malleable than the older ones.

A cracking sound in the ceiling drew his eyes upward. The panels glowed red at the peak, and fingers of flame poked through the roof as if trying to pry the lid off the room. Yes, he noted, Janeal saw it too. This would create an interesting complication. He couldn't have guessed this fire would start at the top and work its way down. A spark from the living quarters must have leaped onto the old barn shingles.

The floor felt hot. Maybe the fire was also beneath them, or in the walls, climbing.

Like he was. Climbing the walls in need of his money. In need of those bills.

Sanso needed a million dollars like he needed a boat in this desert. And this was what Janeal Mikkado and the rest of this sorry band were too stupid to understand. That his need was not financial, but practical.

Practical. *Practical.*

A section of the roof collapsed onto the pool table, sending Janeal reeling away. The felt ignited first, spewing smoke back up into the night sky. Other pieces of roofing began to fall between them like meteors.

The money was not his only in the sense that it belonged to him. It was, as literally as one could get, *his* money, his creation. He had printed those bills, and only sheer luck and the stupidity of the American government had failed to detect the fraud yet.

Instead, the DEA was so narrowly focused on their own mission that they had decided—so said one of his sources—to document the serial numbers and put the money back into circulation. Back into circulation with Jason Mikkado, the way-station master, and hoped to trace the money to other drug sources in the network.

Like Sanso, the DEA didn't care about the actual amount of money. To them, as to him, a million dollars was insignificant. A speck of dust on the $70 billion annual American drug empire, a microscopic atom in the international market. But a million dollars put back into circulation that could be traced back to his cartel? Now, that was worth more.

If they discovered the bills were counterfeit, generated by one of Sanso's profitable printing ventures, that particular discovery could form the lyrics of Sanso's swan song. In the end, the best thing that could happen tonight would be for the money to burn. Sanso's peace of mind, however, needed more certainty that it had actually happened.

All this was too much for Janeal's minute, female, childish pea brain to grasp.

"Let's tally the score!" he yelled over her wail and the crackle of flames that had begun to spread across the room. He approached Janeal's friend—Karen, was it? Kathy? "Salazar Sanso, one; Janeal Mikkado, zero! This is a handicapped game, Janeal. An easy win for you. You only need one right answer to get out of here alive."

The dark-haired girl—ah yes, it was *Katie*—eyed him with the passion of a zombie, dead already after the shooting of her father. How ironic that Janeal would be responsible for all this death tonight, the death of men so much more brilliant than she.

Maybe he should have shot the friend first.

No matter now.

He realized that Janeal's cries had fallen silent, and he turned to look in her direction. A low wall of fire rose between them.

Sanso raised the gun to Katie's head and stared Janeal in the eye.

What he saw there caught him off guard. A flash of alertness, of bright light behind her shadowy gaze. Ingenuity perhaps. He had expected despair, not this courage before death. He found the surprise titillating.

"You don't care about the money," Janeal said.

Sanso cocked the gun for effect. "I care much more than you know."

The corner of her mouth twitched. "I mean you don't care about the quantity. You said the money has symbolic value. It's counterfeit, isn't it? You print counterfeits that you don't want the government to know about."

Sanso found himself overcome with a desire to kiss that sassy, twitching mouth. "Come with me and we'll see."

"It's in the canyon," she said. "A quarter mile north, and a fifteen-minute hike in at the point where it narrows. Under the lip of the flat rock. But I'm not coming with you."

If she had looked at him when she answered, he would have called her answer a lie and killed the coal-headed beauty on the spot. But Janeal had locked eyes with her friend, pleading with her words and her heart that he spare her life. This was the truth, plus another layer of something he couldn't discern.

"You'll come," he said. "They always do."

Flames from the roof descended and met the blaze rising from the floor. Smoke puffed up and out of the open room.

"Go now," Janeal said. "You have what you need." He hesitated one more time, hung up on whether she was playing him.

"Get out!" she yelled.

Sanso exited by the back stairs, wondering if the Gypsy chef was a mind reader.

If she was, she would understand that he'd left her and her friend alive only so they both would die. Janeal Mikkado, at least, deserved to burn in a blaze of glory. With her father dead and the money out of her reach, she had been reduced to ash already. It was the least he could do to give her a noble death. A beautiful death.

15

Thirty seconds. For a life-or-death choice, for Janeal to flee the front staircase before it was fully engulfed, for Sanso to return to the main door below, for him to lock her in.

Thirty seconds for Katie to die on the metal and vinyl stool she was tied to, for Janeal to burn alive with her if she stayed. Because in the time it took Janeal to pass through that wall of fire and free Katie from the ropes—if that was possible—there would be no time to leave.

Thirty seconds for Janeal to retrieve the money and flee this camp, survive this nightmare.

"Janeal, help me." Katie's voice was weak but calm. Much calmer than the lightning storm in Janeal's brain, firing its prickly energy at random. Janeal could no longer see her friend. Her mind went to the shock she'd received at the stairs yesterday. Then to the zinging touch of Mrs. Marković's hand.

"Can you bust up the stool? Bounce it, break it, something?" Janeal said.

Janeal could see Katie's shadowy form rocking atop the rickety thing, swaying enough only to fall sideways into a Coke machine. Katie's shoulder landed in it, sounding a metallic *thud*.

"My ankles . . . they're locked in."

"Keep trying."

Twenty seconds. The flames fanned out from the center of the room. If she went now, she'd never get back across.

"Janeal. I need you." Katie coughed.

"Is my father . . . ?" Dead for sure, but Janeal couldn't think of any other reply to Katie's plea.

Katie didn't answer.

Smoke expanded, clogging its upward escape, and filled Janeal's head. She could hardly breathe. Would the smoke kill her before the flames reached her? She dropped to her knees.

"Janeal, we could still get out through the door back here!"

She felt her head sway slowly from side to side, heard the words she hadn't dared speak aloud. "I can't. I'm so sorry, Katie, I can't." Not when she could almost certainly save herself. Any other choice had an unknown outcome. She would burn alive. They would both die.

Sanso would win.

"You can't? You can't because you have to save your precious money!" Katie shouted.

The metal and plastic frame of the foosball table started to pop and snap.

"You found the money! You took it already! Janeal, what have you done?"

Tears welled in Janeal's eyes. "I—yes, but it's not that!" What was it, then? *Daughters, you are full of deceit.*

Ten seconds.

"Janeeeeeal . . ." Katie's plea turned into a moan, chilling Janeal in the blazing room. Her friend, her best friend since they were five, was about to die.

"Please! Pleeeaase!" Katie started to shriek. Janeal's tears evaporated in the heat. "Pleasepleaseplease!"

In a moment of pristine clarity, she knew that she must attempt to save Katie, no matter the cost. She could never live with herself if she turned her back now.

Janeal stared at the rising flames and felt her certainty pushed back by the heat. A million dollars and a chance to survive. A suicidal effort—or was it a mental obstacle?—to save a dear friend's life. The slimmest possibility that they could both live.

She wished for a chance to turn the day back, to stand on that mesa and refuse to go with Sanso.

A groan escaped her. Katie, Katie. Janeal couldn't do this. Wouldn't. There was nothing she was honestly willing to do but buy her own survival.

Janeal raised her palm toward the fire. The heat pushed back in visible rippling waves as if it were liquid. She could smell the singed crispness of her own hair. She coughed and coughed.

In her mind's eye she saw herself leap to her feet and rush at the fire, screaming for her friend to hold on. She saw fire blister her skin the moment it made contact.

She couldn't do this. Running into the flames was lunacy!

A white light flashed on her horizon, then collapsed to perfect darkness, as if the flames had melted her eyes. The air cracked over her head, striking down as though it possessed hands and a whip. She dropped to her hands and knees, absorbing the shock of the explosion. The room went silent. Perfectly still and completely black.

For a moment she knelt unmoving in the darkness, wondering if she'd been killed, if this absolute darkness was death. Her life at age seventeen had come to a flaming end and her last act had been to turn her back on her closest friend for the promise of a fortune.

Emptiness swallowed her. Fear coiled its long fingers around her throat and chest, a wraith that was claiming her as its own.

But she was shaking, so she couldn't be dead.

The darkness faded and she found herself facing a wall of flame waiting to consume her. She was alive. She was alive, but something had changed.

She sensed this truth in the blood that pounded through her veins, tasted it in the choking air she drew into her lungs. The fire roared, licking hungrily at the walls and ceiling. She had to get out! She pushed herself to her feet, scrambling for orientation. The wall of flame was impenetrable now, no chance to—

Movement caught her eye. A figure staggering across the room.

She blinked, and when her eyes opened again, the shadow through the flame was gone. Someone had been watching? Katie had managed to break free? Or Janeal was seeing things. Either way it was too late; she had to get out, leave the dead to the dead.

Janeal swiveled her neck to see the stairs. Miraculously, the way was still clear. She fled.

The clock of her beating heart ticked, a two-faced time bomb.

Five . . . four . . . three . . .

16

Red light pulsed like loud dance music behind Robert's eyes, expanding into his brain with every beat. He rolled over, tasting dust, gripping the side of his head where he'd been hit.

Tacky half-dried blood stuck to his fingers. It took several seconds before his eyes obeyed his command that they open and examine the damage.

His hand was a shadow, black and textureless in the foreground of a bonfire. The tent next to him was engulfed in flame, and his body would be its next source of fuel.

Robert rolled up onto his palms and knees, swayed there for a moment, then managed to get a foot under him. One. Two. His tall frame threatened to topple when he first got upright, but when the sickening waves in his head stopped crashing, he was able to get his bearings.

The camp's central corridor was empty. The smoldering ruins of burned tents glowed under a black sky. Where had Sanso and his people gone? The dealer's car was no longer there. There were no shouts or shots, no sign of friend or enemy. Robert wondered how long he'd been unconscious.

Where was Janeal? Katie? Jason? Robert's family? Mrs. Golubovich—he saw in his mind her dead body under the stairs and prayed to a God he'd never believed in that they had made it out of the camp alive.

Staggering out into the exposed space between the central rows of tents, Robert dropped to his knees. Everything in the camp was on fire or smoldering. White flakes of ash drifted down from the cloudless black sky like lazy snow, dusting his arms and face. The stench of burnt wood and canvas made his eyes water.

He bowed under the force of possibility that he was the sole survivor of this Armageddon.

To his left, a couple hundred yards away, the meetinghouse was nearly engulfed in hungry flames. The towering building crowned the corridor in which he sat, and the heat from it pulsed past his face.

Fiery tongues darted out of the windows and flickered upward, looking for fuel that hadn't already been consumed.

Boom.

The dull, unexpected concussion knocked Robert flat. If he hadn't already been on his knees, the force would have thrown him backward by yards. The heat intensified and then retracted, and Robert thought he smelled his own singed hair.

The propane tank.

From a disconnected place in the back of his mind rose the question of whether Janeal might still be behind the garage.

He couldn't imagine that she was, considering that Katie had entered the fray alone some time ago—an action he interpreted as proof that Janeal had gone off on her own before that moment. Katie was no coward, but Janeal was the reckless one.

Even so, Robert willed his body to rise. The old meetinghouse had been leveled by the explosion, reduced from a billowing barn to a flaming heap. Skirting the demolished building enough to avoid being burned, he pointed his steps in the direction of the garage.

The ramshackle structure was fully lit, and the wide doors had been rolled open. Surely it was the only structure on the property that had not ignited. The blond woman he had seen earlier and one other man were tearing the place apart, looking for something. Janeal's money, most likely. Jason's tan Lexus sat in the farthest dock looking like a bird in flight—trunk, hood, all doors wide open. A third person was cutting open the leather seats.

That man, the one who had confronted Jason.

Salazar Sanso stormed into the light from the direction of the canyon, a string of men with flashlights and guns trailing behind him. Robert dropped behind a boulder, shielded by the night.

The blond woman stopped what she was doing and studied his face as if sizing up the reason for his mood. Then she turned back to the cupboard she'd been searching and slammed the door shut.

"It's not here either," she said.

Sanso cursed and propelled his own Maglite across the garage. The man slicing through the Lexus had emerged, but ducked as the flashlight whizzed by his head and crashed into a Peg-Board lined with wrenches and screwdrivers.

"After five hours of searching, you're still blind? You people are worthless!"

The woman faced Sanso and folded her arms across her chest, the calmest figure in the bunch. The others fidgeted.

Sanso seemed to regroup under her unflappable stare and after a few moments said, "It's just as well. If we haven't found it, it's burned out there by now."

"No chance she hid it off the property?"

"No one's left the property all night. Or entered. The men at the poker game?"

"We took care of them on their way in, around three thirty. No money on them either, except some paltry winnings." The woman came to stand next to him. "No chance she's buried it in a hole and will come back for it later?"

Sanso shifted to look at the meetinghouse. "Not a chance."

"She died in the house?" she asked.

"All three. The old man and both girls."

Robert closed his eyes as if that would quell the sickness rising up from the bottom of his stomach.

"You should have kept her alive until we had it in hand," she said.

A timber groaned and cracked.

"That's not what you suggested earlier." Fury escaped the cage of Sanso's teeth. "I made my choice. She made hers." He paused. "She would have died before telling me where the money was no matter how long I waited."

"So how much longer shall we look?"

"We quit now," Sanso said. "DEA comes at daybreak. If we haven't found it yet, they won't find it either."

17

Robert awoke on his stomach, his forehead pressed into the dry red dirt between his fisted hands. Someone was tugging at his shoulder and shouting, "Live one!"

He heard the sound of running feet coming in his direction.

Robert rolled left onto his back, shielding his eyes from the bright morning.

"Don't move."

He had no desire to do anything but die. Die like his family, his friends. He smelled smoke as strong as it had smelled the night before. It saturated his clothes, his nostrils. He would remember this permanent stink for the rest of his life.

In an unmemorable haze of information gathering, the men who surrounded him in short order identified themselves as DEA and him as the only survivor who hadn't needed to be airlifted to the hospital in Santa Fe. They couldn't give him any names until the victims were identified. They weren't sure those folks would survive. It would be some time before they could assess the body count. Local law enforcement and other agencies with jurisdiction were on their way.

After a lengthy period of questioning, a field agent named Harlan Woodman gave Robert a card and instructions to stay close while Woodman made arrangements to shelter Robert during the investigation. After learning of his connection to Jason and Janeal Mikkado, then hearing his account of Janeal's encounter with Salazar Sanso, they decided to keep word of his survival out of the press, to protect him as a witness. Robert welcomed the privacy for different reasons.

A medic tended to the gash over Robert's ear, then left him alone to stare at the remains of the meetinghouse.

The charred skeleton of Jason's office desk still glowed red. The fire department poked around in the ash, squelching hot spots, while investigators trailed behind, looking anxious, as if the fire crew might destroy some critical piece of evidence.

On the far side of the collapsed structure, a threesome stopped poking and crouched with their backs toward him to examine something. He rose and moved toward them, putting himself within earshot of their discussion.

"Survivor said there were three. Two women and a man."

"We'll have to take his word for it. The place is incinerated."

"No way to tell a bone from a cue stick in this pile of ash."

"What is this thing? A pool table?"

"Where there's cue sticks . . ."

"Hey guys, check this out." The one who'd walked away held something up with a long pair of metal tongs.

"Put it down," another complained. "You're not supposed to touch—"

"Lighten up," the third said. "We know what happened here."

Robert looked at the object, then doubled over as his vision tunneled.

"Best ten dollars this person ever spent on their feet," the tong-holder said. "Are these things indestructible now or what?"

"No way. Why didn't those melt?"

And though he shut his eyes, Robert could not stop seeing the slightly distorted but unmistakable shape of flip-flops that had once clad Janeal Mikkado's feet.

He staggered out of the camp and never looked back.

18

Try as he did to convince himself that the money had been incinerated, Sanso could not fully rest that afternoon, not even in his favorite room of his favorite hotel.

So he was doubly annoyed when Callista barged into the curtain-drawn suite with her phone open and extended, saying, "You'll want to take this call."

"I told you not—"

She tossed the phone with precise aim, hitting him on the chest. The phone bounced onto the bed, and Callista left the room.

He loved her brazen ways. He couldn't help it.

Sanso found the phone, dropped back onto the stack of pillows, and put the receiver to his ear.

"What?"

"I have your money."

Janeal. He shot up on the bed and turned, placing his feet square on the floor, smiling.

"You're no Gypsy. You're a sorcerer."

"I'm whatever you want me to be. Anything but your friend."

"So what exactly did you think I was, then? The first time you met me?"

"A businessman. Are you a good businessman, Salazar Sanso? Because if you are, I believe you'll want to do business with me."

"The quality of my business dealings isn't determined by the interests of other parties," Sanso said, rising to pace.

"Then I won't waste your time."

"Wait!" Sanso took a breath, irritated with himself for sounding desperate. "I'd like to hear your proposal."

"Oh, I have no proposal to offer you. I have terms. Requirements."

Sanso strode to the door and threw it wide open, looking for Callista so that he could direct his fury at some object. She was there, sitting in a club chair with her feet propped up on the ottoman. She acknowledged him by raising one unsurprised eyebrow.

"What are your *terms*, then?"

"One million dollars, in fifties. Real fifties. I want it by midnight."

"And why would I hand over a million dollars to you, little girl?"

"You're not going to hand them over. We are going to trade. A million for a million."

"You keep your million." *And I'll find out where you are and come get it myself.* "If you don't like the denominations, I can't help you. I'm not a banker."

"No, you're a printer. And I'll bet you wouldn't want anyone to know that. It wasn't so hard to figure that out, once I had time to think it through. "

Sanso's fury left him, and his body began to tremble—with excitement. Anticipation. Satisfaction at having finally found a worthy adversary. He glanced at Callista and she nodded. She appreciated what Janeal represented to him, or she would have handled this call herself.

He blew Callista a kiss.

"I want a million dollars. A million real dollars. In exchange, you will get these counterfeits back. I don't care what you do with them."

He would stretch this game out if he could. "It's a lot of work for an even exchange. But if you're willing to negotiate some of the terms—"

"If you don't give me what I want, I'll take these bills to the Secret Service. They have reason to make you one of their top clients. And then I'll devote my life to hunting you down and—"

Sanso laughed so hard he snorted.

"Sorcerer or not, you'll have to work on your threats. You're not so good at that part of this."

He heard the heavy breathing of a person trying to stay in control of a flyaway temper. "If you don't care, then I'll tell the DEA that the bills are fake. Isn't that what you're trying to avoid here? Isn't that why you don't want them to get their hands on it?"

That was precisely why he wanted those bills. If the American government lopped off this leg from beneath Sanso's empire, it wouldn't be able to stand.

"Janeal, dear, I can see the value of your *proposal*—let's call the spades *spades*, shall we?—and I accept it."

"I am not finished yet."

Sanso grinned at Callista and rolled his eyes. "Then you had better wrap up," he said. "I'm a busy man."

"In exchange for your counterfeits, you agree to leave me alone. You agree never to seek me out, never to do business with me or my people again, never to show your face within a hundred miles of wherever I might be."

"I don't know. Some of those promises might be hard to keep."

"And I will promise never to betray you."

Sanso sobered. "You are easily bought. Your character is no greater than mine in the end, is it?"

19

The front fender of Jason Mikkado's vandalized Lexus nearly touched the support post of the pay phone. The swinging yellow pages dangled from a cord at the base and bounced off the headlight in the breeze, which was kicking up red dust. The driver's door stood open, sending out the dinging reminder that keys still hung from the ignition.

The interior reeked of smoke. In the backseat, a suitcase looked like it was stuffed with youthful dreams instead of a million dollars in bundled bills.

In the front seat, Janeal dropped her dirty face into smoke-stained hands and cried. She cried for her murdered father, for her dead family, for the lost ring of her mother's, which had fallen off her hand in the chaos, unnoticed. She cried for the best friend she could not bring herself to save, for the black-haired beauty who should have lived. She cried for the boyfriend she could not bring with her even if he'd survived, the good guy who would never stoop to any life that involved illegal dealings with a criminal businessman.

Salazar Sanso had been right about her. Like a prophet, he saw her for what she was and named her heart's desires before she could identify them herself. She hated him for it. She loved him too, for understanding her like no one else could.

Janeal cried for the child she no longer could be, and for the despicable woman she had become.

She was soaking wet, crawling on her hands and knees through mud, half of her in water that rushed over her calves. The muddy ground numbed the heels of her hands. She lifted one palm to examine the strange fact that she couldn't feel it. Something about her skin was not right.

Something about her eyes too. She couldn't see her hand. She blinked several times and squinted, yet she couldn't bring anything into focus. In fact, she really didn't want to see right now. She wanted to fall asleep, feeling light. So light that she might have been picked up by a breeze and drifted here without her knowing, senseless. But the rushing water and the sensation of pebbles pressing into her kneecaps held sleep off.

Other than the impression she had of these textures in the ground, she couldn't feel anything. Why couldn't she see? She raised one hand and poked herself in the eyeball. That stung, but tears didn't run down her cheeks. She widened her eyes in case that would help, and her lids seemed to lodge under her brows. She touched her face. The pads of her fingers were sticky.

Her cheeks, her jaw were sticky. And uneven. Lumpy. Very unlike the smooth lines of her skin she remembered.

She felt no pain and wondered why she thought she should.

She smelled wood smoke and something stronger—smoke from rubber or chemicals or something man-made. And something stronger, a stench. She could not place it, sensed that she didn't want to place it.

A sound reached her ears. A low rumbling, as of distant engines. A crunching, as of tires rolling over unpaved ground. A shout. Several voices shouting. She couldn't make out the words, just the tone. Something boisterous. The vocals morphed into surprise, then panic.

Their panic became hers, broadsided her like a contagious virus, and she felt her body beginning to shake. She turned her head toward the sounds, afraid of what they might mean. The tilting of her jaw upset the balance of her dark world, and the resulting nausea dropped her into blackness.

PART II

Slow Burn

FIFTEEN YEARS LATER

20

Janeal Mikkado had not gone to Greece right away. That did not happen until several years afterward, when Milan booked the trip, a vacation to celebrate the promotion he had given her.

A promotion she had weaseled out of him without his knowing it.

Instead, when she left her meeting with Salazar Sanso in an Albuquerque sports bar, she took her authentic small bills, rented a car, and drove to Missouri, where she connected with a *kumpania* her father had done business with three years earlier.

She was in this camp only briefly, because she had no intention of staying with them, and because they expressed no desire for her to stay. Her terse visit had the unexpected side effect of injecting bitterness into her grief over her father's death. In this place where people were valued for little more than their business transactions, she found herself angry at her father for his dishonesty. Who he really was, what he really did with his money and his allegiances—he had hidden it from her, the one person who loved *him* above all else.

Somehow, allowing bitterness to overshadow her loss made it easier to move on. To forget what she had left behind. To believe she had left it unwillingly.

The little community had been welcoming of her money, what she told them she had, which was a fraction of the truth. But it was enough to fund their resources and secure for herself a new name, a birth certificate, and a functioning social security number, the first personal documents she'd ever possessed.

When summer waned and September leaves turned gold, Jane Johnson bought a cheap but reliable used car and pointed it in the direction of New York City. Janeal never came to think of herself as Jane, though no one had called her by her given name afterward—not even Milan, who neither knew nor seemed to care about the details of her past. That was as she wanted it. But Jane was a good, invisible name that would be of use in a city where she wanted to be invisible.

Vanishing turned out to be easier than she imagined, a magic trick facilitated by her funding, which she invested and rationed strategically. Within the year she rented a nondescript studio apartment, secured a food-prep job in the kitchen of a small family-run restaurant, enrolled at New York University, and began to work on creating her new life.

At the center of her vision for this life was a dark hole. She intended to fill it with her regrets, her loss, and her choices, then use her new life to form a lid that would cap it, seal it, and obscure it from anyone who dared to look.

She planned to do this alone and had a good running start. But four years later, as she prepared to enter NYU's graduate publishing program, she met Milan Finch.

Janeal had become an apprentice pastry chef at an upscale restaurant by then and was summoned from the kitchen at the request of a patron. He wanted to meet the person responsible for the astounding sweet-cheese pastries, *kalitsounia kritis*, the likes of which he had not tasted since his recent visit to Crete.

When Milan saw Janeal emerge from the kitchen, he stood and stared without saying anything for several long seconds. She glanced between him and the man he dined with. A business associate, she assumed by the suit and tie and the portfolio that balanced on the corner of the table. Janeal had to break the silence, not because she was embarrassed but because people were starting to look.

"I hope everything is agreeable?"

"Everything," he finally said. "Especially the stunning color of your hair."

The remark struck a chord of loneliness in Janeal that his stare had failed to trigger. She involuntarily reached up to tuck a strand back into her toque, then returned his stare to compensate for her momentary lapse of composure. Janeal found him to be handsomer than she had first noticed. Late thirties if she had to guess, but he was fit and might be older than he appeared. Italian descent maybe, with those olive-colored eyes and square face. Wealthy, judging by the tailored suit.

"And the food?"

"What are they paying you? Tell me and I'll pay you double to be my private chef. My employment package is very appealing. I offer many fine benefits."

Janeal had chosen pastries and publishing over her more likely choice as a chef in part to avoid, as much as possible, the gas stovetops, open flames, and flambés of nearly every professional kitchen. Yet she was too amused by his brazenness to be offended. "Your money would be better invested in a native Greek," she said.

"You're not one?" He feigned surprise.

She would swap mockery with mockery then, if that was what he wanted. "No more than you are. I've never been there." Maybe she had meant to boast.

"Then I'll take you," he announced. "I really must take you." And she believed he was fully conscious of his double entendre.

He did take her, in both senses, and she let him because it served her purposes. Milan, it turned out, was a rising star in the world of periodicals, and she soon convinced him that she was more talented in his editor's chair than in his kitchen.

Janeal recognized many years prior to seeing the Acropolis, though, that he was even more motivated by selfish goals than she was. She also recognized the black hole at the center of his own life. Unlike hers, his hole was uncapped and bottomless. Insatiable.

Even so, she leaned into it quite daringly.

Janeal could not say why she had chosen this day, some fifteen years after the death of her father, to review the path her life had taken. Maybe the flashback was a longing, or maybe it was some kind of misplaced hope, or maybe it was a temporary balm, like the cool emptiness of the elevator she rode in as it zoomed up to the twenty-first floor of her workplace above Manhattan.

Or maybe the memory had merely escaped from that pit she had spent so many years failing to seal off. The nightmares, recurring with increasing regularity, oozed out from under the lid like steam escaping a manhole cover. The headaches, too, drove memories of the past into the center of her brain, threatening to split it apart.

Whatever the true explanation for her reminiscing this evening, she understood the memories to be a symbol of an old transition in her life—and a harbinger of a new transition she would soon have to make.

Janeal gingerly touched her ribs. Milan was always careful to bruise her where no one would see it. He'd never raised a hand to her face, never pinched her throat, never mangled her wrists. The violence had started out years ago as play, as a twisted fantasy that always teetered at the edge of a cliff, with pleasure on solid ground and terror on the drop-off. All this time they had balanced there, mutually demanding, enjoying the danger of a possible freefall without ever having to encounter it.

Until last night, when Milan shoved her over the edge, replacing the thrill with the certainty that death was rushing up to meet her. If Milan had not removed his knees from her lungs when he did, she surely would have hit the earth hard enough to plunge six feet into the soil.

He had been upset over a failed business acquisition.

Janeal transferred her designer bag to the other shoulder and checked her posture.

The elevator dinged, and its doors parted onto a gray ocean of cubicles. Her corner office was farther than any other from the elevator, and getting to it would be nothing short of a fifteen-hundred-meter gauntlet. At seven o'clock on Friday evening, the floor should have been fairly empty, populated only with workaholics and a few less dedicated who simply didn't have a life outside the office.

Like her. Especially now that Milan would no longer be a part of it. Maybe she should have gone home after making her appearance at the mayor's cocktail party. How predictable of her to return to the office.

Indeed, she was faced with a crowd of people who seemed to know they could find her here now, people who mistakenly believed that she was more readily available during this late end-of-the-week hour than at any other time.

Mandy, the art director, headed toward her with several sheets of paper in hand, as if she'd been waiting for the elevator light. In another cubicle, the managing editor stood, wearing a resigned expression for having been beaten out of the starting gate. His eyes turned toward the clock mounted on the far end of the room before he sat again.

Janeal exited, placing her full weight on her right leg to avoid limping, in spite of her swollen kneecap. The phone in her office was ringing as if it hadn't stopped since she left at four.

She saw her assistant's straw-haired head bobbing above cubicle walls, coming toward her. Alan Greenbrook cut Mandy off as Janeal reached her own glass-boxed office on the other side of the room. He held Janeal's black coffee in one hand and extended the other to take Mandy's designs.

"I'll call you when she's ready," Janeal heard him say as she took the more circuitous route to her own door.

She had occupied the corner office in Milan's high-rise for four years now as editor in chief of *All Angles*, an acclaimed social-interest magazine that had been described as "an everyman's rendering of the less accessible giants." The publication was simply worded without being simpleminded. It was, in truth, as liberal as many newsstand bestsellers, but its name and its reputation mandated that its pages be shared equally with complementary conservative viewpoints. Not because Janeal believed in it, but because there was money in it.

Conservatives had as many dollars to spend as the liberals did, but fewer options to spend it on when it came to printed material. Until Milan Finch conceived of *All Angles* sometime during his undergrad years. His business plan, which started out as a senior thesis and then morphed into an MBA venture, had little to do with ideology and much to do with capital return. He delivered what people wanted to hear, included conservatives and liberals and those who avoided labels in one big happy audience where all agreed to disagree, called it objective and balanced, and accepted their money for articulating their positions without assessing them or forcing them into head-to-head debates.

All Angles never broke stories, just talked about them. The magazine exposed nothing and investigated little. There was nothing hard-hitting about it. Only an appeal to the individual rather than the collective whole. A promise of representation. Milan had been the self-appointed publisher since the magazine's inception, but in the four years since he had promoted Janeal to editor in chief, its circulation had quadrupled. In the last two years, the interactive online site had rivaled YouTube in traffic.

It was all the result of Janeal's long-plotted ten-year plan, based on her clear sense that all people wanted these days was to be heard rather than to listen. That very fact was what had allowed her to fly under Milan's radar for so long; he was no different from the average Joe. The moment Janeal had realized this, she saved herself from becoming the average Jane: she recognized and put a stop to her journey of becoming someone who wanted others to hear the pain of her beating heart. Her transparency in those days sickened herself. It was why Salazar Sanso had wooed her all those years ago. It was why Milan Finch started her off in this line of work as a department head.

"You understand my readers better than anyone else," he had said.

Yes. Milan Finch was right about that much at least. But he was wrong to believe she had not changed. That was one of his many mistakes.

Janeal felt the onset of her nightly migraine. The thought that Milan might have ever been right about anything inflamed her brain cells.

"Ms. Johnson." Alan tucked the stack of papers between his elbow and ribs and held her door open. How he managed to get there in time to open it for her impressed her without fail each week. As always, he would be grinning. Grinning in spite of her.

"Alan."

His failure to ever be publicly unhappy, especially on a Friday night, both inspired and annoyed her. Alan was neither a workaholic nor a social outcast. He never said he could be spending these evenings with his cute girlfriend at his brother's nightclub, no matter how late Janeal kept him.

He swept into the room behind her, graceful as a dancer, doing everything simultaneously and without appearing frantic: shut the door, place the coffee on the coaster, lay the papers on the blotter, pick up the ringing phone and nestle the receiver between his jaw and shoulder, reach out to take her coat before she fully shrugged it off.

"Jane Johnson's office," he said.

Janeal loved Alan like she imagined she'd love a son if she had one. Not that he needed to know it. At age thirty-two, she had plenty of years left to think of sons, provided Milan was not their father.

"Yes, sir, the interview will appear in Monday's edition."

Provided Milan was not their father. She clutched her bag, a seven-hundred-dollar tote gifted to her by its designer, and brushed past her personal assistant, mentally reviewing what she had spent the day deciding to do. Her time had come.

Alan continued to talk. To Senator Lynch, she presumed. "Nothing is printed without her approval, sir."

Someone had delivered a gift basket, which sat on the credenza behind her desk, under the exterior window. New York's version of stars—checkerboard squares of illuminated high-rise offices—dotted an otherwise black cityscape. She looked at the note. It was from a physician at St. Luke's involved in the misadministered-drugs scandal of last month, thanking her for her fair representation and blah blah blah.

"I'll pass along your message. Thank you." Alan hung up the phone, probably before the caller had stopped speaking, and placed her coat on the door hook.

Champagne. Dark chocolate. Imported grapes. Caviar. She threw the caviar in the trash.

"Senator Lynch would like to review a copy of the article before we go to press."

"Why doesn't his assistant already have it?" She turned back to her desk, champagne bottle in hand.

Alan pointed to three sheets on her blotter. "Mandy had to redesign. Apex Electronics pulled their ad."

"Why?"

"Something to do with Mr. Finch's pending acquisi—"

"Angelo didn't find a replacement?"

"He's working on it."

"Call Templeton & Wallace. They'll come through."

"They don't want to be on the same page with Lynch."

"We don't really care if they see eye-to-eye with the senator, do we?"

"Of course not."

"*All Angles* is about representing all angles, isn't it?"

"It is."

"And I'm scheduled to attend their fund-raiser next month, am I not?"

"You are."

"So Angelo can call them again."

"I'll let him know."

Janeal extended the bottle to Alan. "Take that home to your girlfriend tonight."

His lips parted. "This is a four-hundred-dollar bo—"

"Trust me, the expensive stuff is rarely worth the fanfare. What's next?"

Alan didn't seem to know what to do with the expensive bubbly but settled on leaning forward and placing it in front of him on the wide cherry desk.

"Mr. Finch asked me to pass along a message."

"Like a boy without the guts to call me himself," she murmured. Alan's smile neither confirmed nor denied he had heard her. In truth, Milan had left three messages on her cell since leaving her loft apartment last night, and she had ignored them all. "And?"

"The meeting with the board has been moved up to eight o'clock tomorrow morning."

A Saturday board meeting. As if that move would work against her. It wouldn't, though the change would make her course of action slightly trickier.

"The presentation packets will have to be ready before you leave, then."

"They're ready now."

Alan was a good boy, he was. Barely twenty-two and indefatigable.

"Fine. Get Thomas Sanders on the phone for me. I need a private meeting with him. Now."

Milan never spent Friday evenings at the office. Tonight, though, he might be motivated to come in.

"If he can't, perhaps we—"

"I don't need to know all the possible contingencies, Alan. Just make it happen."

Alan picked up her phone again and dialed a number. Outside her office, two people stood at the glass door waiting for permission to come in.

"You know, Ms. Johnson"—Alan held the phone between his ear and his shoulder—"our lives around here would be considerably easier if they'd make you president of the board."

Janeal bent over her handbag in search of the PDA to prevent Alan from seeing her smile. He was the only person in the office she would allow to speak to her that way, mostly because he was the only one who had the guts to do it.

"Not president." She kept her tone flat. "Publisher." She straightened and twisted her torso to look at him across her desk. "But then you wouldn't be rid of me, would you?"

21

The back of Robert's neck dripped with streams of sweat. At 109 degrees in the shade and climbing, the Chihuahuan Desert sun would cure his skin into leather. Robert and his colleague Harlan Woodman had been there six hours, which was not long by stakeout standards, but this particular Friday afternoon seemed endless.

Their shade was man-made, generated by a white-tarp lean-to propped up inside a wiry tangle of mature creosote bushes.

Robert sneezed for the umpteenth time, overcome by the plant's pungent odor, and Harlan said, "If we don't get word in five minutes, I'm sending you out."

"That's what you said five minutes ago."

Harlan trained his binoculars on a boulder fifty yards off. "Allergies like that have got to be contagious."

"Consider yourself inoculated."

The boulder was no mere rock, but the marker for the entrance to a tunnel that dropped twenty feet down into the ground and then ran due south for three quarters of a mile, out of Arizona and into Mexico.

This tunnel was one of a huge network that connected Mexico to the southern United States. Miles and miles of tunnels dug out and exploited by everyone from solo coyotes to gangs to cartels with the intention of avoiding border patrol. No one this side of the border knew for sure how extensive they really were. Robert liked to imagine that the tunnel system was so pervasive that one of these days the whole unstable border would collapse and turn the route into an impassible ravine.

Three days ago, Harlan's team had received a tip from Mexico's federal police that the notorious Salazar Sanso would be personally involved in a border-crossing drug run sometime today. The criminal mastermind was wanted in twelve countries for the sale and distribution of some billions of dollars of illegal substances. Sanso lived like a nomad lizard, never staying in the same hole long enough to be tracked.

Harlan was the only man who fully understood Robert's personal dedication to cornering the man and bringing him to justice.

"So when this is over, what's next for you?" Harlan asked, lowering the binoculars and turning over onto his back. His boots broke off several brittle branches.

Robert rubbed his eyes. "There's always another Sanso."

"Somehow, for you, I don't think that's true."

"It'll have to be. I'm too young to retire."

Harlan's radio crackled, and the voice of their task force commander came over the waves. "Sanso and company are in. Undercover officer is with them. ETA to your location ten minutes."

"Copy that," Harlan responded. The other surveillance teams echoed their awareness. Robert checked his watch.

"What's it going to cost us to bring this one in, you think?" Harlan asked.

"If AFI does its job, we should have a zero casualty rate."

"Optimist."

"I'm just saying. Their agent has put Sanso in our crosshairs faster than any other informant we've recruited." Robert sneezed again.

"Which makes me wonder if Sanso is really in the dark about him."

"Well, the rabbit's in the tunnel now with foxes at both exit holes."

"*Rabbit* doesn't match his profile."

"When did you stop being my enthusiastic mentor, O wise one?" Robert checked his pocket-size GPS console to verify the positions of the six other surveillance teams in the area. Two choppers were at the ready but keeping their distance. With Sanso's Mexico-side tunnel entry less than a mile away, all operations would have to go down on the Q.T. today.

"You never needed a mentor. You are hungrier for justice than anyone else I know. That's all you ever needed to do well at this job."

"What about fear? Gotta be a little afraid, you always told me."

"Yeah, well that was for my sake."

"Misery loves company."

"Twist it how you want it, Lukin. The more aware you are of the fact that cockiness will get us all killed—"

"*The better chance I have of staying alive.*" Robert mimicked Harlan's voice. "You look undead enough by my standards. You might have to revise your little rule."

"If I'm still undead when I retire, I'll think about it."

The friends fell into an easy silence and trained their attention on the small, irregular slab of limestone that covered the tunnel entrance while the minutes ticked by and Robert's nose twitched with the need to sneeze again.

The Mexican AFI—their Federal Agency of Investigation—had been working with the American DEA in a cooperative effort to corral Salazar Sanso for the past twelve years. This tip that Sanso would make a rare journey to accompany a payload into Arizona today had come from Javier Alanzo, an AFI special agent who'd devoted two years to infiltrating Sanso's cartel. Because Sanso's American citizenship was his only authentic one among dozens of false passports, the AFI had agreed to an arrest on American soil and later to extradite him to Mexico—then to the long line of other countries that wanted a piece of his skin.

The possibility that the man who had murdered Robert's family was in reach caused the second hand to tick around the clock in slow motion.

When eleven minutes had passed, Robert wiped the sweat out of his eyes. "Something's wrong."

Harlan radioed his officer. "No sign of the target."

"Hold your position."

Robert got off his stomach and crouched instead, studying the limestone for movement. A fly bit him on the neck. He slapped at it and swore.

"Patience," Harlan said.

"I have about thirty seconds' worth left."

"He'll show in thirty-two."

A soft *thwack* sound caused Robert to stand. Harlan's radio lit up with surveillance teams shouting for Robert to hold his cover.

Another *thwack* penetrated the chatter. The sound of a roofer throwing old tiles off a roof three blocks away. But there was no residential neighborhood in this sprawling wasteland. *Thwack, thwack.* The sound of paintballs jettisoned from an air pistol.

No recreational areas around here either.

Or the sound of a gun going off underground. Robert plunged through the creosote and dodged Harlan's hand, outstretched to restrain him. The spiny tip of an ocotillo branch caught his cheek, drawing blood as he flew by.

"Hold your position!" Harlan hissed.

"He's not coming up," Robert shouted. "I'm going down. I want him on my turf, Woodman."

"Agent, stand *down.*"

But Robert did not stand down. He reached the limestone cover in four seconds and had it hauled off the entrance in two. In two more he swept the vertical hole with his gun and a flashlight, determined it to be empty, and began his descent on the rungs of an iron ladder.

When he was halfway down, a beam from Harlan's light blinked over Robert's head.

"You're gonna blow the past fifteen years in fifteen minutes."

Robert took the last four rungs of the ladder in a jump and hit the ground, then looked up.

"Three quarters of a mile and he's back in Mexico. Don't hold me back." Robert bolted into the passageway.

This particular tunnel was one of the more elaborate that Robert had been in. He ran on a concrete slab under lights powered by some unseen generator. A filtration system pushed fresh air past his face, and sump pumps placed at intervals along the ground rattled and vibrated, sending the summer rains back to the surface.

Robert supposed a billionaire like Sanso who slept in snake holes rather than haciendas would invest in creature comforts where he could.

The tunnel was more or less straight for a hundred yards, then curved west about thirty degrees. At the turn, one of the fluorescent lights mounted high in the wall had gone out, casting the angle into a shadow.

Robert sprinted through it and found himself airborne before his mind registered that he had tripped. He sprawled, his palms and chin taking the brunt of the concrete, then was back on his feet with the agility of a cat.

He would not have stopped to see what took him down except for a sixth sense that the information was important. He turned, using his flashlight to cut through the shadows until it caught the shape of work boots and the hem of worn denim jeans.

A body. His flashlight traced the figure up to the man's face.

Javier Alanzo's body, with a blood-black gunshot hole in his right cheek. A pool of blood beneath his head. Not far from the body, a pair of leather cowboy boots lay on their sides, ruined with blood spatter and muddy blood caking the soles. Robert raised the flashlight to the light panel in the wall. Its plastic covering was shattered. From one of the gunshots that he had heard maybe, sent off in a scuffle.

He did not have time to do more than assess these basic facts as he bolted toward Mexico, no time to speculate what might have gone wrong, because after he had run a mere fifty more yards, the tunnel forked.

This was new information. Javier had never said anything about branches off this particular tunnel; maybe he didn't know about it himself. Maybe this lack of knowledge had been his undoing, the surprise that blew his cover.

Which way? If Sanso was the rabbit with foxes at both ends of his hole, and the foxes didn't know but two of these paths, the rabbit would go where there were no foxes.

Robert turned down the branch that led west. He radioed Harlan but did not get a response. This far underground, he'd have no backup but his own instincts.

The concrete paving down which Robert ran ended in dirt at yet another fork. The dirt that lined these branches looked darker, recently cut, but the illusion could have been caused by the temporary lighting, low-wattage bulbs in cages strung every ten to twelve feet. Stale air rather than fresh came out of these passages, and Robert realized he had not seen a water pump for nearly three hundred yards.

He believed he was still heading west. Maybe west by northwest.

Robert stopped to bring his breathing under control so he could hear. He listened for footsteps, talk, the rustling sound of pants as a man walked. He closed his eyes. Nothing.

He removed his flashlight from his utility belt and turned the beam onto the ground, looking for shoeprints or some other disturbance. Five desert pocket mice scurried away from his light in single file.

Finding nothing, he turned his attention to the walls, still listening. Halfway up the far wall of the left fork, at about shoulder height, he saw a smudge darker than the dry red soil. Blood?

Had Sanso been wounded during the confrontation with Javier? Was Robert following Sanso anymore, or someone else? Confident in the likelihood that the drug lord wouldn't have exited these tunnels by the same entrance, Robert followed the blood smear like a road sign, taking the route as silently as a sidewinder down the center of the corridor. It took a sharp left—south—and Robert's heart rate spiked at the prospect of losing Sanso to Mexico and another fifteen years of searching.

It stayed elevated when he rounded the corner and a metallic punch caught him square between his eyebrows. Robert reeled and hit the opposite wall but kept his feet.

A gun went off. Not his. Rock spray from the wall hit his face and got in his eyes. He shouted a protest, trying to locate his attacker with his other senses. Impossible.

A body slammed into his and clipped his wrist, making him lose his gun. Robert heard it bounce. Dropping the full weight of his body to his knees, Robert broke free of the grip and landed on top of his firearm. His eyes were running with tears to rinse out the grit, but he couldn't will his lids to open.

A hard blunt object—the butt of a gun?—came down on Robert's spine and he yelped. Fire shot down both legs and instantly flared into a tingling chill. He rolled, coming up with his gun. A voice that he imagined belonged to Salazar Sanso swore under his breath as if the words were a prayer.

Robert aimed at the voice and pulled the trigger, then rolled again, three times until he hit a wall. His boots scrabbled on the dirt, pushing him to slide up the wall and stand, leg nerves still buzzing, one hand on the gun, one hand working furiously at his eyes to clear them. He had to see his target.

The cursing intensified, then waned. Robert blinked until the dark tunnel formed shadows.

Ten feet away, his attacker had doubled over on his knees like a grief-stricken boy, clutching his stomach and mumbling. A weak lightbulb shone on his stocking feet, and Robert thought of the boots by Javier's body, perhaps kicked off to avoid creating a blood trail.

The man swayed on his knees, then collapsed on his side, sweating and unconscious. Robert jumped to the body and turned it over, groping for a pulse. Salazar Sanso faced him from the ground, his hand falling away from a bloody wound in his side.

The enemy he'd hated for so long had become a mere man.

22

The gunmetal gray PDA phone did not belong to Janeal, but it came to be in her possession as the result of Milan's carelessness. She might have given it back if he had not been so careless with her heart and body as well last night—but no, it was time. So she gave it to board president Thomas Sanders, who left a movie with his wife in order to arrive at her office within twenty minutes.

Which meant that when Milan Finch paid her a surprise visit at eight forty that night, twenty minutes after Thomas had departed with Janeal's information, he was the one to be surprised.

Milan closed the door. Through the glass panels that overlooked the newsroom, Janeal saw the lingering workaholic heads turn in their direction.

"You have my PDA." He spoke as if they were in a public café and didn't want to be overheard.

Janeal sipped her coffee. "I don't."

Her lover—ex-lover, she would think of him forever forward—sat opposite her, his back to the panes of glass, and crossed an ankle over his knee. This chess game they had played for a decade, as amicable opponents content to use each other and be used, was about to come to an end. The rubberneckers in the newsroom returned to their work, unaware of the pinched frown that contradicted their publisher's easy body language.

"I left it on your coffee table last night."

"Do you also remember where you left me last night?"

She had found the PDA after picking herself up off the floor, nursing a goose egg at the back of her head where her skull had met an oak armchair.

Milan had not exactly forgotten the device on the table; he had slammed it down onto the glass with such force that she found a chip in the shiny surface after he was gone. It was a wonder the electronics hadn't shattered.

"Do *not* misrepresent what actually happened, Jane."

"What is there to misrepresent? You were so emasculated by losing that acquisition that you thought beating me within an inch of my life would somehow restore your manhood. Tell me if I misunderstood."

"You like it rough."

"You're lucky I'm not pressing charges."

Milan sneered. "Like anyone would believe it."

"Thomas Sanders was credulous enough."

"You talked to *Thomas*? When?"

Janeal leaned back in her chair and waved a hand to indicate her impatience with Milan. "I thought he was on board with your acquisition effort," she said, knowing full well that Milan's attempt to take over the nation's second-ranked publisher of porn had been an entirely private investment attempt.

She thought Milan's eyes might fall out of his face. "Really, Milan. Don't overreact. What's the harm in one publisher wanting to expand his domain?"

"Jane Johnson, where is my PDA?"

"Are we talking about the one you use for *All Angles* business? Because I'm pretty sure I can see the outline of that one staring out at me from your breast pocket. Or is there another one, Milan? One you use for purposes illicit enough that you have to pretend you're not affiliated with it?"

Milan's hands were shaking and his face was a shade darker, though he had not moved since sitting down. "I am not a man you want to mess with."

"No, you have that backward. I am not a woman you want to abuse. Do you know why I never moved in with you after all these years? Because I am not a kept woman. Ironically enough, standing just outside of your grasp was the best way to get you to think I was. Do you think I have done a single thing in the last ten years that was not planned?"

"For all your planning, you've turned out to be one of the most dissatisfied women I have ever met."

"I'm happier than I've ever been, now that I'm free of you."

"You're a victim of your own ideals. Your level of misery goes up with every goal that you set."

"Ha!" She slapped her palm down on the desk. "Well said by the man who's about to lose everything he's worked for. Let's speak frankly: a man like you has no need of a woman like me, not really, not unless you believe I'm better than you are and present a challenge to you worth conquering."

Janeal cocked her head to one side as Alan walked past the office on the other side of the interior windows. He should think they were discussing where to go for dinner, not the pending upheaval of the magazine. That, after all, was where this would end.

"You're sitting in that seat because of what I have done for you," Milan whispered.

"I'm sitting in this seat because of what I'm capable of doing for myself. And you know it, or else you wouldn't be so distressed over what will happen now that I have your private PDA, the one you use to operate that little moonlight venture of an escort service—oh, don't look at me like I'm the brainless one! I've known for months."

Janeal stood to indicate that their meeting would end now. She felt tired, having spent the last ten years of her life waiting for the right time to tell this little weasel of a man to step aside. But that was the nature of this game, in which the trophy went to the most strategic and most patient. Until last night, she hadn't minded the wait so much.

"Our board meeting has been delayed until Monday. Expect Thomas to request your resignation tomorrow afternoon, before the story breaks and *All Angles* gets the wrong kind of publicity."

Milan sighed and closed his eyes. "No one cares about sex scandals anymore, Jane."

"Really? Thomas was just here wondering how many different points of view we can spin out of this one. Three cheers for lawbreakers! Perhaps if you had come earlier—"

"I'll fight you all."

"Fight away. I'll be sitting at your desk upstairs by Monday morning."

Milan did not have the boldness to look at her as he left the room, smoothing the sleeve of his jacket and tugging at the cuff.

Janeal resisted the urge to place her palm in the center of her forehead to calm the pounding. Her phone was ringing again. Instead of answering it, she scanned the AP feed coming across the bottom of her computer monitor.

The first headline caused her to gasp. Like a remissive cancer rearing its ferocious head, Salazar Sanso couldn't have reentered her life at a more inopportune time.

23

Javier Alanzo's death hit international news as a tragic act of heroism.

As for why Robert found Sanso alone, the prevailing theory among the DEA was that either Sanso had sent his unwitting minions back to Mexico while he slipped away unnoticed, or the cowards had abandoned him. Robert favored the latter idea. DEA agents found a total of seven miles of tunnel in that one network, and the branch Sanso had taken emerged less than a quarter mile from a busy Mexican highway.

Regardless, without Javier's insider view or Sanso's cooperation, the details of how the bust went awry would take some weeks to sort out. Not that Robert cared about them, now that he finally stood in Sanso's secure hospital room. A beeping monitor kept track of the criminal's crooked heart. Morphine dripped into his bloodstream via IV and held his eyelids at half mast. Two FBI agents manned the hallway outside his door.

When Sanso focused on Robert, the drugs did not prevent him from smiling.

"You recognize me," Robert said.

Sanso turned his chin slowly left to right, then back to center. "I do not waste my time memorizing faces as uninteresting as yours."

"Then wipe that stupid grin off your face."

Sanso's smile broadened. Robert checked his annoyance. It would only give this worthless piece of roadkill the upper hand.

"Let me introduce myself. I am—"

"A lovesick puppy who has no purpose in life but to follow me around." Sanso chuckled, then gasped for breath. "I can lead you around like a submissive dog without even knowing you. You go where I go." He clenched his jaw—against pain, Robert thought. "I know who you are. I have known a hundred other men like you." Sanso blinked once. "They're all dead now."

Robert dragged a chair to Sanso's bedside, then sat on it, leaning an elbow on the bedrails.

"You want to know who my suppliers are," Sanso said. "You want to know who my distributors are and where they operate." He licked his lips. Robert leaned over and touched the plastic tubing that led from the bag of morphine into Sanso's hand. "Your type has been asking me these questions for years, and you're no closer to the truth than anyone else has ever been."

Robert held the tubing up for Sanso to see and pinched it in half. Sanso's eyelids rose slightly. Robert had brought his anger under control. "I'm not here to listen to you talk, Sanso. It took me fifteen years to find you, and if it takes me that much longer to find all the answers to those unimportant questions, I can wait. For now, I want you to know who I am."

Sanso blinked again but didn't speak.

"My name is Robert Lukin, and fifteen years ago you destroyed my home and murdered my family."

Sanso closed his eyes and sighed as if he was bored by this. "It happens in my line of—"

"My parents, grandparents, four brothers, and two sisters."

No response.

"You shot my neighbors and burned their homes. A hundred and thirty-four people, squashed under your bloody heel."

Robert saw Sanso's brows arch over his closed lids, as if the hidden eyeballs darted around in his brain, looking for the memory.

"A whole village of people who didn't even know your name."

"Which was as it should be," Sanso murmured.

"For a million dollars." Robert's throat closed, constricted by anger. "You are the devil himself."

Sanso chuckled again. "Yes, yes. The devil himself, igniting infernos in the desert." He opened his eyes and stared directly at Robert's face. "I rather like that image."

Robert gripped the morphine tube in his hand and whipped his arm back over his shoulder as if he were starting a lawn mower. The IV tore out of Sanso's skin, and the man shuddered. His body stiffened as blood oozed from the back of his hand.

"My only regret in this operation is that Javier didn't actually kill you."

"You could finish it," Sanso whispered through gritted teeth.

"Tempting. But I'm not like you, devil. Justice still matters to me for some reason, and I want you to know me because I will be the one who sees it come to pass for you."

"It's a rather difficult proposition to squeeze the blood of a hundred and thirty-four people out of a single man."

"But it'd be worth trying."

Sanso shook his head. "You'll be disappointed. I'll become dust and ten other men will rise from it to take my place. You think I'm nothing more than an arrogant swine, but there are rulers and there are subjects, and nothing you can do in this lifetime will change the fact that I am a ruler, for whatever amount of time has been ordained for me. Send me to the gallows or the guillotine. You can't change what is."

Robert leaned across Sanso's bed, bracing himself on each side rail. He spit in Sanso's face. "I'm no subject of yours."

Sanso let the spittle drip down his cheek. "And yet you have devoted your life to me, haven't you?" The corner of his mouth twitched, and Robert faltered in the face of the truth. "There are all different kinds of servants, Robert Lukin. You are my servant."

"I'm a survivor. The only survivor of the Mikkado Massacre. If I serve anything, I serve the memory of the dead, not you. I am the last one who remembers them."

"But you're not." Sanso raised his bloody hand to Robert's cheek and stroked it. Robert pulled away, disgusted. "You are not the only survivor, my passionate little puppet. I know of another."

Robert's composure snapped at this lie. A hundred thirty-one men, women, and children had been corralled and shot or burned alive by Sanso's gang. During the first and most gruesome investigation of his career, Robert identified every body that was still identifiable. Most of those that were not he identified by their jewelry—the Rom loved their precious metals and stones—or by DNA profiling when possible, though the limitations were considerable.

Only the identities of three had to be assumed: Jason Mikkado, Janeal

Mikkado, and Katie Morgon were believed to be completely consumed in the destroyed meetinghouse. Without official dental records there was no way to be sure, and the few remains investigators did find were too degraded and too scarce for a conclusive DNA test. Robert had not actually seen any of his friends enter the building. He had only overheard Sanso's word that all three of them were there.

"Who?"

"Ah." Sanso's smile condescended. "Privileged information for the puppeteer. You think you have power over me, Robert Lukin, but whether I live or die, I am the one who will pull your strings for the rest of your life." Sanso closed his eyes. "Watch me."

24

Disturbed by his first encounter with the man who had, in fact, directed the course of nearly half his life, Robert took long strides into the hospital corridor outside Sanso's secure room.

It was nearly midnight. At the end of the hall, Harlan waited for him. He was talking with a shorter, youngish-looking man, a kid really, who held an electronic device about the size of a paperback book.

Harlan turned toward Robert at the sound of his shoes tapping on the linoleum. The shorter man turned too and stuck out his free hand. A badge swung from a striped lanyard that hung around his neck.

Robert ignored him and spoke directly to Harlan.

"One hundred and thirty-four people," he said.

Harlan blinked.

"We confirmed that number, right? No survivors? No one showing up at your office ten years later claiming to be the freaking Grand Duchess Anastasia?"

In the silence that followed, Robert heard the man with the badge swallow.

"Is it possible we missed anything?" Robert's voice had risen enough for him to notice it himself. He dropped his tone a notch. "Is it possible there was some . . . detail we overlooked?"

"What exactly did he say to you?" Harlan asked, directing Robert away from the other man. The guy turned his back as a courtesy and fished a cell phone out of a pocket in his cargo pants. He flipped it open and started punching keys. In a few strides the DEA agents were standing next to a vending machine. Robert stared at a yellow bag of Funyuns while he relayed the bottom line.

"He said someone else survived."

Harlan leaned one shoulder against the machine.

"Who?"

"Won't say. Or doesn't know. Or is making the whole thing up."

"He has plenty of reason to be ticked off at you."

"I couldn't possibly be worth his time."

"You humiliated him in that tunnel."

"He's beyond the reach of humiliation."

Harlan gestured toward Robert's face. "You . . . uh . . . something on your cheek."

Robert rubbed the place where Sanso had touched him and felt the dried smudge of blood. He scowled, then spit on the cuff of his sleeve and wiped it off.

Harlan did not need to ask Robert why this claim, whether truth or fiction, was important to him.

"I'd be asking why a survivor wouldn't have identified himself. Or herself," Harlan said.

"What would be the point? After a loss of that scope? We kept my name out of the press. In fact, they came right out and said everyone died."

"Ten to one he's baiting you."

"Why?"

"Power. Basic, caveman-101 power."

Robert scoffed. "A Neanderthal megalomaniac."

"I think my diagnosis was more to the point." The corner of Harlan's mouth twitched.

"But mine is a better visual." For one moment he let himself admire the mental image of Sanso as a bow-legged, flat-faced doofus carrying a club. But then in his mind the hominid heaved the club at burning tents and sent ashes scattering like fireworks. Robert rubbed his eyes, all humor gone.

"He only said it because he knows I'll try to verify it," Robert admitted.

"Well, it's something to do now that Neanderthal man's in custody."

"Not exactly what I had in mind."

"What did you have in mind?"

"Dropping my work week from eighty hours to fifty."

Harlan slapped him on the shoulder. "I'll ship your butt off to Philadelphia to train recruits before I'll let that happen."

"I'm gonna look anyway."

"Bet your BMW you will."

"I'll need your help getting authorization to reopen the case."

"Easier said than done."

"So I'll have to look outside the files maybe. It's been done."

The men turned around.

The guy with the badge was standing right behind them. Robert's eyes dropped to the ID. *Arizona Daily Star.*

"Whoa." He directed a gaze of accusation toward Harlan.

"Pull your pants out of your backside," Harlan said. "I only told him a couple lies about you."

The reporter stuck his hand out toward Robert again. "Brian Hoffer," he announced. "*Daily Star.*"

Robert grudgingly shook the man's hand.

"Couldn't help but overhear you might need a research assistant to look into this Sanso claim." Brian held his phone up for them to see as if it were applying for the job.

"You ever hear of a private conversation?"

"No conversation I hear is private."

"He's a barrel of laughs," Robert said to Harlan.

"I can help you," Brian said.

"I don't want any help."

"Then maybe I can get you some information." The reporter looked down at the device in his hand and tapped it with a small stylus. Some kind of wireless notepad. Maybe it had Internet access.

Harlan chuckled.

"Don't you have a deadline?" Robert asked.

"Three. Two already filed hours ago. The third at 3:00 a.m." He checked his watch. "Plenty of time. What's it worth to you?"

"What's *what* worth to me?"

"Information."

"You're the reporter. What's it worth to *you*?"

An unreasonably happy grin split Brian's face, shoving aside acne scars. He pointed the stylus at Robert and waggled it. "I knew we could reach an agreement."

Robert threw up his hands and started to walk away.

"Fifteen years ago," Brian said, reading his screen and following Robert by a few paces. "August 26."

The date his family and friends were slaughtered. Robert turned around. "You were what—enrolled in kindergarten?"

"Third grade. There were six hospitals located within fifty miles of the massacre site at that time. Only one had a trauma center fully equipped to treat burn victims."

"And they were overrun with people from my camp who survived only a few days. Or a few hours."

Brian looked up, and Robert thought that this surprised look, this wide-eyed aha moment, was how the kid processed his epiphanies.

"My camp?" Brian asked.

Robert weighed an answer. "I've worked the case for so long I've come to think of it as mine."

Brian looked doubtful. "Uh . . . all eleven—there were only eleven . . . people who survived long en—who were still . . ." Brian scratched an itch on the side of his face. "I'm sorry, man. Eleven people were transported to the trauma center—University of New Mexico Hospital—in the early morning hours of the twenty-seventh, all in critical condition. The last one passed on . . ."

"Four days later," Robert said. But he kept his voice gentle, for some reason feeling the need to be kind to this pesky green journalist who was obviously a skilled researcher but didn't know a hornets' nest from a honeypot. "This is information I already have, Brian."

Brian took a step forward as if it might stop Robert from leaving again. "What I was meaning to get to is that there were three Jane Does admitted to hospitals within two days of the mas—of the tragedy." His eyes were apologetic. "Two at the facility where your family went; one at a smaller hospital in Santa Fe. Maybe one of them was this survivor."

Robert leaned over to look at Brian's small electronic screen. "These are public records?"

Brian cleared his throat but handed the device to Robert. "Not exactly." He shrugged. "It's from a contact."

"All three were burn victims?"

"I couldn't say."

"What about any John Does?"

"Just women."

"Did the Janes survive?"

"I don't know that either, but—"

"Either they're still Jane Does, which means they're dead, or somehow they were identified during the course of their treatment. Which is it?"

"Look, it's a lead. If Sanso's mad enough at you to tell you the truth, the survivor could be an amnesiac. Or a coma patient. Or a wacko."

"Or an ally of his. How else would he know someone got out of that inferno alive?"

"I'll have to visit the medical centers in person to answer questions like that."

"Let's go," Robert said, and he walked toward the exit, still carrying Brian's device.

Brian scurried like a dog on a tile floor. "Now?"

Robert looked over his shoulder. "Not one for road trips?"

"If you're buying the gas—"

Robert held the door open for Brian and turned to wave to his friend. "Heckuva job today, agent."

"Don't waste the night celebrating."

"Wouldn't think of it."

25

In her apartment, a tenth-floor loft with a view down Broadway, Janeal sat barefoot on a microsuede Ethan Allen sofa, nursing a glass of red wine, which paired nicely with her migraine meds.

NOTORIOUS DRUG LORD SANSO APPREHENDED IN ARIZONA

The alert had played itself in a mental loop for the past four hours. Last night she hadn't slept because of one bad-news boy in her life; tonight she would be kept awake by yet another, a ghost she feared but believed would never haunt her.

Salazar Sanso.

And Robert Lukin. Robert was alive, and joined to Salazar in ways Janeal could never have predicted. Alive, though every report she'd ever read since that night insisted that all had perished. She topped off her wine glass for the third time and tried to block out thoughts of what her life might have looked like if she had known. Or if he had known about her.

It was not hard to recall her love for him. Compared to the other men she had used, Robert stood apart as unique. He had been her first love, the man she wanted but couldn't have. Could never have.

Thinking of it that way triggered an irrational desire in her to get him back. It wasn't her fault she had lost him. Katie had taken him away.

But now there was only Janeal and Robert.

She shook her head to clear it.

The resurrection of Robert and Sanso on the same day turned Janeal's mind toward her father, opening a grief in her as fresh as the moment Sanso laid him to rest on that cursed pool table. Her mind strained on its leash: if her father had lived, if they had escaped Sanso together, if she had never taken the hand of her father's enemy . . .

If, if, if.

The word sounded like the ripping of her heart in two. She held it together with a stronger thought: *Never.*

She would never know the peace of her father's love again.

Robert represented other possibilities, none of them as optimistic as her fantasies. She soothed her freshly shredded heart by focusing on what to do next.

What to do if Sanso told Robert she lived.

It would be an unwelcome revelation, from her side of things. He worked for them now, the DEA, whose money she had used to launch this fine life she now led. How far would they go to get it back, if someone told them it hadn't been incinerated?

She had not gotten to where she was by making knee-jerk decisions. This moment of discovery, like so many others over the course of her adult life, needed to be weighed carefully.

Option one: Do nothing. Trust Sanso to keep his word now, as he had for fifteen years, never to pursue her. The problem with that was he'd never been in custody before now, never had to face whatever inquisition American law enforcement had in mind for him. What would they convince him to say about the massacre, about the money, about her, before they were finished?

Option two: Pay Sanso a visit, if she could, under the guise of journalism. Renew their agreement. Offer to pay him for silence—she had a million more to spend these days, and then some—or to secure his legal representation.

Janeal nipped that idea before it fully bloomed. She'd be worse than a fool to reveal herself so completely. For all she knew, he believed she no longer existed. At the very least, he would have no idea who Jane Johnson was.

Or he might have shadowed her every move, waiting for a moment such as this.

In which case she should wait for him to summon her. Make whatever demand he thought he could extract. Because if he knew where she was, who she was, he would summon her.

Option three: Hire a freelancer to cover this story and report directly to her. Keep tabs on Sanso via a third party. His notoriety was outside of the magazine's editorial mission, but she could find the right spin for the right person. Wally Coville came to mind. She could suggest a biography to someone in her book-publisher circle. Amos Sinclair might be up for that. Or Bernard Watkins.

Yes, option three might be her best route for now.

Janeal set her wineglass on the coffee table and opened the laptop that she'd put there, waking it.

The prospect of what would happen to her if she were exposed—no, not only exposed, but exposed as having an affiliation with the monster Sanso—was too far outside the scope of her life plans to contemplate yet.

While the laptop went through its figurative stretching and yawning, Janeal's eyes rose to the wall near the front door. Hanging there, pressed between two panels of glass and surrounded by a whitewashed wood frame, was the packet of sweet peas.

The packet Katie Morgon had given her.

In the beginning, Janeal had hung the seeds there to remind herself of Katie as she came and went throughout the day. More dramatically, she intended to remind herself that a choice she had made so many years ago had actually prevented a life from blooming. It was a small but fitting punishment.

This reminder eventually became pointless, and the guilt faded, replaced by an idea she could more readily appreciate: she *had* saved a life—her own. Only one person had died instead of two. Without knowing precisely when it happened, the seeds became an absolution rather than a memorial. Her choice could have been worse.

It could have been a complete waste.

What about your father? The doubt slapped her self-assurance every time she looked at the seeds. Tonight she considered throwing them out. She stayed put on the sofa, though, and looked away, repeating the mantra she had come to believe.

There's nothing I could have done to save him. He brought it on himself.

Her heart ached. She took another sip of wine.

Her computer beeped, and Janeal logged on to the secure site where she could watch stories come in as they were filed. She pulled up the interactive sites of the top five cable news networks and then started browsing the blogs of journalists on the crime beats.

She would have to make her selection carefully.

"I thought your partner said you drove a BMW," Brian said as they reached the outskirts of Albuquerque. The Saturday morning sunrise was casting a glare across the reporter. He had not stopped tapping on his miniscreen since they'd left Tucson.

That might have been an exaggeration, Robert thought. But not much of one. And the guy could talk and tap simultaneously and probably chew gum too, all without skipping a syllable or a link.

"We don't have partners," Robert said. "We have teams. Colleagues. The DEA isn't your local police."

"Whatever you say. You should drive a BMW. Smooth ride, all that power—you seen the latest M3 convertible? Variable double-VANOS camshaft management, a separate throttle butterfly for each cylinder, all eight of them, ion-current technology—it's *amazing*."

"Whatever you say."

"So how'd this rust bucket come to be known as the BMW?"

It wasn't a rust bucket. It was a perfectly decent set of wheels, a reliable Ford pickup that was brand spanking new not that long ago. Robert did the math and realized that was probably before Brian had decided where to go to college.

"Har used to say the new truck was 'better than my wife.' It became an acronym."

"And I'll bet he became single within a year." *Tap tap tap.*

Robert glanced at him sideways. "Two years. But not because of that one remark."

"'Course not. It's about attitude. You married?"

"Nope. I've been a best man. Nothing more."

"So then we can call the truck the Best Man's Woman, since Harlan doesn't have a wife anymore and you're not interested." Brian laughed at his joke.

Robert sniffed. "How about you call up directions to the hospital for me."

It was nearly eight thirty by the time the men pulled into the parking lot of the UNM Hospital, a teaching hospital on a sprawling medical campus that also boasted the state's only level one trauma center. Robert parked and jumped out, slammed the car door. Brian took his time, stretched his legs, and picked up his gray backpack.

"So you walk in and flash that bright yellow DEA on the back of your vest and they tell you whatever you want to know?" Brian asked when Robert rounded the front fender.

"Getting a patient's name doesn't exactly wander into the territory of patient-confidentiality."

"Right." Spoken like Robert must be wrong.

"I'm looking for a witness to a multiple homicide. It's an easy court order to secure if I have to." They walked from the parking structure across a pedestrian bridge and into the hospital.

"You could secure it? That would fall to you? Isn't the massa—homicide aspect of this incident technically outside of your jurisdiction? Or do you moonlight for the FBI?"

Robert stopped halfway across the bridge and planted his feet in front of the journalist.

"Don't work so hard to convince me you're a bright bulb, Brian. I might decide that it was a brainless idea to bring a journalist on this ride."

Brian's head jutted forward on its spine and his mouth dropped open as if his IQ had dropped fifty points. "It was just a question, man. Why is it so critical that you be the one to—"

Robert rolled his eyes and turned away, biting his tongue and trying to cut the kid some slack. He was barely out of diapers as it was.

At the reception desk in the southwestern-decorated foyer, a volunteer who reminded Robert of Mrs. Golubovich directed them to the records office. It had been temporarily relocated to a mobile trailer unit pending a remodel of its permanent office. They walked outside and got on a shuttle without speaking, Robert's attention having turned to the past, and Brian either too distracted or too offended to argue his point. He had pulled out that wireless doohickey again and tap-tap-tapped away their short journey.

The unit was air-conditioned and crammed full of computer equipment rather than the color-coded manila files of days past. A brunette who appeared to be no older than Brian looked up from the back corner of the office when the pair walked in.

"Yes?"

"Yeeesss," Brian sang low, for Robert's ears only. He beat Robert to the counter and leaned on it, crossing one foot over the heel of the other. The girl stayed put in her seat. Robert could see the name tag pinned to her shirt pocket. Alicia.

Brian turned up his official-journalist volume. "We're investigating a homicide that a certain Jane Doe might have been witness to some years ago. Need to know if she was ever identified."

Alicia's expression turned worried, and she looked around as if she wished she hadn't come in early that morning so someone else could be assisting them. "I'm not sure that I can—"

"All we need is a name. No medical details, no privileged information. We don't need an address. It was so long ago it's probably outdated anyway."

"You can't waltz in here and expect—"

Robert withdrew his wallet from his back pocket. "Of course not. We should have started with ID. I'm Special Agent Robert Lukin, DEA." He fished his badge out from behind its plastic window.

Alicia rose to come toward them. And appeared to keep rising out of her chair. Robert pinched back a smile when he saw Brian's expression fall from slick to startled. The girl was easily six-foot-two, two-thirds legs. She dwarfed the reporter. Brian pushed off the counter and stood to his full, unimpressive height.

While she examined Robert's ID, she said, "Once a Jane Doe is identified, we don't store her records under that label."

Brian was tapping again, apparently content to hand the conversation over to Robert.

"Any help you can offer is appreciated," Robert said. He wrote some dates on a scrap of paper and pushed it across the counter toward her.

"We're looking for a woman admitted here sometime between these dates."

She picked it up, crossed the room to another computer. "Fifteen years ago. I don't know how complete our records are back that far."

"If you don't mind checking. She would have been injured in the north-western part of the state."

She folded her long body back into her chair and began navigating the monitor with her mouse. "We don't pay much attention to where these things happen," she said. "That's a detail for law enforcement."

Robert listened to the keys clatter and the CPUs hum while she searched.

"Thirty-two females admitted during those three dates," she finally said.

"How many of them still in the system as Jane Does?" Robert asked.

Alicia scanned. "Just one."

"Our Jane would have been a burn victim."

Alicia tapped on her mouse, eyes shifting across the monitor. In a couple seconds she said, "Not her."

"How many of those thirty-two were burn victims?"

Alicia scrolled, shaking her head. "Fifteen," she murmured. "All admitted on the twenty-seventh. Must have been an apartment fire or something."

Robert looked at Brian, thinking those fifteen were likely among the last few people to be taken out of the camp by emergency crews.

"Did any of them survive?"

"Privileged information."

"Okay then. Tell me how many of those died."

Alicia sighed and turned somber as she tabbed through the files.

"Fifteen," she whispered.

"Any others admitted the twenty-eighth or twenty-ninth?"

"A Belinda Gray. That's all."

Robert knew no one by that name.

"That file list the cause of her burns?" Brian asked.

Alicia frowned at him. "You asked for a name."

"How 'bout an address?"

"Is there anything else I can help you with?"

"*Your* address?" Brian teased.

Robert headed toward the door, thinking for a fleeting moment about bolting for the truck and leaving Brian at the curb. "Thank you, Alicia. You've been a huge help."

26

Belinda Gray turned out to be the dead end that Robert expected. Brian's resources put their best bet on her in Los Alamos, where it turned out she'd lived alone for the past forty-two years. She was not reclusive but independent, and happy to serve Robert and Brian chili-pepper lemonade while she told her story, which involved an antelope on the highway, a rollover accident, and a punctured gas tank. To this day she swore that it was a coyote that pulled her out of the wreckage, though no one had ever believed her. She didn't care who believed what. She knew what she knew, and that was all that mattered.

It was nearly four o'clock before Robert and Brian arrived at the St. Vincent Regional Medical Center in Santa Fe. Brian gung-hoed his way into the records office, fully expecting to be done with this mini-investigation in time to get back to Arizona before midnight. Robert thought a repeat of their rather breezy experience at UNM Hospital might be too much to hope for.

It was.

The men stood in a hall at a sliding aluminum-framed window that separated them from the records office. On the opposite side of the glass, an offended old lady refused to reason with them.

"You shoo yourselves outta here and don't come back until you can show me a court order for information like that." The woman was probably seventy, and Robert would bet she'd worked in this office for fifty of those years. It would take that long for gravity and a sunless room to have sunk a frown so low, and she kept a typewriter rather than a computer on her desk. A manual typewriter.

"After I get that order, you'll fill out these forms"—she shoved five or six sheets of paper across the counter—"and we'll file the request. You'll have your information in five to six weeks."

The plump lady gave them a backhanded wave, slid the window shut, and turned her back on them.

"Glad she's not *my* grandma," Brian muttered.

"Maybe I can be of help?" The voice came from behind Robert, sudden like an unnoticed spider. He flinched.

"Sorry to startle you." She rested a chubby brown hand on Robert's arm apologetically and smiled at him. Everything about her physical appearance—and her jewelry—was bronze and round except for her pepper-gray hair, cropped short below her ears. The top of her head didn't quite reach Robert's shoulder. Her deep crow's-feet framed her dark brown eyes with good humor.

"She's by the book, that one. Been here a lot of years and has earned her keep." The woman took Robert's elbow as if he had offered it to her and tugged him to walk with her down the hall. Brian followed.

"I was thinking we could work something out," she said to Robert, patting his arm.

"In regard to the records?" Robert asked.

She nodded. "I heard you say you are from the DEA, is that right?"

"It is."

"I have a granddaughter who's been getting herself wrapped up in the wrong crowds, now. And her parents, even me—you know that sweet girl has deaf ears for all of us."

"Sorry to hear it." He said this as noncommittally as possible, not sure of what she was about to request.

"But now, a fine young adult like you"—Robert heard Brian scoff under his breath—"might be able to talk some sense into the child."

"Ma'am, I'm afraid I'm not—"

"I was thinking that my girl's still got a chance to turn her choices around." She tapped her bottom lip with the forefinger of her free hand. "Maybe she could take these street smarts she's got and channel them into something more constructive." She stopped and planted her squat, wide body in Robert's path. "More professional. Maybe get a good job with the government if she was so inspired." Her smile seemed as broad as Robert's shoulders.

"Recruiting isn't my area."

Her laugh came from a deep, rich spirit. "Oh bah. I'm not meaning recruiting, now. Just a little pep talk. A little wake-up call. A fifteen-minute chat over Cokes. And maybe your business card."

"I'm not sure I see what good—"

"And if she won't be listening to anything inspiring, you go ahead and scare her. That's no trouble to me. A little truth and consequences never hurt anyone."

Brian clapped Robert on the back. "A fine young man like this can cover a lot of ground in a short time, although he's not so sharp when it comes to the finer points of bartering."

"Ah." She leaned in and held out her hand, palm up. "Let's have a look at this Jane Doe you're trying to find. I'd say I could find her in about fifteen minutes myself, if she exists."

Robert surrendered and dropped into a waiting room chair while the wily grandmother disappeared to do some research. Brian leaned against the wall, tapping on his wireless.

After several minutes passed, Robert said, "I'm not going to spend the whole afternoon here talking to a druggie if we've hit another dead end."

"Not a whole afternoon. Fifteen minutes is all she asked for." Brian didn't look up.

"Do you ever stop it with that thing?"

"Got another deadline."

"There's nothing new to report."

This time Brian did look up. "There's *always* something new to report, if you know how to spin it."

"That's the problem with news these days, isn't it?"

"You know, until you get over your negative attitude, I don't see that we have too much to talk about."

Which was precisely how Robert saw things.

The waiting and lack of sleep were making him crabbier than usual. He made an effort to set it aside.

"What are you writing about?"

"You."

"No, you're not."

"Okay. I'm taking notes about you. So be nice."

"You said you're on a deadline."

"Blog fans await."

Robert sighed. "Why are you here, Brian?"

"Because I'm the only reporter in the world right now who has an inside track to Salazar Sanso through the only survivor of the Mikkado Massacre—oh wait! There might be other survivors, in which case there might be other witnesses against the most notorious drug dealer in the western hemisphere. The editor likes the possibilities. You old-timers would call that a *scoop*."

Robert was willing to bet the kid was bragging about his "scoop" in his blog posts. *We old-timers would call that hubris*, Robert thought.

In a few more minutes the woman reappeared, still beaming. "Here now," she said. "Very simple. No court orders required and a good deed done."

Robert stood, thinking her optimistic indeed to credit him with good deeds in advance of the fact. Or maybe she was referring to herself.

"August 28. White female admitted at 6:14 a.m. by ATV riders who found her about two hundred miles from here." Robert's pulse quickened. "Air Life would have lifted her to UNM, but they were at capacity. Burned over 40 percent of her body, second and third degree. Medically induced coma for three weeks, inpatient treatment totaled four months."

"What was the cause of the burns?"

She shook her head. "Unknown. There was some speculation that she was a victim of that Mikkado Massacre—same time, located within a few miles—but she denied any affiliation with that group. She wouldn't discuss how she'd been injured."

Robert could understand why a person would choose silence in the face of fear and the belief that everyone she'd ever loved was dead. He held out a hand for the piece of paper she had printed out.

"It's a familiar name to me," the woman said, "but I can't recall why I know it. Here's the address we have. Can't promise it's current, but she did come in periodically up until about three years ago. I wrote my granddaughter's down next to it so you can call on her. I'm Mrs. Whitecloud. You tell her I sent you."

He asked her with his eyes if she understood how many privacy laws she was violating by giving this information to him.

"Sometimes what's right is bigger than any related wrong. You'll keep your end of the deal, now, won't you?"

Robert sensed his head nodding but did not hear the rest of what she might have said. His eyes had locked onto the name at the top of the page. Katy Morgan. Misspelled, and yet the same name of his childhood friend.

27

Katie stood outside her New Mexico home and knotted the belt of her favorite wool cardigan sweater. She turned her face so the brisk mountain air could stroke her cheeks, one of the few parts of her body that didn't suffer nerve damage in the fire. On any other day the sensation would have calmed her spirits, but today a headache overpowered the breezy fingers.

A headache and a sense of unease that she hadn't experienced since the hours leading up to that horrifying night so long ago. Flashbacks, memories she hadn't turned to in years, filled her gut with foreboding. The peace that came so readily when she prayed and read her Braille Bible evaded her today. She needed to talk with someone.

Katie left her white cane folded in her sweater pocket. She wouldn't need it on the trail behind the Hope House, the safe place she had established more than a decade ago for women recovering from alcohol and drug addictions. The endeavor had saved her from despair and given her a place to redeem her shattered past. She understood a thing or two about pain, and about the value of second chances.

Katie knew exactly how many paces lay between the house and the pebble-strewn path, and between the path's three sharp turns, and from the last dusty boulder that always smelled wet up to Donna Maria's back door. Her mind's eye gave her all the sight she needed.

It had been a couple weeks since Katie last visited Donna Maria, the old widow who'd lived on a remote property adjacent to the Hope House for more than two decades. The first time Katie met her, the day the property had been purchased and designated as a halfway house, Donna Maria called and welcomed her with a warm kiss on both cheeks and a plate of *sármi*, which surprised Katie into speechless gratitude. She'd never eaten the dish outside the *kumpanía* and didn't think it was common. The woman claimed it was a recipe handed down from her Gypsy grandmother. Wherever it had come from, the food was more delicious than any batch of cabbage rolls Katie had ever made, and a more effective truth serum as well.

In the years that followed, Donna Maria became one of the few women who knew of Katie's connection to the Mikkado Massacre. Katie generally kept that fact, and a few other details, to herself. No one had survived that tragedy, and she saw no point in revealing her singular experience. It wasn't one she cared to rehash.

"Daughter, I was thinking of you!" Katie heard the squeal of the wood-framed screen door opening before she'd crossed the backyard. Her anxiety eased at the endearment. Donna Maria used it easily and probably didn't know how much it soothed Katie's soul.

"I should have called first," Katie apologized. The porch boards creaked when she stepped on them.

"You never have to call. Come in and tell me if the corn bread I've made is fit to eat. I used blue corn this time."

Donna Maria took Katie's hand in hers, an elderly, soft-skinned hand always scented by lavender soap.

Her kitchen smelled of hot corn and butter, and when Katie sat at a bar stool under the counter, the old woman pressed a cool fork into Katie's hand and slid a plate in front of her. Katie wasn't hungry.

"Washcloth at your left," Donna Maria instructed.

The warm bread was nearly doused in butter, but it helped the coarse ball of dough to slide past Katie's tight throat. She wiped a sticky finger on the damp terrycloth. "It's perfect," she said, knowing that it would have been if she were not so distressed.

"Very good. You've got your bread and I've got my tea, so you go ahead and spill your thoughts now." Katie heard Donna Maria settle onto the stool next to hers.

"How about some small talk?" Katie teased.

"Who has time for that when it's not what you came for?"

"And how do you know what I came for?"

"When you come for small talk, you don't bother tying the belt of your sweater."

Katie touched the knot at her waist. She didn't know that about herself. "I've been found out."

"I daresay you have. So?"

"I've been uneasy lately and thought the company of a good friend would help me get some perspective. Do you have any Tylenol?"

"That I do." Her skirts swished as she walked across the kitchen. For some reason Katie had chosen to think of Donna Maria and her Gypsy grandmother as one and the same. No other image would come to mind. "You're not one to get headaches, Katie." A drawer slid open and a pill bottle rattled.

"Not usually."

"What's your trouble?"

"Nightmares. For two or three days now. I wake up shaking, thinking there's someone in my room. There never is, of course."

Water ran from the kitchen tap into a cup.

"Your past has always haunted you."

"These are worse."

"Tell me about them," Donna Maria said quietly.

Katie took another polite bite of the corn bread. Really, it was good, and she wished she could fully enjoy it. "That's tricky. They're nonsensical. Images rather than information."

"Like?"

"A woman without a face. A desert. A bag of gold coins. A cooking pot." She hesitated before adding, "A fire." Hundreds more images had assaulted her; she probably couldn't remember them all if she tried. But these stood out.

"Fire in your nightmares should come as no surprise."

"It was the woman's hair on fire."

The water glass and pill tapped the counter at Katie's right hand. Donna Maria slid back onto her stool.

"Her hair was like mine," Katie said.

"Good thing you wear a wig that can be yanked off."

Katie laughed. This is why she had come. For Donna Maria's insight and lightness of heart. "At least I don't wear it to bed."

"Yes, you have that too."

Katie felt the space between her shoulder blades relax. She swallowed the Tylenol with her water.

"It isn't the fire that bothers you," Donna Maria said when Katie returned her glass to the counter.

Katie considered this. "No. It's the woman."

"Because she doesn't have a face?"

Katie reluctantly bid the image to mind: the Medusa-like flaming head framed a blank canvas of skin. In her dream the featureless visage would melt like wax, exposing a dark gap like a fencer's mask. A yawning void. A black soul.

"That's disturbing, but it's something else. I haven't put my finger on it yet." Katie set down her water glass. "She's getting closer."

"To you?"

Katie nodded. "In the dream. She's larger each night. Like I'm standing in a fixed spot—"

"In that desert."

"How did you know?" Katie wished she could see Donna Maria's body language.

"It was a guess."

"I think you know more than you let on, Donna Maria. What does the dream mean?"

The elderly woman put a hand on her arm. "I interrupted you. She's larger, you said."

"Like she's advancing," Katie finished.

"Does she try to harm you?"

Katie shivered. The thought had occurred to her and was partly to blame for the terror that followed her into wakefulness.

"Not yet." She paused. "Something happened that night, Donna Maria. I swear something else happened that night and it's still haunting me."

They sat quietly for a moment.

"Who is she?" Donna Maria asked.

Katie fiddled with the tails of her sweater belt.

"I think she's me."

"Ah."

"Now, if that isn't something Jungian or Freudian—"

"Tell me, daughter, do you have reason to fear yourself?"

She hadn't thought she did, not for years. Katie cleared her throat. "We all have a dark side, don't we?"

28

Brian Hoffer. *Arizona Daily Star.*

He'd posted three blogs about Salazar Sanso that Janeal had seen so far. At 3:19 p.m. he filed a story claiming that the drug lord had revealed an outrageous claim, according to a close source.

Someone had survived the tragic Mikkado Massacre.

Janeal broke out in a sweat in spite of her office's climate control. The dog was going to give her up. After all these years, they'd caged him and teased him with raw steaks and he'd given her up.

Clad in jeans and a lime silk blazer this Saturday afternoon, Janeal grabbed the handset and was halfway through placing a call to Alan when her office door opened. She depressed the switch hook and held on to the receiver. She glared at the intruder. If Alan were here, this wouldn't have happened. He usually worked six days but had arranged for time off this morning.

"Jim Northrup wants to see you," said the blond woman. Janeal recognized her as an assistant to the CFO.

"I'm not taking appointments today. Certainly not with Jim."

"He's here."

"Why would that make a difference to me?"

"He's threatening to sue."

That made Janeal laugh. "Over what? Bob can handle that hothead. You don't need me for that."

"Bob was the one who sent me."

"Tell Bob I'm not available. He can send a memo to Alan. I've got two chairs to fill now that Milan's resigned."

"What?"

"Milan's not coming back, dear. I'm the boss you get to hate twice as much now. If Jim or Bob come by, I'll put them to work boxing up this office so I can get moved upstairs."

The blonde pinched her lips together and closed the door.

Janeal released the switch hook and dialed again. She looked down at her desk and saw a list under a paperweight on the blotter. A computer-generated daily planner page, in fact, from the schedule Alan kept for her. *Saturday* filled the top margin.

Alan's phone rang.

3:45 p.m. Steve Newman pitch re: gun law repeal

"Ms. Johnson, what can I do for you?" Alan said after the third ring.

"Never mind." She hung up.

Her managing editor could handle that story pitch.

She had a bigger story to chase right now, and she needed to do it herself.

Janeal scanned the thirty-minute intervals that tripped through the remainder of her overscheduled afternoon and mentally delegated the list. Pitches could go to the managing editor. The videotaping at CBS over the latest immigration controversy would have to be rescheduled. No need to meet with the production manager; Janeal would have Alan tell her to switch to the Ontario supplier regardless. It was something Janeal had decided to do a long time ago. She supposed she had better make an appearance at the American Freestyle Feminists reception scheduled for 5:30 p.m. Annie Mansfield had Washington connections Janeal couldn't afford not to maintain. Alan and girl-friend could take her tickets to the symphony—she'd never planned to go to that anyway.

In this sliver of time, Janeal hated her busy, lonely life.

The feeling passed.

She dialed Alan back and told him what she needed him to communicate to everyone. He thanked her for the tickets. She threw the calendar in the trash and got up to lock her door, then dropped into her chair and swiveled so that she couldn't see anyone who came by.

Someone knocked.

She didn't look up.

From her iPhone she quickly found Hoffer's e-mail address, published at the end of an archived *Daily Star* article for feedback, and sent off a note.

Please contact me ASAP re: Mikkado survivor. Possible human interest story, emergency-response policy story, yours on contract. Jane Johnson, All Angles

She left her private cell number.

With her heart pounding blood through her achy head, Janeal stood and placed her most personal belongings in the one box she'd brought with her, keeping her back to the plate glass windows. Milan wouldn't have vacated his swanky executive suite yet, but she didn't care. Alan would pack and sort the rest Monday. She tried to concentrate on a short list of candidates whom she might bring in to replace her as executive editor. No one from the inside, of course.

Names escaped her. She could think of no other name than Salazar Sanso, snake, who would dare renege on their verbal agreement of fifteen years to negotiate with the feds and save his own skin.

How valuable was she in a plea bargain this monster might wrangle out of the government? Surely not much. She hadn't even circulated the counterfeits.

Though they didn't know that. Sanso had the bills and could circulate them all. Likely already had. Could pin the theft of the DEA's confiscated money on her. She had, after all, stolen it and delivered it to him.

Perhaps, if they learned she was alive, the DEA would also hold her partly responsible for the deaths.

What would Sanso say about her role in that massacre?

Take the death penalty off the table and let me give you the woman who engineered that horrible night, the daughter of their dear leader, the woman whose body you never found . . .

How long would it take them in this day and age to follow her tracks from New Mexico to New York?

What would her father—

She reined in that stray thought. The *ifs* would tear at her shredded heart again if she didn't keep them at bay. Her cell phone was ringing. She noticed her banker's box contained only three items so far.

"Yes?"

"Jane Johnson, please."

"Who's calling?"

"Brian Hoffer, at her request."

"Mr. Hoffer, yes. Thank you for returning my call."

"You have an interest in the Sanso-Mikkado story."

Hearing the two names paired in such a casual fashion sent a wave of nausea through Janeal's gut. She kept her voice controlled.

"Not an interest that would put you in a position of conflict, I assure you."

"That helps."

"We're working on a story set about public policy in regard to victims of violent crime and their obligation—or right to decline, some would say—to participate in prosecuting offenders. Mortal consequence to the victim-witness, right to privacy, identity protection, that sort of thing."

"Mm-hm."

"So of course a survivor from such a notorious incident who has stayed silent for this many years would have something to say about the subject."

"Right on."

Janeal smiled at that. His verbal reflex gave away his youth. That was good to know.

"How can I be of help to you today, Ms. Johnson?"

"I'd like you to consider writing one piece of the story set for us. A human-interest feature about this alleged survivor."

"Her existence is merely speculative at this point."

Her.

"I don't especially care. The story is hot right now, so let's move forward as if it's true. Did Sanso give you a name to chase?"

"Ms. Johnson, I will need to give my editor first right of refusal—"

"Don't give me the party line, Brian. It's my story to assign. You can write it or not. You cannot write it for your paper or your blog or your MySpace page. If you do, I'll have your career on the platter I'm serving up at a dinner party next weekend. You write it for me, however, and there might be a book in it down the road. You are the most logical person to write it, provided you don't find this woman before I do, if you understand me. I have several publishers freshly interested in the larger event of the massacre now that Sanso has been apprehended and these new facts have come to light. Six figures. If you're worried about your editor, I can keep you employed. There's a lot of unanswered questions floating around down there in New Mexico that have nothing to do with Area 51."

She heard Brian exhale and, she believed, mentally accept her offer.

"We're following a lead in Santa Fe," he acknowledged.

"We?"

"Robert Lukin and I."

Janeal felt angry at the possibility that Brian was already a step ahead. He'd found Robert quickly. With Sanso behind bars, his chasing a survivor—chasing her—would be the most logical thing for her old boyfriend to do. How had she failed to anticipate a reporter so obviously close to the story?

Why had Robert wasted his life chasing Sanso? She knew the answer, but if he had chosen a different path, maybe things could be different for them now.

"Robert Lukin," she repeated. "The arresting DEA officer."

"That's right."

"You're with him now?" If they were together, she'd end the call immediately.

"Only women go to the restroom together, Ms. Johnson."

She'd have to make the conversation brief, then.

"What's his interest in a survivor now that Sanso is behind bars?"

"I'm not sure, but if you're going to post any watchdogs over your intellectual property, you'd better give them his scent, not mine."

"He has other connections to the massacre perhaps?"

"Don't know. He hasn't yet written a public word about his experiences as a DEA agent—I've looked."

"I guess you won't know until you learn more about him, will you?"

"What kind of an angle did you have in mind?"

"As we speak, I'm thinking Mr. Lukin's story is of value in this context. He's devoted himself to a uniquely personal pursuit of justice. I'd like to know why he's vested. This other victim—I'm curious about her decision to go into hiding. Maybe the decision has a gender bias. That would be an interesting question—"

"So you want a compare-and-contrast angle within the same article?"

"That depends on the subjects. They should determine the ultimate shape of the story, don't you think?"

"Maybe there are two stories, then."

"I won't know until I learn more about her. It's odd, isn't it, that Sanso would hint at the identity of someone who could put more nails in his coffin? I'd like to know about that."

"Well no one knows much at this point."

She allowed herself a sigh of relief. Maybe Sanso hadn't named her to anyone. Yet.

"What's your lead?" Janeal braced herself for news of tracks that blazed a trail east out of Albuquerque.

"Burn victim from St. Joseph's, living outside Santa Fe right now. Name's Katie Morgon. We'll try to see her tonight."

Janeal's palms dampened and her cell phone slipped. Her mind emptied itself of words. She thought she heard someone pounding on her door again, far away—or maybe that was only the sound of hot blood pulsing through her ears. Katie. Not Katie.

29

The address Mrs. Whitecloud gave to Robert belonged to a halfway house for women in the Sangre de Cristo Mountains. The Desert Hope House, a relatively short drive north of Santa Fe.

From the bench seat of Robert's pickup, Brian used his electronic doohickey to find a listing online. Robert punched the number into his cell phone, dreading what he might learn. Had Katie survived her ordeal physically but not emotionally? Had she gone through so much only to land at a facility for people struggling to cope?

Or possibly the hospital had the name right, and Katy Morgan was not the Katie Morgon he sought.

The phone rang and his thinking backtracked. How could she have survived the worst of the blazes on the property? Especially the tank explosion? How could she have gotten several miles outside the camp on her own? In the half second the person on the other end of the line took to lift the phone off its cradle and answer, Robert wondered if one of Sanso's people had taken Katie, whisked her away and done something unspeakable.

"Hope House," a woman's voice announced.

Robert forgot what he had planned to say.

"I'm looking for a Katie Morgon. Maybe she's a resident there?"

"That's a first."

Robert didn't understand. "Is there anyone who—"

"What makes you think she's a resident?" the woman asked.

"Does she work there?"

"What's this in regards to? Because Katie doesn't have the time to deal with pranks or backdoor methods. If you're a reporter, you of all people should know that. Let me give you the number of our PR agent."

"I'm not a reporter." He shot a look at Brian and hoped that sitting in the car with one wouldn't be used against him.

"Journalist, member of the media, whatever you want to call yourself. If she spends any more time on the phone, this place will go to the dogs. I can't imagine how many other ways you can possibly spin her success story."

Robert scratched his head above his right ear. "I'm sorry. I'm an old friend."

"*Riiiight.*"

"I'm not sure she's the Katie I'm looking for."

"I'll say."

The truck's windshield magnified the afternoon glare and made Robert's face uncomfortably hot.

"Would it be possible to speak with her?"

"Sure. Katie will speak to just about anyone, though I don't understand why. You give me your number—"

"I'll wait."

"Well unless you give me your name you'll be waiting for eternity."

"Robert Lukin."

"And you're calling from?"

Robert's impatience mounted. "If Katie doesn't know who I am, she's not the one I'm looking for."

The woman muttered something that sounded like *Romeo,* only her inflection lacked anything dreamy. A wooden knock sounded like the handset dropped onto a desk.

Robert waited.

Not for eternity, but for several long minutes with nothing but Brian's uneven tapping for background music. The reporter wrote, shoulders hunched and neck bent at an unnatural downward angle that would evolve him into a stooped old man one day. Though Brian acted as if he were alone, Robert had a hunch his ears registered everything.

Robert looked away.

What if this Katie was not his old friend? Disappointment loomed large. Robert braced for it. It would be within Sanso's character to have fabricated the outrageous claim that Robert was not alone. Nothing would change.

Except there was no more Sanso to pursue.

He stepped out of the cab to separate himself from Brian, not able to predict his own reaction to the voice that might come on the line, whether it be familiar or strange. He shut the door and leaned against it, looking out over a flat red plain that rose across the miles to meet the Sangre de Cristo foothills.

The phone rattled on the other end.

"Robert?"

It was a familiar, comforting voice, straight out of the past, a voice he knew. Different in a way—older, wiser, calmer—but the same.

He exhaled audibly.

"Robert Lukin?"

"Katie."

She seemed not to know what to say any more than he did at first. Then they both spoke at once.

"All the reports said everyone died."

And "Why didn't you tell anyone what happened?"

Robert laughed and drew his hand down over his brows, nose, mouth. His eyes watered. He hadn't felt this kind of joy in . . . years.

"It's so good to hear your voice," he said.

"All this time . . . I had no idea. They said *everyone* was gone. That was the hardest news of all. I got over the rest eventually, but that . . ."

"I'm sorry."

"Why didn't I hear about you?"

"Sanso, the press . . . the DEA wanted my help. They kept it quiet. If I'd known, Katie—"

"No. Don't go there now. How did you find me?"

"We arrested Sanso yesterday. He suggested I wasn't the only . . . that you . . . I didn't know what to think. Wasn't sure if he was telling the truth. How he could know for sure. You know?"

Katie didn't reply right away. He wondered if he'd made an ounce of sense.

"We don't get a lot of news up here," she murmured. "Not right away. It's intentional—helps the women focus."

"That's okay. I wouldn't expect—"

"You sound good," she said.

"Older. More cynical."

"No. Grown up. We both have, I'm sure."

"I've missed you so much, Katie. Everyone."

They fell into a silence that called up the memories of all the people lost to them. Robert's heart felt heavy and light at the same time.

"I have so many questions," Robert said.

"I'm sure we both do. Where are you?"

"Santa Fe."

"Can you come up? I'd like to—" Her voice broke. "It would do my heart good to see you."

"Is it a good time?"

"It's fifteen years later than I would have liked." Her laugh sounded more like an attempt not to cry.

"I'll be there in a half hour."

"We have a lot of catching up to do, Robert."

"I have the time."

30

Janeal guesstimated that some three hundred fifty people filled the *Chez Jacques* restaurant, which had been entirely reserved this Saturday evening for the American Freestyle Feminists' reception. At the office, Janeal had changed her jeans for a black pencil skirt and shucked the silk jacket to show off the coordinating green cami. She pinned up her auburn hair, which had darkened over the years, and dashed a matching lipstick across her mouth. Her eyes were gritty but she kept her cosmetic contacts in—those unnatural blue ones that Milan liked because of how her hair set them off. Even she thought they looked good in photographs. She was presentable at least.

Good enough was all she was interested in tonight.

She entered *Chez Jacques* to flashbulbs and turned heads. Janeal was under no illusion of being some kind of J. Lo–Brangelina attraction, but in the circles where she moved, the more sophisticated, less tabloidlike celebrity she had attained in New York's publishing circles was far more enviable. The thing about *All Angles* was that she had her feet straddling both sides of the aisle, as it were, one in the more conservative and long-thinking book world and one in the liberal, reactionary news dailies. Both loved her. She was a veritable bipartisan politician.

Within the first two minutes she had five offers of a table and a drink, and more congratulations on her new job than she could track. Not a single person asked where Milan was. Word in New York still traveled faster than modern technology. She smiled and cheek-smooched and thanked her way to an empty table near the bar, where she could set up her own turf. People would come to her.

Two did, actually, securing her table for her before she sat down. Meredith Swan, who had taken many reporting assignments from *All Angles* and was a decent writer, attached herself to Janeal like a pesky ankle biter. She was here with Bill Dawson, a former assistant to the DA who believed he had found a more fulfilling role as a probation officer and public servant. Janeal could not fathom how Meredith had wrangled him into this event. He pulled out her chair and went to get the women a cocktail.

"You *must* tell me about your new promotion," Meredith said over the high volume of crystal glasses and close-quarter New York City chatter. "People are saying all kinds of things."

"As people do." Janeal leaned back and scanned the room for Annie Mansfield.

"I never in a million years would have thought Milan was one to resign."

"He's been working for a while on a new venture. The time was right."

"What kind of venture?" Meredith leaned forward.

Janeal offered an enigmatic smile. "I imagine he'll announce it within the week. I couldn't spoil his surprise."

"I heard that you forced him out."

"Meredith, honey, do you think anyone could force Milan to do what he doesn't want to?"

Bill returned with two garnished cocktails, set them in front of the women, then waved down a server who had an appetizer tray. Janeal fielded greetings from three more passersby. Annie was nowhere in sight. Janeal looked at her watch and decided to give this exercise thirty minutes. She could be gracious and act engaged for that long.

At the most.

Janeal did not expect sleep that night. It would be the third night in a row. On the bright side, she wouldn't need to be seen in public Sunday if she didn't want to. And better, the one mercy of sleeplessness was dreamlessness. She'd be spared the recurring nightmares.

Either Katie Morgon was still alive or Janeal would have to put her faith in some unbelievable coincidence: that a woman of the same name in the same state suffering the same horrifying trauma would rise to torment her after a decade and a half of silence.

And it was all Salazar Sanso's fault. Stupid, stupid criminal that he'd go and get himself snagged when he had plenty of peons to lay down their lives for him.

But Katie Morgon? Janeal grabbed hold of her cocktail, feeling the chill of the glass charge her fingertips. How would he know about Katie? What would he have to gain from revealing her survival rather than Janeal's?

She drew only a modicum of relief that Robert wasn't looking for her yet—*yet* being the operative word. Katie might not be able to say for sure that Janeal had survived, but she knew about the DEA's money, and she knew, worse, that Janeal had left her to die. She would tell Robert all kinds of things, things Sanso would corroborate . . .

In one of her nightmares—there were three that recurred almost rhythmically—Katie's skeleton hand, tied to the leg of a cursed metal bar stool and encased in a shiny black glove, would start to quiver when it sensed Janeal standing at the rear door of the charred game room. It would vibrate until the movement became a visible quaking, an audible rattling that crescendoed until Janeal clapped her hands over her ears, unable to either enter or leave the room. The soles of her shoes had melted, gluing her to the floor.

Then the ropes that bound the hand would lash out at her, expanding like a striking snake, grabbing her by her frozen ankles and penetrating her thin skin at the bones, yanking her out of the oozing shoes so that she cracked her head on the doorframe but did not black out. In her dream the chains recoiled, dragging her back into the stool, which burst into flame and licked at her toes, then at her feet and her shins.

Each time, as the flames approached her knees, she awoke with a migraine that took two to three hours to subdue.

In fact, she felt one coming on now.

Bill Dawson was setting a business card on the table in front of her and saying something. She smiled and nodded and slipped it into her purse, then sipped her drink, trying to keep her mind in the present.

Annie Mansfield's brilliant white hair appeared on the far side of the room.

Tanya Barrett of *Vogue* placed a hand on her shoulder as she passed by and whispered in Janeal's ear what she thought of Milan Finch and how far Janeal had advanced the cause for professional women by kicking him in the—

Janeal's phone rang.

"I'm so sorry," she said to Meredith and Bill, rising and setting her sights on Annie though she moved as if to go to the women's room. "I really must take this call."

She answered in the hall by an old pay phone that probably hadn't been used in a decade.

"Yes?"

"Ms. Johnson, Brian Hoffer."

"And?"

"You asked me to call you back after our meeting with—"

"Yes, no need to remind me. What did you find out about the Morgon woman?"

"She's willing to see us tonight."

"So why are you calling me now?"

"To let you know that she and Lukin know each other."

Janeal held her tongue and leaned against the filigreed tile wall that ran the length of the hallway.

"Lukin's a survivor of the Mikkado Massacre too. Pretty cool, huh? To find two in two days after all this time when everyone was presumed dead? Apparently only the DEA knew. It's sort of a Phoenix thing, out of the ash—"

"It would be good for the project, for a book deal, if you don't publish word of her until after you establish some personal rapport with Ms. Morgon."

"I know a thing or two about how to keep the cap on a story."

"Really. You've already discussed the possibility of her in multiple blog posts. How long do you think you have?"

The kid was appropriately silent.

"Brian, have you questioned Sanso about—"

"No one's questioning him but doctors and lawyers these days."

"Well maybe Mr. Lukin can get you some special access."

"I'll work on it."

"I'd like to know how Sanso knew about Ms. Morgon while the rest of the world apparently didn't."

"Can't speak to that." He must have interpreted her silence as scolding because he added, "Yet."

What if Sanso and Katie had made an arrangement that protected her? From what? Sanso had tried to kill Katie.

But Katie knew Janeal had run off with his—the government's—money. Had Katie bribed him?

Janeal shook her head. Not one of these questions would make any sense at all until she figured out how Katie survived in the first place. That propane tank . . .

"Where is your meeting?"

"Ms. Morgon runs a small halfway house for women recovering from drug and alcohol addictions. Called the Desert Hope House. Little place in the mountains north of Santa Fe."

A halfway house. Of course. So perfectly suited to the perfectly tempered Katie Morgon, who could turn tragedy to sunshine on any day.

"How long will you stay?"

"Depends on how long it might take to see if there's really a story here."

"Oh, I'm confident there is. Stay in touch."

Janeal closed her phone and stepped into the bathroom, then closed a stall door behind her. She stared at the coral-colored grout between the bathroom tiles, collecting herself before returning to that crowd out there.

Her life seemed little more than the sum of her pretenses right now. Out there, the world she had created for herself stood on a fault line, and the ground was starting to quake.

She could rely on Brian to feed her the story as he uncovered it. She felt pretty certain she would get a decent biography at the very least: what had happened to Katie, how she survived, what paths her life had taken since the tragedy. So far Brian did not seem to have the depth perception of a more mature journalist. He would dig, but not too deep. More important to him, she judged, was the idea that he was first on the scene. King of the mountain for the time being. Which meant Janeal would have a fairly easy job of keeping him on topic.

With the young, life was always about the speed of the race, not the technique for winning it. She would use this to her advantage where Brian was concerned.

There was a chance, however, that Brian would give her information but not control. Her task at hand now was to determine exactly how much control she needed, and when. To what extent could she prevent Katie from disclosing what choices Janeal had made in that fire? Would Robert's arrival end Katie's silence? How far could Janeal go in preventing Sanso from tipping his hand further? What could these people plot against her, and how far ahead of them could she stay before they discovered and exposed her true identity?

She stepped out of the bathroom stall and washed her hands at the basin farthest from the aromatherapy candles decoratively arranged and lit on the countertop. She had no use for flaming candles. She didn't keep matches in her own home.

She smoothed her skirt, straightened her hair, reapplied her lipstick. Her first task, she determined, was to find a way to see Sanso and deduce what was behind this poorly timed revelation of his.

Janeal fished a pill for her migraine out of her purse and threw it back without water.

Yes, she would start with Sanso. Sanso was a worthy rival, an intellectual equal, a challenging partner in a competition. She might even say she admired him on these levels. But he had already taken everything from her, thereby losing his ability to threaten her with anything more. Katie Morgon, however, was a darker adversary cloaked in sweetness and light.

And Janeal feared her.

31

Katie sat in the blackness of her private room and tried to overcome her surprise. Her heart was still racing. *Robert. Robert. Robert.* She'd tried to excuse herself from Lucille's office, where she'd taken the call, without sounding as stunned as she was.

"What was that all about?" Lucille had asked.

Katie turned her face away. Lucille could read her expressions too easily. "It was an old friend," she murmured.

Lucille must have read her body language in spite of her hidden face. Her coworker laughed low and said, "Riiight."

Katie sat on the edge of her bed and hugged herself. Dread brought the faceless woman with the fiery hair to mind. She hadn't prepared Robert for what he would find on this mountaintop. Should she have told him about her scars, her blindness? Should she have told him that she was not the same person he remembered?

He might turn away when he saw her, though Katie honestly didn't believe he'd do that unless the last fifteen years had worked some tragic change in his heart. If they had, she believed she would love him anyway.

Love him still. Yes. She did.

Katie started praying. She prayed until the flaming head of her nightmares finally began to recede.

She considered the likelihood that Robert would be married after all this time.

She swallowed the pain of that possibility. If he was, that would be for the best. Because when he found out the truth about her—if he ever found it out—he would vanish from her life forever.

Robert directed his truck up the narrow mountain road that led to the Desert Hope House. He wasn't sure how to identify the emotion that stirred in the pit of his stomach and was less sure that he wanted to. After fifteen years spent capturing and caging the emotions of his loss, the prospect of reuniting with someone who shared his experience threatened the security he had constructed for himself.

And opened up the possibility that he could finally kill the untamed beast.

"The people at *All Angles* are pretty interested in your friend," Brian said.

Robert had tried to find a way to ship Brian back to Tucson after his call to Katie, but the journalist smelled a story with money behind it. So, apparently, did someone else.

"Katie Morgon is becoming well known in public service circles. Some two hundred fifty women have completed her program in the last ten years." Brian read from his wireless device. "Seventy-three percent are still sober and hold paying jobs after five years. That's pretty high."

Robert's truck hit a pothole and jarred the young reporter out of his seat. Sixteen miles into the mountains outside of Santa Fe, the halfway house would be remote enough to discourage wannabe runaways, but close enough to town to ease former addicts back into the real world by degrees. It was a detail Katie would have thought through.

"She's won four humanitarian and public service awards in New Mexico in the past two years. People who are like her—people like the Mother Teresas and Father Flanagans of the world—fame comes to them whether they want it or not. True goodness is rare enough these days that people will notice it."

"Katie was always like that."

"Award winning?"

"Good."

"She started working at the house thirteen years ago." Brian whistled. "You think she would have been in any condition to do something like that then?"

"What condition?" Robert didn't mean to be accusing, but really, if Brian asked Katie questions like that, Robert would boot him off the mountaintop himself.

Brian looked away and cleared his throat. "She took over the program when the director died in an auto accident. She was only twenty-one."

She'd be thirty-two now. Robert wondered what Katie looked like today, if he would recognize her. If he passed her on the street, would he turn away? The information Mrs. Whitecloud had provided did not offer gruesome details about the extent of her burns. It did say, though, that she had been in and out of the hospital regularly over many years. Robert could only assume what for. Skin grafts. Infections. Pneumonia, which was so common among burn victims. Pain management. Therapy.

And yet he couldn't bring any other image of her to mind except for the teen beauty she had been, with her oak-colored complexion and long black curls.

So unlike Janeal Mikkado in both looks and personality.

Janeal. It had been some time since his mind had flitted to her. His memories moved in her direction less frequently across the years. He had loved them both, which was something Janeal never understood. Maybe it wasn't fair of him to think she could. Though his own heart drew lines between passionate and protective kinds of love, Janeal's heart demanded clearer definitions. The Janeal who knew so precisely what she wanted out of life was the Janeal he loved. She had inspired him to think outside the *kumpania*, though at the time he never thought he'd have to leave it.

Katie, though . . . Katie represented to him everything that was good in the world, pure and joyful and free of the cynicism that was so pervasive it had managed to seep into their isolated community. Into Janeal. Even into himself. Katie was a bright blue sky in a dimming world.

Robert's truck crested a hill and then the road dropped toward a long gated driveway. He passed under a wrought iron archway that bore the house name. The gates stood open.

The halfway house was an adobe rancher shaded by a grove of mesquite trees. The clay-tile roof of the long, low building had been modernized with several solar panels that faced south. Old wooden shutters had been pulled open on the outside of the house to expose new vinyl windows.

Other than a dusty Suburban next to a detached garage, Robert didn't see any sign of life. He parked near the oak doors that he assumed were the entrance and climbed out.

An attractive middle-aged woman, slender and blond, wearing blue jeans and a UNM sweatshirt came through the doors and extended a hand to Robert.

"Robert Lukin?" she asked. He gripped her palm and shook it. "Lucille Adams. You're late."

Robert looked at his watch. Had he told Katie they would come at a certain time?

He apologized because it seemed the right thing to do, then introduced Brian. Lucille gave his arm one firm pump and dropped it. "I'll take you to Katie, see if she's still available."

He was surprised at the bright lighting of the house's interior. He associated such places with bleakness and had expected the dimness of small windows, wood paneling, brown tile. Instead, the house opened into a bright, skylighted atrium where green plants flourished in a garden the size of a living room. Bleached pine lined the walls, which were decorated with brilliant red and turquoise Navajo rugs.

Lucille made her way around the atrium and past a hallway to an enclosed patio on the south side of the building. Robert followed her across the threshold. This area, too, was a lush indoor garden with cushioned chairs and reading lights and coffee tables. Heat lamps suspended over the plants likely kept the place green through the cold mountain winters.

Two dark-haired women bent over the soil at one end of the long room.

"Katie, Robert and Brian are here."

The woman with the longer hair sat back on her heels and pushed herself up.

Robert realized he was holding his breath. He exhaled.

She turned around.

Except for the mane of dark curls, he would not have recognized her if they'd passed on the street. She was thinner now, which made her look taller. Her skin was paler than he remembered, and smoother than he expected. He'd braced himself for something hideous. But her face was beautiful, stunning, maybe because the sweetness of seeing the woman he'd loved like a sister and believed dead was greater than the reality of the past.

A creamy ribbon of scar flowed from her left temple and traversed her high cheekbone, ran down to the underside of her jaw, and dropped into her turtleneck. He finally had the presence of mind to look into her doe-brown eyes—

Dull, flat eyes. Dull where they once had sparkled. Flat where they once had been deep pools.

Katie was blind.

Robert averted his gaze involuntarily. The guilt he had felt for so long at having survived at all multiplied, confronted by having also survived physically unscathed. Whatever he had imagined on the way here did not compare to the reality, which knocked the wind out of him and prevented him from even being able to speak.

He felt trapped in this garden room by the idea that he owed her more than he could pay, and at the same time an overwhelming sense that he shouldn't have come.

Brian covered Robert's hesitation. He stepped toward Katie as she removed her gardening gloves. He took her hand in his so quickly that she gasped, surprised. He pumped her arm and spoke slowly. "Ms. Morgon, I'm Brian Hoffer."

At least the kid didn't yell.

Katie's shock turned into a slightly mischievous smile and she turned her eyes toward his voice. Enunciating as carefully, she said, "It is a pleasure to meet you."

Brian dropped Katie's hand, and Robert noticed for the first time the disfiguring red and white scars that crossed her knuckles and ridged her long fingers as if they were melted candlesticks.

Except for her hands and face, and smooth-skinned feet clad in thongs, the rest of her body was covered: khakis, a plaid cotton shirt over the turtleneck.

She turned her head as if to listen for Robert's location. Or maybe she was worried about why he hadn't spoken.

He cleared his throat at the same time she said, "Thanks, Lucille," and held her gloves out directly to the blonde. "Maybe you and Rita can finish while I show these men around and get them something to drink." Then Katie turned her head toward Robert.

Lucille took the gloves. "I might plant the hostas somewhere other than where you want them."

"I might let you," Katie said. She smiled although Lucille didn't. When Lucille grunted and joined the other woman, Katie took three steps toward Robert as if she could see him perfectly.

"How are you, old friend?" she asked. Katie tipped her head the way she used to when she would ask him to let her practice reading his palm. She extended her hand to greet him, lacking any self-consciousness.

And Robert, still unable to speak, grasped her hand and pulled it to his heart, encircling her with his other arm so that he could bury his face in her hair and hide the fact from everyone—most of all her—that his eyes had filled with tears.

32

Robert followed Katie through the halls of the old adobe, which was originally an art school that had since relocated to Santa Fe. Her graceful body glided like smoke above the brick-colored tile floor, silent and ghostly, the thongs on her feet not even slapping the tiles.

She explained the function of each room, mostly for Brian's benefit, Robert thought. Robert cared about the house, but he would have rather spent the afternoon alone with her, answering each other's questions about their ordeal, about escaping it, about all the ways it had haunted them since.

In this library the residents received peer counseling and support, she said; in that classroom they were taught basic life skills, such as how to manage finances; in this workshop they received job training. The standard program was nine months. Some of the women needed more time, some less. The house, for women only, had twenty-five beds, she told Brian, who talked more than she did. Eighteen were presently occupied. Two residents had graduated last week, after three years of dedicated work, and taken homes and jobs in Albuquerque. She was so proud of them.

Robert listened but did not hear very much. This woman was the Katie he remembered and yet she was not, and the difference had nothing to do with her blindness or her age or her voice, which was in many ways the same and in others deeper and breathier, maybe an effect of the fire. The change that he could not describe was both familiar and foreign, as apparent as her rich dark curls and as hidden as her thoughts about his sudden emergence in her life. He believed if he focused hard enough, he might soon identify this thing, the way one finally recalled an obvious name or fact that had been elusive for hours.

That might have been the case if he could have studied Katie privately, without the constant distraction of Brian. Somehow he would muster the patience to wait until Brian returned to Arizona.

"Out here in the boondocks is a pretty good place for a person to hide if she wanted to," Brian observed. Most of his questions so far had been slanted observations like this.

"That depends on what you mean by *hide*," Katie said, pausing at the entrance to the kitchen and turning her eyes toward the sound of Brian's tapping stylus. "If you mean it in the sense of not wanting to be discovered, like a criminal running from the law, no. That's not why we're here. That's not why these women come. But if you mean it in the sense of finding a protected place where a person can safely recover from wounds, then I could live with a word like that."

She gestured to a wooden plaque above the doorframe. Robert's and Brian's chins turned up simultaneously.

Hide me in the shadow of your wings from the wicked who assail me, from my mortal enemies who surround me. Psalm 17:8–9

"You're a religious group," Brian declared.

Katie's mouth pursed—to suppress a smile, Robert thought.

"We're a realist group," Katie said.

She stepped into the kitchen, an enamel-coated marvel that appeared to be ancient and yet suitable for commercial-scale cooking. Standing over a butcher block, a woman wearing a blue apron glanced up at them. She was crushing garlic, from the smell of it.

"You offer a Bible study," Brian insisted. "I saw it on the weekly schedule."

"Participation in that isn't mandatory."

"What parts of the Bible do you study?"

"Anything that applies to these women's situations. Which is about all of it."

"And I'll bet your funding comes largely from churches."

"What makes you think that?" Katie indicated they should sit at a Formica-topped island, then moved to a cupboard and withdrew three glasses.

"Where does it come from then?"

"People who care."

"Isn't there a shortage of such people these days?"

"Not at all."

"But you said earlier that you were facing something of a funding shortage."

"Money's scarce, big hearts aren't. People help in other ways."

"What kinds of wounds do you treat here?" Robert asked, wishing Brian's tone were less confrontational.

"I've seen all kinds." She turned her head toward him.

Brian reinserted himself. "What inspired you to come work in this place so soon after you were injured? I mean, what's the connection between your experience and substance abuse?"

Katie was so slow to respond that Robert thought she either hadn't heard Brian or was finally offended by his line of questioning. She filled the glasses with ice and removed a pitcher of tea from the refrigerator before saying, "The answer to that is likely outside the scope of your article, if I understand it correctly."

"Not really, if it's true that you and Robert here are the only survivors of the Mikkado Massacre. That's what I'm mostly interested in—what would make one of you choose to hide, if you don't mind me using that term, while the other seeks justice in a comparatively public way."

Katie poured without missing any of the cups and filled them equally. Robert noticed her cheeks blanch.

"You could say we've both devoted our lives to protecting others from similar tragedy," Robert said, keeping his eyes on Katie. At the sound of his voice, she exhaled and seemed to relax. She turned to the windowsill over the kitchen sink and plucked some mint off a plant growing in a small pot.

"But with very different methods," Brian insisted. "Why this one for you, Katie?"

She dropped a few leaves into each glass before setting the men's drinks in front of them. Her eyebrows had drawn together in a contemplative frown, and for a moment Robert thought she would tell Brian that the question was too personal.

But she said, "Tragedy shows us what we really are, Brian. The truest, most comprehensive picture of what's at our core. And if we're truthful about what we learn, the path we must take afterward is usually pretty clear. Do you agree, Robert?"

"I do." He took a mint leaf out of his glass and crushed it between his thumb and finger. Smelled it. Recalled how Janeal had often put mint leaves in her tea.

He stared at the leaf. How long had it been since he'd thought of that?

"So that looks different for different people," Katie was saying to Brian. "No surprise there." She turned back to her own glass of tea and raised it to her lips, then paused. "Most of the women who come here understand the importance of being honest about what we are."

"You mean *who* we are."

"No. *What* we are. Fragile human beings prone to failure. So we have that in common, since you asked about connections."

Robert wondered if Katie had found any answers to the questions he had been asking for the past fifteen years, and if he had any right to ask her to share those with him. He wondered if she had discovered any explanation for the tragedy, any sense in the senseless, any justice or hope. For all the moral goodness of a place like the Hope House, he didn't see how a little hideaway in the mountains could provide the kinds of answers that mattered.

But because he wouldn't ask in the presence of this kid reporter, he mentally urged Brian to ask the bold question that he couldn't—yet. What meaning had she found in this place to salve the pain of their tragedy?

Clearly, Brian was no mind reader.

"You're saying you had addiction problems at one time."

Katie's laugh burst out of her in a spew of tea. Robert saw the woman at the chopping block grin, not at all shocked by Katie's display. He couldn't help but smile himself, mostly because Brian, sitting there looking perplexed, was the outsider in this little joke. The idea of sweet Katie ever being addicted to anything but goodness was outrageous.

"Brian," Katie said, blotting her mouth with the back of her hand, then reaching for a dish towel, "I'm pretty sure I'm not the right person for your article."

"Of course you are."

"I was never one to stand at the center of anything."

"Plenty of people think you deserve to."

"It's not about deserving, Brian. It's about wanting. I know you and Robert came a long way to speak to me, and I'm glad to have you here for as long as you'd like to stay, but I don't have a story to tell the world. My stories are much more private."

"I have the editor of a national magazine and several book publishers who think otherwise."

"Let them think what they like. I don't parade my personal life before a national audience. Whatever stories I do have to tell are only for the people who need to hear them."

"How do you decide who needs to hear?"

"I don't have a formula, if that's what you're asking."

"You realize that the more you protest, the more you make a reporter want to dig?"

Katie crossed her arms. "Poor boy. You haven't outgrown that willful-defiance stage yet, have you?" Impatience had crept into her tone, but she maintained enough kindness to silence Brian. Temporarily, Robert thought.

"You're quieter than I remember you being, Robert," she said into the awkwardness.

"You've changed too."

"For the better I hope."

Robert nodded and saw a shadow pass across Katie's eyes. He mentally slapped himself. She couldn't see his body language, of course, and his remark had been obtuse.

He groped for an appropriate compliment. "You had very little to improve upon."

Katie dropped her eyes and turned her face away from him. She reached for her tea glass and misjudged its location, tipping the cup. It shattered on the tile floor, and everyone watched the brown liquid slip across the tile.

"Oh, Robert." She sighed. "You have no idea."

33

Saturday night—technically Sunday morning now—Janeal boarded an airplane and dropped into her first-class seat. Her PDA had been beeping prior to her call to board, and she'd been methodically answering as many of the messages as possible before having to turn off the device in flight.

Brian Hoffer had sent a note. *Conceptual pitch on your story idea attached. Tough subjects, play close to the chest, not sure they're right for the concept. Speak to me.*

She opened the file and skimmed the two-page synopsis. She'd speak to him all right. There was nothing here. Nothing that sang, anyway, nothing that would make for any story idea she could use in *All Angles,* nothing that would make a publisher drool instead of yawn.

Nothing that she could skim off by way of personal information.

This young reporter obviously would not do. All these decently written words and nothing to show for it but two decently portrayed figures, one Robert Lukin and one Katie Morgon, smiling out of the page like Macy's mannequins.

She'd have to do this herself.

Do what herself? She hadn't been after a story in the first place.

She wanted information. Not information about how this Desert Hope House functioned or how much funding had dropped in the past five years, as Brian had reported. She wanted personal information that only she would know how to ask for. She should have realized that in the first place.

Janeal sent Brian a reply.

Not strong enough, nothing to discuss. Idea's dead at the starting gate. If we decide to revive this thing, I'll call.

She turned her mind toward the next steps. How would she get to Katie?

How could she find out what Katie intended to do with all these cards she held? How could Janeal do it without exposing herself?

No clear answer presented itself.

A second message came in from Brian half a minute later, politely announcing the unreasonable kill fee he expected, along with canned language about how he hoped *All Angles* might reconsider or use him in the future, blah blah blah. She squashed her initial irritation and decided that since he hadn't called to argue with her, he was worth whatever fee he wanted. His own lack of passion was indication enough that he found the story not worth his talents. All the better.

Not only that, but as if aware that his demands were unusually high, Brian had included the following information: *Fee includes one-way ticket back to Phoenix, as my transportation—Lukin—has decided to make a vacation of it here in the Land of Enchantment.*

Janeal replied, *Send mailing address. Allow three weeks for payment,* and set her PDA aside. She didn't expect to hear from him until after he learned that she had not paid for his airfare. He got himself there of his own will; he could get himself home.

She hadn't expected Robert to spend an extended time with Katie either, she realized. His presence might add a fresh wrinkle to Janeal's already rumpled quandary.

34

Over Lucille's objections, Katie made arrangements for Robert to stay in a wing where there were three unoccupied rooms. Robert promised Lucille he would not be a distraction to any of the residents and would stay out of everyone's way.

If he had any say in it, Katie would be the only person in this house he saw for the next week anyway. Brian would bunk with him tonight, then scoot back to Arizona in the morning. He said something about wanting to respect Katie's desire for privacy. Robert didn't believe him, though he didn't care why Brian left, only that he finally did. He needed some time with Katie. Alone.

Sunday morning, Brian used his wireless device to book a flight out of the municipal airport in Santa Fe, then shoved Robert awake for a ride at seven thirty. Katie wasn't out of her room yet, as far as Robert knew, and he drove down the mountain grudgingly without being able to tell her where he was headed. Though Brian had given up on Katie as a potential story, he persisted in bugging Robert to help him gain access to Sanso—a promise Robert refused to make. He dropped Brian in the parking lot, certain he'd hear from the kid again soon.

On his way back, he picked up some toiletries and sundries he needed, then placed an outgoing call to Harlan and made arrangements for a week-long leave.

Harlan told him he'd better stay for two. "You haven't taken a vacation in three years," the man said. "Don't come back here a day sooner."

Robert parked his truck at the Hope House just after ten thirty.

The Sunday morning quiet seemed unnatural compared to the women's chatter and footsteps that had filled the halls last night. The sound of a pan clattering against a metal sink led Robert toward the old kitchen, empty except for Katie. She had her hair tied back and was lifting a steamer basket out of a pot on the stove. On the island where he and Brian had sipped iced tea when they arrived, a mess of cabbage leaves, spices, and a bowl of what appeared to be chopped meat, onions, and cooked rice cluttered the table.

"*Sármi*," Robert said. "I haven't had these since—"

He hadn't eaten them since Janeal last made them, the week before she died.

"I can't promise they'll be great," Katie said, placing the steamer in the sink. "It's been awhile. Not a big demand for stuffed cabbage leaves around here."

She leaned over the stovetop grill and sniffed. Three kabobs loaded with thinly sliced beef and peppers looked about finished. As easily as if she could see what she was doing, she pulled at a piece of the meat with a fork to test it for doneness, and it flaked off easily. Katie moved the kabobs to plates, two for him and one for her, next to helpings of brown rice flecked with herbs. Then she used a pair of wooden tongs to lift out the contents of the steamer.

"Do you mind an early lunch?" she asked.

"I'm starving. When did you take up cooking?" Robert asked. He sat and thought the meal was the most appetizing food he had seen in quite some time.

"It turns out cooking is therapeutic."

He waited for her to explain, but she did not. Perhaps she was inviting him to join her.

"Where do you keep the plates?" Robert asked.

Katie pointed to a cupboard.

Robert pulled out what he thought they needed, wanting nothing more in that moment than to tell Katie everything about his years searching for Sanso, of his single-minded focus, of the week leading up to the day it finally happened. She would understand the emotions he felt but could not express. But where to start? And did she want to speak of the past, of Sanso and what had happened the night that their lives burned to the ground?

They moved through the kitchen in silence while Katie filled the plates and Robert searched for flatware and then helped clear two spaces at the island large enough for them to eat at.

Robert took a bite of the beef kabob. The marinade was spicy and sweet and held a hint of curry. "This is incredible."

Katie smiled.

They ate without speaking for a few long minutes, and the awkwardness cropped up in Robert's mind as a new, unforeseen thing. He put a cabbage roll in his mouth and chewed it slowly.

He studied Katie, who took small bites. She'd taken the band out of her hair, allowing it to curtain the side of her face.

"These taste like Janeal's used to," he dared to say.

Katie's eyes misted.

"I'm sorry. I meant—I wanted it to come across as a compliment." And an invitation to a real conversation.

"It did. That's why I made these, you know."

"Because you wanted a compliment?"

"No, Robert. There's this big elephant in the kitchen . . ."

"Right."

"It's okay to talk about it."

"It's hard to know where to start."

"Do you want to talk about it?"

He did. And he didn't. He chewed slowly before saying, "Sure."

Katie laughed then, and he felt foolish. "I see I'll have to be the emcee at this little reunion of ours."

"You've been the silent one all these years."

"Fair enough."

"I never knew you survived. Why did you tell people you weren't affiliated with the *kumpania*?"

"How did you know about that?"

"Someone at the hospital said."

She set her fork down. "At first, I denied it because I was afraid. The man who killed our families—he was so bent on killing that I believed he'd come after me. It would have been impossible to avoid the inquiries of investigators, the media. He would have found out."

"I wouldn't put it past him."

"You were one of the agents who apprehended him, Brian said."

"I'll tell you about it sometime. You keep going."

Katie leaned her elbows on the table. "As time went on, it got easier to keep the past sealed off. There was a day when I decided to consciously separate myself from that period of my life."

"It was too painful to think about."

Katie bit her lip, then released it. "That might be the simplest way of putting it."

"If I'd known you were alive . . ."

"It was probably for the best. I've needed this time to get back on my feet again. How did you find me? No—first things first. How did you . . . not get killed that night? What happened when you went looking for your family?"

Robert pushed his plate aside and took both of Katie's hands in his own. Harlan was the only other person he'd told, and that was ten years ago. But his account of the horror replayed in his mind often, including the moment he'd seen Katie's father die and Sanso haul her off toward the meetinghouse. Slowly and honestly, he told her everything.

Both their faces were wet by the time he finished.

"Were you . . . ?" Katie reached up to touch his cheek and he grasped her hand, pressing it into his skin and closing his eyes to focus on her warmth. He shook his head.

"And you?" he asked, returning her touch, caressing the scar that ran down the side of her face and disappeared into the high-neck shirt she wore. "How did it happen?"

"It's a mercy I don't remember the bulk of it," she said. She pulled away, running her fingers through her hair. A lock snagged on a ring she wore on her right ring finger, six small diamonds set into the width of a slim gold band. For the first time, Robert realized that the beautiful mane of hair was a wig. "It's a mercy I can't actually see it."

"Why would you say that?"

"My whole body—I'm hideous, Robert."

"You are the most beautiful woman I have ever seen." It was the strongest opinion he'd held about a woman for some time, and it popped out of him without a thought.

"Don't."

Her perception that he was being insincere pained him. Robert wanted to touch her again but didn't want to offend her, didn't want her to stop talking. "What parts do you remember?"

She shook her head and covered her eyes with her scarred hands. "I don't like to talk about it."

"You can talk to me."

"I've never . . . I'm going to need some time to sort it out in my own mind."

Robert waited.

"Janeal," Katie said. And that was all she said for a full minute.

Robert prodded gently. "Janeal what?"

Thirty seconds later Katie shook her head again and wiped her eyes. She stood and picked up their half-eaten plates of food. "Janeal tried," she said. Then Katie carried the plates to the sink and was rescued from saying anything more by Lucille, who burst into the kitchen with smoke coming out of her ears. She demanded Katie's presence for an emergency meeting regarding one of the residents.

"I'll be right there," Katie said, but didn't rush as she placed the uneaten cabbage rolls into small plastic bags. Lucille let the door slap back into place, and Robert watched Katie clean up the rest of her cooking project, paced and calm and thoughtful, moving as if her steps were measured and choreographed. Robert reached out and brushed Katie's hand when she walked by him and suggested maybe they could walk together when her meeting was finished.

Katie squeezed his fingers without committing either way.

"Take as much time as you need," Robert said.

Lucille's voice reached Katie ten paces before she entered the office. It was like Lucille to start without her in cases like this, and Katie was glad for it today. The conversation with Robert had thrown her off center.

"Six thousand dollars!" Lucille was saying. "And you think you deserve to stay here? You're lucky I haven't called the police yet."

Katie entered the room.

"Tell me why I shouldn't hand you over to them," Lucille demanded.

"Lucille." Katie urged her to calm down.

"It's not a difficult question. Tell me why, Rita."

"I'm so sorry."

"Sorry you were caught!"

"No . . . it was only supposed to be a little bit, one time. My brother needed help. I never meant to take so much—"

"You stole from every woman in this house, Rita. As if we have plenty to go around in the first place! As if we didn't already pay for your food and your shelter and your training. You think that's free? You think the government subsidizes everything? Let me tell you what it costs to run—"

"Lucille, that's enough." Katie's words, though several decibels quieter than those of the other two, were forceful enough to make Lucille back down. She heard Lucille move toward her desk and lift the phone out of its cradle.

"We're already two weeks late paying the mortgage, thanks to her," she mumbled.

"Just call the police," Katie said. Then she turned to Rita. "Tell me about your brother." The sound of a tissue being withdrawn from a box was followed by sniffling. "What did he need help with?"

"He . . . uh . . . lost his job. Three kids. His wife has cancer. He needed something to get by."

Katie pulled up a chair in front of Rita, who sobbed on the couch. Warm afternoon sun poured across Katie's back. "Money can be a real Achilles' heel for some of us, can't it?" Katie said. "It's sitting right there within our reach, and we think we need it for a good cause. And before we know it, we've got it in our fist."

Rita blew her nose.

"I understand that kind of temptation. Believe me, I do."

Rita did not reply.

"This house is operating right now on barely enough to 'get by,' as you put it. We trusted your help with the books enough for you to have seen that. Am I right? Yes. So I think you understand what it means to us to have lost six thousand dollars." She paused. "You also understand why we have to report this."

"It will never happen again."

"That's a nice promise, and I believe you're feeling genuine right now, but I can't take a promise to the bank."

More sniffling. "I'll pay you back."

"You might. I believe you might. In the meantime, I can't save you from the consequences of what you've done, Rita. Letting you stay here puts every other woman in this program in jeopardy. They have to believe we take our house rules seriously. And you've committed a crime."

The girl's crying picked up again. "Please don't make me go to jail."

Katie rested her hand on Rita's knee, where the fabric of her jeans was frayed. Lucille had a police officer on the line and was explaining what happened. Katie sighed. She wished she could give everyone a million second chances, however many do-overs they needed to find their feet after a horrifying mistake.

She of all people understood the power of this kind of grace, which was nothing short of a miracle. A miracle that had been granted to her once upon a time; a miracle she did not believe she deserved.

"What happens to you will be for a judge to decide."

Lucille's phone rattled in the cradle as she ended her call. "They're on their way."

"But I'll tell you what I can do," Katie said to Rita. "If you're serious about making this right."

"I'll do anything you want. I'm so sorry."

"I will stick with you through this. I'll go with you to your hearings; I'll visit you if you're sentenced. If you need someone to talk to, you call me."

The air went out of Lucille's vinyl desk chair as she sat, groaning audibly. "I swear, Katie, you are the patron saint of lost causes."

Katie kept her attention on Rita.

"You tell the judge the truth of what happened. I'll vanish if I discover you have told the smallest white lie. You accept these consequences gracefully. Serve your time. Put together a plan to give this money back to the residents here, even if it takes you twenty years to pay it. I can help you with that."

"I will. I will."

"You will attend any rehabilitation programs the judge assigns you to. You won't miss a meeting, even if you're dying of some incurable disease."

"I'll do it."

"And you'll attend church with me once a month. No complaining. No excuses."

Rita did not respond to that one.

"If you do this, Rita, if you prove your apology is sincere and can win back my trust, I will let you come back to this house when it's all over."

"I should have seen this coming," Lucille said.

"She talks mean," Katie said without turning her face from Rita, "but she'll be the first to give you a hug if you make it back here."

"That's what you think."

Rita choked out innumerable thank-yous to both of them.

"Go pack your things and bring them to me," Katie told her. "I'll look after them for you."

"She'll bolt," Lucille said as Rita scurried away.

"Then go supervise," Katie said.

Lucille didn't leave. "I don't know why you do that."

"People visit this house wanting to know what sets us apart from the rest. And you know it's because we see everyone as equal. You, me, the rest of our staff—we're all capable of the worst. Some of us accept grace and mercy when we're given it, and others don't. That doesn't mean I'll stop handing out forgiveness."

"No need to go religious on me again, Katie."

Katie laughed. She loved her thick-skinned colleague like a sister. "It's not religion, it's redemption."

"Rita wouldn't know redemption if Jesus himself presented it to her."

"Some of us require more time than others to recognize it. Or more drastic measures."

"Well if I'm right about anything, that girl will have to walk across flaming hot coals and back before she'll recognize a second chance."

Lucille could not have known the impact of her choice of words. "Some of us do," Katie said.

"I doubt you ever needed a second chance for anything, Katie." She heard Lucille step out into the hall to follow Rita.

If she only knew.

35

Standing outside the hospital where Salazar Sanso was still recovering, Janeal hesitated one last time.

She had spent the morning flight from New York to Tucson in first class staring at her orange juice, considering that a visit might be unwise. She would expose herself, for one, and risked triggering his ire. Or his infatuation, if it still existed. He might, because he could, decide to blackmail her or throw her to the wolves.

Janeal hated to think of Robert Lukin and Katie Morgan as wolves. At present, she was the truer wolf and they were as harmless as *Peter and the Wolf*'s duck. But if they discovered her, those roles would certainly reverse and she'd end up in someone's belly.

Salazar Sanso, lover of "games," as he called them—games that ended in death—would not keep his promise to her. No doubt he saw promises as strategies, and his recent arrest would be reason to reevaluate. To send Robert after Katie was only the first move in a contest that would best all of them if she did not anticipate his game plan, because Sanso was a poor loser, and he would never concede to anyone connected with Jason or Janeal Mikkado.

Sanso would bring her down before he went down himself. She understood this because she had come to operate in much the same way. It had worked with Milan Finch.

She had to preempt Sanso's move. If she was successful, she'd let Robert and Katie ride off into the sunset together while she faded to black.

As much as she didn't want to, she'd have to let Robert go. Again.

At least Sanso couldn't threaten anyone she loved this time, because Jane Johnson loved no one.

No one.

Before her flight touched down in Arizona, she had decided that there were ways around her concerns, starting with a call to one of Milan Finch's friends in the attorney general's office. Jasper Tennant became her friend after she squashed a story that incriminated him in an embezzlement scandal and instead ran an alternate theory that eventually created enough reasonable doubt in court to salvage his reputation. And his career.

Today she called in the favor.

With Jasper's help, she secured a pass to interview Sanso as a defense attorney, as one Lisa Rasmussen, a bona fide partner in the firm that had already agreed to represent the criminal. Except the real Lisa was vacationing in Europe until the end of the week. All this explained why Janeal was here late on a Sunday afternoon, carrying a Styrofoam take-out container in one hand and a Dolce & Gabbana satchel in the other. She wore a cropped almond-brown wig and a pinstriped chocolate pantsuit, both in a style that Lisa preferred, based on photos Janeal had located easily online. A slim pair of Anne Kline glasses completed the look.

Sanso would recognize her mind and voice as Janeal—if he didn't, she'd prod his memory—but if all went well he wouldn't be able to pull her out of an *All Angles* lineup.

As if he read American magazines to begin with, acclaimed or not. She liked the idea that he might read comic books, though.

She wouldn't be running her image in the periodical any longer anyway. That misery would fall to the new executive editor.

Janeal entered the hospital and took the elevator to the fourth floor and then to the secure wing, without anyone informing her that visiting hours were over. At Sanso's door the guard on duty nodded as if he'd been expecting her and didn't check the ID she'd assembled in her hotel room.

Sanso was napping when she entered the room. A weak blade of late afternoon sun cutting through a part in the blackout curtains was the only source of illumination at this hour. Janeal placed her take-out container on the rolling bed table and opened it. The man had aged some since their last encounter. Gray hairs rimmed his temples, and the fragile skin under his eyes sagged. No doubt injury and sleep gave off the appearance of being more vulnerable than he was.

The aroma of grilled tilapia and lemon rice filled the room. Janeal turned away and sat on the wood-and-upholstery visitor's chair, her face in shadow. She did not have to wait long for the scent to wake Sanso. He stirred after only two or three minutes.

"Hungry?" she said from the dark corner.

Sanso did not reply, though she detected his head shift at the sound of her voice. After a breath he started patting the sheets, probably searching for the bed controls.

"Let me," she said, her eyes having adjusted to the darkness. She went to his side and raised the back support, then moved the remote control so that it dangled by its umbilical over the head of the bed, where he couldn't reach it. She returned to her seat.

"I should see what I am eating," he murmured. "And who with."

"You are eating fish and rice. With Lisa Rasmussen."

"I doubt it." His voice was baritone and coarse.

"Taste it and prove me wrong."

"Ah. It's not the food I question." He prodded the Styrofoam container with his fingers and sniffed. "You might have brought a fork."

"You never minded getting your hands dirty."

"True. Nor did you. At least once upon a time. Janeal Mikkado."

He folded his hands across his chest and sighed like a man content with life.

"You remember."

"Child, the number of women I have not forgotten is so small that I have time to name you each in my morning prayers. I've waited for you to come back to me. I looked for you now and then—but not too hard. I'm a man of my word. Did you know I have prayed for you daily since the morning you sold your soul for a million dollars?"

"Did you know that I have cursed you daily since the night you slaughtered my father?"

"Prayers are far more effective than curses."

"Look where you lie, murderer."

Sanso turned his head toward her and opened his eyes wide. They seemed to bore through the shadows, and she wondered how clearly he could see her.

"I'd wager I lie in a bed far brighter than the one you have made for yourself," he said. "Tell me why now, after all these years, you've finally come to me.

Surely you could have found me more easily somewhere else if you had really wanted to."

He reached into the take-out box and broke off a piece of fish. He placed it on his tongue and chewed slowly, licking his fingers before he swallowed.

"Would you like some?" he asked.

Janeal replied softly, measuring each syllable as if she were controlling the conversation. That she wasn't in control bothered her; directing others' words was something she had become accustomed to.

"What was your intent in telling Robert Lukin of a survivor?"

Sanso's laugh was silent, but his chin bobbed. "Just a little harmless fun. That boy devoted his life to hunting me down—do you know what it's like to be so idolized?" He dismissed the question with a shake of his head. "Of course you don't. But what's he got to live for now that he's conquered me? He needed a diversion."

"I'm surprised you concede defeat so quickly," Janeal said. She fully believed Sanso had more sinister intentions for the man who had finally captured him—and in such humiliating fashion, if the stories being reported were true.

Sanso put another chunk of fish into his mouth and talked around it. "True. I think of my situation as a temporary pause in the game. No harm in making him think it's over for now. That's strategy. You're a far more slippery eel than I ever was. It'll take him a bit longer to track you down. I'm thinking twenty, twenty-five years. And if he's looking for you, he's not looking for me."

Janeal had some difficulty following this rambling. Was he saying he had not intended to direct Robert to Katie? If not, how had Katie come to be a part of this scenario at all?

Sanso covered his mouth with one hand, feigning the embarrassment of a shocking realization, then spoke through his fingers. "Oh, I hope you're not angry about me telling him. That wasn't a part of our arrangement, was it? I don't believe it was against any rules to tell him about you. He thought he was the only survivor, you know. Telling him there was another was really quite a precious moment. You should have been here."

In the darkness of this fishy-smelling hospital room, the picture of what Sanso thought he had done became clearer in Janeal's mind. Sanso had no idea Katie Morgon existed, and Robert Lukin had no idea Janeal Mikkado existed.

But Katie knew about Janeal.

She decided that she would have better luck controlling what Sanso revealed to her if she didn't say anything at all.

"When he finds out that you've done business with me, that ought to make your reunion all the sweeter. I saved that information for later, but when he finds out, he'll know he searched with a purpose. Wouldn't it be sad to send a boy on a decades-long hunt for a woman who left him behind on purpose? See, but by me sending him to you, I'll have helped him do *more* justice, even if you've already managed to spend all that money. Tell me you invested it, please?"

"He won't waste twenty years of his life on me."

"If it appears he won't, I'll inform him of your antics sooner than I had planned."

Janeal couldn't keep the fury out of her voice. "We had a deal!"

"And I have kept it faithfully. I keep all deals that serve me well. But once in a while I have to renegotiate."

"Seems a pretty one-sided negotiation to me."

"You have your secret identity, child. That ought to be worth something."

"How much?"

Sanso deposited another bite of fish into his mouth.

"He'll find you," Sanso said, chewing. "Survivors of any tragedy have a connection that draws them together. I've seen it again and again. Yes, he'll find you." He took another bite. "And when he finds you, I'll find him once more."

Janeal stared at him.

"Or maybe you'll find him for me," Sanso said, smacking his lips. "Preempt his moves, save your own skin. You'd save me a lot of time."

Janeal stood and placed her bag on her shoulder. He raised his eyes to Janeal slowly, without moving his head. She must not have taken enough care to hide the fury on her own face, because he laughed at her—a low, soothing laugh.

"Don't be mad. I've only made your life more interesting. You could thank me."

Janeal placed her hand on the doorknob and turned it.

"Janeal Mikkado. Stay another moment." The tone of his voice had changed from teasing to tempting, raising in Janeal's mind the memory of her first encounter with him as a girl. "Tell me what you've done with your life."

She stood in the cone of light that came in off the hall. She was surprised to find herself considering his invitation. She tried to bring her mind back to the urgency of the moment he had put her in.

"Nothing interesting," she said.

"You could scrub a toilet and make it interesting, child. Why are you always running from me?"

Her answer popped out before she could edit it. "I have no desire to be like you."

"I think you're in a hurry to leave because you know you're already *exactly* like me, and it frightens you."

His eyes glinted at her in the darkness, and she realized he spoke the truth. She *was* like him—she could sweep across the surface of the world without concern for any desires but her own.

"You shouldn't be afraid," he said. "We could help each other. Soul mates united."

"Help each other do what?"

He didn't answer immediately. "Find the happiness that continues to elude us, in spite of all our accomplishments."

"I'm happy enough." It seemed necessary to protest, though without conviction.

Sanso's low laugh sounded appropriately villainous this time.

"Don't," she murmured.

"Come put my bed back down so I can sleep again. Though I doubt I'll sleep much tonight."

Janeal did not evaluate whether she should do as he requested or walk out the open door. But when the door closed and latched, she found herself standing at the head of his bed, fetching the controls and returning them to his hand.

His fingers closed around hers and she let them.

"Find Robert Lukin before he finds you. You have the advantage. We can keep what we have. We can have more."

"*We* don't have anything," she said.

Sanso raised her fingers to his lips. "We could have everything," he said after a kiss to her knuckles. "After you deal with Robert, you'll come back to me."

"I don't visit prisons."

"Neither do I."

Janeal snatched her hand out of his and took quick steps to the door. She threw the door open and stepped out into the hall. She was shaking.

"See you soon," he prophesied in the darkness.

36

Sanso knew by the tattoo on the left bicep—a dagger plunged into a stack of thousand-dollar bills—that the orderly who delivered his evening meal was no orderly at all. The sweat beading the man's upper lip and the effort he made not to look into Sanso's eyes confirmed it: he was a low-ranking felon in the Sanso empire, a plebe of a criminal kind, an expendable, untraceable member of the family who could make a risky delivery and be killed if necessary to cover a botched job.

Sanso had been expecting him.

The delivery boy put a covered melamine plate on Sanso's bed table and rolled the meal within Sanso's reach. He wiped the back of his hand across his perspiring brow.

"Took long enough," Sanso complained. He'd ask later why the delivery had taken two more days than it should have, if all had gone according to prelaid plans.

"Chef's apologies," the man mumbled. "The first batch of potatoes was ruined." He backed away from the bed and turned to rush from the room, his foot snagging the chair Janeal Mikkado had sat in. At least the oaf didn't fall.

Janeal, Janeal. She understood so little, namely, that Sanso's driving desire was not for Robert, who wasn't worth Sanso's time, but for her. He had known she would come to him. She had not disappointed.

Sanso lifted the plate cover, still happy to understand that he knew her so well. Gray green beans, a leathery Salisbury steak, a generous mound of leaden mashed potatoes. Jell-O. He had waited these many years for her to grow into her true self, and though he would never have made his own arrest the provocation for her to return, that had worked out nicely enough in the end. The better job he did of convincing her that Robert was his target, the more quickly she would cave to Sanso's will.

To his plan for Janeal Mikkado's life.

His plan to have her completely—not by force, but because she surrendered willingly. She would betray Robert to save her own skin, as easily as she had given him her father and her friend. Then her transformation would be complete.

This was a worthy pursuit.

He lifted the flimsy metal spoon and poked it into the large helping of potatoes. The spoon slipped sideways off of an invisible object. Sanso scooped it out. A syringe wrapped in plastic, and an unlabeled glass bottle. He unwrapped the mess and withdrew the capped syringe, slipping it under the sheets at his side. Then he lifted the bottle, which appeared to contain water but should, if Callista had done her work, contain enough carfentanil to bring down a gorilla in a matter of minutes.

And a man in a matter of seconds. With a potency eight thousand times greater than heroin, it would be quite a trip.

He tucked the bottle next to the syringe and ate the rest of his meal.

A different orderly cleared the uneaten food an hour later, and two hours after that the night nurse came on shift, checked the dressings on his side, and declared him progressing at a fast enough rate to get himself out of this prison and into another one within a day or so. Sanso didn't speak to either of them.

At midnight, as every night, he heard the nurse tell someone outside his door that she was heading downstairs for a coffee. Did he want her to bring back the usual? Sanso couldn't hear the answer but did hear the ding of the elevator doors tell him when she was gone.

He withdrew the glass vial and filled the syringe, then placed it in his left palm, needle down and thumb on the plunger. His left wrist was attached to the bedrail, which he lowered so that he could sit and swing his legs over the edge. His side burned where the bullet had clipped his liver and passed through. A minor injury, in his mind.

Sanso hollered. When the guard did not respond, Sanso fished the clean bedpan out of the foot of his bed and hurled it at his closed door.

The guard, a clean-cut, federal-looking guy with tidy black hair and shaven cheeks, leaned into the room, one hand holding the outside doorknob.

Sanso rattled the cuffs that kept his left arm attached to the bed. "Get a guy to the john?" he asked.

"I'll get the nurse." The door started to close.

"You seen her? You think you could do anything in a bathroom with her breathing down your neck?"

"You'll live."

"Cut me a break, please. Man to man."

The FBI head reemerged. "Use the bedpan."

"If I do that, what d'you think will happen next time I have to get your attention?" Sanso gestured to the place the pan had landed. "Get your partner to do it if you don't want to."

"If I were lucky enough to have someone else here to do your dirty work, I would." He stepped into the room and leaned over to swoop up the pan, then took three steps toward the bed. The door swung closed and clicked.

"Throw this thing again, empty or full, and next time you can go in the sheets. That ought to endear you to the staff."

His right arm swung to release the pan, sending it toward Sanso's chest. Sanso leaned forward and let it bounce off, focused instead on the man's outstretched wrist, which came close enough for Sanso to grasp with his free hand. In a swift move assisted by the element of surprise, he twisted the agent's arm and spun the man around, pulling him toward the bed.

The guard reacted as fast, using the momentum of his spinning, falling body to wrench his wrist free of Sanso's grip. The man got an extra quarter turn out of the spin, no doubt trying to prevent himself from landing on the bed with his back exposed, but that was all he accomplished. Sanso, having rotated the syringe in his cuffed hand so that it pointed upward, depressed the plunger at the same moment that the needle penetrated the fleshiest part of his opponent's hip.

The man's eyes went wide and he gasped, and Sanso threw the full weight of his body over the man, sending an elbow up under the agent's chin to prevent him from shouting out, and thrusting a knee into the guy's groin. A few repeated blows were enough to minimize the impact of the man's flailing fists for the thirty seconds or so that it took him to wilt.

The agent was conscious but mostly paralyzed when Sanso released him and started patting his pockets for a key to his cuff. He hadn't expected to be so winded. Sanso's wrist was bleeding where the metal had cut him in the contortions of the scuffle, and the syringe was bloody. He let it drop and kicked it away under the bed.

Sanso found the key quickly, released himself, and started to strip the immobile man of his clothes. Lucky for him, the agent was about his size. Unfortunately for the agent, that meant he would undoubtedly not survive this ordeal. His eyes had already closed, and his breathing had become labored. The shirt cuff button snagged on a wedding ring when Sanso tugged it off. Nothing he could do about that. These men should marry their jobs and nothing else if they cared about anyone in the world.

He mentally judged that he had about four more minutes before the night nurse returned. Not that he was concerned about what it would take to put her out; it would merely be inconvenient.

In one minute he was dressed. In less than two he was in the elevator, headed for the lower level garage, using the agent's phone to summon Callista and willing the wound in his side to stay closed.

37

Janeal needed time to think.

Foremost in her mind was deciding which was in most immediate need of defense: the world she had so carefully and successfully constructed around herself these past fifteen years, or the very self that world protected. The *All Angles* board would frown on her running off to New Mexico for an indefinite period during this critical transition, and who knew what Milan might engineer in her absence, either for reinstatement or for revenge.

Then there was Katie, the woman who had held her tongue for a decade and a half. If she broke her silence the moment she saw Robert, however, those two wouldn't know the first thing about where to look for Janeal if they wanted to. Maybe they wouldn't want to. Maybe Janeal was far less of an important figure in their world than she assumed she might be.

She wasn't sure whether to feel relieved or disgruntled by that possibility.

Janeal returned to New York considerably distracted. Though Sanso's plan to put Robert on her trail had been foiled by Katie's surprise survival, Janeal could not put the thought out of her mind that Katie and Robert *would* talk about her. Eventually. And when they did, what would Katie say?

Janeal had to know. With every passing minute, her need to know grew. Katie held the power to ruin Robert's memory of her, to turn former friends into foes, to end the dream life Janeal had created for herself.

Monday morning, her head started pounding earlier than usual. She staggered into her new office—which today seemed unnecessarily large and staggeringly bright—at nine o'clock. Alan Greenbrook met her at the door, and she ignored his immediate suggestion that she advise him of new routines he needed to put in place. Instead she groped for the bank of light switches inside the door, flipping down two of the three.

"The firecrackers going off inside my head take priority over everything else right now," Janeal said, reaching out for the balancing stability of the desk. "For now, the extent of your routine is to keep a semiautomatic weapon trained on my pharmacist until he refills my prescription for Fioricet." She rounded the furniture and dropped into the brown velour desk chair, eyes closed.

Alan stood his ground in the doorway, arms crossed and feet planted wide. They'd had similar conversations before. It was one of the few topics that wiped the smile off his face. "That refill is not due to be filled until—"

"A gun, Alan. Use a gun if you have to. I'm not leaving this office today." She tilted her head back against the headrest, eyes closed. "Why do I sense you still standing in the doorway?"

"Ms. Johnson, your episodes are getting more frequent. And if they are also getting more intense, you may need to consider that Fioricet puts you at risk of—"

"Are you a physician, Alan?" Janeal managed to open her eyes and find the general shape that marked his location. The light that found its way to her brain pulsated. "Because the last time I checked, you were a worthless assistant. Do what I've asked so that you're no longer worthless, or give me your resignation and I'll drop-kick you into medical school myself." She had to close her eyes again and hope that the meds she had taken while on the elevator would kick in soon. She simultaneously hoped that he understood her sarcasm for what it was. He was not an employee she wanted to lose.

Alan sighed as if he were a long-suffering son of an unreasonable old hag— really, she could probably date him if she wanted to—but he left without saying anything more.

"Ms. Johnson?" A female voice intruded.

"Not now."

"I've been sent to ask you—"

"I said *not now.*" Janeal's hand closed around the nearest object on her desk, her morning coffee, and with her eyes still shut, she hurled it at the voice.

The splash of coffee was matched by a gasp, which was followed by Alan's low tones. Janeal imagined the boy taking the ignoramus by the elbow and leading her away, explaining the rules of office communication.

Janeal sat, willing the aura of this headache to fade, willing strength back into the plans she needed to make to protect her future, willing Katie to forget Janeal had ever existed.

She dozed.

She placed her hand on a wood door and pressed it inward. A hospital room, lightless and rank with the smell of charred flesh. She stepped into the blackness.

A strong wind sucked the door shut behind her. Her entire body twitched at the bang, which acted like some kind of ignition. Light jumped into the room: flames, licking at the hem of drawn curtains in the windows. Within seconds all four panels were blazing.

She turned back to the door to get out of the room and grabbed the knob. The metal burned and the palm of her hand sizzled like grilled meat. She screamed and pulled away. Bits of her flesh stuck to the smoldering hardware. She gripped her injury and watched the knob turn molten.

Someone was calling her. Katie. Katie was calling her, and Sanso. She spun around, noticed a figure in the hospital bed for the first time. Sanso lay there, beckoning to her with seductive fingers. A flame from the curtains jumped to the corner of his sheet and began to spread, an uncontained blaze in a field of cotton fibers.

You should not have left me, Janeal, Sanso said. Sanso said it, but the voice was Katie's.

Janeal closed her eyes, breathing hard, backing to the closed door that she could not exit.

She bumped into something—some*one*—who gripped her shoulders. Robert. She knew him without looking and began to sag with relief. Her head ached; her hand stung fiercely. He would rescue her. He would love her.

Robert shoved her.

Straight toward the burning bed.

Janeal flung her hands out in front of her, though there was nothing in her path to stop her trajectory. She hit with her elbows locked.

And awoke on all fours on the floor of her office, the palms of both hands stinging with the friction of a rug burn.

Breathless, she opened her eyes. Nothing in her new office was on fire. No one else occupied the large room. Her head was clear and light.

She unlocked her joints and lowered her forehead to the carpet as if it were the tarmac of a homeland she thought she'd never see again. If anyone walked in, she'd claim a lost earring.

Janeal breathed deeply for several seconds. Maybe several minutes. This, too, was a nightmare she had had before, but not for a few years. The hospital room was a new setting, though, and the roles were mixed up. Previously it was Katie in the bed, and Sanso who shoved her.

And Robert who caught her before she was engulfed by fire.

Janeal's phone was ringing.

She let it beep while she settled back on her heels, then gripped her desk to pull herself up and return to her chair, which had rolled backward a few feet. The sudden break in the usual stream of human interruptions made her consciously grateful. It could have been divine intervention.

Or a spilled cup of coffee. The brown liquid still dripped from her door.

She remembered Robert's hands on her shoulder blades, shoving her, and she involuntarily shivered.

Janeal rose and went to the freestanding closet adjacent to the office's private restroom, thinking that maybe Alan might have thought to hang a jacket or sweater in advance of her arrival. She pulled the mirrored wardrobe doors open.

What the cabinet held was not at all what she had expected to find. Taped onto the back panel was a grotesque picture of herself—not her really, but her head, electronically manipulated to fit onto the naked body of a contorted woman. Milan's doing. The photo illustration was among the more vile and violent that Janeal had seen, making her almost immediately close the closet doors.

She opened them again only to tear the photo off the walnut surface and quickly read the message that had been scrawled with a broad-tipped marker across the image.

No forgiveness.

Janeal folded the paper in half and walked across the room to feed it to the shredder. The last of it was devoured before she realized she ought to have kept it as potentially incriminating.

On the other hand, if Milan was serious, he would provide her with plenty more evidence. She wondered in passing how bad Milan's animosity might get.

No forgiveness.

So what? Janeal did not need Milan's forgi—

And in that moment, Janeal understood what she needed to do to secure Katie's silence and maybe Robert's. If she was successful, she would protect this happy little life she had created for herself.

38

Katie and Lucille and the three other full-time staff members each took one afternoon a week off and rotated weekends. Katie had Monday afternoon and so suggested to Robert that they go down into Santa Fe to browse an art gallery that was featuring the work of a sculptor she admired.

Robert agreed, though he cared little about art and knew even less about sculpture. On this Monday, though, he'd go anywhere if it meant being alone with her.

As Robert shaved before breakfast, he'd heard the five-second headline on network news—no satellite or cable TV out here—that Sanso had escaped. If he hadn't been using an electric razor, he surely would have cut himself. Instead he rushed to finish and made a sloppy job of it, wondering why he'd bothered to shave in the first place, as he was relegated by Lucille to taking meals in the kitchen.

The Desert Hope House had a strict no-cell-phone policy, even for guests, which meant that Robert had to keep his phone in the car and make calls off property or from the landline in Katie's office. Robert rushed to the office to call Harlan. He wasn't optimistic about what he'd hear. The immediate problem of Sanso's getaway would fall to the FBI, and chances were that until they picked up his trail again, Robert would have to stare at the dirt and wait for the gopher to pop back up.

Harlan told Robert exactly what he expected: nothing to do now, nothing until the feds picked up Sanso's trail, so sit tight and check your messages once in a while.

So much for his one-time, satisfaction-guaranteed life experience of ending Salazar Sanso's career once and for all.

He felt restless and vaguely irritated, angry that the one stellar day of his professional life had been reduced to insignificance so quickly.

With several hours to kill before Katie would be through with her morning, he caught himself wandering the house halls, catlike, in search of a glimpse of her. His intensified yearning for her company surprised him. This was crazy. He was assuaging his disappointment with the warm comfort of an old friend who knew him better than anyone else.

He found a Clive Cussler book in the house library and tried to bury himself in it. Robert turned ten pages of the book before realizing he couldn't recall a word he'd read. He was thinking about her. He wanted to hold her and forget the last fifteen years of his sorry life. He wanted to pick up the pieces with someone who knew the happier part of his history and could help him re-create his life. He wanted her to tell him that his life wasn't the exercise in futility he believed it to be.

Stupid, stupid, stupid. He forced his mind into the book.

He considered leaving early, leaving New Mexico this evening, going back to his DEA division in El Paso, picking up Sanso's scent again. He packed his duffel.

But fatigue anchored him to his bed. The kind of fatigue that hit athletes mid-event if they took too long a rest break. He couldn't get started again. He had no momentum.

"Everything okay at work?" Katie asked from the doorway.

"It's been better." He swung his legs off the bed and tossed the book onto the pillow.

"You sound annoyed."

"Just frustrated."

"You never were very good at hiding the way you feel, Robert."

"Not around you anyway."

He told her about Sanso's escape. She offered her sympathy but didn't say more.

Later, with Katie on the seat beside him, he drove down the mountain and into the community of artists, and his lethargy seemed less ominous. The sun baked his neck as he drove, turning it, he was sure, into the same color as the red clay adobe art studios on the road where Katie instructed him to turn.

"You're quiet this afternoon," he said when she rubbed the back of her neck as if it was stiff.

"Didn't sleep too well last night."

"What kept you up?"

"Nightmare."

"Does that happen often?"

"Almost never, fortunately."

"Want to talk about it?"

Katie considered this. "Only if you promise not to try to analyze it."

"Promise."

"I was in the game room at the *kumpania* meetinghouse. You remember it?"

"Of course."

"I was standing in the doorway and the whole place was—on fire, up in a blaze. But there was a stool at the back wall, not burning at all, and ropes attached to one of the rungs at the bottom. And a skeleton hand lashed to the other end. Bones in a black glove."

Robert looked at Katie from the corner of his eye, thinking this sounded like a twisted recollection of what might have actually happened.

"I opened up a closet of bad memories by showing up here this weekend," he said.

"Shush. You promised not to analyze."

Robert cleared his throat.

"I tried to run out, but the soles of my shoes melted and I was stuck. Glued to the floor. And while I was trying to get out of my shoes, that hand reached out and snatched me off my feet. Dragged me through the fire."

She waved her hand as if that was all she had to say.

Robert looked at her again, wanting to keep his promise not to analyze, but also wanting to comfort. The smile on her face was meant to downplay the real terror of the dream, he was sure of it. The quiver at the corner of her mouth gave her away.

He reached over and squeezed her knee and decided not to let go.

"So tell me about this sculptor you're so excited about."

Katie's face brightened, genuinely this time. "Her name's Kristen Hoard. From Sacramento. She does the most amazing things with salvaged metals. And the rest you're going to have to see for yourself."

"Don't take this the wrong way, but I wouldn't have pegged you for an art aficionado."

"Don't take this the wrong way, but you have a lot to learn about me."

"So sculpture's your thing."

"Just this sculpture."

Katie reached out to him as they approached the studio, and he took her hand.

She squeezed his fingers, and he decided to put off his premature return to El Paso.

An artful sign announced the display of Kristen Hoard's work, which would be here for one more week. Inside, white pedestal boxes of varying heights supported tabletop pieces of art, mostly metal sculptures—faces, hearts, abstract shapes—that had been cut, ground, variously textured, and welded together with minute seams. The materials varied: copper, aluminum, steel, iron, some of which had been coated in colorful patinas. Reds, greens, blues. On the walls, mirrors of all shapes and sizes framed in similar metals multiplied both the size of the room and the number of pieces on display. A few contemporary aluminum steel tables held informational flyers about the artist.

"Is her fire art here?" Katie asked a woman who was approaching them from the back.

Fire art?

"Yes. But we don't keep it lit all the time." The woman, whose flamboyant dress and bearing suggested she might be the studio owner, pointed and caught Robert's eye. He acknowledged that he saw the sign and the room where the pieces would be.

"Is it lit now?" Katie asked.

"No, but we'll move the pieces outside for a night show this weekend if you can come back."

"Oh please—I can't come back this weekend. Is there *any* way you could light the sculptures for us? He's never seen them, and I think they're the most beautiful . . ."

She seemed to lack the word to express herself, and the curator's surprised gaze lingered on Katie for a few seconds, openly wondering about her remark and her blindness. An awkward silence filled the gap before the woman picked up a safety lighter off the reception desk and smiled at Robert.

"Give me two minutes."

"What's fire art?" Robert asked Katie as the woman went into another room.

"Let's go see." Her voice played with his curiosity.

Katie bounced on the balls of her feet until the studio owner called them in.

Robert stepped into the room ahead of Katie without meaning to be rude, but the sight pulled him in.

Large pockets of fire—real flames, not cheap paper-and-light tricks—punctuated the room from within their metal frames and containers and cages and shapes. Flames flowered from the inside of a larger-than-life lotus blossom. Fingers of fire waved from the top arcs of nested circles and flickered within a perforated and torn globe. He could not imagine what it had taken to secure a permit to display such work, five pieces ranging from one to six feet, blazing and contained and stunning.

"Isn't it amazing?" Katie whispered, as if talking too loudly would disrupt the impact.

He looked at her. Her face was attuned to the five pieces in the center of the room. The flames lit her bright eyes so that they seemed to light up from the inside.

"How can you see it?"

"I feel it." She approached the tallest piece, which stood over her head in the very center of the room, and lifted her hands toward the fire, palms out. Robert couldn't understand her fascination with the heat.

"This one is called *Origins of Fire*," she said. A fissured orb, like a volcanic-split earth, sat atop a dagger-shaped pedestal and seemed to ooze molten rock.

"How did you know that?"

"It's the tallest. I've seen this one before. Her work was here two years ago. She was here then, too, let me touch many of the pieces. When they don't mind me touching them, I can see a lot."

"I imagine the metal gets pretty hot."

Katie laughed. "I did my seeing before they lit up. Every once in a while I have Lucille read the artist's blog to me. She wrote once that she likes working with recycled metals so much because she loves the idea that she can transform something gone to waste into a beautiful piece of art."

"I guess there's a fine line between art and trash."

Robert moved to stand next to her, more moved by her appreciation for the dangerous beauty than by the display itself.

"Why do you like it?"

"Because she took something that was wasted and turned it into something worth hundreds of dollars."

"So she's a kindred spirit of yours when it comes to lost causes."

"Something like that."

"Do you ever wish you could really see them?"

"No. I think the sight wouldn't really compare to what I've got in my head."

"I don't know. They're pretty impressive. The fire doesn't scare you?"

Katie shook her head.

"That's incredible, after what you've been through."

Katie took one step closer to the artwork. "Honestly, I've never thought about being afraid of that. Not when it's so stunning."

Robert looked over his shoulder. The owner stood in the door, watching, but she seemed unconcerned by Katie's behavior.

Robert felt compelled by Katie's fascination. He closed his eyes, lifted his palms, and tilted his face toward the orange and blue heat.

He tried to keep a picture of the sculpture in his head but couldn't. It was overwhelmed by another idea: he was standing in the darkness shoulder to shoulder with a woman whose spirit burned more brightly and with more mysterious heat than any other object in this room.

39

Janeal went about her Monday afternoon as usual. Except working at the desk that Milan used to occupy had not yet developed into usual.

And the fact that her migraines were flaring earlier and lasting longer than they had six months ago was not something she considered usual. Yet.

She felt a cold coming on, an ache in the top of her throat like a stuck fist, the result of a string of sleepless nights and two germ-filled flights in twenty-four hours.

Alan had secured the Fioricet refill for her before lunchtime. It was delivered along with a stern voice mail from her doctor informing her that she would receive only half the usual number of tablets and needed to make an appointment with him before he renewed her prescription. He reiterated her dosage and urged her not to take more.

Janeal had already increased her own dosage by half as much and would have doubled it today if not for her need to remain clearheaded rather than sedated. She took enough to hold the demon at bay.

She moved through her afternoon hours with smiles and graceful acceptance of those necessary congratulations. She sat through regularly scheduled meetings that were familiar enough, though she wore a different hat now. She met with the board and ran through a list of potential candidates to be sought as her replacement, and she met privately afterward with Thomas Sanders, who advised her to avoid being alone whenever possible until the ordeal involving Milan Finch had blown over.

Throughout these events, Janeal did little to conceal the appearance of not feeling well, though she milked everyone's sympathy with a brave face.

At five o'clock, Janeal removed three of the ten pills from her prescription bottle, stashed them away in her bag, and placed the clear plastic container on the desk in plain sight.

At five fifteen, she summoned Alan into her office for their daily debriefing. She had drawn all the shades and turned off all the lights save the one on her desk, which she kept on for Alan's benefit.

"Until we find a new executive editor, I will have a foot in two worlds," she said to Alan. Her voice had turned hoarse in the waning hours of the workday. He nodded. "So I'll be relying on you more than usual"—his grin popped up sideways, challenging the possibility that she could rely on him *more* than usual—"to be my eyes and ears in the editorial department."

"Your clone."

"Be yourself. The world certainly doesn't need two of me in it." That may have been the truest thing she'd ever said.

"This morning I was a worthless assistant."

"That was the migraine talking."

"I don't suppose I'll find a pay raise in the double duty?" His joking indicated his acceptance of her halfhearted apology. "A Christmas bonus?"

She tipped her head to one side. "Fridays off at four for a month after we hire."

"Deal." He withdrew a cigarette from his breast pocket and put it in his mouth, then took a lighter from his pants.

What on earth was he thinking? "When did you start smoking?"

"When I was seventeen."

"You've never smoked here."

"All these long hours you need me to put in now"—he flashed a boyish grin —"seems like a good time." He flicked the dial on the lighter with his thumb.

"You see an ashtray in here?" She was aware that her voice sounded shrill.

His eyebrows arched above the dancing flame. She stood and thrust out her hand.

"Give that to me."

"What?"

"Give me the lighter."

Like a schoolboy not understanding why it was such a bad idea to stash a dead mouse in his lunchbox, he handed the device to her. It was a cheap plastic Bic.

She hurled it into the wastebasket. He stared at her.

"So, first: editorial calendar."

His eyes refocused, and she gave him points for not saying what was surely on his mind. "You want me to go get Max?" he asked.

"No. From now until I say so, you outrank Max. Think you can handle him?"

"What's a lowly managing editor compared to you?"

"Precisely." She closed her eyes now and rested her head, tilting her chair back until her heels came off the carpet. She swiveled her computer monitor on its base to face him so he could see the ticker running across the bottom. "Let's review the headlines." She took a peek at him from under her lashes. His eyes were on the medicine bottle. If he were her age, she might find his concern . . . endearing.

"Read."

"Before that," he said.

She opened her eyes fully.

"Milan Finch," he said. "How do you want me to handle him?"

"There's nothing to handle."

"I shouldn't expect him to pop in at unexpected moments—"

"Security should have that covered."

"—or make threatening phone calls? Or leave dead rats on your doorstep?"

Janeal raised one eyebrow.

Alan looked down at the pen he held. "Or post violent images of you online? Or in your coat closet?"

Janeal leveled her chair and clasped her hands in front of her, leaning forward to demand that Alan look her in the face. When he did, she said, "You shouldn't expect it. But in the event he exceeds your expectations, you can let me handle him."

"Thomas said—"

"Thomas spoke to me already. I appreciate all the concern, but it's pointless. I had nothing to do with the burning bed he made for himself to lie in. He knows it. Right now he's mad and needs an outlet. That need will smolder out soon enough."

If Milan Finch were Salazar Sanso, Janeal would be less certain of this. But the two men were as comparable as a guppy and a great white, and she knew which one was worth her wariness.

"He hasn't really posted anything online, has he?" The possibility that Sanso or Robert or Katie might recognize her outweighed any fear of public humility.

Alan shook his head.

"Good then," she said. "Now, headlines."

"The president has declared an embargo on Chinese imports."

"About time."

"The senate doesn't think so."

"Put Douglas on that one. Tell him I want story set concepts on my desk by three tomorrow." She wouldn't be here at three tomorrow, but that was the point of this exercise—to make herself surprised by and opposed to the turn of events that was about to occur. "Next."

"An environmentalist has been accused of shooting and killing the lobbyist who introduced the latest bill to drill for oil in ANWR."

"I can't think of a single fresh way to spin that old topic."

"Drilling in Alaska or gun control?"

"Either one. Skip it."

"Educators in Massachusetts are demanding the right to add transgender discussions to their sex education classes."

Janeal snickered and leaned her forehead in her palms. "Give that one to Sam."

"Not if you want an objective—"

"Give it to Sam." She stood slowly and made a good show of swaying on her feet.

"You okay?"

"Fine." She gripped the desk with one hand and sank back into her chair. When Alan didn't keep going with the list, she figured she'd made her impression. She frowned at him and motioned him to keep going.

"Let's get through it so I can get out of here at a decent hour."

Alan looked back at the screen.

"Internationally wanted drug dealer escaped from medical custody early this morning, leaving one dead. Salazar Sanso."

Janeal had originally planned to stage her collapse, but the shock of this news made pretense unnecessary. If she'd been standing, her plummeting blood pressure would have driven her to the ground of its own accord. As it was, she slumped forward onto the desk, her head thundering. That much wasn't an act.

Alan jumped up, dumping papers on the floor. She heard him grab the phone and punch in some numbers, then explain to someone where he was and what had happened. She could have corrected him then; instead, she breathed shallowly and felt Alan come closer, heard the phone base scraping across the desk blotter as he stretched out the cord.

He sounded truly worried, especially when he told the operator she might have had an unintentional overdose of her migraine meds, and she was willing to bet he wasn't smiling. She felt a twinge of guilt. Alan didn't deserve the lie.

But all these observations were eclipsed by a creeping question that turned her feigned frailty into real, breathless fear.

Where had Sanso escaped to if not to a place where he could wreak fresh havoc on her life?

40

Outside a bar, Sanso stood under an awning that shielded him from the monsoon rain. The fresh air and a visit to one of his favorite clubs, where he'd received private care from an excellent physician, had done wonders for his spirits. When he saw Callista's black SUV, he stepped out, and she pulled to the curb.

He climbed in to the sound of squeaking wipers. The car idled while she leaned across the seat and greeted him with a long, slow kiss.

"Where is she?" Sanso asked when they parted.

"Cozy little place in New York City."

"You find her alias?"

"And so much more. She's made quite a life for herself."

Callista and two others on Sanso's payroll had picked up Janeal's identity after her hospital visit by following her back to the airport, purchasing a ticket on the same flight, and then hacking into the airline's flight manifesto with her seat assignment information. From there it was an easy matter to connect the Jane Johnson of West 69th Street, Manhattan, to *All Angles* magazine.

When the alerts attached to her credit card activity signaled she had purchased a ticket to New Mexico the day after Sanso's escape, Callista was notified right away.

She sent a woman with a photo of Jane into the baggage claim area where Janeal was expected to arrive.

Sanso laughed aloud. "We should go fetch her. Make ourselves a threesome."

Callista cleared her throat. "We need to get you across the border."

"That's exactly what the rest of the world is thinking. So why don't we do something else? Like follow Janeal around for a while. It would be entertaining."

"I've had enough entertainment for the week. Amos has his eye on her. She's on her way to Albuquerque."

"Of course she is. She's leading me to Lukin."

"We know where Lukin is. We don't need her to lead us anywhere."

Callista could be quite annoying when she wanted to be. There was a time when he found this an ironically attractive quality. Lately, though, it tended to sap the fun out of things. Now, as he had several times in the last forty-eight hours, he imagined Janeal Mikkado's face in place of hers.

"You've missed the point, I'm afraid."

"The Mikkado woman is trouble."

"Why else would I be so infatuated with her?"

"Leave her in the ashes, Sanso."

He looked at Callista and said, "Let's all take a vacation. A vacation to Santa Fe."

It gave Sanso no small satisfaction that Callista adjusted her grip on the steering wheel and refused to look at him for the entirety of their eastward drive on I-10. He loved nothing more than a jealous woman.

Sanso reclined his seat and closed his eyes, a spider content to wait for the fly to vibrate his web.

41

Another day, another flight, another night of snatched, broken sleep. Janeal arrived in Albuquerque Tuesday morning, medicated and headache-free.

It had not been difficult to stage a miraculous recovery in the ER after Alan left her in the doctors' care. She "awoke" feeling a hundred percent better, her claim aided by test results so normal that the physicians couldn't explain why she'd collapsed in the first place. She suggested stress, low blood sugar. With all the events of her job transition, she had forgotten to eat that day.

When pressed to answer Alan's theory that she had taken too strong a dose of her Fioricet, she produced all but one of the pills, explaining that she always separated them in the event she accidentally left the bottle at the office or at home. Alan must have seen the half-empty bottle and worried. He was such an attentive, thoughtful person.

After a couple hours of this back-and-forth, she politely demanded to be allowed to go home.

From Albuquerque she rented a car, drove to Santa Fe, checked into a hotel, and called Alan.

"I'm being sent down to Bethesda. They want me to be evaluated for some clinical trial conducted by . . . what on earth are they called? The National Institute of Neurosomethingorother."

"The NINDS."

"If you say so." She sighed heavily. "See if I qualify. It might take a week. I can only imagine what kind of torture chamber they've got for it to take that long."

"Don't worry about us. You take the time you need."

"You'll let Thomas know for me? I don't think I can survive another phone call."

"I'll tell him. You sound hoarse."

"Not enough sleep."

"Try to catch up, or you'll have laryngitis by the time you're back to give the keynote at the NYU seminar. Max and I will hold down the fort."

"I have every confidence."

"Bye now."

She hung up before Alan would think to ask which hospital she was going to and when, threw her cell phone into her shoulder bag, and reached for the door. Alan wouldn't call to check up on her so long as she kept in regular touch.

The first few things she needed to do were easy.

She scoured the AP and every network, cable, and Internet newswire in her database for information about Salazar Sanso. Nothing. The man had vanished. Janeal hoped he had gone back to Mexico or Canada or one of a dozen other places. If she had to place a bet on it, though, she'd wager he had not left the country yet. Not within the hours when every U.S. border patrol agent had eyes peeled for him.

What she didn't know was whether he'd be brazen enough to go looking for Robert.

Or whether he'd come for her first.

No. He couldn't know who or where she was yet.

Find Robert Lukin before he finds you. It was either a threat or an invitation to join Sanso in a new phase of the game. Perhaps both.

Was she angry enough with Robert for threatening the safety of her world that she would be willing to walk Sanso to his door? Did her romantic love for her childhood friend still have a pulse after all these years?

She didn't know the answer to either.

For two reasons, then, she'd have to take extra precautions: She would need to watch and move as if Sanso already knew who she pretended to be, as if he would recognize her in any identity she took, as Janeal or Jane or Lisa or anyone else. And depending on how things went, she would need to prevent Robert from ever learning her assumed identity.

Her plan to buy Katie's silence, however, would require self-exposure.

How long would Robert stay at Katie's little halfway house? She would wait for him to leave if she had the time.

She didn't have the time. Janeal had to get to Katie before she told Robert everything. Before Sanso found Robert. Before Sanso found her.

Janeal paced her bathroom, smooth pedicured feet kissing the cool tile floor. How to accomplish so much so quickly? Maybe she had been too quick to dismiss Brian. He might have been an entrance.

She turned on the shower and stepped in. The hot water vibrated her brain cells into some measure of clarity, holding off a genuine headache for the time being. By the time she had shampooed her hair three times and let the water run cold, she had assembled some options.

Option: Go directly to Katie as herself, no pretense, no disguise, no guile. Beg her forgiveness. Offer to get Desert Hope House out of the financial hole Brian had said they were in, in exchange for never speaking of her to Robert. Vanish. Disappear into the abyss that was New York City and leave Janeal Mikkado behind forever.

Problem: Katie might refuse. Even if she hadn't abandoned her morally questionable fortune-telling days, which Janeal doubted—she was running a halfway house, for crying out loud!—bribery might be beneath the goody-goody. Very risky. Not to mention humiliating. Still . . .

Option: Use the Lisa Rasmussen getup to gain access to Robert.

Problem: Robert would be familiar enough with due process to refuse to speak with Sanso's attorney without his own present. How about Katie, though? Janeal might be able to start with Katie, as a potential eyewitness, if she could keep Robert out of the way. Depending on what Katie revealed during the meeting, Janeal would decide then whether to reveal herself.

Forget it. They'd see right through her. They knew her too well.

Option: Janeal could get Brian back in the saddle. Retract her rejection of his work. Go with him as his publisher, fully disguised, on the grounds that she could help persuade Katie to be more forthcoming and—

Problem: It was way beyond *problem*. It was untenable. Too complicated. *Ridiculous.* She'd expose Jane Johnson, if not her true self. And if anything went awry . . .

Janeal towel-dried her hair and settled on option four by the time she was dressed. Grabbing up her purse, she found the business card Bill Dawson had slipped to her Saturday evening.

He answered on the fifth ring.

"Bill! Jane Johnson."

"Jane . . . *All Angles*, yes. How are you? What can I do for you?" He was too enthusiastic.

"Bill, dear, I'm so sorry to interrupt your busy day. I wouldn't do it if I wasn't absolutely desperate on behalf of a friend of mine. She's in such trouble—I won't bore you with her saga, but when I heard what she's up against, you were the first person I thought of. You're such a miracle worker."

"That's . . . kind of you to say."

"I hate to impose, and I hope you'll tell me if I'm being absolutely out of line. I will compensate you for your trouble, of course."

"What can I do for you, Jane?"

"I was wondering if you could make a call . . ."

In the online yellow pages, Janeal searched for a salon and found one a block away that accepted walk-ins. Of all her physical traits that needed disguising, Janeal's hair would be the first. Her stylist at home could help her recover when the whole ordeal was over. She'd brought those hideous blue contacts with her to hide her brown eyes. At least they wouldn't go to complete waste.

Then she searched for a Goodwill or ARC. Her clothes, too, would need a higher scruff factor.

Armed with the addresses she needed to plug into the rental car's GPS, Janeal slung her bag over her shoulder, grabbed her card key off the dresser, and flipped back the door's dead bolt.

And was knocked to her knees by a wave of nausea and a pulsing, spearing pain behind her eyes.

Janeal cursed these headaches and groped into the bathroom, eyes closed, groaning her way to the toilet. She would have been disgusted by the number of germs she was crawling on if not for the overwhelming ache.

She vomited, which only helped her feel better by a degree. She still couldn't stand and didn't dare open her eyes.

Walking, let alone driving, was out of the question.

With fumbling motions she managed to locate her medication and a paper-capped water glass. She spilled the pill bottle across the counter and picked up the first tablet she touched, leaving the others spread out. She downed it, considered taking two, found the question of whether she should too big to answer, and instead ran a washcloth under cold water.

She wished she had fetched ice before now.

Somehow Janeal drew the blackout curtains and fell across the foot of the bed while holding on to the semi-cold cloth. She pressed it over her closed eyes with the heels of both hands and begged the pain to stop.

The pounding in her head sounded like a knocking on her door.

42

When Robert stepped out of his room at the sound of Katie's footsteps in the hall, he thought he'd surprised her. She was carrying a set of clean towels for him, and at the same moment he appeared she halted, threw up one hand, and averted her eyes as if she'd stepped in front of an oncoming car and was resigned to being hit.

"Didn't mean to scare you," he said. Robert moved to her quickly and took the towels. "My timing can be—"

She lowered her arm. Her eyes were wide. The shocked gaze and her slightly parted mouth concerned him.

"You all right?" he said.

She rubbed her eyes, then pressed her palms against her cheeks and exhaled. "Yeah."

"What happened?" He took her elbow with his free hand.

"A flash of light. I saw a flash of light coming at me. A big one."

"Like headlights big?"

"Like dying-sun big. Galactic-explosion big."

Robert guided her to his room's only chair, which sat beside a desk in front of a narrow floor-to-ceiling window. The light streamed onto her face, but she didn't seem to notice it. He allowed himself to stare at her scar and could not explain why it made him want to touch her.

"Do you want me to call a doctor or someone for you?"

"No. I'm okay. It's gone now."

"Has it happened before?"

"Never. It reminded me of the spotlights that used to swing around at the summer carnival. Remember those dares?"

"To stand close and look without blinking when it crossed your face? I do. It's been awhile since I thought of that."

"Did anyone ever actually do it?" she asked. "Without blinking?"

"You did once—don't you remember?"

She shifted her position on the chair and dropped her eyes. Robert thought he saw confusion cross her features. "No," she said after a long pause. He tried to ease her discomfort.

"Maybe I made that up."

"Maybe that was when I started going blind." She offered him a half laugh. Robert didn't find it funny.

43

Janeal was pretty sure she slept off and on, though she couldn't say for sure without a clearer indication of the time. For a while she didn't dare open her eyes to look at the clock, or swivel her head, or move her big toe. But the pulsating agony seemed to have lessened. She tested this impression. She moved her arm and it did not hurt; then she moved her legs; then she turned her neck one inch and did not get the sensation of a knife being run through it.

After a few minutes—or it might have been an hour—she opened her eyes as well.

They couldn't penetrate the pitch blackness of the room. The heavy air pressed down on her as if the darkness had weight, and she didn't fight it.

The wet cloth had slid off her face and now lay in a damp heap against her cheek. She reached up to move it away, taking deep breaths. So far so good. Janeal considered opening a window but hesitated for a reason she could not place.

It was the smell of the air, which she couldn't name.

An undercurrent of sound that she couldn't identify.

She shivered although she was warm, and her palms turned clammy. Her head was clear now, but she willed herself to a new level of stillness—opossum-like, near-death stillness.

Breathe. Smell. Listen.

Janeal broke out in an involuntary sweat. Another person sat in the room with her.

She swallowed.

"I can outlast you at this contest, if you're wondering," a man whispered.

Sanso.

She opted not to respond, not sure if fear or thrill was responsible for kicking her heart into her throat.

Fear, most definitely.

And some thrill.

During her visit to his hospital room, she had the upper hand of surprise and the security of a guard within range of her voice. But now she was an injured bird knocked out of her nest to be stalked by a snake. How had he gotten past the locked door? She shuddered to imagine.

"Hungry?" he asked. He taunted her. "I can call room service."

"I'm not well." Her throat felt dry and scratchy and swollen.

"Sometimes food helps. Eat with me. We've never shared a meal. Not really."

"You shouldn't be here."

"Why? Because I'm an international fugitive or because you don't want to be perceived as harboring an international fugitive?"

"Because you should never enter a woman's room uninvited."

"I didn't."

She didn't have strength to argue.

Sanso must have dragged the chair he sat in close to the bed, because she heard him shift and place a foot on the ground, and when he spoke again his hot breath caressed her forehead.

"Your deal—our deal, my beautiful child—gives me an all-access pass to you. Fifteen years ago you surrendered your right to restrict me. You sold yourself to me."

"I don't remember it quite the same way."

"Doesn't really matter, does it?" His fingers pushed her hair off her forehead and painted her skin with dread. Her clammy perspiration chilled her.

"I never sold any part of myself," she tried to argue, not entirely convinced it was true. "Especially not to you. You stole my father from me, my very life. You paid me back. Our accounts were settled."

The remark struck something in Sanso that caused him to stand abruptly, shoving his chair out of the way with a noisy *thunk*. "Let's get straight who is the thief." Scorn replaced the seduction that had underscored his words. "You seem to have forgotten who you are, Janeal Mikkado. And who *I* am."

"You're a bully who frightens young women—no, you're worse than that.

You're a killer who values life less than your own sense of entitlement." Her head felt painless enough that she pushed herself up onto her elbows. The clarity of mind emboldened her and gave her anger a chance to blossom fresh. "What's a million dollars to you? *Nothing.* It's your pride that you can't seem to put a price on."

She heard him drawing deep, measured breaths in through his nose.

"It's true," he eventually murmured. "Everything you say is true. And I will tell you something truer."

He moved around the bed. Though Janeal's eyes should have adjusted to the darkness quite awhile ago, she still could make out only dim shapes. She sensed him standing in front of her.

Sanso struck a match so close to her face that she felt a spark from the strike hit her nose. She cried out as the flame flared between her eyes and Sanso's. The blaze dancing in the reflection of his glistening irises demonized him.

"You admire me," he said. The stench of the initial burn coated the inside of her nose. She turned away, fearing she'd be overcome by panic.

"You admire my willfulness and my confidence and my ability to seize exactly what I want out of this life." He waved the match in front of her eyes. She snapped her head the other direction, needing distance from the flickering light.

"You have spent every day of the last fifteen years trying to be like me. And that is as selfish as a woman can get."

The flame came to the end of the little wood matchstick, and Sanso dropped it over Janeal's chest. She shrieked. The light petered out before it hit the skin at her throat, but she felt its stinging heat.

Tears escaped her pinched eyelids then, a mercy that they finally surged when Sanso couldn't see them. She controlled her voice. "What do you want?"

Sanso placed a fist in the bed on each side of Janeal's shoulders and hovered over her form.

"I want Robert Lukin."

"I don't know where he is."

"You know where he was. That works for me."

Janeal's ears filled with her salty tears. Her throat throbbed and snagged her words. "I c-can't. He was my friend."

"Present trumps past, child. He *is* my enemy. He will not rest until he succeeds in throwing me into a pit to rot. Ergo, I must take a similar approach with him."

"Why would I do this? Why would I help you?"

Sanso's laughter rang loud in her head and threatened to shake loose another mind-splitting episode. "See there! You want to know what's in this for you? It is true how much you have made yourself like me. Ah! This is beautiful, exactly as I had hoped!"

"Stop!" Janeal reflexively braced her wrists to shove him away. Her palms met his chest, a concrete wall.

"What's in it for you is the continuation of a nice little undisrupted life. Another decade and a half, if you're a good girl, of my silence and your pitifully false sense of security—which I can turn into a reality for you." His voice dropped so that she could barely hear him. "For you, there is nothing I wouldn't do."

He pushed himself off the bed and she took a deep breath—to fill her lungs, to settle her heart, to focus her mind. The close flame of that burning match was seared into the back of her mind. It had taken her several years of therapy to overcome her pyrophobia, and it would take days to put that tiny flaming stick into its proper perspective.

"If you were the sole person responsible for my security, I'd weigh your offer seriously," she said.

His delayed reply told her she'd caught him off guard. "And who else, pray tell, can possibly hold as much power over you as I do?" The center of the rope in this tug-of-war shifted an inch in her direction.

"Give me twenty-four hours to consider your . . . proposal. And then I might tell you."

In this blackness where she could see neither body language nor facial expression, his silence concerned her more than his verbal threats. She hoped he would play along. The smoke from the extinguished match was still strong in her nose.

She heard the metal grating of the doorknob turning, the latch sliding back against the strike plate. A beam of yellow light sliced through the room and across the bed, not quite touching her.

"Twenty-four hours," he said. "This is far more exciting than I had thought you capable of, my dear." Then he stepped out of the room and let the door float shut.

Janeal rolled onto her side to see the tall red numbers of the hotel clock—9:47 p.m.

She looked down the throat of another sleepless night.

44

By the time the sun came up, Janeal had formulated a plan to get herself out from under Sanso's all-seeing eyes, at least temporarily.

Bill Dawson had left a message for her confirming an appointment at the Desert Hope House for Jane Johnson's "friend" early that afternoon.

She made a hair appointment, hung up, consulted the phone book, and programmed the number of a taxi service into her cell phone. She donned a pair of jeans and a black T-shirt, then went through the items she had brought with her from New York. She transferred from suitcase to satchel only what she couldn't live without: cash, credit cards, false ID, PDA, phone, keys, contacts care kit, and ultraslim laptop. Prescription pills. Anything that could be identified as belonging to Jane Johnson. When she left the hotel at ten, she also left her clothes, makeup, accessories, and toiletries.

She'd buy replacements when she returned to New York.

She drove her rental car to the Goodwill store she had located the previous night. Keeping an eye on her rearview mirror, she narrowed her potential Big Brothers down to a silver Escalade—subtlety, Sanso style—or a blue Camry. Not that she actually cared who was following her.

At the secondhand store, she selected a set of wicker baskets and a denim tote bag and took them into the dressing room, where she shucked her Jimmy Choo sandals and slipped into a pair of blue canvas tennis shoes. When she exited, no one appeared to notice the switch. From there she went to the clothing racks and quickly picked out a pair of olive green pants and a pink blouse in her size, both clean and presentable but slightly dated. She grabbed a pair of sunglasses off a revolving display before reaching the cashier.

Janeal purchased everything but the shoes—she figured the store got the better end of that transaction—and before leaving the building she put the clothes and the tote into her roomy satchel. She carried the baskets in their oversize plastic bag out of the store and threw them into the backseat of her car. Their only purpose was for show.

At the salon, she parked in a space that faced the street where anyone driving by could see it clearly, and then went into the shop to surrender to the stylist.

This was no New York studio. Linoleum flooring and wood paneling from the seventies still served their function. The hairdresser who greeted Janeal introduced herself as Carol, then sat her down in the vinyl chair and examined her auburn locks with unnecessarily long plastic fingernails. A cigarette smoldered in an ashtray on the cluttered shelf. Silk flowers had been draped over the tri-fold mirror at the station.

It was perfect.

"I want to go short," Janeal announced. "I want a towel-dried look. And dark. Not black, but maybe chocolate."

The overweight woman picked through Janeal's hair like an ape, grooming. "Short will be nice. But you've got some pretty good-looking highlights in here to be covering up with chocolate."

"I'm ready for a change."

"Change is what I do, honey. Can I talk you into some lowlights?" Janeal shook her head. Carol went to a drawer and withdrew a white plastic card with synthetic hair in various shades looped around the edges. "Got one here called burr noyer." She showed it to Janeal.

Beurre noir, she read.

"No idea what that means, but it's dark. Where do you think they come up with these names?"

"That'll do fine." Janeal didn't honestly care how she ended up. In fact, if this woman butchered her locks, so much the better.

Leave it to her luck at this stage that the stylist would be a genius.

"You sound like you're fighting a bug," Carol said. Janeal didn't have to reply. Carol kept up her end of the conversation without needing a partner.

As it turned out, the woman, while no award-winner, was no hack either. She worked quickly, applying color first. She touched up Janeal's brows. The yellow undertones of the brown made Janeal's skin look slightly sallow, but that wouldn't hurt when it came to the impression she wanted to make.

Carol cut Janeal's shoulder-length waves to follow the line of her ear and nape, then coated them with a heavy mousse to give them a windblown look. Or a slept-in look, depending on one's point of view.

She turned Janeal in the chair to give her a front and back view, and Janeal caught sight of the silver Escalade in the parking lot across the street. She was so pleased to see her plan working that she tipped Carol ten dollars before asking if she could use the restroom. Carol pointed it out before launching into a new monologue with another customer.

Behind locked doors, Janeal dialed the cab service and gave them her location. She pulled out her "new" clothes and changed, then shoved everything she'd been carrying around into the old denim tote.

She shoved the empty Dolce & Gabbana satchel behind the toilet and only felt a small pang of disappointment about that. Someone would snatch up that find no matter where it had been.

Sunglasses in place, she slipped out the rear door of the salon and hoped the cab would be as punctual as their yellow pages ad declared them to be.

In fact, the driver beat his ETA by three minutes.

Better and better.

She rifled through the floppy bag as if looking for something and climbed into the cab without raising her head.

"Desert Hope House," she said, giving him the address.

The driver nodded understanding and pulled out of the lot, not needing to chat with her like all the New York cabbies she'd ever encountered. Thank goodness for small gifts.

He turned left so that he passed directly between her rental car and that conspicuous silver Escalade. Janeal dared a look out the corner of her eye.

The driver was reading a newspaper.

45

Robert didn't see much of Katie on Tuesday. She had a full day moderating peer group sessions and conducting individual resident evaluations for the women she supervised. But his own feelings about Sanso's escape had quieted during that time, though Harlan had no optimistic news to offer.

Oddly enough, Robert's thoughts kept turning to *Origins of Fire*. He tried and failed several times to make connections between the horrors of that blazing night at the *kumpanía* and the beauty of fire's power and the peace that Katie managed to embrace in spite of those conflicting realities.

Wednesday afternoon, he and Katie returned to the Hope House in Robert's truck after transporting three of the women to their various jobs in Santa Fe.

"How do you do it?" he asked. She sat with her head tipped back easily against the headrest, her eyes closed.

"Do what?"

"Reconcile what happened at the camp to the life you're living now?"

"You see a disconnection?"

That wasn't what he'd meant to imply. "The morning after it happened, the morning I realized how much I'd lost, and I thought everyone was dead—my parents, my siblings, you, Janeal—the first thing I wanted was justice. I never stopped wanting justice."

"That's all most of us want, Robert. No matter what our situation."

"You want justice against Salazar Sanso?"

"Of course I do."

"Doesn't it bother you that we don't have it yet?"

Katie took a few seconds to ponder this before saying, "I can't afford to devote too much time to wanting things I don't have. I have my life, after all, when logically I shouldn't have made it through that ordeal at all. They kept saying I shouldn't be alive—through the dressing changes, the skin grafts, the physical therapy. You hear that often enough and you start to ask God why you are, what it means that it wasn't your time to go."

"And he said . . . ?"

She laughed. "It wasn't like I got a FedEx delivery of stone tablets or a visit from a prophet or anything like that."

Robert turned left off the highway.

"But over time it became clear that justice wasn't . . . that I wasn't the one to . . ." Katie cleared her throat and looked for the right words. "At some point I became more captivated by the miracle of grace than by wondering what God was going to do to Salazar Sanso."

"I don't know what you mean."

"I realized—and maybe it's because I lost my sight or because I had to rely so much on other people those first few years—that what's more astounding than justice is mercy. The times when we *don't* get the consequences we deserve."

"Some people get lucky breaks."

"I'm not talking about those. I'm talking about moments when you know what *you* deserve, and you agree that you deserve it, and some person or some circumstance comes along and lets you off the hook."

"Sure. I guess we all run into that now and then. But you're talking about little stuff, aren't you? Not Sanso-scale murder."

"I'm only speaking for myself. I'm not going to claim I'm any better a person than he is."

This statement shocked Robert. "Nothing you've ever done comes close to what Sanso did that night, Katie. I have to side with Lucille on this one. The Katie I grew up with was pretty close to perfect."

Her mouth formed a half smile and she looked out the window. "What we do . . . who we are . . . I'm not sure we get to measure our relative goodness by comparing it to others'," she said.

"Where do you get that idea?"

"'Every inclination of the heart is evil from childhood.'"

"Sounds like cynical psychobabble."

"God. Genesis."

"I still say some people are worse than others. And you're an angel," he said. He took his eyes off the road for a second to look at her, then turned back. "You're a model of peace. I wish I could have some of what you've got."

"You could."

He shrugged. "Maybe if I hang around you long enough. But after fifteen years of thinking a certain way, I think it would take me some time."

"Maybe you can. And maybe it will. But if you want to change gears . . ." She left her invitation open-ended, and he was relieved.

Robert pulled into the Hope House drive and found a place to park in the small guest lot near the main entrance. Robert jumped out and met Katie on her side as she closed the door. Robert stopped her from moving toward the house by placing a hand on her arm.

"I was not teasing you when I called you beautiful," he said.

Katie dropped her head. "I'm nothing like what I was."

"You are so much more than what you were, Katie."

"Robert, if you knew—"

"I do know." He swept his arm toward the house even though she couldn't see him do it. "You live for these other women when you could hole yourself up somewhere and wallow in everything you've experienced. Somehow—and this is what's really amazing—you live free of your pain, though I know it must still hurt you. I know because people like us have that ability to recognize the real deal." Robert leaned against the car.

"It doesn't fade, does it?" he asked. "The pain doesn't hurt less as time goes by, you learn to live with it. But you do so much more than that, Katie. So much more than I could dream of. I can't imagine anyone not wanting to be like you."

A yellow cab came down the dusty driveway and pulled up to the front porch of the house.

"Robert, I'm not all that you think—"

"You are all that and more," he said.

He bent and kissed her lightly on the mouth and felt her short gasp of surprise. He cared little if anyone was watching—the person getting out of the cab, maybe Lucille from the office—though he did hope as he pulled away that what he'd done wasn't a terrible idea that would inflict another wound in either one of them.

He tried to gauge Katie's reaction.

She was holding her fingers to her temple and looking pained, as if she had a headache coming on. And yet something told him the gesture had nothing to do with him. She shifted and turned in the direction of the cab as if she could see it, as if she recognized the dark-haired, skinny woman exiting the rear door. His eyes followed hers.

46

Though it was Janeal's intention to find Katie and possibly Robert here, she hadn't expected them to be the first two people she saw.

And she definitely hadn't expected to see them doing anything so intimate as kissing.

She stood there at the open door of the yellow cab, clutching her cheap tote bag and feeling frumpier, homelier, and plainer than ever before. Janeal raked a hand through her overdark hair and self-consciously smoothed her wrinkled blouse before catching herself.

With any luck she had appeared appropriately nervous, nothing more.

A flash of light burst behind her eyes, warning of a potential headache. Not now, of all times. She had to hold it off, not that she had any real power over these things. Still, she tried. She closed her eyes and held still for several seconds, and when the flash did not recur, she slowly refocused on her surroundings.

She closed the cab door and pointed herself toward the entrance of the house, risking another look at the pair by the truck.

Robert was definitely Robert, a manlier version of the Robert she had loved. He had filled out, had picked a profession that broadened his shoulders and hardened the lines of his mouth and jaw. He glanced at her and seemed to dismiss her as a stranger, then returned his attention to Katie.

Katie. Janeal wouldn't have recognized her except for the head of curls, the trademark beauty Janeal had coveted as a teen in spite of her own attractive auburn hair. What kids ever wanted what they had until they were older? But the way Katie stood there with Robert, it could be no one else.

An emotion stabbed Janeal with the sharp pain of surprise. Jealousy.

Jealousy? After all these years? But there they were, all her old feelings for Robert in living color.

Katie was still ruining everything. Everything. A knife of anger plunged into her heart with the jealousy. All her old feelings for Robert came rushing back.

Katie was taller than Janeal recalled, and there was something about her build that seemed unlike her old friend, but she couldn't put a finger on it. Maybe it was the years, or the clothes. That neck-to-toe coverage was out of place in such a southwestern location on such a blue-sky day, though the mountain air was brisk. Or maybe it was the body language. Katie, too, showed no sign of recognizing Janeal or acknowledging her as the afternoon appointment.

In fact, Katie wasn't looking at Janeal, though her face turned toward the cab. Janeal found this both irritating and unnerving.

She consciously shut out the sight of the couple, focused on reaching the front door of the house. She had to stay on track.

She saw a doorbell and punched it.

In a reasonable amount of time, a dour-looking woman—otherwise attractive except for the frown—opened the door.

"I'm Janice," Janeal said, making sure to look down. She'd go for insecure, nervous. "A friend made an appointment—"

"Right. Come in then. I'm Lucille." She opened the door wider and stepped back. "You're a little early. Better than late. Are you ill?"

"It's just a sore throat. Sounds worse than it really is."

Janeal clutched her tote, following Lucille down a brightly lit tiled hall. It occurred to her then that they might require her to surrender the bag to a search. Or surrender it completely. Of all the details to overlook—

She held on to her mousy demeanor. "You got a bathroom?"

"Go right at the end." Lucille pointed up the hall. "Second door on your left. Come back here when you're finished." Lucille stepped into an office on the front side of the house.

The rest of the house did not quite match the bathroom's décor: white paint, tarnished chrome fixtures, one-inch black-and-white checkered tiles. Janeal supposed the house had to set its priorities. The pedestal vanity stood under a cracked mirror. There were two bathroom stalls and one shower stall and a free-standing cabinet with a key lock but no handles. Locked, probably.

Janeal tested it.

The doors swung open.

Inside, two shelves, each about ten inches deep, held paper towel bundles, boxes of tissues, tampons and pads, and large plastic bottles of liquid soap.

It would work.

Working quickly, she emptied one shelf and stood her laptop up against the back wall of the cabinet. It was almost too tight, but the snug fit would keep the thing upright. Then she debated between a tampon box—roomier, but there was only one—and a tissue box. There were six of the latter on the bottom shelf. Much safer.

She partially lifted the perforated lid off one box and emptied more than half its contents into her tote. She replaced the tissues with her wallet, PDA, keys, medication, and phone. These she covered with a thin layer of tissues, cramming them back in through the plastic and then returning the cardboard cover to its original spot. She held it in place by putting the box at the bottom of the stack.

Risky, but not as risky as carrying it around with her. She'd come back after she had a room.

She flushed the toilet and washed her hands and returned to Lucille's office. Lucille sat behind a metal desk under a window overlooking the parking lot. Katie sat in a faded upholstered recliner. She stood when Janeal came in.

"Janice"—Lucille looked at a calendar that also served as a desk blotter— "Janice Regan. This is Katie Morgon, my codirector."

Katie held out her hand a few inches to the left of where Janeal was standing. "Good to have you here, Janice."

From this distance, Janeal thought that the woman looked more like her old friend than at first. She registered several facts quickly. The wig. The burns, hidden except on the side of her face by all those clothes. The incredible ordeal Katie must have gone through to have survived.

The blindness.

That Katie couldn't see was both a relief and a devastation. Janeal's disguise, such as it was, need trick only one person—Robert—instead of two. But to lose one's sight after so much other loss! Janeal's sympathy overtook her worry.

For the first time, the reality of Katie's survival knocked the wind out of Janeal. The horror of the choice she had made fifteen years ago marched up to the forefront of her mind and started screaming at her as if she'd abandoned Katie an hour ago.

She began to quiver with fear, the surge of fight-or-flight adrenaline acting like a shot of caffeine straight to her heart.

She grasped Katie's scarred hand and shook it weakly, saying nothing. Her fingertips brushed against a ring Katie wore, and she looked at it to avoid having to look at Katie's face. Katie's open, kind, nonjudgmental face.

Janeal's grasp tightened on Katie's palm. That ring, six diamonds in a gold band—that was her mother's wedding ring. The band Janeal had slipped onto her own hand, the band that she believed had fallen off her finger and melted in the flames with everything else.

Six diamonds glinted as if they were living things, one diamond for Jason and Rosa and each of the four children they'd always planned to have—and did. The pristine jewelry represented a cruel contradiction of reality, in which five of the six stones had been crudely pried out of their settings and crushed underfoot while the sixth stubbornly remained, a pointless and off-balanced solitaire.

How Katie had come by it was only one of many questions that could not be asked this moment. Janeal let go. Katie's hand stayed suspended in the air for an extra second, and Janeal thought she understood what was really happening here, thought she might expose Janeal as an imposter and a criminal and a would-be killer who had abandoned her to smoke and ash.

If Janeal believed in all that cosmic-energy, fabric-of-the-universe, supernatural-sensation hocus-pocus that was trendy, she might have believed Katie had caught a glimpse of Janeal's innermost mind. That Katie once was a fortune-teller, con or not, sent a shiver up Janeal's back.

She expected Katie to point a finger and shout, "Don't think I don't know exactly who you are!"

Her sympathy for Katie evaporated like droplets of water in a hot cast iron skillet.

Janeal held herself together under the assaulting possibility of what would happen if Katie had one more moment to think—

". . . don't usually take new residents without a referral from a personal PO," Lucille said as she tapped her pen tip on the desk blotter, challenging Janeal to defend her desire to be accepted here.

"I . . . I'm waiting on a new one to take my case file," she croaked. She placed a hand around her raw throat. "They said by Monday I should have an assignment."

Katie was watching her with those frightening blank eyes. Janeal doubted that her carefully fabricated story would ever pass Katie's instinctive lie-detector test.

Lucille huffed. "So you have friends in high places." An accusation. "Lucky you. Here, though, such friends are pretty much worthless. You will not be seeing any friends for the first six months of your stay, during which time you will be expected to attend every session we schedule you for whether you think it applies to you or not. We have a strict rotation work roster and a stricter curfew. Do your work without complaining and you might get to choose your jobs in a year. If you think I am the warden of your prison now, you will think of me as your fairy godmother by the time Frankie has had her way with you."

Janeal looked for a chair to sink into and found she was standing in front of a well-worn sofa that faced the door.

"If and only if she approves you for work at the end of that time, you may take a job outside the house so long as your shift gets you back here by four thirty on any given day, no excuses."

Janeal took a deep breath and decided that her chances of slipping under Katie's radar would be better if she didn't have to speak, although her illness made her voice nearly unrecognizable. She hoped.

"We conduct random urine tests," Lucille went on. "You'll comply on demand, or you'll be back to using public restrooms within an hour of your refusal. There are no cell phones allowed. No electronic devices. Television time is an earned privilege. So are phone calls. Not that you'll have anyone to talk to."

Janeal glanced at Katie, who had returned to her seat in the recliner, so intently focused on her that Janeal had to look away. Her eyes went to the wall by the door. A short bookshelf stood there, and a key rack hung above it. Three of the seven hooks held rings. *Van, Kia, Master Room* the labels said.

"Let's see your bag." Lucille came around to the back side of the desk. She stuck her hand out and waggled her fingers for Janeal to hand it over.

Lucille hefted the tote onto the coffee table and plowed through it.

"You travel light."

Since it wasn't a question, Janeal didn't offer an answer.

"You got a suitcase?"

Janeal shook her head.

"Well, I guess we've had people come in here with less than one change of clothes and a head cold." Lucille picked up some of the tissues Janeal had tossed into the tote. "At least you'll have something to wear on laundry day. Which reminds me: you don't get paid around here, but we do have a points system that will allow you to make 'purchases' from our donations pile. So you can build up a closet as you go."

Janeal was about to ask how that worked when Lucille added, "You also have the chance to lose points faster than you rack 'em up."

Janeal could feel Katie's cool gaze burning into her soul like some comic book hero's x-ray vision.

"Where's your ID?" Lucille asked.

"Stolen," Janeal said.

"Bogus. I've heard it all, Janice. You'll have to come up with another story."

"I'm telling the truth. I took a shower at the hostel downtown last week—someone walked right in and took it."

"You got any money?"

"I—it all went for the cab fare."

"And how do you plan to get home if we don't let you stay here?"

Janeal was dumbstruck.

Lucille threw the tote bag down at Janeal's feet. "If we're going to start off this relationship by you thinking you can waltz in here and yank my chain, you need your head checked more than most. You play me straight, girl, or you don't get to play at all."

It wasn't often that Janeal was caught without words, but Lucille's impatience and Katie's silence—why was she here for this interview?—rendered Janeal undecided about how she should answer. Which woman did she need to play most strategically?

Lucille, she decided. For now. She definitely needed to be allowed to stay.

Janeal rubbed a hand over her face and tried to conjure the closest thing she could to contrition. She hadn't had a lot of practice with that one.

"I hid the money in the bathroom. I thought you'd take it."

"How much?"

"Forty-two dollars and seventy-six cents."

"Well that was an unnecessary little spat we had to get into, then. You keep what you come with, though there isn't anything to spend it on here."

Janeal nodded, eyes on her feet.

"How about that ID?"

"I *swear* I don't have any ID," Janeal rasped.

"And that PO?"

"I'm supposed to see him Thursday. Or Friday, I don't know." Janeal's frustration started to rear its head. "I don't really care if they ever get me someone."

"She's a liar," Lucille said to Katie.

Katie folded her hands in her lap.

"Better than some but not good enough to say I've never seen the likes of her before."

Katie didn't reply.

"I got enough liars on my hands to keep me all wrapped up for the next six years. I'm not looking to acquire any more."

This was going far worse than Janeal had envisioned.

"Please"—she dropped her face into her hands and tried to summon tears—"if I can't stay here I don't know where I'll go next . . ."

"Right. Not too many places offer free room and board for six months in exchange for a good attitude."

Janeal couldn't find any real tears in her acting repertoire and so resorted to a tantrum. She had not expected this inquisition.

"This is *so unfair*. I am at the bottom here! No one else is willing to help me get back on my feet, and why?" She stood and yanked her tote off the floor as if to leave. "What have I ever done to you? And you think you—"

"Janice," Katie said. "Why do you want to be here?"

Janeal whipped her head around to face Katie. She took a deep breath to center herself and refocus. She searched her mind for an appropriate cliché.

"Because I think I have it in me to get it right this time."

And when it was spoken, she wondered if she had pulled that out of some subconscious desire to apologize.

Or not.

Katie smiled for the first time and looked at Lucille.

"I think I can handle one more liar," she said.

Lucille shook her head and went back to her desk. "Then have at her."

47

Because Sanso understood what role he played in this battle of wits with Janeal, he couldn't have been happier to discover her "disappearance." It would work to his advantage if she believed she had slipped through his net, which in truth had been cast much wider than she knew. But because he was the only one privy to his real intent, he put on a good show of coolheaded fury for the sake of his subordinates.

For fun, he stripped the men who were supposed to be trailing her of their vehicle, money, and clothes and left them to find their way back to wherever they came from in boxers and socks. Delightful.

The assistants who'd accompanied him now escorted them out to I-25. Sanso stayed behind to place a call.

"She's changed her appearance," he told Callista.

"Enough for you to quit following her around like a slobbering puppy?"

Sanso leaned against the hood of Janeal's rental car in the salon parking lot and tipped his phone between his ear and shoulder. "Your envy becomes you, sweet. Her car is still here, and she's looking for Robert alone."

"So she would have called a cab."

"Obviously." He withdrew a pistol from his waistband and checked the magazine. Full.

"And they're at the Hope House."

"More than likely."

"So I assume that's where we're headed next."

"Let's let the pair have time for a happy reunion first."

Callista exhaled. "Yes, Master."

Sanso cackled at that. He closed his phone and dropped it into his breast pocket, then leveled the gun at the tires of the rental car. He took his time, walking around the car in broad daylight and shooting out each tire. And the rear wind-shield, because he could, and because Janeal could afford to pay for the damages, and because the shocked souls rushing out of the strip mall storefronts wouldn't dare try to stop him.

Life could become so dull if one didn't take advantage of every opportunity to make an impression.

Then he climbed into the idling silver Escalade he'd confiscated from his men and drove off to meet his associates and ditch the car. Maybe they'd indulge in a little tequila while they waited.

Katie walked Janeal to her room, a shoe box at the end of a long corridor, flanked on each side by two larger rooms.

"There are six other women on this wing of the house counting me," Katie explained. "My room's at the top of the hall where it meets the other corridor." Katie pointed in the general direction. "Smallest rooms go to newcomers, then you move up as you stick with the program and others graduate. After you're approved to take a job outside the house, you're expected to pay rent on a slid-ing scale based on how long you've been here and how much you earn."

The room contained a cot with a single mattress, a four-drawer dresser and mirror, a table and chair, and a rocker that sat by the window. An old rag rug covered the center of the hardwood floor.

"Spartan," Janeal said.

"Your first week of chores is kitchen duty," Katie said as Janeal threw her tote on the bed. "You can pick food prep or dishwashing."

"Food prep." Janeal lifted the dusty curtain to a view of a clay hillside strewn with cacti.

"Popular choice." Katie paused. "You like to cook?"

Janeal dropped the curtain. "I don't like to do dishes."

Katie remained standing in the doorway while Janeal examined the one-door closet and opened the dresser drawers. When she finally sat down to test the rocker, Katie stepped into the room and leaned back against the wall with her hands flat behind her hips.

"Can I have car privileges?" Janeal asked.

"Not until you're within three months of graduating or file a special petition. We have two group cars available for things like doctor appointments."

"So I'm stranded here."

"You sound like you're fighting a cold. Is there anything I can get you?"

"I don't suppose you keep echinacea on hand."

"I ran out of my supply, but I'll ask Frankie for you. She's our staffer with a love for all things homeopathic."

"You use it too?"

"Since I was a baby."

The herbal immune booster had been a staple among the *kumpanía* for decades.

"Medication will kill you, I always say," Janeal said.

"Everyone who comes through these doors knows how to medicate themselves one way or the other."

Janeal mentally scolded herself for not having been more careful. "You always make your residents feel so welcome?"

"We can't help you if you aren't honest about what you're going through."

Janeal scoffed. Honesty was not a valuable asset in the world she operated in, at least not since she had run off with Sanso's money. In fact, one's survival seemed dependent on playing a strategic game of deception.

"It's like this," Katie said. "You respect the other women here and they'll respect you. We look out for each other. The ones who have been here longest understand what's at stake. So don't take offense if anyone gets in your face."

"Sure." The easiest approach, of course, would be simply to steer clear of everyone. Not make waves. Find out the information she needed. Make a plan, make a deal. Fall off the wagon. Vanish.

If she wanted to get out of here quickly, she'd have to start quickly.

"I couldn't help but admire the ring you're wearing," Janeal said. Katie released her hands from where they were pinned between her and the wall. Her fingers went to the diamond-studded band.

"Thank you."

There was an awkward pause.

"I would think there'd be some policy around here about flaunting valuables."

"It was my mother's."

Heat flashed through Janeal. How dare she make such a claim?

"A gift?"

"An heirloom. She died a long time ago."

"So did mine. Freak accident. The story of my life."

Katie tipped her head to one side. "Maybe we have more in common than you think, Janice."

They most certainly did.

"What happened to your mom?" Janeal asked.

"Tornado," Katie said, speaking toward the floor now. "Impaled her on an oak tree. Killed my three sisters too."

Janeal shot out of the rocker so suddenly that its momentum caused the furniture to hit the wall and then smack the backs of her knees. Katie Morgon's mother had been alive and well until the night of the massacre. What was Katie doing, stealing Janeal's story as if it were her own?

This was some twisted coping mechanism for a burn victim, for any kind of victim. It would have made more sense to Janeal if Katie had blurted such lies to a newspaper in a conscious effort to get in some cheap shots at the woman who'd betrayed her.

Katie must have sensed Janeal's reaction. She came off the wall, standing straight. "That was more than I needed to say. I'm sorry."

Janeal stepped out of the window's afternoon light, glad Katie couldn't see the contradiction between her words and her furious face. It took an effort to manage her tone.

"Don't be. What kind of world is this where two people can meet by chance and have such similar tales?"

"Suffering is suffering, though it takes a lot of different forms. I'm not so sure that the depth of pain any one person feels is unique to a given experience. We seem to understand it universally."

Of all the weak justifications. Janeal tried not to be snide. "I would imagine those scars you bear hurt worse than most."

Katie touched the side of her face. "I wasn't meaning physical ones. What kind of scars do you have, Janice?"

"Topic off limits. For now."

"That's fine." Katie moved back toward the door. "You can wash up. Dinner prep starts in thirty minutes."

Janeal fidgeted, unwilling to let Katie leave so soon. "What's your story?"

"Which part?"

"The burn part."

Katie put her hand on the doorknob. "It's not something I usually talk about."

"Why not?"

"I try to focus on other people's stories. That's usually more helpful to them."

"How long have you been here, Katie?"

"Thirteen years."

"In all that time have you ever told your story?"

"Abbreviated versions."

"Honest ones?"

Katie's pause was the only sign that Janeal's challenge had taken her aback. In a moment she said, "Of course. Honest."

"Could you spare me an abridged version then?"

If Janeal could get this much out of Katie, she might have an inkling of how much Robert would know. Or eventually learn. She might also—no guarantees here, but maybe—get a clearer picture of how slanted Katie's version of the story had become after a decade and a half. How accusatory of Janeal Mikkado.

"Abridged."

"So long as it's honest. That's what this place is all about, right?"

Katie took a step away from the door, halted, then two more steps to the foot of the bed, where she stood with one arm level across her ribs and the other hand raised to grip the side of her neck as if it ached. That ring glinted on her finger, winking its secrets at Janeal.

"Fifteen years ago I met a man who asked for my help in retrieving something another person had stolen from him. I had access to it that no one else in my . . . family had." She shook her head as if she'd started out with unimportant information. Janeal crossed her arms and leaned against the wall by the window. She tried to remember if Katie had ever told her such a story, or if her older brothers had ever been in criminal trouble.

"What was it you were supposed to recover?"

Katie shrugged. "That doesn't really figure into the story in any meaningful way, except that I was able to find what the man needed. I made arrangements to get it back to him, but . . . well, my plans didn't hold together. I was too young then, I guess, too naive to understand what he'd asked me to do. I didn't mean to do anything but save . . ." She took a deep breath. "I mean I tried to do exactly what he asked, but there were other people involved."

The nerves in Janeal's abdomen twitched as she realized whose story Katie was telling. Katie was playing her! She had perceived the truth about Janeal in spite of her blindness and was getting her revenge!

"He thought I betrayed him," Katie went on. "It was really a horrible misunderstanding, but he became angry. He took my father and one of my dearest friends as hostages. He imprisoned them in my house and burned the place down."

Janeal started to pace. A sweat broke out at the base of her hairline as she tried to reconstruct how much she had told Katie about what Sanso had done within the twenty-four hours of her first encounter with him. She didn't think she had offered Katie enough information to construct such a bare-bones tale.

Katie wouldn't know of her plan to return the money to Sanso. And Katie would never have characterized the events of that night as "a horrible misunderstanding." Janeal doubted Katie knew Sanso's name. Confusion settled over her mind.

Katie licked her lips and Janeal thought that maybe she planned to end her story there. Janeal pressed her thumbs into the base of her skull and linked her fingers behind her head as she paced. This method sometimes worked to prevent the onset of a headache.

Janeal prodded. "You got caught in the blaze."

"Not exactly."

Janeal's breaths shortened and quickened. She anticipated Katie's blame. What would she do when Katie pointed the finger? She couldn't snap. *Steady now.*

"I had the chance to get out. My father was already dead."

Janeal sat heavily on the bed. *My father . . .*

"But my friend . . ."

Katie did not speak for a full minute. Janeal closed her eyes to try to regulate her breathing, and when she opened them, Katie's cheeks were wet. What was Katie trying to do? Janeal wondered if she should demand an explanation or wait for it to reveal itself.

"He would have burned her alive," Katie said. "He wanted her to die in the fire." Katie lifted her face. "Do you know what happens to a person who dies by burning, Janice?"

Janeal stood and paced again. "I don't want to know."

"If they aren't fortunate enough to die by asphyxiation first—"

"What was your friend's name?"

Katie's lips parted and she seemed to snap back to the present. "I tried to get her out."

What was going on here? Why was Katie telling Janeal's story, and why would she change it to protect Janeal from the truth of what had really happened? Or had Katie snapped and concocted a version that helped her to cope, a version that she wanted to believe, unable to come to grips with Janeal's betrayal?

And what had she meant when she said that Sanso's money didn't figure into her story in any significant way?

Janeal dropped her thumbs from the top of her spine and flexed her fingers, mentally grasping for answers. Katie moved from the foot of the bed to the nearby desk chair. She hiked her pant legs at the knees to sit and extended her sandal-clad feet into the middle of the little room. Placing her hands on her thighs and locking her elbows, she leaned forward in the chair so that her shoulders nearly touched her ears.

"I tried to get her out but I couldn't. I dragged her to the door. I—we fell, and after that . . ."

Janeal didn't say anything.

"It's a horrific story. People don't like to hear it, which is why I'm reluctant to tell."

Janeal's eyes drifted to Katie's feet. The pattern of burns on Katie's body, what was visible anyway, didn't make sense. To have been in that meetinghouse, to have fallen through fire, to have escaped an explosion of that magnitude— how had any of her body gone untouched? The right side of her face, the tops of her feet? It seemed likely that Katie's choice of clothing covered a mangled mass of flesh, but that any of it was as pristine as those feet . . .

Her gaze rose to Katie's ankles, exposed when she sat down in the chair.

There, beneath the ridges and seams of discolored scar tissue, was the green ink of a tattoo. A flame, melted into an asymmetrical mess.

"You have a tattoo," Janeal whispered.

Katie's mood shifted and she reached down to run her fingers over the top of it. She brushed aside the fabric of her pants.

"I do."

A melted sun with a wavering flame that would have matched the one on Janeal's own left ankle, were Katie's in pristine condition.

A copy. It had to be a copy. How far had Katie gone with this pretense? And why?

It couldn't be a copy. Katie had never seen the tattoo Janeal so boldly acquired.

It couldn't be.

"It's a sun," Janeal said. She felt all the blood rush out of her head as if the gravity from that very ball of fire commanded it.

"You can tell what it is?" Katie seemed surprised. "You're the first person who hasn't asked me. A burned sun. Ironic, isn't it? My last juvenile stunt before . . ." Her expression turned sober again. "I didn't have time to show it off."

You showed Robert, Janeal thought, staring at the deformed skin. *Not you. I. I showed Robert.*

She lifted her own pant leg to see the tattoo's twin, which she typically covered with heavy makeup.

"What did you say?" Katie's question was barely audible. Janeal's head snapped up. Her companion had paled.

"What?"

"You said something."

"I didn't." Had she spoken aloud?

"Something about a Robert?"

"No. I didn't."

Katie opened her mouth, but her words did not come out right away. "How did your mother die?"

The starting point of this discussion had fallen far from Janeal's mind in the presence of this new mystery. She rifled through her brain for some believable headline. It took longer than she meant it to. "She was . . . she was shot. Some random bullet fired during a drug bust at a neighbor's."

"Is that the honest story?" Katie's frown accused. Janeal's composure flagged.

"I'm not a fraud, if that's what you're suggesting." Janeal wished she hadn't said it so harshly and that she'd chosen some word other than *fraud.*

48

After Katie left, Janeal stood paralyzed in the center of the room. She was going insane. The headaches or the drugs or the nightmares had finally scrambled her brain cells into an incoherent, illogical mess of thought and possibility. Her eyes were unreliable. Her ears too. Nothing Katie had said could possibly be true. The story was . . . crazy.

Yes. Katie was the crazy one. She'd snapped from her experience and turned into a wily predator, waiting with eternal patience for her prey to finally arrive so she could rope it in with this sweet, delicate, sad sob story. This *act*. Everyone thought she was heaven-sent, this miracle worker, this Princess Diana Florence Nightingale Angel of Mercy *saint*, when she was really a pretender. An imposter.

A psychotic but brilliant mental case who'd concocted the story of all stories, having been locked up in the insanity of her own mind long enough to sound believable.

It couldn't be true. It couldn't. It couldn't.

The story was a lie.

No, the story was as true as if Janeal had told it herself—all up until the part where Katie claimed she went to rescue . . .

Katie?

It can't be true.

What can't—?

Don't say it don't say it don't say it!

It can't be true that—

No!

It couldn't be true that she and Katie were the same person.

Janeal dropped to her knees and grabbed her head in both hands, entwined her fingers through her hair and pulled as if the physical pain could make more noise inside her head than that lunatic thought.

Impossible.

There was no explanation for this. Nothing so absurd.

She had to explain it. She needed to grapple with every possibility and come up with a reasonable reason, a believable reason for what had happened in this little room with an old friend who didn't know whom she was talking to. Bending forward with her hands still entangled in her dyed locks, Janeal dropped her forehead to the rug and tried to breathe. She inhaled the scent of dust and lint—it grounded her in the physical world. She breathed it in deeper and allowed reality to bring her back to focus.

Somehow, Katie had survived the fire.

There it was. Janeal exhaled. A reasonable thought she could hold on to. The very thought that had brought her and Robert here.

A fact.

A piece of objective reality.

Katie *had* survived.

That was a thought she could follow in a straight line, compared to this circular tail-chasing her mind had become trapped in.

It was possible that Katie had made it out. Janeal had seen her, after all, free of that stool in the final seconds before she made it out herself. And although Janeal had spent at least a year following the stories before concluding Katie had died in the building—or had not survived the ensuing explosion—she had never possessed definitive evidence.

Katie could have fallen through the floor, gone down with the weight of that soda machine before the fire reached her, miraculously tumbled into a spot that had yet to ignite, or had already burned out.

Janeal's eyes opened a half inch away from the blue rug loops with a more startling idea: Sanso had watched Janeal flee and stepped in to get Katie the moment Janeal was gone. He'd rescued her himself. Played executioner and savior in the same moment. Created an elaborate scenario designed to push Janeal toward the money. Toward *him*.

He could have fed Katie the story. He could have tattooed her and burned her and . . .

. . . and why?

Sanso didn't even know Katie was still alive.

What did it mean?

Nothing sensible. And it didn't explain how Katie had come by the ring. *Her* ring.

She had noticed it missing when she wrapped her fingers around the Lexus's steering wheel after Sanso left. The meetinghouse smoldered and cast an orange glow through the tinted windows of the car onto her filthy, sooty, ringless hands. Janeal had allowed herself three minutes to grab a flashlight from the garage shelf and retrace her steps in search of her one connection to her mother before determining it must have slipped off in the blaze.

Right onto Katie's finger.

Someone in the room adjacent to hers dropped a book on the desk. Or the floor. The noise was electric, a popping snap that brought an unbidden image to Janeal's mind: a red Tiffany lamp swinging over a pool table. Her arm tingled as if she'd been shocked.

What had happened in that room the day she fell into Sanso's web? Something electrical. Spiritual. Magical. Something Mrs. Marković had anticipated and understood and tried to explain to Janeal, something about two chambers in the heart. And she'd referred to her as "you two."

Impossible.

In her little desert shoe-box room, Janeal released her hair from her fists and pressed herself up onto all fours, staring at the tight blue fibers until they blurred.

She was going insane. She was insane.

Janeal got up and staggered to the bathroom to retrieve her pills.

A triple dose might help her fake her way through the evening meal.

Janeal Mikkado—the blind, scarred, Hope House Janeal Mikkado who had spent the last fifteen years learning to think of herself as Katie, who had presented herself to the world as Katie—could not have been more shocked by the conversation she'd had with Janice Regan.

"I showed Robert," Janice had said. Clear and loud and unmistakably to

Katie's sharp ears. *I showed Robert.* Katie had never been more certain of what she had heard. Nor more worried that she had misunderstood.

On the surface, the remark was senseless. Janice showed Robert what? The tattoo? How could she have shown someone else Katie's—Janeal's—tattoo?

Did Janice know Robert? Could it be that they knew each other and Robert told her about Janeal, and about the green sun on her left ankle? If they did, and if he had, Janice's remark still didn't make sense to Katie. *I showed Robert.* As if she herself were Janeal Mikkado.

An irrational idea. An impossibility. Surely Janice had meant someone else, not the Robert Lukin here in the same house at this very moment.

But Janice had denied saying anything at all!

I showed Robert. Katie sat on the edge of the bed in her private room, mulling over the emotion the remark had ignited in her belly. What was it, precisely? Curiosity? Anxiety? Fear?

No, not fear. What could she have to fear anymore, after having had her life literally, physically, irrevocably purged by fire? She had nothing more to lose, ever again, and by that she didn't mean material things, but all the intangible valuables of her life: the security that came from knowing she had done something right for once, the understanding that nothing else mattered.

Fifteen years ago Janeal, who now called herself Katie, had stood to her feet in that game room of her *kumpanía's* community center, hands facing outward toward the blaze, and done what she knew she must. The air split with light and noise, but there was no turning back for her. She turned her back on the money, on Sanso, and on the idea that she could live after abandoning Katie in such a horrible, unforgivable way. All her indecision, which had seemed so compelling a heartbeat earlier, vanished. She had to try to save her friend.

That was all the thinking she'd had time to do. She ran toward Katie, who was engulfed by the flames, only momentarily aware of the intense burning. She had not lied to Robert when she said the course of events was fuzzy. One of the reasons the tale was so hard to tell was because she recalled so little of it. She did not remember having any sensation of being burned at that time; she did not remember if she and Katie exchanged any words, or if Katie was still conscious; she did not remember any images from the encounter.

What she remembered was that she chose not to try to free Katie from the stool. She intuitively understood that time spent separating body from chair was certain death for both of them. She hugged Katie and grabbed the seat and felt the hot squishy vinyl melt around her hands as she dragged everything toward the burning doorframe.

She remembered that she went out the doorway first, backward, dragging Katie after her.

She remembered stepping out of the passage into thin air, the exterior staircase already consumed, and then falling with Katie and the stool on top of her.

How she survived the fall was a question she had never been able to answer. It seemed unimportant now, compared to the questions she had about Janice. When Janeal rolled Katie off of her, the stool fell away to the other side. The ropes that had held Katie in place had finally disintegrated, but not before the beautiful teenager died.

What Janeal felt then was the purest kind of despair she had ever known, before or since. The emotional pain of her failure went so deep that the realization that she was on fire came as a delayed reaction to the scent of burning hair. Her burning hair.

That she shouldn't have started running was a truism she didn't think of until later. At the time, all she considered was how to reach the river as soon as possible. She did reach it, though what happened when she got there was not a part of her memory.

The current must have carried her downstream.

The next thing she remembered was waking on her hands and knees, balanced on a muddy riverbank surrounded by the shouts of surprised people.

She was told later that she had been babbling when they found her. *Katie, Katie, Katie.* They thought it was her name. She let them think it, in honor of her friend. In that moment she put to death Janeal Mikkado and resurrected Katie Morgon. She made an unspoken commitment to live a life worthy of the cheerful, decent girl who hadn't deserved to die.

It no longer mattered that she had survived and the real Katie had not, though this fact had sent her into a personal crisis during her recovery. She did not question the purpose of the burns—that God had used them and her blindness to draw her to him. What she did question was why he couldn't have saved Katie too.

What had it mattered to lose all this if she couldn't win the most important prize of all: her friend's life?

It mattered, Katie came to realize over a period of years, because she had made the right choice, with no guarantee of the outcome, and she came out of the ordeal spiritually, mentally, and emotionally whole. This was why she loved fire the way she did. To her, it represented the beauty of freedom—not from trouble or grief or sadness, but from fear, from true loss, from regret.

Until tonight.

Katie had spoken of the Mikkado Massacre to only one person in fifteen years, and only after their friendship had blossomed. But tonight, in five minutes, she found herself speaking to this stranger as freely as if she were talking to herself.

Herself.

A disturbing thought blossomed in Katie's gut. Something about Janice had troubled her starting with their meeting in Lucille's office, and she tried to put a finger on it now. She remembered the odd way Janice had gripped her hand for an impolite amount of time, then let go as if Katie's palm had seared hers. In light of the inquisition over Katie's ring, maybe Janice had noticed it. Studied it.

Both their mothers had died in freak accidents.

Katie shook her mind to clear it of that coincidence. Something else was bugging her. Something about the way Janice spoke.

I'm telling the truth . . .

This is so unfair. I am at the bottom here . . .

I told Robert.

The inflection was her own. Janeal's.

What a ridiculous idea. It couldn't be.

Katie got off her bed and smoothed her pants, then made a conscious effort to relax her shoulders. She tipped her chin up to the ceiling, stretching her neck. She clenched her fists and released them three times, then shook out her fingers loosely.

Katie opened her door and exited, taking brisk steps to the kitchen. After the meal, she would take her overactive imagination to Donna Maria and put these crazy thoughts in their place.

49

Dinner preparations were a near disaster. In the kitchen, Janeal could barely hold on to her knife while she cut carrots and bell peppers. Her hands shook while Katie—*I still must think of her as Katie*—worked next to her, silent and focused.

Or silent and distracted. Three times, Katie lost the grip on the potatoes she peeled.

An image flashed through Janeal's mind: herself, raising the quivering knife and plunging it into Katie's back. She gasped at the vision as Katie turned to face her.

Katie hesitated as though to speak, then concentrated on her potatoes again. Janeal wondered what she suspected of their earlier discussion, if not the psychotic possibility that they were both standing in some soup kitchen staring at each other as if they stood before a mirror.

The more Janeal pondered the impossible, the more the kitchen closed in on her, oppressing her with other details. Katie had stood next to her in the doorway and looked Janeal in the eye—Katie had never been that tall and wouldn't have grown two or three inches since her eighteenth birthday. Janeal, not wearing her usual high heels, hadn't thought of that until now. At the time, they were both flat-footed in sandals and Keds. At first glance, Janeal had credited Katie's slimmer frame to the frugal way of life at the house, or to the trauma. Janeal herself was thinner than she had been as a teen. She had attributed Katie's lighter complexion to scars, to fifteen years of indoor living and perhaps a damaged immune system. It wasn't a dramatic change of skin tone, but it was enough.

Enough to match Janeal's biracial tan.

Had Robert noticed these changes? Did he suspect that Katie wasn't Katie at all, but . . .

Janeal's knife hovered over a pile of vegetables while she studied Katie. That ring kept glinting as if it were a crystal glass filled with wine and Janeal were an alcoholic in need of a drink.

Let's just say, for the sake of letting this ridiculous idea run its course, that you and I are the same. Let's just say that I am standing here looking at myself, talking to myself. What would it mean?

It would mean Janeal needed to check herself in to a wholly different kind of treatment center.

Robert came in then and went straight to Katie. He didn't greet anyone else. Janeal turned away. What would happen if he got a good look at her?

Though Janeal's goal had been to be completely unnoticed, she hadn't anticipated the pain of coming close enough to touch him and having to keep her distance. She was not able to prevent herself from staring at him, staring and remembering.

He leaned in close to Katie's ear. He touched the small of her back. Janeal chopped vegetables within tossing distance of those two and felt the blade of old emotions slice a jagged tear down the center of her sternum.

Robert belonged to her. Had belonged to her since they were twelve and fourteen and had hiked that red mesa together for the first time, hand in hand, while Katie straggled.

When had Katie caught up and separated them like a yolk from an egg white?

It had happened long before now, Janeal was forced to admit, long before the arrest of Sanso or the destruction of her father's *kumpanía*. At the time, the reality of their separation had made it easier for Janeal to leave the way she did. Of course, she had thought Robert and Katie were dead.

Katie *was* dead, wasn't she?

Janeal's knife came down on her finger as if it were a stalk of celery, but she didn't notice it until someone exclaimed and rushed over with a dish towel. Robert glanced at her then. *I'm so sorry,* Janeal sent out with her eyes while the person gripped her hand in the towel and forced Janeal to apply pressure, *I thought you were dead.*

There was no point in trying to justify that claim, though, because she knew she would have left him anyway. When she held his eyes too long, he looked away.

Another resident rushed over with a first-aid kit. Janeal wondered if the tables had been turned and Robert had discovered her first, would he have come to her side as quickly?

Yes. She liked to believe he would have.

Robert was the real reason her love for Milan Finch was no love at all. Because she had Robert to compare him to.

Was her plan to find out and bury whatever Katie might tell Robert about the money pointless or essential now? While her fellow cook examined the knife wound and declared it didn't need stitches, Janeal toyed with the idea of telling Robert who she was. She could make him choose between Janeal and Katie. She could confront him with the truth that Katie was an imposter.

Katie and Robert talked in low tones near the stove, and Janeal decided she could not afford the risk of losing Robert again. She had lost Robert to Katie fifteen years ago, and he'd never return to her as long as Katie stood between them.

50

After supper, Robert went looking for Katie and found her in the enclosed garden room where he had been reunited with her. She was shrugging into a light sweater.

"That new resident of yours is a bit unnerving," he said. Katie jumped and placed her hand at her throat. "Sorry."

She waved him off. "My fault. I was distracted. You were talking about Janice?"

"Is that her name?"

"What unnerved you about her?"

Robert shrugged. "She keeps staring at me."

"You have those rugged good looks." Katie wasn't smiling. Robert couldn't tell if she was teasing.

"Not that kind of stare."

"Then what kind?"

"Like she knows me, though I don't know her."

Katie tied the sweater's belt at her waist. "Tell me what she looks like."

"Tall. Skinny. Unfortunately skinny. What is it with women who think—"

"You don't really have to ask that question, do you?"

"Okay. But she could use some meat on her. Short dark brown hair. Unnaturally blue eyes."

"Might be contacts."

"Maybe. They take the creepy factor of her staring to a whole new level. I didn't want to encourage her by studying her too closely, you know?"

"I'm sure many of the other women who live here find you a sight for deprived eyes."

Robert laughed. "I haven't noticed anyone but you."

Katie fell silent. He'd said too much. She wasn't ready to reciprocate. Of course she wasn't. She didn't have the benefit of having nothing else to think about but a long-lost friend, miraculously rediscovered. He wondered if she ever took vacations—as opposed to an afternoon off now and then.

"I enjoyed the sculptures you showed me Monday," he offered.

"They're beautiful, aren't they?"

Their conversation stalled again.

"Could I ask you a favor?" Katie said.

"Anything."

"Janice needs echinacea. We're out of it. Could you run down to a Walgreens for some?"

"Tonight?"

"A little outing might do you good."

"I know. I meant—never mind." The ease of their prior conversations evaporated for reasons Robert couldn't pinpoint. The earlier connection he'd felt to her seemed threatened, and he reached out to touch her, then stopped himself.

"Of course I'll go. Echinacea—that's the stuff our mothers used to make us swallow all the time, right?"

"Brown bottle, orange label."

"You want to come?" he asked.

"Staff meeting at eight thirty. You could possibly get me back in time, but I've got something else I need to do first. Thanks for doing this."

"No problem."

Katie left the garden room through an exterior door into the back of the property. Robert almost asked if she had a flashlight along. What could she have to do out there in the dark?

Instead, he left in the opposite direction. He circumvented several sets of tables and chairs, then stepped into the hallway that separated the garden room from the atrium in the entryway. From the corner of his eye, he spotted a figure walking toward the end of the hall, as if she had passed the point where he was standing seconds ago. Janice.

Had she been listening?

When he hesitated, she turned her head to look at him. Shadows from the setting sun reached in through the windows and cloaked her eyes and propped them up on deep, dark circles, but Robert could imagine her blue stare easily enough. She continued walking, and after a few seconds she looked away.

Robert picked up his pace and crossed the tile toward the exit.

51

Donna Maria was standing on her squeaky porch when Katie approached her house. The light breeze rustled her skirts, startling Katie.

"I've been expecting you," the old woman said.

Though Donna Maria had never indicated that she'd heard of the Mikkado Massacre, for a long time Katie couldn't shake the fact that the woman reminded her of Mrs. Marković, who had paid a visit to their camp and spoken so cryptically to her the very weekend of the disaster. In many ways the two women were similar—elderly and soft-skinned, prone to perplexing statements, and scented with lavender soap. But they differed in at least one significant way: Donna Maria never frightened Katie. The part of her that was Janeal recalled Mrs. Marković as being creepy at best, and too strange to be considered friendly.

Donna Maria took Katie's hand and guided her to a wobbly folding chair. Katie heard moths fluttering against glass. She guessed the kitchen window. Donna Maria sat too, in a chair that creaked.

"You have more trouble," Donna Maria said.

Katie touched the knot in her sweater belt. "I hate to come only for trouble."

"Bah. You come for any reason, daughter."

Katie pulled the sweater sleeves down over her cold hands. "A new resident came to the house today. She hadn't been there an hour before I found myself telling her my story."

"Then she's more gifted than I at drawing you out."

"I don't think it's that. It's more like she and I have this bond. Like I've known her a long time."

The boards beneath Donna Maria began to knock rhythmically. She must have sat in a rocking chair.

After a few seconds the widow said, "Like sisters."

Katie hadn't thought of Janice as sisterly, though the comparison seemed helpful. But the word made Katie self-conscious of how little thought she'd given to explaining herself. The ludicrousness of her private thinking would embarrass her once she said it aloud.

"Out with it, daughter."

"Identical sisters," Katie said. "Almost . . . the same person."

She expected Donna Maria to laugh, or to challenge her. She did neither. "What makes you think you and this woman are so much the same?"

"It will take some explaining."

Donna Maria patted the back of Katie's hand. "See? This is why we have no time for small talk."

That made Katie smile.

In halting phrases, Katie explained Janice's preoccupation with her ring, then realized she'd have to explain first that her name wasn't really Katie, and why. She finished that and began to relay Janice's remark about Robert, then realized she'd never told Donna Maria about him, let alone that he'd shown up at the house coincidentally close to Janice's arrival. All these details took some time to unravel. It was backward, circuitous storytelling. Donna Maria let her go about it without interrupting.

"I'm not sure what I'm trying to express," Katie finished.

"You think you and Janice are the same person. This Janeal."

Stated in such frank terms, the idea caused Katie some panic. Did she want to put it that way? She wasn't sure. "I know *I'm* Janeal. But Janice is an unknown quantity."

"Have you asked her?"

Katie barked out a laugh. "No! I'd lose money from my donors if word got out I was asking questions like that." Her humor passed. "They'd think I have a psychological disorder. MPD or something like it."

Donna Maria did not reply.

"You don't think . . ."

"Lucille interviewed Janice, you said."

She nodded and added, "I was with them."

"Then Lucille can confirm that—"

"—there were two of us in the room? How do you propose I go about asking her such a thing?"

"Tough problems call for tough questions."

"Donna Maria!"

"This could be nothing more than a freak coincidence, Katie."

"I'd be willing to entertain that possibility if Robert and Janice hadn't knocked on my door within days of each other. That's coincidence enough, don't you think?"

"I've had stranger experiences in my long life."

"What if Janice is an imposter?"

"Yes. What if?"

"How would she have known what my tattoo was? How could she have known I showed it to Robert?"

"Maybe she wasn't talking about your Robert."

"He's not *mine*."

"Or maybe she knows Robert."

"He had no idea who she was."

"Then maybe they are both playing a trick on you."

Katie threw up her hands. "Why would they do that? Robert and a woman I've never met before in my life?"

"So we're down to two options: she's a complete stranger, or you and she are the same person."

"There have got to be other choices. Maybe I do know her somehow. But one person can't inhabit two bodies! That's insanity."

The widow stayed silent.

Katie lowered her voice. "I apologize. I didn't mean to be rude. But listen to us talk!"

"I have seen stranger things, daughter. I've seen miracles. I've seen God's hand at work in the world."

The quiet settled between them and Katie waited for her to explain.

" 'And the Lord said unto Satan, Hast thou considered my servant Job?' " The breeze carried her words away.

Katie waited for her to say more, and when she didn't, Katie groped for some meaning. "I'm not Job."

" 'And Satan answered the Lord, and said, Doth Job fear God for naught?' "

Now Donna Maria was sounding more like the Mrs. Marković Katie remembered. She shivered. "I don't understand."

"Who can imagine what God and Satan discuss? Certainly Job had no idea God was gambling with his life," Donna Maria said. "What other deals might they strike involving us? Tell me again about the night that this happened."

"Sanso found me at the front of the community house. I followed him upstairs—"

"Before that."

"I found the money in Dad's cabinet. I set the house on fire."

"No, earlier still."

Katie frowned and put her fingers at her temples. "When I went with Sanso?"

"There was a visitor at your camp. She spoke to you."

"Mrs. Marković?" Katie searched her memory. Had she told Donna Maria about her? She would have sworn she hadn't before now.

"What did she say?"

"When did I tell you about her?"

Donna Maria rested her hand lightly atop Katie's. This time she laughed, and Katie's fingers tingled as if they'd been asleep.

Why Donna Maria would dodge the simple query made it hard for Katie to recall the long-forgotten conversation. But the electric sensation in her fingers brought to mind Mrs. Marković's shocking touch, the connection that seemed to split her head in two, and the static that charged the air of the game room, cracking like a whip. Katie experienced no such headache now, only the unusual warmth of Donna Maria's soft skin.

"You've always been my favorite," the old woman whispered. "A good child. Now, the devil—well, he would place his bets on the other side."

Katie snatched her hand back, alarmed. "What do you mean?"

"There are two chambers in every heart," Donna Maria said.

Katie remembered now. She drew in a sharp breath. "One for Judas and one for John. She said one must be pumped out or both would die."

The sound of Donna Maria's chair rocking across the weak porch boards ceased. "Perhaps God arranged for them both to live."

52

Sanso might have taken his Jaguar XKR convertible up to the Desert Hope House if the car were here in the States with him rather than in Brasília. But short of time to find a car of similar quality to rent, he secured a Mazda Miata, which would do a sufficient job of being quick and quiet if it so happened that was what he needed.

A black Ford pickup was the only other vehicle he encountered on the way up the hill, and that one was headed down, away from anything that concerned him.

Callista had not laughed as expected when he showed her the car and asked if she thought it would work as a chick magnet at the Hope House. Poor Callista. She did know him better than most of his employees and probably knew by now that he was only putting her through the paces. She wanted him back in Mexico. Needed him in Mexico to preserve her station in his hierarchy before Janeal Mikkado commandeered it. Sanso respected Callista's sharp mind, which surely had detected all these minute details. But it could not compel him to change course. Not in this case.

Instead Callista only mentioned, wryly, how fitting it was that Sanso would follow Robert into a houseful of solitary women. Maybe the DEA agent had a lover here. Or a snitch. Or a sinfully bad habit.

Well now—could the mystery person be the one Janeal had referred to as somehow "responsible for her security"? Perhaps she could arrange for Sanso to meet this person during his visit.

Sanso was having more fun than he'd enjoyed in years. He rolled the possibilities around in his mind.

A lover for Robert. Mm. That would be optimal. Someone to kick up a little more dust in Janeal's anxious, disguised, jealous face so Sanso could wash it off. He would caress it and kiss it away and reveal her true self, the self that was interested in dodging Robert's authority and preserving her own power and money and influence.

Interested in him, to put it bluntly. If her passion matched even half of his, they would live happily ever after.

Oh yes. Robert was nothing more than a pesky fly that made a lot of noise. But Janeal! In his fifty-three years he had never met such a perfect match for his own devious heart. Janeal would be his trophy. His unprecedented conquest. If he maneuvered as he was wont to do, she would never know there had been a battle for her soul.

53

Robert's cell phone rang as he left the drugstore with the small brown bottle in a plastic bag swinging from his fist. He recognized Harlan's phone number.

"Woodman, you have news?"

"Not sure, but I don't want to deal with your sourpuss face if it turns out to be viable."

"So what is it?"

"There was a shooting today in Santa Fe on Cerrillos Road. Happened around three at a strip mall. The only victim was a blue sedan, a rental registered to a Jane Johnson, whom authorities haven't located yet."

"And the DEA is involved because . . . ?"

"The description of the shooter matched Salazar Sanso."

Robert exhaled and mentally ran through all the reasons why Sanso would be in this area. "There are plenty of Latino men who'd fit a similar description walking around this town." Robert climbed into the cab of his truck and slammed the door.

"He was driving a silver Escalade, which they found ditched out of town, south of Route 66. It's registered to a Callista Ramirez."

Robert paused with his key in the ignition. Ramirez was long thought to be an associate of Sanso's, though she kept a low profile. The one time she had been apprehended, she was released in a few hours for lack of evidence to charge her.

"You think he's on my trail?"

"Why else would he head for Santa Fe?"

"I'm not worth his time. I'm an annoyance from his point of view." Robert wanted this to be true, though it apparently wasn't. For Katie's sake. If he'd led Sanso to her doorstep . . .

"Maybe. Maybe not. We're sending some agents up there to poke around. Should arrive first thing in the morning. If you're looking for something to do . . ."

"What's the address of the shooting?" It was only seven thirty. On the off-chance that he might get firsthand info from an eyewitness who was still there, he decided to drive over and satisfy his own show-me tendencies.

It took Robert about twenty minutes to cross town and find the strip mall Harlan had described. The car in question had been towed, but a dusting of fresh glass between two orange parking lines indicated where it had been parked. Robert stood in the slot and checked the shops most directly behind it. A liquor store. A bookstore. A hair salon. A vacuum and sewing machine repair shop. The repair shop was closed, but lights still shone out of the other three.

The cashier at the liquor store hadn't been on duty when the incident happened, but she gave him the number of the store manager, who had apparently seen the whole thing and would be glad to tell his story again. She'd heard it enough times to give a summary version to Robert.

He stepped out onto the concrete walk, planning to go into the bookstore next, when he saw a woman exiting the salon, keys jangling from a spiral band on her wrist as she prepared to lock up.

"Excuse me, ma'am."

She looked at him, her eyes judging in a flash whether he was danger or mere stranger. He pulled out his DEA identification and her cautious gaze turned fatigued.

"You guys have been around here all day. Haven't you asked enough yet?"

"I'm sorry to inconvenience you"—he looked at her name tag—"Carol. But I'm from a different agency. If I could ask you a couple questions."

Carol leaned her heavy frame against the storefront window and pulled out a cigarette, then her lighter. "What's another twenty after two thousand?" she said.

"I'll be as quick as possible. You saw the shooting today?"

"Plain as day. I was standing at the cash register when it happened." She jerked her thumb over her shoulder.

"Tell me about the shooter."

"Not bad looking. Latino maybe, middle-aged, tall, wavy hair. Real pretty hair. Still nice and thick; you don't see that much. Graying at the temples. If

I could touch up those locks—mm-hm. I bet I could take off ten years. Oh, and he had a beard."

Robert asked her questions about the shooting that she had likely been asked all day. Her answers were immediate and mechanical, having been uttered multiple times, and he didn't learn anything Harlan hadn't already told him.

Until he caught her off guard with a new question.

"The sedan was rented to a woman named Jane Johnson. You know anyone by that name?"

"Jane Johnson? Must be hundreds of women named that in this country. But no, I don't know any of them. Had a client in here today named Jane though." Carol took a drag on her cigarette and frowned. "Is that right? Or maybe it was something similar. Janet. Janice. It all runs together."

The name revived Robert's attention. "Did she have an appointment?"

"Sure she did. Cut and color."

"What time?"

She shrugged. "Around noon."

"Would it be possible to check her name?"

Carol sighed and took the keys off her wrist. "Come on in then. We almost done?"

"Yes. Would you describe the woman to me?"

"She was one of those super skinny chicks. Too thin to enjoy life if you ask me. I did her up real nice in a whole new look—cute short hair. She was a redhead, wanted to go dark. It turned out."

Carol turned on a light and went behind the reception desk to the appointment book. She ran her finger down a column and paused.

"Janice. I guess my memory's running out for the day."

"You have a last name?"

"Nope, just Janice. She paid cash."

"Did you see which car she got into when she left?"

"A car? Oh no. She must have had a ride here. Took a cab when she left."

Robert's stomach plummeted. He checked his watch. Almost eight thirty. If he raced, he was looking at another forty-five minutes back to the Desert Hope House.

Where some woman named Janice had lured Salazar Sanso, who was about to stumble onto Katie Morgon, sitting in the dark, alone.

Back in her room, after Robert had dodged her in the hall, Janeal broke into silent tears. Why? Why? Why, after Milan and Sanso and a handful of other men she could have as she wanted, did she feel this longing for someone who had buried her with the rest of his past?

She had never felt more dead than she did in that moment. How could she feel this way, if her love for Robert was clearly so alive?

She needed to stay focused on the task at hand. The conversation she'd overheard between Katie and Robert in the garden room had revealed nothing of significance except that they didn't connect Janice to Janeal. At least Robert didn't. As for Katie . . .

Thieving, lying, self-righteous, smug Katie. Janeal couldn't read that woman's mind.

Janeal spent five minutes practicing a deep-breathing exercise her doctor had recommended for the headaches. As her mind settled, she recalled that all her personal items were still hidden in the bathroom. She jerked back into an alert state, hoping Lucille hadn't already gone fishing for her things after finding out about Janeal's money.

While the other women who lived on her hall watched *Survivor* reruns in the common room, Janeal retrieved the collection and returned to her private space. For the time being she would rip a twelve-inch seam out of the side of her cheap mattress and stuff everything in there, then cover it all with the fitted sheet. Not original, but short of burying the stuff in the dry clay outside, it would have to do.

The phone vibrated in Janeal's hand as she slipped it through the gash in the polyester. She pulled it back out and glanced at the number. Not one she recognized. The area code was unfamiliar as well. Certainly no one from New York or D.C. She risked answering it.

"Yes?"

"Janeal Mikkado," a woman's voice said.

Of all the people who had this number, none of them would have known her previous name.

"I'm sorry, I think you have the wrong—"

"Callista Ramirez. It's been awhile."

Janeal recalled with some surprise the blond woman who'd visited her on the mesa with Sanso all those years ago. The one who'd drugged her.

She lowered her voice and pointed it away from her roommates' walls. "How did you get this number?"

"Does it really matter? Jane, Janice, Janeal—Salazar Sanso gets what he wants. He knows where you are and enjoys the game of making you think otherwise."

"Why are you calling?"

"He's on his way to pay you a visit."

"Then he must also know that Robert Lukin is here."

"He does."

"He enjoyed his hospital stay, did he?"

"Look, Janeal—"

"What do you want?"

"I want Salazar back in Mexico, and walking uphill to pound on the DEA's door isn't going to get him there."

"Obviously. You're talking to the wrong person then."

"No, I feel pretty confident about this. I don't know why your boyfriend picked that particular place for his little victory R&R, but I guess you wouldn't have followed him there if you weren't hoping for some sweet reunion yourself. Where is Robert now?"

With Katie, probably. "How should I know?"

"Listen to me. This is the only time you and I will ever have a goal in common. We do not want Salazar on that mountain. But he's coming up there with Robert in his crosshairs."

Bitterness rose in Janeal's throat. "He always was a little extreme in his view of revenge," she said. "There's nothing I can do about that."

"You can convince him Robert's left and that he tipped off his colleagues to Salazar's whereabouts."

"You want me to tell Robert that Sanso's coming? That's not the way to get him back to Mexico, dear."

"Don't be smart. That's not what I said. All I'm asking you to do is lie."

Janeal decided to drop the sarcasm. "Sanso won't believe me."

"He doesn't believe many people, but you seem to be an exception to the rule."

"What's to keep me from tipping off the DEA before Sanso arrives?"

Callista laughed. "I call your bluff. You can't talk to them without implicating yourself. In fact . . . that's interesting. Nothing like a little matter of a million dollars to stand between you and Robert. Does he know?"

"You don't know what you're talking about."

"You still love Robert, don't you?" Callista asked.

"After all these years?" Janeal faked.

"Some loves never die. I'm going to bank on it." The older woman sighed. "Unfortunately, I have to."

"Don't you know by now?" Janeal said. "Hate is more powerful than love, Callista."

"Maybe. I don't care whether you love Robert or hate Salazar more. Find a way to get Salazar back down that hill and I'll guarantee you Robert's safety for as long as I'm alive."

"What about *my* safety?"

"He wouldn't harm a hair on your pretty little head."

"He was ready enough to let me burn to death."

"That changed forever when you turned the tables on him. Are you so blind?"

Katie's the blind one. Katie, who is not Katie, but is . . .

Janeal slammed the lid on that recurring, disturbing thought. This entire mess was Katie's fault. Katie was why they were stuck in this house for losers. Katie was why Robert had fallen out of love with her. Katie was why Janeal felt like she was losing her mind.

Janeal was not entirely sure why Callista had made this call. It wasn't as if Janeal had refused to help Sanso; in fact, based on their latest encounter, she believed that Sanso had interpreted her demands as a type of cooperation. Maybe Callista was operating on her own with this phone call.

Maybe she was worried about something else.

Losing her coveted spot as Sanso's right-hand woman?

Yes, Janeal decided, this was a power play.

She was a pro at such games herself, and happy to participate.

"You can count on me, Callista. Can I count on you?"

"I've been doing this longer than you have, Janeal."

Janeal disconnected the call first to make her point.

The conversation, though pointless in Janeal's mind, had raised an interesting idea. If it was possible that hate was more powerful than love, maybe the answer to her crisis could be found not in loving Robert, which would only frustrate her desire, but in hating Katie.

54

Robert tried to call Hope House repeatedly on his way up the mountain, but no one answered. He recalled Katie saying that she had a staff meeting and hoped that it—not something awful—was the reason for the lack of response.

He turned off the paved road and onto the dirt drive that led to the halfway house at 9:17, having broken a few speed limits. About five hundred yards into the trees he saw the house, lit as normal by porch lights and lamps in the offices and rooms.

Only then did he admit to himself that he had thought the house might be ablaze.

There were four cars in the unpaved lot, which he recognized as the community van and Kia, plus two vehicles owned by residents who had jobs in Santa Fe.

Maybe Sanso had not arrived.

Maybe Robert's mind had made connections that didn't really exist.

He slowed the car as he approached and made the final curve before the lot. His headlights caught something reflective on the opposite side of the drive, and he braked. Put the truck in reverse and backed up until he spotted it again.

A convertible, parked between two pines, top down.

A Mazda Miata, here, hidden.

In a flash of memory Robert remembered passing a car like this on his way down toward Santa Fe. He could not recall the driver.

Robert looked at the house again and decided that Sanso was there, playing a game of stealth this time rather than acting out a pyromaniac's fantasy. Waiting, no doubt, for Robert's return. Which meant that Sanso might prefer hostages over dead bodies. Something to hope for.

Was Janice one of Sanso's lackeys? Had she found Robert here and told the drug lord? How? And what was their connection to Jane Johnson's car? Robert didn't have the time to sort any of this out, but the sense that Janice knew Robert and that he ought to know her continued to gnaw at him.

Robert cut the lights and the engine and decided to leave the truck right where it was, blocking Sanso's exit. He retrieved his firearm from under the seat and climbed out of the cab, then retrieved a spare bulletproof vest from the tool kit suspended across the truck bed.

He did a quick scan of the convertible and found nothing that tied the car to Sanso. But keys dangled from the convertible's ignition, and he took those too.

His hiking boots sounded loud on the coarse red dirt as he approached the house's long porch. He stepped up onto the concrete slab and looked through each window that he passed, gun out and pointed down, trying to gather as much information as he could. Most of the curtains had been drawn. The office that he believed to be Lucille's was brightly lit but empty. No sign in any of the front rooms of Sanso or the staff.

Robert began to build a strategy in his mind. He decided to find Katie first, hoping that Janice had no connection to her that would explain why Sanso had come here of all places. Secure Katie's safety, then find out where Janice's room was.

He slipped in through the front entry and listened for voices that would indicate a meeting. When he didn't hear anything, he moved across the atrium and adjacent hall and into the garden room. Two table lamps had been left on, and he saw the rear door ajar. He wondered if Katie had returned.

In the hall again, he caught a sound in the direction of the kitchen. Cups being set out on the counter maybe. He entered from the back, under the plaque about God's protection from enemies, and judged by the tenor of voices that if they were in any danger, they didn't know it.

The five women on staff, including Katie, were gathered on stools around the kitchen island, sipping coffee and flipping through notebooks and talking in low, happy tones. Lucille jumped up at the sight of him, almost knocking her stool backward.

She recovered quickly. "If you'd give us a few more minutes we'll be finished and you can—"

One of the other women gasped at the sight of Robert's gun. Katie stood and said, "What is it?" Robert thought she had gone pale.

"You've got an intruder on the grounds," he said to Lucille. Two of the women started murmuring.

"One of our girls probably brought someone home," said the one he thought was Frankie. She stood and took one more sip of coffee. "I'll find out who."

Robert held up a hand to stop Frankie at the same time Lucille said, "Whoever it is, I'm sure a gun isn't necessary, Lukin."

He ignored her. "Katie, I need you to explain to your colleagues who Salazar Sanso is." Her hand went to her mouth. "And then I want you all to go outside. Take a flashlight. Start walking out to the road and stay there until I come get you."

Someone said, "The residents—"

"Are safest in their own rooms for now."

"One of us needs to stay with them," Katie said.

"All of you will go. And you'd better be the first one out that door, Katie." Robert left no room for argument, but he didn't know whether she would actually do it. "Tell me where Janice's room is."

"What?"

"The woman who arrived today. I think she might be connected to Sanso. Or me."

"She's at the end of my wing. Room 28."

"I think Janice is using an alias. That she goes by the name of Jane Johnson and that somehow I should know who that is. You ever heard of a Jane Johnson?"

Katie shook her head.

"Go with them and I'll come get you. How many women are here tonight?"

"Nineteen," Lucille said.

"How many on your hall, Katie?"

"Six."

"Okay. Sheriff's on his way. Go on and leave now."

He headed toward Katie's wing without waiting for them to obey, hoping they had a strong enough sense of self-preservation to do what they were told.

Salazar Sanso. For fifteen years she had hidden from him behind the identity of a woman he couldn't possibly care about. How had he found her? Why was he here, on the heels of Robert and Janice? He couldn't possibly know her true identity.

Unless . . . Sanso wasn't here for her. He was here for Janice. For Janeal Mikkado. The one Janeal Mikkado he knew about.

Sanso's presence became the deciding factor Katie needed, confirmation that there were two Janeal Mikkados walking the earth at the same time. As it had the night of the fire, the moment she chose to save Katie's life, all her indecision faded away.

Right now, the only thing she couldn't understand was why the drama was unfolding in this simple little desert home, where she had finally extracted a purpose from her reborn life.

Frankie was practically yelling at her. "I said *who* is this man he's ranting about?"

Katie turned slowly toward Frankie's voice. "He's a drug dealer."

"And what's your involvement with him?" Lucille asked.

No answer was brief enough for the time they had. "I'm not involved with him. We need to get the women out."

"Wendy and Trish have already gone for them."

"I need my cell phone," Katie said. She walked out the kitchen door.

"Katie," Lucille protested.

"I'm the only one who's got one," Katie said without looking back. "I told you we'd need it someday."

Right now, Katie didn't care that she was right. She was more concerned with Sanso's arrival, and why Robert thought he was here. How was she going to explain all this when she barely understood it herself?

Was there any reasonable explanation for what had happened to her? No. There was only the spiritual at work here. A battle of unearthly, paranormal proportions.

A battle between the light and dark halves of a heart.

Now, as she raced toward her room, grief over losing the real Katie overcame her in a fresh wave, because now she feared she was likely to lose Janice too. The other Janeal, her mystic twin, who had listened to Sanso's lies again and again until they became her truth and he became her master.

Janice, not Katie, was the one who needed saving now. After she found her phone, she would find her other self.

55

Sanso was coming.

What did he think he would do? Knock on the front door and ask to see her?

Janeal took short, agitated breaths and linked her hands atop her head as though that might stop it from floating away. These side effects of the Fioricet only bothered her when she took her doses too close together. The atypical stress she was under might have something to do with it too.

So this was what it felt like to slip off the edge of sanity into a black, overwhelming river of doubt.

What to do about Sanso?

What to do about . . . *Katie*?

Janeal growled like an angry cat and took three long steps to the window. She needed air, but her hands shook so badly she almost couldn't get the stubborn thing open. When the sash finally lifted, squeaking, Janeal half expected Katie—blind but bionic-eared—to come ask her what all the ruckus was. When Katie didn't knock, Janeal lifted out the dusty screen and slipped out the window. The mountain air, free of city exhaust and eastern humidity, renewed Janeal.

She couldn't wander too far from the house, as it was her only source of light and she didn't know the area. But she stayed to the nearby shadows cast by evergreens, stepping slowly to avoid turning her ankle on some rock or impaling herself on a cactus.

Slowly, Janeal's heart rate calmed and her breathing deepened. Her poise returned. Out here, at least, she could formulate a plan.

She wished Callista had said how long it would take Sanso to get here.

Sanso wanted Robert. Janeal had Katie, a wild card, an element of surprise.

Would Sanso negotiate with her? She doubted it. Why would he care at all that Katie had lived?

But Janeal cared. She cared with a passion that surprised her.

It could mean that Robert would be lost to her forever. That he had fallen in love with someone who reminded him of both Katie's goodness and Janeal's strength and would never cast a glance at another woman. It could mean that Janeal's resuscitated love for Robert would be stolen away by this version of herself whose best qualities—humility, modesty, isolation, servitude—were far beneath Janeal's aspirations.

She hated Katie.

Janeal had everything, had always secured everything she'd ever wanted. Everything but the man she had loved from childhood. Why would she treat Katie differently than she would treat any other woman in this kind of scenario? She'd routed plenty in her conquest of Milan. There was never enough room for two women in one man's life. Never.

The emotion that was birthed in Janeal's heart at that moment was unlike any she had experienced before. It was a kind of self-hatred she could not describe. A jealous loathing of a woman who was her but not her.

Not her, not her.

But Janeal couldn't make her denial stick.

There was a period in Janeal's life when this nighttime hour was her favorite part of the day, when she'd seek out the solitude of a high-desert night and climb to the top of that mesa overlooking her father's camp. Somehow the environment, noisy in its own way with crickets and scuttling bugs and night foragers, quieted the restless frustration of her own heart.

But tonight even this peaceful place could not penetrate the hardness of Janeal's heart.

She moved around the house to a hidden spot where she could see the parking area in front, then found a rock and sat. Waited. Listened. Maybe she could recapture some of the peace she remembered if she tried hard enough. She heard a breeze through foliage. A squirrel or raccoon shimmying up a tree. Branches cracking. Close.

It remained for her to decide what interest Sanso might have in Katie, and if Janeal could strategically negotiate to rearrange the pairings in her favor: Janeal and Robert. Sanso and Katie.

She sensed the warmth of a body behind her at the same time that a hand snaked around her face and yanked her back into someone's firm chest. She gasped, her shout muffled by the palm, and started thrashing to free herself. Instead she managed only to get herself turned around to face this person. She was not strong enough to break free of the hands that now gripped her by each bicep and yanked her close.

Her fists and arms, bent at the elbows, were all that separated her from Sanso's handsome face. His skin smelled faintly of fish and lemons. She relaxed. He sensed her muscles yield.

"You realize now there is nowhere you can go to hide from me," he whispered.

"I knew you were coming."

"And yet you wanted to come here without me. You wanted to be alone with your old flame." His breath blew on Janeal's forehead as he spoke. She closed her eyes and could feel his body quivering.

"No," she whispered, not immediately sure why she had denied it. It had something to do with self-preservation, and with protecting Robert. It was true enough that he wasn't the first reason she had come to this place. "I didn't come here for him."

"You'll have to prove it to me. I'm a jealous lover."

She didn't feel the need to argue with the title he had bestowed upon himself. Her terror of him had vanished. For the first time, she saw him as more of an equal than an adversary. This time, for once, she sensed she was a step ahead of him.

Sanso pulled Janeal in and kissed her on the mouth, gently at first but with increasing force until she could barely breathe. His breath muddied her head, caused her mind and muscles to soften until she couldn't quite remember what it was she needed to accomplish.

Sanso let her mouth go and kept hold of her arms.

"Prove it to me," he said again. "Give me Robert and show me where your love really lies."

She focused on clearing her head, on staying in charge of this confrontation. "You think that if I give you Robert, you will have finally conquered me."

His eyebrows shot up, and he didn't contradict her.

"I'm sorry to disappoint you, but Robert isn't here," she said.

Sanso's mouth parted slightly.

"Like I said, I didn't come here for him."

"Then why are you here?" Sanso asked.

"There is someone else."

"You're a bad, busy girl."

Janeal allowed herself a flirtatious smile.

Sanso shook Janeal with such force that her head snapped back, then her chin hit her chest. She'd been here before, with Milan, when the possession of power began to change hands. Sanso jerked her body toward his again and he pressed his cheek against her temple. The diamond stud in his ear grazed her skin.

"It seems someone else has made promises that you think might be more valuable than mine."

"Why do you care?"

"Because I want you with me and no one else. No. One. Else. I will have you for my very own."

"I'm out of your reach. I have been since the night of the fire."

"That's only what you think. You've been under my thumb since that night. You're lonely and miserable. Your life is worthless without me."

Janeal wriggled out of his grasp. "I've made my own way without you. I don't need you."

"But you need this other person?" He raised his voice and Janeal feared someone would come out of the house to identify the shouting. "*Tell me* who it is."

"Katie Morgon." She steadied her gaze. "The girl you chained to the stool and left me to die with."

Sanso's teeth showed through a wide grin. "Ah yes. The girl *you* left to die—she survived?" He sent a sigh toward the stars. "She's found you and wants her revenge."

Janeal was happy to have him believe it.

"She'll kill me if someone doesn't kill her first."

"Please. Allow me."

PART III

Blaze of Glory

56

Katie Morgon. That she and Janeal had both survived his inferno amused Sanso to no end. What remarkable women to have bested him in his younger, more devilish years. Killing her would be all the more rewarding now, because her death would secure Janeal Mikkado as his. Forever.

A promise of new life shot into his old veins. Janeal might keep him going another decade at least. Based on what details Sanso had gathered about Jane Johnson, she had nearly arrived at his level. He was so eager to welcome her fully. She alone had a mind to match his. A spirit as diabolical as his, willing at every opportunity to sacrifice someone else to save her own skin.

That was, truly, Sanso's primary interest in Robert. He was the Jesus to Janeal's Judas. Her treatment of Robert would be the indicator of how far Janeal had sunk since the day she first abandoned the Morgon girl.

Sanso dropped into the darkness of Katie Morgon's room from the unlocked window. Janeal closed it behind him and stayed outside. He didn't have to hide if he didn't want to. He could do this with the lights on if it suited him.

He left the lights off and chose to stand in the closet behind one of two sliding panels that she had left open. When she closed her bedroom door, it would be easy enough for him to step out and draw the nylon ligature across her throat. There would be no need for the mess or noise of the gun he carried in a holster at his waist.

So few things in his life were this easy.

Janeal raced back toward the open window of her own room. Better to be there than anywhere else when this sheltered little house exploded. She shivered, but she wasn't cold. Her nerves rattled with the uncertainty of what she had asked Sanso to do.

If Katie dies, will I?

Of course I won't. We are separate. Even if we are . . . the same.

She had foolishly allowed her overstressed mind to lose sight of the end goal. She could come back to earth now that Sanso was here. With Katie out of Janeal's life, it would become simple again: no fear of exposure, no fear of betrayal, no competition for Robert. As the minutes passed, she calmed. Sanso was obsessed with her, which would make it easier for her to control him—an important detail, because Sanso had discovered her identity as Jane Johnson, a wrinkle she had hoped to prevent. But such a small wrinkle.

So small, compared to this unfathomable encounter with Katie. Temporary encounter. Janeal could not hold her hands steady. She fumbled with the window screen. It must be temporary. If it was temporary, then it would never matter if it was real.

The death of Katie Morgon wouldn't be too much for him, she hoped. She had never meant to hurt Robert, and that would be her main regret of this unfortunate dilemma.

She certainly didn't want him dead. Yet Sanso would see to it that Robert died as soon as possible, and his twisted love for her would almost certainly correlate with the amount of pain he'd inflict on her until he took Robert's life too.

She stepped out of the mesquite trees and had her right leg slung over the sill of her open window when it occurred to her that she could kill Sanso. He would take Katie's life and escape the same way he entered, expecting Janeal to be in her room or in his car.

Not standing there waiting for him in the dark.

What would she use as a weapon?

She was running through a mental list of options—a knife from the kitchen, a rock from the hillside, a gun from Robert's truck (he would travel armed, wouldn't he?)—when the door to her room opened.

Katie's wing was on the south side of the house, isolated from the main living areas and the other residents on the north side. Robert touched the numbers on her apartment, 21, which stood at the top of the hall. Beyond it, three rooms flanked each side of the carpet runner, which led to a seventh room at the end. Number 28. A light shone out from under the door.

He approached silently and put his hand on the knob and his ear to the hollow-core panel. No sound. He eased the door open, gun up and ready, expecting Janice to scream or to bolt free of Sanso's threatening—

The room was empty. Robert swept it anyway, starting with the closet. One pair of pants on a hanger. One T-shirt on the bed. A flat denim tote bag on the floor. He lifted the blankets off the mattress, then the mattress off the cot. Nothing. He dropped the mattress back onto the springs and it bounced once.

Something hit the ground and rolled, rattling. Robert picked it up. A translucent brown pill bottle prescribed to Jane Johnson. Fioricet. Prescription painkiller. He pocketed it to show Katie.

Who are you, Jane Johnson? What do you have to hide?

He stepped back out into the hall and closed the door, eyeing the other rooms. Light spilled out from under five of them, casting narrow bands of gold onto the carpet runner. Two were black: one on the left, and Katie's room.

If he were looking for a place to hide, it wouldn't be in the light with strangers.

He pushed open the unoccupied room and flipped on the overhead bulb. The room was so spare that a spider couldn't have hidden in it. He checked the closet. Four wire hangers shifted and chimed together in the vacuum created by the opening door. He checked the window. Locked.

At the sound of feet running and then a doorknob turning, Robert shot out into the hall, head turned toward Janice's door. It was closed. He snapped his head and gun in the other direction.

Katie was opening the door to her room.

"What on earth are you doing?" Robert said past a clenched jaw. In two steps he was next to her, pulling her away.

"I wanted to be able to contact you," she whispered, yanking her arm out of his and reaching for her knob again. "My cell phone—"

Robert blocked her and used his body to direct Katie into the unoccupied room. "Do what I say this time and don't come out until I come get you myself."

"I'm fully aware—"

"Have you forgotten what Sanso did the last time we met him?" He was angry that she had risked coming down here. No, furious. "Don't be an idiot, Katie. Don't go where I can't find you, like last time."

She confronted him with her confident face, and Robert was pricked with some guilt for having spoken so cruelly of the night they lost their families.

"I'm not the idiot in this situation, Robert."

He flipped off the light and pulled the door closed with as little noise as possible, shutting her in the room.

A hard-soled shoe connected with Robert's armpit, sending currents of pain across his rib cage and down into his elbow. He spun to face the direction of the attack while he reeled. The gun he held flew upward and hit hard, raining down a shower of curd-shaped ceiling texture into his hair.

His head cracked into the doorframe, splitting the wood at the same time he heard the gun land. Katie cried out from inside.

"Don't open the door!" he shouted.

He lunged in the direction of the gun but misjudged, kicking it with his toe. It skittered down the hall between the carpet runner and baseboard.

Another kick landed in Robert's stomach before his defensive training found its footing. He successfully blocked a blow aimed for his face, then lashed out with his fists, having no clear idea what he was aiming at, hoping speed if not accuracy would count for something.

It did. His knuckles hit teeth, which broke open the skin on the back of his hand.

Robert was familiar with the streak of Spanish curses that ensued. He'd found Salazar Sanso.

The man's ankles swept Robert's out from under him and he fell sideways. He lifted his arms instinctively and landed sprawled out. He scrabbled out of Sanso's reach to get up, leaving Katie's door exposed.

Doors were opening on the hall. A woman screamed.

"Stay inside!" Robert's thundering voice was chased by the sound of panels slamming into their frames.

He registered Sanso's form coming down on him, knees first. They caught him in the ribs and knocked his wind out. Robert shuddered.

Sanso leveled a gun between his eyes and Robert would have resigned himself to an immediate death if not for Sanso's fantastic hubris: the criminal could never resist an opportunity to boast.

Robert dragged air into his lungs.

"You're not . . . the one I was looking for," said Sanso between breaths.

"Who then?" Robert's arms were pinned under Sanso's knees. His head was pointed toward Janice's door, but his gun was closer to Katie's. There was no way he could get to it. He saw blood on Sanso's shirt. From the gunshot wound Robert had given him back in Arizona? It could prove to be a weakness.

Sanso used his free arm to wipe sweat off his forehead. "You'll do." The hall had fallen silent except for their voices.

"You're here with Janice."

"Who?"

"Jane Johnson."

Sanso laughed. "Yes. Jane Johnson. She's why I came."

"Who is she?"

"An old flame." He sniffed. "Of yours."

Robert measured his strength by squeezing his hands into fists. "What do you mean?"

"You'll be sur—" A gunshot obliterated Sanso's answer, and a spatter of blood hit Robert's cheek at the same time the Sheetrock next to his head exploded. The concussion of the shot lifted Robert's hair off the side of his skull. The drug lord's face changed from smug to pained, and he dropped his weapon. He shouted and rolled off Robert, clutching his right shoulder, finding his feet and staggering toward room 28. Another shot rang out. Robert covered his head.

The sound of cracking wood was followed by a tumble of toppling furniture.

Robert's strength surged and he bolted upright. The gun Sanso dropped lay at his side. He seized it and raised it in the direction of the shots and found himself looking down the barrel at Katie, who held Robert's lost firearm level and steady.

Katie. He pushed himself off the floor and she trained the gun on the sound of his movements. "Robert? Robert?"

"It's me. Put that down!" He kept an eye on her gun.

"Did he hit you?"

"No." He grabbed her at the wrist and disarmed her. She could have killed him. He didn't try to hide his accusation. "But you might have. What were you thinking?"

"I was thinking he was about to kill you," she said, matching his frustration. "I aimed for his voice. I couldn't have missed that voice."

57

At daybreak, Janeal curled up in a fetal position on her cot, gripping the sides of her head, facing the wall. Her brain seemed to be on fire, and she had no pills. Robert was such an opportunist; she'd watched him go through her things and take the pill bottle as she stood outside the window. How long would it take him now to find out who Jane Johnson was?

What happened last night was so far from what she had envisioned that she couldn't think straight. She couldn't sleep. She was a walking zombie. Her empty stomach heaved at the thought of food. But this confusion was only temporary. Soon she would have another plan.

Sanso had broken down her door and tumbled out her open window, landing at her feet, at the same moment sirens lit the main driveway with screaming light. She didn't wait to ask him what he would do; this mess was his to fix. She'd raced for the garden room door and made a show of emerging from the library as the entire house lit up with officers and frightened women.

Robert put himself at the center of their activity. He insisted on being present for every interview and also insisted that Katie not leave his side. He allowed local law enforcement to do its job while keeping his finger in this pie as an authoritative, relevant party.

He had stared at Janeal for the duration of her ten-minute interview. She tried to keep her head down, her eyes averted. She lost her focus several times, lost her words, lost her confidence and could only hope it came across as trauma.

To Robert, though, she believed it came across as revelation. His eyes bored into her skull like laser beams, igniting her latest, unbending pain. He knew she was not Janice, and yet he didn't ask her a single question. Was he protecting her?

She could leave now, as the chaos of the evening dissipated in the dawning sun. But if she left, she would have to utterly vanish, as she had the first time, fifteen years ago. Jane Johnson would have to disappear and Janeal Mikkado would have to start a new life all over again as yet another woman.

After all that she'd accomplished!

As Janeal's headache intensified, her hatred for Katie grew. The sense of fury that welled up in Janeal was unexpected and inexplicable. This woman who should have died in that fire had lived to take it all back—Janeal's mementos, Janeal's one true love, Janeal's carefully constructed life.

Katie Morgon should be twice dead by now.

She heard women coming down the hall, talking in low voices. Breakfast would have ended by now. The scene had been cleared about two hours ago. Janeal got up, rode out a wave of nausea, and pressed her ear to the door. They paused right outside her room, presumably because they occupied the shoe boxes on each side of her.

". . . off-site," one said.

"Why?"

"To keep her from having a breakdown I guess. Or maybe they're worried someone will retaliate and come after her."

"So they're going to hide her?"

"I think they want her to have some space. I know I wouldn't want to look at that bloodstain right outside my door."

"She's blind, remember?"

"Still."

"I can't believe she almost killed someone."

"Well it's lucky for you she scared him off. Who knows how many of us that creep might have taken out?"

"Where are they taking her?"

"Some top-secret bunker? How should I know?"

Janeal withdrew her ear. Katie was leaving. And Robert was probably going with her. Who knew where Sanso had gone? If he found Katie before she did, he'd kill Robert too. She had to move quickly.

As quickly as possible under the weight of this staggering headache.

She cursed Robert for having taken her relief.

In thirty seconds she loaded her tote bag with her few items and walked out of her room, heading in the direction of the first morning class she was supposed to attend, which was three doors on the other side of Lucille's office.

Which happened to be empty when she passed. She paused, leaned inside the entry, and checked out the key hooks hanging above the bookcase.

A single key still hung under *Kia*.

Janeal lifted it swiftly and dropped it into her tote. After Katie left, she'd follow.

The morning sun was still cresting the tops of the trees when Robert attempted to help belt Katie into the Hope House van and closed the passenger door. She yanked the buckle out of his hands and held on to it while she argued.

"It's unnecessary to whisk me away like some damsel in distress."

"I told you she'd buck," Lucille said from the driver's seat.

"Getting you out of here makes sense," Robert said. "Don't take it personally. I'd do whatever I had to to protect anyone in your shoes."

"What if I'm not the one who needs protection? He could have come for you, or for—"

"Sanso came out of your apartment. He left a ligature inside the door. He might have choked you."

"He couldn't have known it was my room."

Robert closed the van door and leaned in through the open window. "Let's argue about what he was really up to later, okay?"

Katie frowned and continued to turn the diamond ring on her hand as she had for the past several hours.

Lucille held on to the steering wheel, looking softer than Robert had seen her this week.

"My guys will be here in another hour," he said to Lucille. "I need to walk them through their investigation and then I'll come down." He reached out to tuck Katie's hair behind her ear, hoping it would be a comforting gesture. She withdrew, and Robert found her irritation endearing. Strong woman.

"Thanks for what you did last night." He could offer her that much, now that it was over and they had emerged unscathed.

She lowered her eyes and buckled in.

Lucille reached across Katie and gave Robert a sheet of paper. "Here's directions," she said. "I wouldn't take her there if I didn't think it was the best place for her to be."

"Will she rest?"

"I'll rest. No need to talk about me like I'm not here."

"I'm sending an officer to follow you and set up camp until I can get there. I don't want Katie anywhere near this place."

Lucille's face hardened. "Lukin, if you have put my girls in any more danger than they've already experienced—"

"I will surrender my hide to you myself. Try not to worry, Lucille. A half-way house is the last place in the world most of these people want to be. Their sights won't be on you."

Robert turned to Katie. "Try to sleep. I'll come as soon as I can." She nodded and he stepped back from the van and leaned against the Kia's hood while Lucille pulled out.

Back in the house, he turned down the first hall that led to Janice's room and pulled out his cell phone. He withdrew Jane Johnson's prescription bottle from his shirt pocket. It had cracked during his confrontation with Sanso, and the lid no longer stayed snug. But the pharmacy label was still intact.

Itching to finally confront Janice now that the locals had gone back to their precinct, he called Harlan. He needed more information about this woman.

Sanso said she was an old flame. That was a riddle Robert would have a hard time cracking, considering he didn't recognize Janice. He'd dated only a handful of women in the last fifteen years. She didn't look a thing like any of them.

Although . . .

She bore some similarities to Janeal Mikkado. But it would be like his mind to play that kind of a trick on him, wouldn't it? He'd been thrown forcefully back into his past since arresting Sanso. Maybe this was another one of Sanso's games, a low and dirty trick.

"Any leads on Jane Johnson yet?"

"Our guys out there tell me the address she used to rent her car turned out to be bogus, and the credit card goes to a PO box in Manhattan. But your friendly neighborhood pharmacist was more helpful."

Robert tapped the bottle with his finger, rattling the pills.

"The meds are for chronic migraines. Our guys in New York went to her address, a swanky Broadway apartment, but no one answered. Neighbor said the Jane Johnson who lives there works for *All Angles* magazine. You ever read that?"

Robert's mind had already left the conversation and gone in search of something Brian Hoffer had said during their drive up to the house. Something about the publication being interested in Katie.

"I don't suppose the warrant covered a search of her home."

"No way, nohow."

"You check out the magazine offices?"

"Yeah. She's one of their power players. Her personal assistant says she's on medical leave. Went down to Bethesda for some testing or a clinical trial or something. We're looking into it."

Bethesda, his foot.

"Did you get a physical description?"

"About five-nine, one twenty-five, age thirty-two. Auburn hair, dark brown eyes. You think she could be your mystery resident?"

"The height and weight fit, but not much else. Janice looks older."

"I'll send a photo to your phone."

"I'll look for it."

Robert clapped the phone shut and proceeded down the hall. Time for Janice to explain a few things.

Her door was standing open when he arrived. The room was empty, not only of her, but of her things. He saw the fitted sheet peeled off one corner of the mattress and lifted the pad off the cot. A torn edge and loose filling suggested that something had recently been pulled out of it.

The pants hanging in the closet were gone.

Robert headed toward the rooms where the morning sessions were being held. He passed Frankie, who carried an armload of linens, and asked if she'd seen Janice. She shook her head.

Classroom 1: no Janice.

She was not in the library either, where the other meeting took place.

Robert checked the garden room, the bathrooms, Lucille and Katie's office, then glanced out the window at the parking lot. The Kia was gone.

Who was driving it?

Only staff members were authorized to drive the community cars, and all five—

His phone chirped to alert him to the arrival of a photograph. Half certain that the Kia was in the possession of one Jane Johnson, Robert ran to his truck, forced his key into the ignition, and swung the truck into a reverse arc that put it on the winding dirt road down the mountain.

Holding his phone on the top of the steering wheel, Robert punched through his menu options to retrieve the new photo. A circling clock indicated it was loading. His eyes flickered to the road, then back.

The two-inch display wasn't designed for high-resolution digital images, but the face that appeared there could have been a fax of a postage stamp and he would have recognized it. Robert hit the brakes to prevent his shock from taking him off the edge of a curve, then pulled over and stopped.

Janeal Mikkado was as beautiful as a thirtysomething as she'd ever been as a teenager, with that stunning auburn hair, cropped to her shoulders in this photo. Smiling brown eyes, full lips, wide-set cheekbones. Robert stared until the phone's battery saver caused the photo to blink out.

He called the image back up.

How had she survived too? Why hadn't she tried to find him?

Why had she taken another name? Janeal was Jane Johnson . . .

. . . who was Janice.

Who was connected, in ways he didn't understand until now, to Salazar Sanso.

She had betrayed them all. And she would do it again to preserve this deal she had struck with the devil.

Robert let his phone close as his ire increased. He pulled back onto the road. He saw it now, the similarity between Janice and the teenager who had been buried so long in his own mind. If Janice had smiled even once, that might have made her artificially blue eyes and dull hair color look like the Halloween costume that they were.

He wanted to sob and scream at the same time. He found himself capable of nothing more than squeezing his phone and the steering wheel in a death grip. The truck moved down the dirt road at an unsafe speed.

He opened the phone again and punched in Katie's cell number, but she didn't answer. Given all the events of the previous night, Katie probably never retrieved her phone from her room, and Lucille didn't carry one. The women had been gone at least ten minutes. He checked the Google map Lucille had printed out for him. Their destination was listed as twenty-four minutes away. He accelerated and looked at his useless cell phone.

He called Harlan again.

"What can you do to find me a cell phone number for Jane Johnson?" he asked.

Harlan didn't have a quick answer.

"Someone at the FBI?" Robert prodded.

"I'll see what I can do," Harlan said.

"You've got ten minutes."

"Hey, you're talking to your superior, buddy." And Harlan belly laughed.

Robert couldn't laugh with him. "Then don't let me keep you."

When he hit Highway 68, he turned north toward Taos, exceeding speed limits by at least twenty-five miles per hour. If he was lucky the highway patrol would be elsewhere today.

He hoped and hoped that Lucille was a law-abiding driver, and that Janeal was following at a distance that would help him to find her before she caught Katie. It was clear enough that Janeal was following her. The only question he couldn't answer was why.

He waited for his phone to ring, doubting Harlan would be able to put him in touch with Janeal in time.

58

Janeal concentrated on the van that carried Katie, pondering the idea that she was chasing herself.

What a silly idea. A lunatic idea. But she indulged in it a moment, allowed herself to feel intrigue rather than repulsion and fear. What laws of the universe had to have been violated for such a split to take place? What were the long-term consequences of such coexistence?

Janeal had not been joking with Alan when she said this world did not need two of her in it. And if Katie really was Janeal, it was to be expected that this whole public-servant act was merely part of a larger scheme to gain the upper hand in the world.

Katie would be competition. For more than Robert.

Lunatic or not, Janeal believed she must approach Katie in this way, as competition, from here forward.

She was slightly concerned that Lucille might see her in the rearview mirror, so she hung back as far as she dared, keeping two or three cars between them as the van headed into Taos. This strategy worked until they arrived in the small mountain town and Lucille turned off the main highway into the residential areas.

She let the van move ahead as far as she dared through the forested properties, which were large and buffered from each other by generous acreage marked off by split-rail fences and narrow gravel drives. Whenever Lucille made a turn, Janeal accelerated through the corners, worried she might lose her at another turn before the Kia caught up.

She almost did lose them once, at the end, when Janeal took a corner onto an empty street. She swore under her breath, afraid to have come this far without another way to find out where Lucille was going. She raced to each cross street, hoping for a glimpse of the van. Janeal was rewarded a half mile later, when she spotted the burly vehicle pulling into a long driveway. The van rounded a bend, to the front of the house, Janeal presumed.

After a few seconds of deliberation, Janeal directed the Kia past the gravel driveway at a crawl. She spotted the van, parked near the front door of a small log cabin. They must have gone inside. Outside the fence, a mailbox told her the house number. She made note of the street, took a U-turn another quarter mile down the lane, and mentally mapped her way back to the highway.

At a gas station perched at the edge of the busy road, Janeal pulled off and took out her cell phone. She scrolled through her list of calls received until she found the number she was looking for, then dialed out.

A woman answered. "Who is this?"

"Janeal Mikkado."

"Why are you calling?"

"Where is Sanso?"

"As if I would give that information to you."

"Callista, I made you a promise that I intend to keep."

"He's with me now, so I release you from your worthless promise."

"But *he* still has a promise to keep for *me*."

"I don't care."

"When he's of sound enough mind to care himself, we'll be right back where we started."

Callista did not reply to that.

"He told you about Katie Morgon?" Janeal asked.

"He finds that *funny*. The humor practically killed him." She said it slightly off of the mouthpiece, as if talking to him. Janeal pictured a shadowy, unsanitary dive and some rough-jawed bartender stitching up Sanso's gunshot wound with whiskey and an upholstery needle. It would serve him right.

"Katie has left Hope House," Janeal said. The line was still live, and Callista still mute, so she continued, "Tell Sanso I expect him to finish what he started. I have an address."

"Give it to me."

"First, I need you to get me a hotel room in Taos. I want you to reserve it in your name, because Robert will have his friends looking for me. How far are you and Sanso from Taos?"

"A couple hours."

"Hours?"

"We couldn't exactly patch him up in Santa Fe, now, could we?"

"When will he be ready to go?"

"When he says he is."

"Make a decision, Callista. I need to know when you're going to be here."

The woman sighed. "Give us until tomorrow night."

Tomorrow night? Janeal would have to come up with a plan to get Robert out of Katie's company by then. They'd be joined at the hip otherwise.

An idea came to her.

"Fine. Make my reservation for two nights. Call me when you have it booked."

Janeal hung up and considered that she needed to move the Kia off the main drag. She might have to ditch it completely, as it wouldn't take long for the Hope House staff to notice it missing and Robert to connect its disappearance to her.

She was contemplating the best way to do this without stranding herself when her phone rang. She checked the ID, having let numerous calls go to voice mail during the last couple days, and didn't recognize the number. She didn't answer. Seconds after it went to her voice mail, the phone rang again. Same number.

This pattern repeated itself two more times. She would have shut off the phone if she wasn't awaiting Callista's call. As it was, whoever couldn't live without the sound of her voice would block Callista from coming through at all.

The fifth time the number rang in, Janeal lost her patience.

"Who is this?" she snapped.

"Robert Lukin."

Janeal swallowed, having expected anyone but him. She calculated what posture he expected her to take in this conversation. Without knowing precisely what Robert knew, she was lost.

"Who?" she said lamely.

"Is this Jane Johnson?" he asked.

Go with the flow. "Yes."

"But you're Janice Regan."

Janeal groaned inwardly. "I'm sorry. Do I know you?"

"You knew me once, but I can't say I know you anymore. Janeal Mikkado."

Janeal's breath left her. She almost hung up the phone but sensed he would only call back.

"I don't know what you're—"

"Don't you dare pretend not to know what I mean. Lying to your best friends about who you are is exactly the kind of thing you'd do after fifteen years of practice. You're Janeal all right. You're Janeal to the nth degree."

She couldn't see any way out except via a road she had navigated many, many times over her life since leaving the *kumpanía*: the road that put her in control of the conversation.

"I'm sorry, Robert."

"For what? For pretending? For bringing Sanso to Katie's door and almost getting her killed? For slinking away while your family went up in flames and letting us think you were *dead*?"

Janeal closed her eyes. "You didn't know Katie was alive either."

"Katie has a pretty good excuse. What's yours?"

"Sanso took me, Robert. He killed my father and took me and threatened to kill Katie if I didn't come with him. He . . . he shot Dad and tied Katie to a chair and set the building on fire. I didn't have a choice."

"We always have a choice."

Her anger flared. "Well what would you have done?"

Robert dropped the volume of his voice slightly. "You tell me."

"He promised," Janeal said. "Sanso promised to let her go, but I . . . I never saw her. Callista told me Katie burned to death."

"No one thought she survived."

"I died too, Robert. I thought I had lost everything." She strained her voice as much as possible. "Including you. Seeing you yesterday . . ."

"How long were you with Sanso?" he asked.

"Two years. I was his prisoner." Would he believe her?

"How'd you get out?"

She imagined him in this mode with some of the drug dealers he had brought down. It irked her that he might place her in the same category of people who needed a full inquisition.

"Very long story."

Neither of them said anything for a moment.

"Did Katie tell you how she got out?" Janeal asked through conjured tears.

"She doesn't like to talk about that night much." This information gave Janeal some relief. At least Robert's anger didn't stem from some revelation of her guilt in everything. She wondered if Robert had questioned Katie's identity in the way she did.

Of course not. Why would he, if she didn't talk about that night much? Maybe she didn't talk about herself much.

Talk about herself. Janeal almost laughed at that.

Maybe she really was going nuts.

"I'm sure you don't like to talk about it either." She was intentionally open-ended, believing that he would tell her as much or as little as he wanted.

He said nothing.

"But you escaped okay," she prodded.

"Define *okay*."

"Robert, this is so hard for me. I wish I had known. I would have done anything. For you, for Katie . . ."

"You could have found me if you wanted to."

Was it an accusation? Janeal blinked and opted for defensiveness.

"How? How could I have done that, with the DEA practically setting you up in a witness protection program? Sanso has eyes . . . everywhere. If I had gone back to New Mexico, he would have followed me, found me . . ."

"So instead you changed your name and took a high-profile job in New York City, where you'd be in the public eye."

"Why are you so angry with me?"

"Maybe because I'm just now discovering that you walked away without looking back. I can't imagine it was that hard for you. You never wanted to stay in that camp anyway—"

"What else could I have done?"

"Wasn't it the perfect opportunity for you to get out into the big world, have some sugar daddy to pave your way?"

"Robert."

He took a deep breath. "When did you find out about Katie and me?"

"When you arrested Sanso. I contacted Brian Hoffer about doing a story—"

She caught herself. If Brian had explained anything about the story to Robert, she might have tipped her hand.

She filled her cheeks with air and then let it go.

He didn't seem to notice. "He told me you called the story off," Robert said.

"When I realized who we were talking about, I did. To put you and Katie in the spotlight like that—Sanso already had his eyes on you, and then he escaped."

Her lies were spinning out more easily than she anticipated.

"So why didn't you come? Why didn't you call the house, tell Katie everything, get us together? You went to a lot of trouble with that getup of yours. Why?"

"I had a flight booked when the news about Sanso's escape broke. It wasn't too hard to guess that he'd go searching for you right away. And if I showed up looking like Janeal . . ."

"Did he know you as Jane?"

"No. But my appearance hadn't changed much. I lost some weight, gained a few lines on my face."

Robert's tone softened. "That hair color is terrible."

"It works."

"Maybe you should have stayed in New York. Waited him out."

"I had to at least see you. And Katie." She tinted her words with worry. "I can't imagine what she's been through."

"She's an amazing person." The admiration in Robert's tone rubbed Janeal the wrong way. She couldn't prevent the thought that Katie's death fifteen years ago might have been the more merciful outcome for everyone.

"You've had some time to catch up with each other."

"A couple days."

"She talk about me?"

Robert hesitated. "When were you going to tell us who you were?"

"I don't know. I couldn't . . . When I saw what had happened to Katie, I didn't know if I ever could." She didn't like the way the conversation had begun to slide.

"Not even to warn us that Sanso was on his way?"

"How could I have known? You knew that he'd escaped. What else could I have told you?"

Robert's sigh pressed down on her. "Everything you're saying . . . you've got to know that it looks like you're in bed with Sanso. It's so easy to believe, after everything you've done, that you would—"

"Oh, Robert. No. It's not true. I'd never—"

"Where are you?"

"I had to get away. I had to think about what to do next. Do you know where Sanso is?"

"Not yet."

"I took the Kia. Can you get Lucille to give me a day to get it back to the house?"

"That's not my call."

"Please. I'll report in to you. I couldn't stay there, and I don't know where to go as long as Sanso is . . . unaccounted for."

"It's not for me to promise."

"Please. If I mean anything to you."

"Janeal . . ."

Oh, it felt good to hear him say her name! Her heart filled with a warmth she hadn't felt in years. Maybe she could find her way back to the person she used to be, the person she was when he was near.

"Janeal, look. You're on your own here. I need to take care of Katie right now. She's my first priority."

The warmth that had filled her turned frigid. *You don't know what you're saying. You may think you love her, but she's not the girl who vied for your attention back when we were kids!* She stared out the windshield at a couple walking by, holding hands. How could Katie have worked her magic over him so quickly?

The phone beeped to indicate an incoming call.

"You love her," she mumbled.

"What? I can't hear you."

You love me. You think you love Katie Morgon but you love me. That scarred piece of trash is me, but she's not the one you want, Robert. If only you knew how deceived you are! I'm the real thing; she's nothing but a conniving imposter. A deformed, lying witch who has her spell over you. She has nothing to offer you. But I do. I know what it takes. The men love me—Milan, Sanso, a dozen others who have recognized—

"Janeal?"

"What?"

"You're not going to vanish again, are you?"

"Where do I have to go, Robert?"

The phone beeped again.

"Off to some new life, new name, whatever it is."

She pondered this. "That's not the answer, is it? I can't keep running."

"Eventually your sins catch up to you."

She bristled at his implication. Maybe because it was true.

"I'll call you." She hung up before he could say anything more, and checked the incoming number. Callista.

"Yes."

"You're at the Pueblo Vista Lodge." The voice was Sanso's. "Callista will text you the reservation number."

"You'll meet me there tomorrow night?"

"Sometime tomorrow. I'm full of surprises." Someone close to Sanso made a remark that caused him to laugh. "My Callista thinks we should leave you to handle Katie yourself and head south."

She was certainly capable of taking matters into her own hands, except that her life would be simpler if someone else would kill Katie. If she did it herself, Robert would never look at her again.

On the other hand, killing Katie would be like a suicide rather than murder, wouldn't it? Now there was an interesting idea. Of course, Robert wouldn't buy it.

"Do whatever you want."

"I want to keep my promises."

"Where are you?"

"Las Vegas."

"Nevada?"

"New Mexico. A good surgeon isn't *that* hard to find, my love."

"I'm surprised you don't keep one on your payroll."

"Too much ego for me. These little after-hours centers are much more manageable."

"And I'll leave you to work your magic. How do I know you won't stand me up?"

"The same way I know you won't vanish into thin air."

"You trust me?"

"No. No, not at all. I only know that you need to know Katie is dead as badly as you once needed a million dollars."

Janeal shook her head. She would stick around long enough this time to get Robert out of harm's way and ensure Katie died. Then Sanso would never see her again.

As for her and Robert, she could only hope he'd come around eventually. They'd have time.

59

Robert parked his truck in front of the modernized log cabin where Lucille had brought Katie, not quite ready to go in. The house sat on several acres in Taos Canyon, at the crest of a hill that dropped off into a narrow stream. He watched two elk drink from the water. The intensity of the night's events, the morning's pursuit, and the blindsiding revelation called Janeal left his head foggy. He was only slightly relieved that Janeal had not taken the Kia in pursuit of Katie.

He was still angry at Janeal, and why? Was any of what Sanso had engineered her fault? Even if it wasn't, this woman he had once loved so much had lied to him outright, coming in that dyed-hair disguise yesterday and staring at him forever. Maybe she was still lying. He had no way to know for sure.

Fifteen *years*. Gone. What had she been doing this whole time? Whatever it was had aged her. Not physically, but some aspect of her personality had turned ugly. He thought back to the DEA's interview with Janice: the tone of her voice, her posture, the way she dodged questions and moved her hands as if they were working on some magic trick.

Would he take those years back if someone offered them to him? And if Janeal could be a part of them, would he want her to be?

Kind of a dumb question right now. Robert didn't trust her.

Also, despite the shock of rediscovering Janeal, Robert's mind kept going to Katie. He pictured her enduring the earliest days of her burns alone, and he wished he had been there with her. For some reason he found that he could easily wish back *those* fifteen years. Not so she would have to go through it all again, but so she wouldn't have to go through all of it with people who never knew her in any other condition.

All of the energies he had once poured into hunting Sanso down had morphed overnight into an equally driving desire to protect Katie and give her the kind of secure life she deserved. Not because she was incapable or somehow lacking, but because . . .

Just because. Just because he could, and he wanted to. Because it would be a more rewarding way to spend his life than the way he'd spent the last decade and a half. This reality seemed especially profound right now, with Sanso gone again, having slipped through his fingers twice. The possibility that he might stand in this same situation at age forty-nine held no appeal.

He recalled Katie standing in front of the *Origins of Fire* sculpture with her hands raised to feel the heat, smiling. Self-confident and happy to be with him.

Janeal didn't need that kind of security from any relationship. He knew this because, now that he thought about it, that had always been the truth. Maybe that was what had divided his own heart. She could protect herself with this plan or that one, never needing anything from anyone beyond a promise to obediently play their part in her production.

Robert stepped out of his truck and entered the cabin. Lucille greeted him in the kitchen and showed him around. In spite of her protests, Katie was sleeping. Stubborn as she was, Lucille said, she knew the value of rest.

The modest three-bedroom home was owned by a grandmother who usually would be here to cluck over the Hope House staffers, Lucille explained, but she'd gone back to California to visit a grandbaby for a couple weeks.

Lucille left within minutes of Robert's arrival and returned to the halfway house, where her help would be needed in Katie's absence.

When she was gone he called Harlan, and then the agent leading the investigation into Sanso's activities of the previous night, answering what questions hadn't already been addressed. Around two o'clock he wandered back into the kitchen, planning to find some coffee to brew and then go look in on Katie.

"It was sweet of you to come," she said from the hallway. He turned to look at her and smiled.

"You shouldn't sneak up on a guy like that," he teased. She wore pajama bottoms and a cotton T-shirt with three-quarter-length sleeves that exposed the scars on her forearms, dark ridges of tissue mixed with pale seams like a topography map. Robert crossed the room, took her by the hands, and kissed her on the cheek.

She withdrew and tugged at her sleeves with one hand, head down. "I'll make some coffee."

"Wait." He kept hold of her fingers and pulled her back to him, encircling her in a secure hug. He held her head against his shoulder gently until he felt her shoulders relax. When he dropped his hand to her waist, she stayed there.

They didn't say anything for several seconds.

"You sleep okay?" he finally asked.

She nodded. "You could probably use some sleep yourself."

"I'll get to it."

"I never asked you how long you plan to stay," she said as she went to a cupboard and reached up for a wide coffee can sitting right at the front.

"It depends," he said. The prospect of his four-hundred-mile drive back to El Paso made him feel tired. She scooped grounds into a paper filter, her back turned to him, and didn't say anything. Katie filled the coffeepot with water, then turned it on, and they listened to the machine start to suck up the liquid.

"But I've been thinking," Robert said.

Katie turned around, her arms tucked behind her as she leaned into the counter. "About?"

"About what I really ought to do next."

"Do you mean like 'Should I eat a sandwich or soup for lunch?' or like 'How should I spend the next forty years of my life?'"

He laughed. "I was thinking about my job."

"You've built quite a career for yourself."

"It's not quite what I expected."

She waited for him to explain.

"I'm starting to think the only reason I joined the DEA was to find Sanso."

"Ah."

"But we're locked in this cycle that is going to repeat itself."

"I would think in all this time you have done far more than be frustrated by the career of one criminal."

He shrugged. "Maybe."

"Maybe," she teased, going to a cabinet for mugs. "What's so bad about all this great work you've done?"

"The fact that I've done it all out of anger."

The answer surprised him; it was the first time he'd thought of it consciously in those terms. He debated whether to try to take it back as he watched Katie tip her head slightly and set the mugs on the counter.

"What are you angry about?"

Her ability to draw truth out of him made him uncomfortable. He shouldn't have brought it up. "Well, Dr. Morgon, I'm angry about the ATM machine that chewed up my bank card last week, and the price I have to pay to fill up my gas-eating truck, and the fact that I can't get my cell phone company to straighten out some charges . . ."

He stopped at Katie's expression, which was disappointed. When he didn't finish, she said, "I see."

"I'm sorry," he said.

"You don't have to explain yourself."

"But I want to."

Her eyebrows arched. "Before you do, I should tell you—"

"No, let me spit it out." He raced ahead before he lost this opportunity to speak honestly with someone who would understand him like no one else could. "Everything I did, I did because I wanted justice against Sanso. I did it because of the satisfaction I thought I would feel when he finally went down. I did it because I was angry, and that was all the fuel I needed to keep me going. Anger's like nitro in a street racer. There's a lot of power in it, enough to keep you going for a long time. But when it burns out—what's next? Where do you go after that kind of a rush?"

The pot gurgled.

"Do you know what I'm talking about, Katie? Were you ever angry about what he did to us?"

"Of course I was."

"But you never were the street-racer type, angry like Janeal and I could get sometimes."

Katie turned toward the coffeemaker and fiddled with the handle of the carafe.

Robert continued, "I never expected this . . . this complete dissatisfaction with getting the thing I wanted so much, and then losing it right away. Twice! I keep thinking, *That's it? This is what I've spent my life aiming for? This pursuit that might never end and certainly won't matter if it does?*"

Katie shrugged. "I don't think I have a magic answer for you."

"Maybe it's not magic, but you know something I don't."

Katie snapped back to face him. "Robert, the truth is—"

"No, wait. Hear me out. I watch you with these women at Hope House and it's so clear. You have something so few people have. You've lost everything that anyone values—your family, your home, your sight—but you still keep giving and giving. You seem happy! But they keep taking. Don't you feel robbed?"

"Not at all."

"Why not?"

"Because I *am* happy. What I'm doing isn't about me, Robert. It never was. It's about these women. They've lost so much more than I ever have."

"That seems impossible."

"It's true."

"What is?"

"When we quit trying to meet our own needs, we find more satisfaction in meeting the needs of others. God shows us how much we have to offer the world, and how unimportant our own desires are."

"I'd say you've mastered that."

"If you knew the truth . . . I work in a comfortable house with a small number of women. It doesn't take a saint."

Robert moved across the kitchen to pour the coffee. "I like your brand of sainthood." He lifted the carafe and poured the steaming liquid into cups. "It's funny that you and I both ended up working on the drug problem in such different ways."

She nodded and he risked an idea without looking at her.

"Maybe I could see myself doing something different from now on. Maybe here in New Mexico. With you."

Katie blushed. "I think you would miss your old life. It can get lonely in the mountains, stuck in a house with a bunch of loopy women."

He held her cup and lifted her hand to place her fingers on the handle, then paused, studying her face. Her beautiful, strong face. "Maybe taking that loneliness off your shoulders is something I could do for you. My first small act of selflessness." Not that it would be a huge sacrifice. He bent and kissed her on the mouth, and when she put her fingertips to his jaw, he let himself linger. For just a second this time, though in his mind he decided that he never, ever wanted to leave her.

Her eyes were glassy when he pulled away.

"I want what you have, Katie. You are . . . you are the brightest example I've ever seen of a life that matters. How did you ever get to this point, after all that you've been through?"

Katie sighed and accepted her cup from Robert, letting the steam caress her nose.

"A part of me had to die first."

The answer confused Robert. "You mean that metaphorically."

She took a sip of the scalding drink.

"Not exactly."

"Tell me more."

Katie frowned and touched the ring on her right hand. "We were together in the fire. Janeal and I."

"Janeal was there?" Janeal's shopworn but flawless complexion sprang to his mind. The story she had told about Sanso abducting her before Katie's death heaped more questions on the pile. He wondered if he should disclose that Janeal was alive. "You mentioned Janeal the other night. What did you mean when you said she 'tried'? She tried to help you get out?"

"In her own way. I don't know what I meant to say."

"What happened? Did she leave you there?"

"No! No. But she couldn't . . ."

Her struggle was so apparent in her flustered shake of the head that he would have let it go if not for the hope that she was ready to talk. All the anger that had driven him to hunt Sanso down had burned out, and he felt stalled on the side of the road in the middle of the desert. Katie, he believed, was the only car that could stop and help him. Maybe they could help each other.

"Katie. Janeal is alive."

Katie set her coffee on the counter. "I know," she said.

"You know?" Robert sloshed some of his coffee onto the floor. "When did you . . . Did you always know Janice was . . . When were you going to tell me?"

"There's so much we haven't had time to talk about." Katie shook her head.

"I talked with her. I'm so ticked. Why would she go to all the trouble of a disguise, and why is Sanso after her? I mean here, now, after all this time?"

Katie's hands dropped to her sides, and her lips parted. Robert tried to decipher her expression—anxiety?

"Maybe the three of us should sit down and talk," she said. It sounded lame once it was out there, hanging in the air in front of Katie's blank eyes.

"Robert, there's something I need to explain."

60

Janeal moved through the next few hours without feeling anything but hatred toward Katie Morgon and a desire to confront this alter ego and be done with her forever. She bought a prepaid cell phone from Walgreens and a decent change of clothes from a small boutique before she checked into her hotel. She would stay only long enough to change and make a phone call. She hoped the detour wouldn't cut into the time it would take for her to stay one step ahead of Salazar Sanso.

It was good he would not arrive before tomorrow. She dropped the clothes she'd been wearing into the trash can under the bathroom sink and changed into fresh clothes.

The hotel had free Wi-Fi service, which she used to locate the urgent care clinics in Las Vegas, New Mexico. There was only one, which would make this task much easier than she could have imagined. She looked up the local police department next and found a tip hotline. Janeal was about to call it from her disposable phone when a call came in on her personal line.

She snatched it up.

"Yes."

"Ms. Johnson. How are you feeling?" Who was this? Alan?

"What are you . . . I asked you not to call."

"An urgent matter—"

"Not now." Urgent? What could be more urgent than her present situation?

"Milan Finch has filed a complaint with the board and asked them to—"

"I said not now. I can't . . . It will have to wait."

"But Mr. Sanders—"

Janeal closed the phone. Mr. Sanders? Ah. Thomas. She didn't really care.

Janeal put Alan behind her and placed her call to the Las Vegas police.

"Hi. Yeah. I'm calling about that guy who's been in the news, that drug guy who escaped a few days ago?"

"Salazar Sanso."

"Yes, that one."

"May I have your name and number, please?"

"Oh no. I mean it took my husband all kinds of persuasion to get me to call you at all. This doesn't sound like a man I want to run into."

"What information do you have?"

"Our daughter—well, we were out for a hike before we went into Santa Fe for a vacation. She got quite a gash in her arm on a fall, so we took her in to the urgent care center there in your pretty little town."

"What time was this?"

"Oh, I don't know. Around nine or ten this morning. But as we were going in, you know that man, the one on the news, he was coming out of that center with a blond woman. Bold as day!"

"You're certain it was him."

"As certain as I am that he didn't see *me,* if you know what I mean. He got into this pretty little car, a silver sporty thing. What was it again, honey?" She covered the mouthpiece, then said, "A Miata. A Mazda Miata."

"Did you see which direction they headed?"

"Oh no. I was afraid he'd spot us staring, you know? And then where would we be? Poor victims on some homicide documentary, I'm sure. No, I've told you everything I know. My civic duty for the day."

"We'll look into it."

"Well then, you've been real nice. I hope you have a very nice day."

Janeal ended the call and threw the phone into the trash on top of her clothes. She mentally calculated how long it would take the tip to filter out to Robert's people at the DEA, and then to Robert. There was no way of knowing for sure.

She supposed it didn't matter in the end. Her first objective was to get Robert away from Katie, and she had more than twenty-four hours to make that happen. She'd be patient.

In fact, she'd be patient by waiting with them. What did she have to lose at this point? If she knew Robert at all, he'd already told Katie about her.

And Janeal wanted to set her own version of the story straight.

Callista sat in the driver's seat of the Miata and refused to put the key in the ignition.

"You're risking everything for a stupid, stupid girl," she argued. "We could be across the border by nightfall, but you want to stay here, where the world is crawling with agents who have a much better idea of where you are, thanks to that bungled tryst last night."

Callista's tirades were stale now. Sanso found he had come to prefer Janeal's mode of argument, which was calmer and sharpened by her like-mindedness.

Sanso adjusted in his seat to make himself more comfortable. The gunshot had gone clean through the fleshy part of his bicep, lucky for him. The wound in his liver still had quite a bit of healing to do, in part because the scuffle with Robert had aggravated the damage.

"I'm not driving this car until you agree to leave the States today."

Sanso opened his car door and swung his legs out to the curb of the abandoned lot where she'd pulled off. If she wouldn't drive, he would.

"Don't even think about it, Salazar." She twisted in her seat, following him with her eyes as he walked around the back of the car. He'd taken the top down, also against her objections, after leaving the urgent care facility. "We had two days' lead time to get you out of here, and then you went and told her where we are. How long do you think it will take her to call the cops and get on with her life? An hour? Maybe less?"

Sanso opened the trunk and leaned into the compartment on both hands. It was here somewhere. He allowed himself a snarl in Callista's direction. She didn't understand the bond he and Janeal shared. She couldn't possibly imagine that Janeal would not betray him in such a fashion. Janeal had *chosen* him over Katie, over Robert, and she would be his in the end. In fact, she already was.

It was hard to forgive Callista's ignorance, though.

"This is not the time to be a brickhead," she was saying.

There was the leather bundle he was looking for, hastily crammed under the carpeting that hid the spare tire. He pulled it out and untied it, then unrolled the casing slowly.

"We need to go," she insisted. "Now."

Sanso straightened and shut the trunk, then approached Callista. She twisted forward to watch him in the rearview mirror. "Get in the car, Salazar. You rest. I'll drive. To Mexico. Do you hear me?"

He reached the driver's side and leaned over her, bending to kiss her on the forehead.

"Oh, I hear you," he said. He sensed her relax, then he drove the six-inch knife he'd retrieved into the back of her neck. "The problem is, you don't hear me."

Callista slumped against the wheel, paralyzed but not dead. It wouldn't take long. Opening the car door, he lifted her petite frame with his good arm and resituated her in the passenger seat.

"I'll give you a good burial, my dear. You've been good to me through the years. But you seem to have forgotten your place. You'll pardon me now while I go pay a visit to my love."

61

Robert paced in front of the window, feeling as if the morning had stretched into days. He wasn't sure what time it was. Time had stopped and the world no longer made sense. The woman he loved had told him a story he couldn't believe in spite of how much he tried.

Katie faced Robert on the sofa, not speaking. After explaining her reaction to the revelation about Janeal, she stilled and seemed to wait for Robert to respond.

The dry mountain air scratched Robert's throat. There wasn't enough oxygen in it to help his brain make sense of her claim.

What did she expect him to do? Buy the whole unfathomable explanation and go on with life as if it weren't extraordinary? Call her a liar and demand she prove her claims?

Those were only two of a thousand possibilities. And he wasn't sure his response mattered.

Robert's cell phone rang. He ignored it.

After several minutes of silent musing and stolen glances at the woman on the sofa, he narrowed down what *did* matter to two things:

The identity of the woman he had fallen in love with this week.

And whether he could still love her if her story was true. Or a lie.

"You're not Katie," he said for the fourth or fifth time.

She shook her head patiently as if he'd only asked her once. "Katie died."

"So who are you?"

"Janeal."

"And who does that make . . . the other woman?"

"Janeal."

"You can see the problem I have with that."

"It's a difficult claim, I understand."

"It's an unimaginable claim. Physically impossible. How did it happen?"

"I don't know."

"When did it happen? And don't tell me during the fire. I want to know the precise moment. Because I can't believe . . . well, I can't believe any of it, but I don't see how you could become . . . disembodied, or whatever you want to call it, without knowing it was happening."

Katie nodded. "It must have happened when—"

"You're telling me you don't know the precise moment?"

"Precise? No. But I sensed something . . . supernatural happen. The moment I decided to help Katie."

Robert couldn't help it. He scoffed.

She pressed ahead. "I can't explain why that was such a hard decision to make, but the mental strain—"

"Mental strain is a much more reasonable explanation for why you think you're Janeal. I've had my own experience with survivor's guilt—"

"That's not what this is. And it can't explain why two of us are claiming to be Janeal. Or why I'd empathize with someone who supposedly abandoned me to die."

Robert didn't have a comeback for that.

"Things harder to believe than this have happened," she said.

"Like?"

"How does the Red Sea part? How does the sun stand still?"

"Stories."

"Truth."

"For you maybe."

Katie sighed. "I couldn't have made this up. *Why* would I have made this up?"

"Why have you pretended to be Katie?"

"I was ashamed of who I'd been, of the part of me that didn't want to save her. I only tried to live in the way we know Katie would have lived. It was an attempt to keep her goodness alive."

Katie's goodness was in fact what Robert had loved, then and now.

"Please forgive me for not telling you right away," she said. "I couldn't think of how."

If she had told him the truth then, would that have changed the nature of the wild story she was telling now? He wasn't sure which was the worse offense: withholding the truth or making up a fantastic lie.

His phone rang again on the heels of the first call.

"I think you're Katie but don't want to admit it," he said. "I can't guess why."

"Considering I've been using her name for the last fifteen years, that doesn't add up."

"You look like Katie."

"How much? Think about it, Robert. Hair is easy to duplicate. My eyes might be any color. My skin tone is damaged. I'm taller than Katie was. You see what you want to see."

Robert turned around and studied her. He leaned against the windowsill and crossed his ankles and his arms. How closely had he looked into her face in the past several days? He'd made assumptions based on her hair, her speech, her gestures. His eyes had been trained on her heart.

She showed him the melted tattoo on her ankle. "I showed this to you the morning of the massacre," she reminded him. "Janice has one like it. Except hers isn't scarred."

Robert ran a hand through his hair. There was so much he couldn't explain. "Would you be willing to have a DNA test, compare your DNA to Janeal's?"

She nodded. "Do you think she'd agree to it?"

A test would satisfy his first pressing need—to know whether these women were actually the same—but no science existed that could tell him whether his love was resilient enough to withstand the results. He needed time to process this bizarre claim and wished he had known it before suggesting he might stay here in New Mexico.

When Robert's phone rang for the third time, he crossed the room and snatched it off the table. Harlan Woodman.

"Lukin."

"Robert, we have a tip on Sanso. Someone spotted him up I-25 in Las Vegas, and local police confirmed a description of him at an urgent care center. They could use your expertise trailing him."

"How long ago?"

"Couple hours."

Robert hit a wall of fatigue. He was tired of chasing this man and didn't care if he never heard the name Sanso again.

"Let me get on the road and I'll call you back," he said.

He tucked the phone into the holder on his belt and began to collect the few things he'd brought with him. Katie stayed attuned to the window, but she tipped an ear in the direction of Robert's movements.

"I have to go up to Las Vegas. It's what—a two-hour drive from here?"

Katie nodded.

"Will you be okay here by yourself?"

She turned her face at a slight angle to him then, and he saw that she was crying.

There was nothing he could do about it.

He walked to the entryway behind the sofa, stepped into the hall that led out to the front, and paused.

"If someone told me a week ago that I wasn't the only survivor of that massacre, I would have given him a piece of my mind."

Katie bowed her head.

"Now I'm standing here and there are three of us. And two of you. There's a part of me that thinks I might be hallucinating. Maybe I made this all up after I arrested Sanso because putting him in jail wasn't what I ever really wanted for all my efforts.

"Maybe I wanted something entirely impossible. A different outcome. Friends and lovers resurrected from the dead."

He was about to leave behind a flesh-and-blood hope or a doomed wish. He couldn't be sure which one.

62

Janeal sat in the blue Kia behind a tree at the end of the lane, where she could see the cabin's driveway. She was surprised when Robert climbed into his truck and pulled out within an hour of her arrival. A part of her had wondered if Robert would leave Katie at all, even for Sanso.

But he was gone now, and provided that Katie died before he returned, Robert would be safe.

He might be going into town for food. Janeal followed him to the highway, and when he turned south and passed Taos's major shopping areas, she decided to hope that he'd be gone awhile. Katie would know.

Janeal drove back to the cabin and parked on an adjacent street to make the car less noticeable if Robert returned. It was time to sort out the lies from the truth, retrieve her mother's ring, and ensure that Robert would not be present in this cabin when Sanso arrived tomorrow night.

Then Janeal could get on with her life.

She walked in without knocking and followed a narrow entry hall into a long living room area. Floor-to-ceiling picture windows lined the wall that overlooked the sloping hillside.

Katie sat on the sofa, her back to Janeal.

"I was hoping you would come," Katie said.

Not the conversation starter Janeal had anticipated. She rounded the sofa and took a seat on the other side of the coffee table, her back to the window.

"Do you want to start or shall I?" Katie asked. A beam of light from the afternoon sun cut right across her face. She stared through it without squinting. Her eyes looked bloodshot and her nose was red; otherwise, Katie was eerily composed.

"I don't know what Robert has told you," Janeal started.

"I didn't realize you two knew each other, Janice."

Janeal could not be sure, but she believed there was something close to sarcasm in Katie's tone, only less biting. "From a long time ago."

Katie nodded. "We go way back too. You still sound a bit hoarse. Feeling okay?"

Janeal shifted in her chair. "As well as can be expected. Things haven't been good for sleeping lately."

"Yes, well, I'm sorry about what happened at the house last night." Janeal thought she didn't sound sorry at all. She cleared her throat.

"Do you know who broke in?"

"Almost as well as he knew you," Katie said. She rose and went to the tall window and rested her hand on the pane.

Janeal wiped her hands on her pant legs. There was no point in pretending anymore.

"How about we start telling each other the truth, Janeal?"

Janeal stared at this reflection of herself, this reflection with flesh on, wondering if she should be frightened. She was talking to herself in a way she was sure few people had ever experienced.

Not even hallucinating people.

"How long did it take you to find out?" Janeal asked.

"Robert told me. But I knew something was off the moment you walked into Lucille's office. Most of what's happened has become clear to me in the last few hours, including why Salazar Sanso would show up there on the same day you did, trying to kill me."

Janeal was unprepared for Katie's awareness, and she took too long to formulate an answer.

"We are the same person, and you would like to see me dead." She turned her head toward Janeal. "Isn't that right?"

"No! No! I don't know what you mean. When I found out you were alive—Katie, I had to come back. I had to see you. I am so sorry that I failed you that night. If there was anything I could have done differently . . ."

"Let's not do this dance. We can't explain what happened, but we can try to sort out what it all means."

"You're talking in riddles."

"You understand me."

"Prove it. Prove that you're who you say you are."

"Katie told you she knew you took the money."

"You're Katie. You'd know that."

"I'm you, Janeal. I know where you found it."

Janeal blanched.

"You found it in the medicine cabinet. After you looked for it in Dad's room—in the safe, the light fixture, the floorboards."

"I might have told someone about that."

"No, you didn't. Did you also tell them you took the bowie knife, the wedding ring, the stones, the seeds—"

"Stop!" Janeal took a long, slow breath. "What do you want from me?"

"I want you to tell me about your life since the fire." She leaned back and put her feet on the coffee table as if Janeal had already agreed to launch into an entertaining story. "I want to hear about everything that's happened to you since that night. Every relationship you've had. Every choice you've made. Every moment you've ever felt happy. Or sad."

Janeal might have imagined it, but she believed the temperature in the room dropped twenty degrees. She felt sick—not with the sickness of a pending migraine but with a sinking realization: whatever she had envisioned about the direction this conversation would take, she had failed to anticipate what it might be to duel with someone of an equal mind.

Of the same mind.

She needed time to gain control over what was happening. Janeal stood to go.

"Sit down," Katie said. "Robert doesn't know about what you did yet, how you betrayed him and Katie all for a little drug money that you most certainly never returned—"

"You don't know what I—"

"I *do* know!" Katie shouted. "So if you don't want me to expose you to a man who will have your hide faster than he ever had any criminal's, sit down and start talking."

Janeal lowered herself back onto the cushion. She considered killing Katie now, here, with her own hands and quick thinking. She hated this woman in front of her, hated with an energy not even Milan or Sanso had tapped within her.

Janeal started talking, if only to give her time to sort this out. Katie closed her eyes and leaned her head back against the cushion. Janeal repeated the story she had told Robert, then told about going to New York, enrolling in school, working as a pastry chef, dating various men, and eventually entering a long-term relationship with Milan. As she spoke about working her way up the corporate ladder at *All Angles*, Janeal was surprised to find the truth-telling a comfort, a catharsis. As if she was talking with an old friend.

A true friend. How easy it became, almost without her realizing what words spilled out of her mouth, to talk about the abuse. She confessed to her own use of Milan to achieve her ends.

Even more surprising to Janeal was the heartache she felt in telling these stories. It had been a long time since she considered the pain and solitude she'd felt through each step of her journey. It was something she consciously buried.

At the very least, this conversation was better than any therapy session she'd invested in.

For an hour Katie listened without interrupting, and Janeal wondered if she'd fallen asleep. But when Janeal reached the night of Milan's final beating, Katie raised her head and opened her eyes.

"I don't envy you a single minute of your life," Katie said.

The condescension of that remark, the smug superiority of Katie's tone, shut off Janeal's storytelling tap. She stood and looked down on Katie.

"Of course you don't. You couldn't wish up a life for yourself as successful as mine. I've seen and done things you could only dream of, Katie Morgon."

"What I meant was, you don't sound happy. Successful, but never happy."

"Success *is* happiness."

"Not always."

"What would you know about it? Look at you. You hide here in the mountains acting like your suffering has made you noble and good, when in reality you're a cop-out."

"I pity you, Janeal."

That four-letter word *pity* stirred Janeal's anger with such vigor that she couldn't contain it anymore.

"You disgust me. Is that what you wanted out of this story, Katie? To make yourself feel better about your own small life?"

"If that's what I wanted, I would have arranged a public venue for this event."

"You're sick."

"No, you're the sick one."

Janeal fumed over the sugary-sweet, calm voice Katie used.

"And you've been sick ever since the day you made your decision that a few bucks is more valuable than a human life. The reason I wanted you to tell your story was because I wanted you to hear it for yourself. I wanted you to think through this way of life that you seem to think is so valuable."

"You have no right!" Janeal shouted. "I'm not one of your addicted residents."

"No, you're *me*. Which gives me every right. You've turned your back on the truth and your life is miserable because of it. Face it, Janeal. Face what you've done and what you've become."

"Why? So I can be like *you*? I don't want what you have! There is nothing about you that I would ever envy! I *hate* you!"

"You hate yourself."

Janeal yelled a note of frustration. She didn't have to listen to this. This was not why she had come here. She could walk away. Should walk away.

Her feet wouldn't move.

Katie stood and leveled her blank eyes at Janeal. Janeal turned and Katie followed her. "You're addicted to a far more powerful drug than anything any of our residents have ever used."

"And what is that?"

"Yourself. You live for yourself and no one else, and you don't recognize how it's reduced you to a shell of the person you were."

"You're crazy."

"I care about you."

"You *can't*. You want me to be like you."

"I do. Janeal, I want you to know the peace I've known."

Janeal put her hands at the sides of her head. "Stop it! I wish you'd *died* in that fire! Both of you!"

"Listen to me, Janeal. Don't hate me. I am *you*, and I am the better version of you. I am the person you wish you had become. I'm the person you *can* become."

The claim cut Janeal to the core. "How dare you? How *dare* you?"

Janeal's back hit a wall and Katie reached out to her. She placed her hand in the center of Janeal's chest, right over her heart. Janeal shrank down into a squatting position and Katie matched her movements.

"You don't have to stay on the path you chose that night. You could pick a different course."

"Why should I? I'm *happy*. I've made my own life!" Janeal threw up her hands to knock Katie's palm off her chest, to break this connection that was killing Janeal's very soul.

Was that what Katie wanted? To kill Janeal? Fear flared in Janeal's chest. Why had it not occurred to her that she had endangered her very life by coming here, that her alter ego had as strong a desire for Janeal to die? She had been a fool. A stupid, stupid fool.

"Get away from me," Janeal spat. "Get away."

63

Robert stopped by Hope House on his way out and returned to the empty wing where he had been staying, then packed up his things. It took all of three minutes.

He headed out of his room, duffel over his shoulder, and wondered whether to go back to Katie—or Janeal, however that worked—after his visit to Las Vegas. He supposed his decision would depend in part on where Sanso led him from here.

He wondered if he should call Janeal but put it off. How exactly could he pose the question of whether she and Katie were the same person? Even if it was true, would she know it?

The truth was, he didn't want to leave Katie. A few minutes of honest thought made it clear that what he really desired was for things to be the way they were, with him and Katie in their self-contained world of possibility and Janeal and Sanso firmly locked away in a separate compartment. An entirely other universe.

Instead, he and Katie had been sucked into a black hole of confusion right alongside those two. The mystery of how it had happened was so far beyond his ability to solve that Robert didn't see the point in applying his mind to it.

Which was one reason to leave and go back to his life and career as if the past week had never taken place.

He didn't want to hurt Katie.

He couldn't think of her as anyone *but* Katie, no matter how he turned it over in his mind.

He poked his head into Lucille's office on the way out.

"You able to look in on Katie tonight?" he asked.

"What's that about? Isn't that for you to do?"

"I have to take care of some business."

"I can't do it tonight, Robert. I'll go get her tomorrow afternoon, but tonight you're it." She frowned at him. "You two didn't have some stupid fight, did you?"

"Nothing like that."

"Good thing for you. If she comes back from Taos worse than when she went up, I'm going to have to rethink my open-door policy where you're concerned."

"Got it. You recover the Kia yet?"

"Oh, it'll turn up eventually. I filed a report as soon as I got back and figured out what happened. If Janice is still here in New Mexico, our officers will find it."

Salazar Sanso covered up the bloody seat in the Miata with a dry cleaner's bag from the hotel, then prepared to return to Taos. It had taken him a few hours to arrange Callista's transportation. It was no easy feat in the middle of the day, no easier than bandaging his bicep single-handedly with his teeth. But he'd done it.

He made arrangements for Callista's body to be sent home to Mexico with his chief operator—the man he appointed chief operator in Callista's place. The guy was not incompetent. At Sanso's request he quickly acquired a twenty-pound tank of medical-grade nitrous oxide from a connected physician and loaded it into the back of the Miata. He also provided the extra gas cans Sanso would need. Still, Sanso would have to think through whether to make the appointment permanent or allow Janeal to fill Callista's shoes after he'd secured Janeal's companionship. Now that Robert was certainly up to speed on Janeal's latest identities, the woman might have to give up her glamorous New York job.

He'd certainly give her a more attractive employment package than she'd received from anyone else.

The thought of working side by side with Janeal for the rest of her life brought the first smile of the day to his face. He picked up his phone. He needed to talk with her.

64

Janeal stormed out of the house, catching a glimpse of herself in the hall mirror on the way. She looked awful. Her brown eyes were the color of a murky sewer. Flat and sick. She hadn't washed her hair in two days, and it was coming out of its clip in oily strings. Her new clothes didn't fit her right.

Janeal averted her eyes. Worse than her physical appearance was the condition of her heart, which was braking and railing at such a spasmodic pace that she felt faint.

I have to go. I hate her. I hate myself.

But she knew not all of it was true, that she didn't hate anyone but Janeal Mikkado, Jane Johnson, Janice Regan—the beast she had willingly become. She was miserable and lonely and broken and everything else Katie had said she was. Good, wise Katie, who had from the beginning only spoken the truth.

Janeal had never wanted to be anyone other than herself. Never. What was so wrong with that? What was so wrong with what she'd become?

She muttered aloud as she headed for her car. "She's nothing, nothing, nothing. I did the right thing. I did. It was best. I'm okay."

But deep within her, not even Jane Johnson could pretend that Janeal was okay. She was divided, worse than a split personality, standing against herself and—worse—faced with the possibility that her other self was wiser, superior, and more powerful in every way.

What if *that* was true? What if Janeal had, in fact, reached the apex of her power while Katie was still shooting upward toward the stars? What if Janeal spent the rest of her life running from horrors she'd created for herself, having to waste precious energy conspiring against people like Milan and evading people like Sanso and lying to people like Robert?

All to preserve this miserable life.

The what-ifs only made her head murkier.

She fished her keys out of the bag as she marched down the driveway and walked the distance to the Kia. It seemed farther away than she remembered. When she came around the corner, a crumbling asphalt pavement that gave way to a sloping bank of grassy dirt, she stopped short. A police officer was speaking to a tow-truck operator, who was raising the Kia onto the truck's flatbed.

They'd found her already? Robert had promised!

She dropped her head and turned around before she was noticed. The truth was, Robert hadn't promised her anything.

She headed back toward the cabin without intending to return there, but she didn't know where else to go. Her mind was confused, her heart still palpitating, and now she was in a sweat without her transportation.

Without her freedom.

Had Janeal ever truly been free? She thought she had, ever since she drove away from Salazar Sanso the first time with a real million dollars in the trunk of her father's vandalized car.

Janeal stopped walking. Stopped in the middle of the road and wondered what her life might have been like if she'd never gone with Sanso the night he first approached her on the mesa.

A flash of fuchsia and gold drew her eye to the home she was standing in front of. An old woman sat on the porch in a rocker. The late afternoon sun glanced off her brightly colored skirt, which is what Janeal had noticed. The clothing seemed familiar.

So did the wrinkled brown hands, folded across the wide lap. And the long gray hair brushed smooth down the woman's breast to her lap. She smiled at Janeal, a smile that should have been decayed at her age but instead was supernaturally straight and bright.

Mrs. Marković.

There are two chambers in every heart, one for Judas and one for John. One must be pumped out, or you will both die.

A car horn screamed behind Janeal. She whirled to face it. The impatient driver shrugged as if to say, *Are you gonna stand there all day?*

Breathless, Janeal took three steps out of his way, three steps toward Mrs. Marković, who should have been long dead.

The driver made a point of aggressively accelerating, and Janeal ignored him. She looked back to the porch, where an empty rocker now tipped back and forth.

This time, Janeal would not let her go so easily. She burst through the chain-link gate and the front of the yard and ran up the path to the swaying chair, then pounded on the door behind it. When no one answered, she pressed her forehead to the sidelights, trying to detect movement inside. She pounded again.

"Hello? Mrs. Marković?"

Janeal could be a patient woman when she wanted to be. She kept at it.

After several minutes, the door opened. A harried young woman with a baby on each hip glared at Janeal. One of the children was screaming. The other eyed Janeal curiously.

"I don't want what you're selling. I just want these guys to nap more than five minutes."

"I need to speak to the woman who was on your porch."

"What woman?"

"Mrs. Marković. She was right here."

"No one here by that name."

"I saw her—"

"I don't know what you saw, okay? I don't know who she was or why she was here or where you can find her."

The screaming baby kicked it up a notch. The other babbled and handed a teether out to Janeal like a gift.

She looked at him and said to his mother, "I'm sorry I woke them."

The woman set her lips in a line. "If it hadn't been you, it would have been something else."

Janeal's gaze shifted to the unhappy child. "Twins?"

"Yeah. As alike as angels and demons. I really have to go."

She shut the door.

Janeal stood immobile on the porch for a full minute before her ringing phone snapped her out of her thoughts.

65

Sanso turned up the radio in his car and thumped his thumb on the steering wheel, more energized than he had felt in years. Janeal's fiery spirit would be good for him, and he wouldn't snuff it out. He called her.

"What?" Her tone was distracted rather than typically brusque.

"I must see you, my dear. I don't think I can wait until tomorrow."

"You need to wait. Tonight is not good for me."

"Which makes it all the better for me. That is, if you're not putting me off because you're entertaining our friend Robert."

"*Our friend* Robert is in love with *you*, Sanso. He's off chasing you again, as far as I know. I doubt he's still in town."

"Wonderful, wonderful. Listen, we must speak, but I refuse to do it over the phone. So much has . . . changed in the past few days. So many new opportunities await us. I'll come to you."

"Not tonight."

"I'll come when I want."

"You'll come when I tell you!"

Sanso howled, delighted. There was the Janeal he needed. "That's my girl. That's the one I want to speak with. I'll wait for you. Call when you're ready."

Janeal hung up on him.

While he waited for her call, he'd pay a visit to Katie Morgon.

Janeal reentered the cabin and listened to the still house, wondering where Katie had gone. It was too hard, too painful, to think of the woman as herself, the self she could have been if she'd only made different choices.

She padded into the kitchen and poured herself a glass of water, then wandered out through the dining room before noticing Katie asleep on the living room sofa.

Her wig was on the cushion next to her, a mound of sleek black curls. Seeing her without her hair for the first time, Janeal saw the heart-shaped face that looked so much like her own—that was, in fact, her own—but had been cloaked by the hairstyle.

Janeal set the water on the coffee table.

Katie's body was still seated but leaning sideways onto the arm of the couch. Janeal's eyes filled with tears at the sheer mass of scars that crisscrossed the left side of Katie's scalp and deformed her ear. She stood behind her and reached out to touch the lumpy skin. Her hand froze in place an inch away from Katie's head. Janeal couldn't do it. She had plenty of desire to know what this meant, to touch her alter ego, to verify that she lived and breathed and was made of soft warm flesh. Did she doubt it? Even if she did, she had no right. Janeal had divorced herself from goodness years ago.

She sat in a chair and studied Katie sleeping, curious about the foreign emotion that crept up from the bottom of her rib cage into her lungs.

Envy.

As ugly as the scars were, as repulsive as that hairless head might look to others, Katie had so many things Janeal had never been able to possess. The unconditional love of a man. The fearless admiration of people. The confidence to act without ulterior motive.

Katie didn't envy Janeal a minute of her life, she had said a short time ago. Could it be possible that Janeal was jealous of this blind, bald, scarred woman sleeping with salt trails running down her cheeks? Janeal had never envied anyone, let alone such a pitiful figure.

Janeal slipped off the chair onto her knees, inches away from Katie, feeling regret for the first time in years. Regret for every decision she had made since deciding to broker a deal with Sanso for his money. And for the decisions that had led to that one. She reached out and touched Katie's shoes, which had walked such a different path. A path Janeal could have taken.

What good was regret on a day like today, after so long?

The sun began sinking and the room dimmed. She rose and turned on a table lamp in the corner. Katie stirred and Janeal thought she had awakened, though she kept her eyes closed. Maybe she was listening. Janeal walked back to her chair and sat.

"I thought you left," Katie said.

"I don't have a car."

Katie sighed and straightened into a sitting position. Her hand brushed a lock of her wig. She picked it up and held it out toward Janeal, then shrugged.

"It must get uncomfortable in the summer," Janeal said, hoping Katie could hear some lightness in her voice.

"My one vanity." Katie dropped it back onto the cushion.

"You're gorgeous without it."

"That's a vain thing to say." This time Katie smiled.

They fell into a silence that was, miraculously, comfortable. A clock ticked in another room.

"I'm sorry," Janeal eventually said.

Katie cocked her head to one side—a gesture that Janeal recognized as once belonging to the Katie who had died.

"For leaving you—for leaving Katie in that nightmare."

"I'm sorry I couldn't save her," Katie said.

"That's nothing to be sorry about. I mean, it's not a true offense on your part. What I did was unforgivable."

"Nothing's unforgivable, Janeal."

"I'm beyond forgiveness."

"God's grace is never out of reach."

"I don't have a single cell of goodness in me anymore."

"That doesn't matter. God is bigger than you, than the sum of your choices. He can overcome anything."

"I've spent fifteen years living like I could never be forgiven."

"What are you going to do with the next fifteen?"

The question came across as a challenge rather than a curiosity. Janeal had no adequate answer. The next decade and a half of her life seemed as disconnected from this place as her New York office. It was hard to think of any of it as real now.

"Tell me what happened the night Katie died," Janeal said. "Tell me about the choice you made."

"If I hadn't waited so long to make it, maybe she would have lived."

"I'm not interested in the ifs. Just the actuals."

Katie touched the scars behind her left ear and told her story, interspersing the tale with apologies for the blur of her memory. And though the account took only a few minutes to tell, Janeal was in such tears by the time Katie finished that she could not speak.

Katie pushed herself up off the sofa and walked to Janeal's chair. She tugged at the ring on her finger, their mother's ring, until it slid off into her palm. Bending at the waist, she located Janeal's hand and placed the jewelry in her palm.

"You take this for a while. We can share it."

Janeal let go of a sob and grabbed Katie's hand—her own, unscarred hand—squeezing it between her palms. She pressed it against her cheek, right where her tears would douse Katie's fingers. Katie didn't pull away. Instead, she rested her other hand on the top of Janeal's disheveled hair.

Janeal felt like a child and didn't resist the sensation. She leaned into the security of being so small in the presence of someone so much stronger than she. Janeal closed her eyes.

"How do we fix this, Katie?"

"What is there to fix?"

"I don't know what to do next. I don't know where to go."

"You can go anywhere except back to where you've been."

"What does that mean?"

"You have to pick a new path. You're dying, Janeal. Inside, I mean. Your heart is dying. Will you choose to keep it alive?"

Janeal shook her head. She didn't know where to begin looking for an answer to that question. But her mind was clear for a change, and her headache nonexistent, and that gave her somewhere to start. She let her mind begin to drift and fingered the perfect circle of her mother's ring, allowing it to remind her of the place where all this had begun, a place she might somehow be able to get back to. A place of innocence and purity and openness to the idea that anything was possible.

66

At 7:45, as the sun dropped over the Sangre de Cristos to his left, Robert received a phone call from the Hope House landline.

"You miss me so soon?" he said kindly, expecting Lucille.

"They found the Kia," she said brusquely.

"That's goo—"

"They found it a quarter mile away from the cabin, Robert."

Robert's mind started flying through explanations. Janeal had never actually told him where she had gone. He had assumed . . .

"No sign of Janice, though," Lucille complained.

"Call Katie."

"I did. She said she's fine, that everything's fine."

"Is Janice with her?"

"Katie said she wasn't, but Robert—"

"I know. I agree. I'm on my way back."

Robert pulled off I-25 at the nearest off-ramp and made a loop back into the southbound lanes. He berated himself for having left. It was going to take him an hour to get back.

It was nearly eight thirty when Janeal decided to take a shower while Katie went to see if she had a change of clothes to offer. But first, Katie went in search of something to eat. In spite of the day's emotional stress, she could feel hunger eating away at the inside of her stomach while her blood sugar dropped. Her head felt light and wobbly when she stood.

She opened a cupboard door and heard Janeal turn on the fan in the bathroom as she searched the cupboards for something bland and dry. Saltines or rice cakes would work.

She found peanuts. Not quite the fast-acting blood-sugar stabilizer she hoped for, but decent protein. She popped a couple in her mouth and considered calling Robert.

A gentle *pop*, a soft hiss, and a light thud sounded from the back of the house. She turned her head toward the sound. Her ears picked up something that sounded like a window closing.

Water started running in the shower, covering the sound. Katie went down the hall to investigate.

Katie hadn't meant to mislead Lucille when she'd called. It was true that Janice wasn't here—Janice would never be seen again, Katie believed—but Lucille was not the type to understand the kind of story Katie and Janeal had to tell. That was something they were going to have to work out.

Katie imagined the possibility that Robert would not come back. She wouldn't blame him for that. How would any man react to her tale of being . . . what? Split in two like Solomon had butchered them himself? Who wouldn't run from that kind of horror?

The scent of gasoline passed over her, bringing her to a halt in front of the bedrooms at the back of the house. Or was it natural gas? She returned to the kitchen and checked the burners. All off. She stood in front of the living room fireplace but didn't smell anything unusual there. She moved through the house, ending up in the laundry room behind the kitchen, until satisfied that nothing was out of order.

Sometimes her mind did that to her. She could think of a truck zooming down the highway and she could generate the scent of its fuel as if she were drafting it on a bicycle.

Katie decided to go back to her room and see what she had to offer Janeal to wear. Katie had no idea what Lucille might have hastily packed for her yesterday.

Katie had stayed in this room often, as many of the Hope House women had, and knew the layout well. It was small, smaller than her little room at the Hope House, but entirely sufficient for a restful getaway. Four steps toward eleven o'clock put her at the bed on the left wall, under a window. A bookcase that doubled as a night table abutted the bed. The reading chair was two steps to the left, at nine o'clock, between the bookcase and the door. The closet: three steps ahead in the right wall, at the foot of the bed.

The air of the room smelled sweet, pleasant. Heavy. Katie wondered why she hadn't noticed it when she napped earlier. Sometimes fatigue took the edge off her senses.

She went to her travel bag from the reading chair and leaned over it to rifle through the contents. A fresh pair of denim jeans and cotton khakis, socks, three T-shirts. A Braille book she'd been reading. Lucille had packed all this for her. Most people found Lucille callous and unthoughtful, but she paid attention to details like this. She wasn't all sharp corners.

Katie felt light-headed and knelt in front of the chair. The sweet smell of the room seemed almost overwhelming.

She fished the jeans and her most comfortable cotton tee out of the bag to take to Janeal. She took a deep breath and shook her head. It seemed to be filled with cotton. She must be hungrier than she realized.

Holding the clothes on her lap, Katie leaned forward to rest her head on the cushion of the chair. She'd close her eyes for a minute.

67

Maybe it was that the muscles in the back of her neck finally loosened up while she stood under the scalding hot water, allowing blood to flow freely to her brain. Or maybe it was the shock of the water finally running cold, not gradually by degrees, but all at once, like a tossed bucket.

Janeal understood the significance of Sanso's desire to see her tonight. He wouldn't wait for her to contact him. He had Katie's address.

She gasped and fumbled for the faucets.

She needed to call him off. Which essentially meant she needed to get Katie out of the house. Where could they go? And how?

More fully alert than she had been all day, Janeal started to formulate a plan.

She would call a taxi as soon as she was dressed. She'd have it take them to the hotel—no, all the way to Santa Fe; she could afford it—where it would be harder for Callista or Sanso to find them. She'd need to withdraw enough cash in Taos to avoid a credit card trace after she left. What was her daily limit on that? It would have to get them through the next few days.

Janeal didn't think too much farther down the road than that. She saw Sanso adding Katie's name to his list, pursuing her in much the same fashion as he'd pursued Janeal, but without the love. That sick, twisted love.

Too much to think about now.

She stepped out of the shower and wrapped her wet body in a bathrobe she found hanging on a garment hook. Katie had not brought in the promised change of clothes yet.

Janeal opened the door and was rushed by thick black smoke that choked and blinded.

What?

"Katie?"

The smoke quickly filled the bathroom, drawn in by the fan. Was something on fire in the kitchen? Katie had said she was hungry . . .

"Katie!"

No answer. Janeal grabbed her pink blouse and tied it around her nose and mouth, lashing the arms together at the back of her head. There was nothing to help her eyes, which already burned.

In the hall her feet, still wet from water dripping off her legs, slipped a bit on the laminate flooring. She felt her way along the walls in the direction of the kitchen, already afraid of what she might find.

If she could see anything at all.

Janeal rounded the corner of the hallway and screamed. Flames, brilliant orange and blue fire, licked at every wall of the living room. The glass of the big picture window had already started to sag in its panels, creating vents at the top that allowed some of the smoke to escape.

Fear took over Janeal's body. Her will separated from her limbs and she collapsed on the floor, shaking. Numbness overtook her hands and feet and a chill rushed her body. An overwhelming belief that she was going to die pushed every other thought from her mind.

Lying on her back, she saw an upside-down view of the front door. Already the flames had consumed it and reduced the wood panel to a charcoal frame. If she could get through the flickering remains, she could reach the midnight blue air on the other side.

She closed her eyes to shut out her surroundings and flipped her body over onto her stomach, driving her elbow into the floor. A shooting pain zipped up her arm, forcing back the panic for precious seconds. Janeal found her hands and knees, and then her feet, and bolted out the door. She fell into the space where the porch had been and jarred her ankles, then scrambled onto the gravel drive, flipping herself over and doing a crabwalk to safety.

To her right, flames gained height in a dry pine tree. If no one had noticed the blaze before, they would now. Beneath it, the flames rose around the house like a tomatillo husk, rising out of the ground and stretching in an effort to peak over the roof.

She was hyperventilating.

Where was the fire department? Had anyone called? Her phone—was in the tote in the back bedroom. She couldn't see the room from here but thought the back of the house would probably look the same as the front.

Maybe Katie had a—

Katie.

Where was Katie?

Janeal began to shriek, barely getting her cries out on the wave of each fast breath she took. "Katie! Katie! Answer me! Kaaaatieeee!" She began to run a circumference of the house, hoping she had escaped through a window, a back door, anywhere.

In seconds she was back at the front of the house. Her feet were bleeding. Katie was still inside.

Janeal, help me. It was a memory, but as loud as if Katie had breathed the words right into her ear. Only this time the plea begged her to save herself. Janeal watched the flames turn blue. A window popped like a bubble. Wood groaned.

I can't. I'm so sorry, Katie, I can't.

Janeal raised her face toward the fire and closed her eyes, surrendering to the panic and the fear. The heat pushed back on her skin in pulsating waves. She could feel the steam rising from her damp hair. She took one step forward toward the burned-out front door. Miraculously, the hall beyond it had not ignited.

A gap opened up in the roof like a gateway to her own mind.

You can. You will do it because you want to live—and tonight, if Katie dies for the second time, so will you. You'll die right in that safe little place where you stand, and the rest of your life will be a living death.

Janeal's eyes snapped open. Her feet carried her back into the crackling house.

———

The ring of gasoline Sanso had poured around the little house was scaling the outer walls when a woman burst out the front door in a cloud of smoke. Katie?

Sanso raised his binoculars. The woman was screaming and running around the perimeter of the blaze. How in the name of everything he held dear had she made it out alive? Again! She vanished around the back side of the house and then returned to the front, stared at the door that had burped her out. The nitrous oxide should have knocked her out for as long as—

It wasn't Katie. Sanso dropped his binoculars into the grass and started running at the same time Janeal stepped back across the threshold of the death trap.

68

About a mile from the cabin, Robert noticed people standing out in their yards in the darkness. A couple here, a family there, a pocket of teenagers, all looking in the same direction. Eventually he made out what they were staring at: an orange glow that pulsed red and yellow.

When it registered that the light source was likely a fire, and that it didn't budge from the direction in which he was headed, Robert stepped on the gas. Then, when it became clear that the fire was his destination, he called 911 and reported that not only was there a fire, but an arsonist to be caught. The lengths that Janeal had gone to now had crossed all boundaries of decency. She would go to jail for this. Forever. He would not show up too late to catch her.

He refused to think that he was already too late for Katie.

His truck skidded on the gravel as he braked as close to the inferno as he dared. No sign of either woman in the—

Boom! An explosion rocked his vehicle and blew out the window, throwing shatterproof pieces of glass toward Robert. He threw up his hands to protect his face, then, as he dropped his arms and his jaw, he saw a black cloud rise over the west half of the house.

Maybe two minutes had passed since Janeal stepped out of the bathroom. In that wink of time, the outside of the house had become a blazing sun, and the inside a black pit of smoke.

The explosion changed everything.

Janeal was in the first of the three bedrooms when it happened, rocking the house and throwing her onto the bed. A rush of fire raced down the hall, a demon's breath, poking its head into the room for a terrifying second before getting sucked back out again. Janeal covered her head and groaned.

A flame leaped from the wall onto the bedspread.

Janeal rolled off, dropped to her belly in an attempt to stay beneath the smoke, then crawled to the door. She looked in the direction of the kitchen but couldn't see the end of the hall. The flames were moving outward, toward her.

Where was Katie? She didn't answer at the second bedroom.

Above the smoke, Janeal saw an orange glow that was the ceiling. Or had been the ceiling. A picture frame in the hallway lit up and began to disappear as if eaten away by acid.

Katie woke to thunder, then heard someone screaming. *Eeeeee! Eeeeee!* Then clearer: *Aaaaa—eeeee!* Eventually the long vowels turned into a name. Her name. *Kaaatieee!*

Her lungs needed air and drew it in hard. But there was no air, only smoke. The jolting coughs that followed hurt her head. Katie tried to sit up, but dizziness forced her back down.

Where was she?

Mrs. Weinstein's house. The living—no, the guest room. An intense heat to the right of her body forced Katie to roll to her belly, away from it. It. The bookcase. On fire.

"Janeal?" she said. The word scraped against her throat. "Janeal, the books are on fire."

"Katie!"

"Janeal. The books."

Wheezing and crying, someone dropped to the floor next to her. "Katie?"

"Why are the books on fire?"

"What is that tank on your bed?"

"What?"

Katie tried to make a connection between these two things as Janeal gripped her by the wrists and yanked her upright.

"Crawl!"

"Dizzy."

"Katie, we need to crawl out!" She shoved Katie between the shoulder blades. "I can't carry you! The whole house is on fire!"

Katie's head cleared to the degree that she found the strength to move her legs. When Janeal shoved her back again, then slipped a hand around her waist for support, Katie was on her hands and knees.

"Which way out?" she said.

Janeal started to sob. She pulled Katie toward her and gripped her in an embrace, pressing her wet cheek against Katie's dry skin. "I don't know," she said. "Something exploded out there."

Gas lines in the kitchen and laundry room, Katie thought.

"We can't go back that way."

To the front or back doors, Katie realized.

"I don't know if there's another way out."

69

The bookcase was a curtain of fire in front of the room's only window. The windows of the other rooms were similarly inaccessible as the house burned from the outside in.

Janeal couldn't imagine what that cylindrical green gas tank on the bed contained. Had contained. She hoped it was empty.

Katie had started to shake, maybe from shock or fear, and her coughs became more violent. Janeal's awareness of Katie's physical response to the crisis dried up her own tears. Katie had been here before, nearly eaten alive by Janeal's selfishness.

The fire was Janeal's fault.

Katie's burns were Janeal's choice.

Katie's life was Janeal's to save. This time, she would.

She unwrapped the blouse from her own face and tied it around Katie's to help stem the coughing.

"Let's go," Janeal said, not knowing to where. She took the lead. "Hold on to my ankle." They crawled off the braided rug Katie had been kneeling on, and Janeal dragged it out with them. Maybe she could use it to beat a path.

The hallway had become a burning tunnel now, and pieces of the textured ceiling were falling down like flaming rain. Their slow progress was made slower as Janeal kept stopping to beat fire like mosquitoes out of her clothing. Her own hair, now nearly dry, ignited more than once.

Halfway down the hall, in front of the bathroom, Janeal confirmed that their situation was worse than she had originally thought. The gas that had exploded in the kitchen hadn't burned itself but instead provided a continuing fuel to the front end of the house. She couldn't see the floor or the walls or the ceiling, only this inferno.

Janeal tried to beat it back with the rug, but in a cruel twist, the action only acted like a fan, feeding the hungry beast the oxygen that made it thrive.

She dropped to her elbows, breathless, coughing, eyes barely able to see anymore.

"How bad?" Katie said.

"I see a way out," Janeal said. It wasn't a lie. It was, maybe, the first honest thing Janeal had said to Katie since they'd met. She did see a way, a path to safety, a door to Katie's freedom, and it would be open for only seconds more.

There was that clock again, ticking down in Janeal's mind. *Ten . . . nine . . . eight . . .*

This time, she'd make a different choice. This awareness that there was nothing else to decide freed Janeal in that second to do the very thing she had become so good at in the last fifteen years:

Succeed.

No matter the cost.

"Stand up," she ordered Katie. When Katie didn't jump to her feet, Janeal yanked her up. She wrapped Katie like a burrito in the braided rug and forced the edges into her fingers. "Hold this." Katie gripped it, crossing the edges over her chest.

Janeal slipped the bathrobe she wore off her shoulders. Her skin was long dry on her exposed face, neck, and legs, but the heavy terry robe still had a little moisture in it. Not much, but enough.

She threw it over Katie's head.

"What are you—?"

"You can't see anyway. We're going through the front door. I'll show—"

An arm snaked out of the bathroom doorway and gripped Janeal by the hair.

"Must I keep bailing you out of trouble?" Sanso hissed.

Janeal gasped. Her hands went to her hair as he began dragging her away from Katie.

"Janeal!" Katie shouted.

"What are you doing?" Janeal cried.

"There's room for two in the bathtub," he growled. "We'll breathe air from the drainpipe. Old fireman's trick."

"Katie!"

"Where are you?" Katie screeched.

Janeal fell to her hands and knees, and her neck snapped back under Sanso's grip. She threw out her arms as he pulled her backward toward the bathroom, trying to make herself too wide to fit through. She held on to each side of the doorjamb with blistering fingertips.

She felt no shame over her nakedness. It seemed a fitting way to fight this particular battle, stripped down to the core of her true self.

"Katie, listen to me," she shouted above the fire's rumble.

Sanso roared and kicked at Janeal's hands. "Don't you understand what's happening, woman?" She felt the knuckles in her right fingers crack. "I'm trying to save your life."

No, I'm trying to save my life. And I'm the only one who can do it.

"Katie, you're between the bathroom and the kitchen. Three steps forward, sharp left, then straight out the front door."

"It's burning," she said, fear in the tremors of her voice.

"Yes. You've got to throw all that stuff off the second you're outside."

Janeal's left hand was losing its grip. Sanso had released her hair and was tugging at her armpits. She thought he would have overpowered her by now if he hadn't been weakened by the smoke himself.

His fury gathered steam, however, and he shouted at her. "Would you come any more quickly if I killed her first?"

"You hear me?" Janeal repeated to Katie. "Throw it off."

"What about you?"

Janeal saw the fire dancing in front of them, an excited, evil toddler anticipating the chance to pull the wings and legs off a bug. She lost her grip on the doorframe and her body jerked backward onto Sanso, toppling him. He crashed into a towel bar on the opposite wall and fell, smacking his head on the toilet seat.

"Janeal!" Katie shouted.

"I'll be right behind you," Janeal yelled, scrambling to her knees. She wouldn't be, of course. That was as she had planned it to begin with, knowing the flames would immobilize her unprotected body before she crossed the threshold. But she hoped that Katie would finally go.

Sanso was dazed but not out. He started to rise.

"What will you—"

"Get out! Go now!"

Janeal grabbed the knob and slammed the door, separating her from Sanso. Separating Sanso from *Katie.* The hot metal seared her palms. She planted a foot on each side of the frame and leaned back like a mountain climber in rappel.

Katie was still standing there.

"Go!" Janeal screamed.

Katie vanished into smoke.

On the other side of the door, Sanso jiggled the knob. "Janeal Mikkado!" he bellowed. The door rattled in its frame. "Don't waste your life."

Oh, she wouldn't. Not anymore. She could count on Sanso wasting his, though. He would spend his breath trying to sell her his lies and forget that bathtub drainpipe until it was too late. Indeed, he continued to jerk on the door.

Janeal had to close her eyes against the thickening blackness. It was harder and harder to breathe. She might not be strong enough to keep this devil of a man trapped.

The door, the door, the door. Focus on the door instead of on the pain. The pain will pass. It will burn away until all that is left is the only thing that matters: the best part of you, the only part of you that should be saved.

The best part.

The only part.

The rest, the waste, will burn away.

70

Robert was standing at the truck with one hand on the top of his head and the other on his belt when the flaming figure burst from the house and headed straight for him, blind and aimless, the sight of silent panic.

He caught the bundle and threw it to the ground. It flailed, trying to escape. He clawed at the fiery wrapping until it parted. A rug. The woman inside tore at the clothing over her head and ripped it off, coming up gasping.

"Katie," he breathed.

She panted for fresh air.

Robert pinned her legs and beat at the orange tongues in the hem of her pants until they turned smoky. He reached for her shoes and burned his hand on the melted soles. He grabbed the towel. Or whatever it was. He used this to pull the shoes off her feet before they, too, started to ooze like wax.

The pads of her feet were merely pink. She had fresh burns on her ankles. Her clothes were blackened but intact. Her hands untouched. Her face—he could think of nothing else he wanted to look at.

Robert raised her by the shoulders and pulled her to his chest awkwardly on the ground, kissing every inch of her face. He laughed at the same time tears spilled onto his cheeks.

"Not again," he whispered. "I couldn't have gone through that again."

Her breathing began to settle down. She placed her hand on his arm that surrounded her. "Where's Janeal?"

71

In the end, investigators never did find a trace of Janeal Mikkado or Salazar Sanso. Just ash—everywhere, ash—and one yard from the cast iron skeleton of the bathtub, a pile of six small diamonds embedded in a metal puddle of gold.

Two months after the fire, Katie turned the rehardened mass over in her fingers. She and Robert sat on padded wicker chairs in the garden room of Hope House, their feet stretched out on ottomans. Her bandaged ankles had nearly healed.

Robert had come up for the weekend with the results of the DNA test, which confirmed that Katie's saliva matched hair samples taken from Jane Johnson's apartment.

"You know what this means?" Robert said.

"That you finally believe there were two of me?"

"I guess I have to. It's still tricky though."

"You'll grow into the idea."

"But that's not what I was going to say. Guess again."

"It means that I've been fired from my New York career for going AWOL?"

"Nope. It means that the value of Jane Johnson's estate will be transferred to you."

"How will that work, if they think Jane is a missing person?"

"She's not missing. She suffered a tragic accident and has taken up a new life helping others."

Katie's mouth slackened. "It will take one talented attorney to explain that to a judge."

"One already did. The evidence was pretty convincing."

"So how much am I worth?"

"Enough to open a halfway house in every state if you want."

She gasped. "Enough to give the DEA their million back, then."

Robert laughed. "That would be the right thing to do."

"When did Harlan say he wants you back?" Katie asked.

"Today."

"But here you are."

"There's this girl I promised to meet. The granddaughter of someone who helped me find you. I worked it out with Lucille to find her a room at the house."

"And she agreed to bring someone not accompanied by a PO onto the property?"

"Your soft heart seems to be rubbing off on her," Robert said.

"And is it rubbing off on you too? Or does El Paso win the battle for your heart?"

"Oh no. You won that battle the first day I saw you here. Actually, I was thinking El Paso might need a Hope House of its own."

Katie rested her head against the back of her chair and smiled.

"I was thinking of changing my name back to Janeal," she said.

"You're messing with my head."

"I'm serious."

"Tell me why."

She dropped her jaw in exaggerated disbelief.

"Because that's who I really am."

"The better half of her."

"The half that lived."

Robert nodded and took her hand, squeezing it in his. "The half I loved from the beginning."

His winnowing fork is in his hand, and he will clear his threshing floor, gathering his wheat into the barn and burning up the chaff with unquenchable fire.

MATTHEW 3:12

Reading Group Guide

1. In an early draft of *Burn,* Janeal was kidnapped by Salazar Sanso in chapter 3. Later, the authors decided that Janeal would have willingly gone with him at his request. Why would she have done this? How were the choices Janeal had to make after her encounter with Sanso affected by her willing relationship as opposed to a forced confrontation?

2. Janeal hates Sanso but also is attracted to some of the very qualities she despises. What are these qualities? What causes her feelings about him to be divided? Why does he later become obsessed with her?

3. What or whom does Sanso represent to Janeal? Why?

4. What does Mrs. Marković mean when she says, "There are two chambers in every heart, one for Judas and one for John"? Do you agree with her?

5. Do you see Janeal's abandonment of Katie in the fire as a moral choice (to save or not to save a human life) or a practical one (to preserve one life rather than destroy two)? Or would you describe that moment of decision in other terms? Explain.

6. How is Robert's years-long pursuit of Sanso like Janeal's attraction to Sanso? How is it different? Does his commitment to bringing Sanso to justice bring out the best in Robert or the worst?

7. The Katie who lived represents the best of both women, Janeal and the Katie who died. Does this make her better than both women, or merely different from them? Which of Janeal's personality traits are preserved in Katie's

post-fire life? Was the price she had to pay to achieve her maturity worth it? Explain why or why not.

8. What blinds Robert to the truth about Katie and Janeal, before and after the fire? Why is he torn between his love for each of them?

9. Katie says to Robert, "What's more astounding than justice is mercy." What did she mean? How would Janeal have reacted to this remark if Katie had said it to her?

10. Imagine a choice you made in your past that, maybe in retrospect, has moral implications you didn't realize at the time. If you'd made a different decision, how might your life be different than it is today, for better or worse?

Q & A with Erin

1. What's the process like to write with a *New York Times* best-selling author like Ted Dekker?

Erin Healy: It's a little bit like following Tyra Banks down a runway in a bikini. Very intimidating! But it's also wonderful and exciting. Ted is as gracious as he is talented, and he's been patient with my sometimes-bumbling early attempts at novel writing.

Each of our stories has come about in its own way. For *Kiss,* I sent him several story concepts, and he pulled from one of those a device he liked: the idea that a woman could steal memories from other people. Then he built a story out of it that was quite different from the one I envisioned, but of course it was spectacular. *Burn,* interestingly enough, emerged from two ideas we had independently of each other that had similar themes of regret and second chances. We married those concepts and got a pretty baby out of the union. So the process has reinvented itself each time.

Ted and I spend a lot of time on the phone hashing out ideas. We talk and talk and talk. I've lost at least three phone batteries to Ted alone. Then I write and he reads and we talk some more. Then I write and rewrite, and he writes and rewrites, and we go back and forth like this until the story is born. It's a real synergistic endeavor, and each time I learn something new—like what not to eat if you want to look good on the runway in a bikini.

2. How will your solo novels be distinct from your novels with Ted Dekker?

EH: In many ways my solo novels will be similar to the co-authored books, which should create continuity for readers. Ted and I intentionally created novels that hearkened back to *Blink* and *Thr3e,* which were popular among Ted's female readers and weren't as dark as his more recent works. The co-authored novels are stories I wanted to tell: supernatural thrillers with strong Christian themes featuring strong female protagonists.

My stories will share these features. They'll continue to be commercial page-turners, but they'll also be distinct from Ted's solo fantasy and thriller brands.

I think of Ted's novels as **parables**. They say to readers, "The kingdom of heaven is like this," or, "The love of God is like this." I see my novels as **fables**, stories that explore the value of a character's choices. Such stories say to readers, "What is the significance of one choice over another? What is the impact on a physical life? A relational life? A spiritual life?" The answers won't always be black and white. *Kiss* is a fable about losing and finding memory. *Burn* is a fable about dying to self. *Never Let You Go* is a fable about forgiveness and bitterness.

The action of Ted's novels is largely **physical**. In my novels, the action will be more **psychological** and spiritual, driven by relationships and feminine sensibilities. If Ted's stories are like the films *300* or *The Gladiator,* mine will be like the psychological thrillers *House of Games* or Hitchcock's *Sabotage.*

In my novels, the suspense will driven by **high spiritual/moral stakes** but not necessarily **darkness and death**. I do think as Christians there are so many things that are worse than death. With the promises we've been given by Christ, we shouldn't fear death. We don't long for it necessarily, but we shouldn't fear it.

3. Talk to us about the "thin places" you like to explore in your novels.

EH: If you've read C. S. Lewis or anything about Irish history, you'll know that "thin places" is a Celtic idea. It describes locations in the world where the veil between physical and spiritual realities is so thin that a person can see through it—or perhaps even step between the worlds. Figuratively speaking, thin places represent moments of spiritual revelation, a connection between the seen and unseen elements of our lives.

The Irish girl in me has long been fascinated by this concept. My married name, my maiden name, and my given name are all Irish, so perhaps it was inevitable. As a young adult I spent half my waking hours in the Pentecostal church, and I came away from that tradition with an unshakable belief in the existence of an active spiritual world. I was a high-school sophomore when my mother gave me a copy of the new book *This Present Darkness,* and the imagery of the spiritual world invading this one stayed with me.

I don't expect my stories to be as literal as Frank Peretti's. But I do hope that they will have a similar shoulder-shaking effect. Early in my editorial career Dean Merrill challenged me with a critique of books published in the Christian marketplace. The weaker ones, he said, cause readers to say, "Amen, I agree with you!" The stronger ones, on the other hand, cause readers to say, "I never thought of it that way before."

I hope my exploration of fictional thin places will cause readers to think of their spiritual and physical lives in new, desegregated ways.

4. Give us a sneak peek into how you came up with the concept for your first solo work, *Never Let You Go.*

EH: Have you ever been in a relationship that made you think, *So and so is a good person, but man, I hope I never do anything to get on their bad side!* These are nice people, mature adults, but they have an edge about them that is bitter and unforgiving. They don't easily let go of offenses. I've known a few people like this. I could name them but won't—they'd never forgive me. What's unique about the people I'm thinking of is that I've also had the opportunity to meet their parents. In one particularly startling encounter, one of these parents began rattling on about an age-old resentment, and it was so clear to me as an outsider that the child's bitterness was rooted in the parent's. It was as if it was genetic, not just learned, but ingrained.

These people are Christians, by the way. As a Christian parent, the revelation caused some soul searching. My wheels started turning: Why do some Christians find it so hard to forgive? I think it some cases it's because the harm done to us is real and our offense is justifiable. In some cases it's because we see ourselves as good people; we don't necessarily grasp the magnitude of what we've been forgiven. And in some cases it's because we honestly believe that unforgiveness doesn't harm anyone except (maybe) ourselves.

So I created a character who believes all these things and then challenged her with a notion: What if your justifiable bitterness cost you the one treasure you hold dear in the world—the life of your only child? And *Never Let You Go* grew out of that question.

5. Tell us more about the spiritual elements of Never Let You Go.

EH: I have a 15-month-old who is at the stage where he wants to hold all of his toys at the same time. He can manage to get one or two of them in his arms and then I just enjoy watching him as he tries to pick up another one and one of them falls. He does this juggling act trying to hold on to things. The story *Never Let You Go* is about what you choose to hold on to and the idea that we can't hold on to everything. You can't have your cake and eat it too. You can't hold on to bitterness and unforgiveness and love at the same time. Which one are you going to hold on to? *Never Let You Go* refers to a lot of different things depending on the character that it's in reference to so it's a multi-layered title, but that's the key spiritual element: are you never going to let go of love or are you never going to let go of bitterness? And the costs of both are very high. It's not an easy choice.

6. What's the most unexpected joy of being a published author?

EH: Having meaningful encounters with complete strangers. In the name of transparency, I have to say: Social media freaks me out. I've hired someone to help me cope with the bigness of it. I'm a very private, introverted person. Until very recently, if someone said "Facebook" my left eye would start to twitch and my shoulder would spasm. Against all odds, I've learned how to update my Fan Page, I'm blogging sporadically, I have a Twitter handle, and my Web site is undergoing a complete redesign after only eighteen months of life.

It has come as a complete surprise to me that people really want to connect. When a fan asked if Ted and I would keep writing together, the guy was thrilled when I suggested he should poll other fans to see if we *should* keep writing together. (Still awaiting results!) I've been encouraged by people who don't know me but feel they do, through reading *Kiss*. I've received invitations to write. My favorite so far is an e-mail from a sixth grader who is 100 percent sure she wants to be an editor when she grows up. She wrote to ask me for advice on how she should go about it. Go figure: I dropped everything to answer her right away.

6. What's your perfect day as a writer?

EH: My perfect day is an Irish day: cold, wet, and gray, with the family tucked in at home and a bottomless pot of coffee on hand. On a perfect writing day there is time to read for pleasure and inspiration. There is silence and space to hear what God might want to say. There is opportunity to be surprised by a new idea, maybe a new connection within a story. Perfection is 3,000 clear-headed words and a pretty good idea of where they're leading me. I wrap up in time to make dinner for my family. Hubby tells me what I need to know about a particular firearm or a sports scene I'm writing. Daughter tells me the latest details about the story *she's* writing. And son brings me *Brown Bear, Brown Bear* to read to him before bedtime.

Before *Burn* . . . there was *Kiss*.
Don't miss the first Dekker/Healy novel.

SOMETIMES DYING WITH THE TRUTH
IS BETTER THAN LIVING WITH A LIE.

Losing everything has made Lexi
hold those she loves tightly.
Hell is determined to loosen her grip.

NEVER
LET
YOU
GO

ERIN HEALY

The suspense of Ted Dekker
The spiritual warfare of Frank Peretti
The relational drama of Karen Kingsbury

IN STORES MAY 2010

{ An excerpt from *Never Let You Go* }

For seven years, Lexi Solomon had been as cold as the chill wind that raced down the mountain above her home. She was not ice-in-her-veins cold, or I'll-freeze-you-with-a-glance cold, but numb with the chill that came from being uncovered and abandoned.

Only the love of her daughter, a warm and innocent love that was so easy to return, had prevented her from dying of exposure.

At the back of the Red Rocks Bar and Grill, Lexi checked to make sure the rear stoop wasn't icy, then exited and pulled the kitchen door closed. The blustery elements had spent decades huffing and puffing on the backside of the local haunt with nothing to show for the effort but a tattered awning and a battered screen door. The stalwart cinderblock, painted to match the russet clay dirt that coated Crag's Nest, was as stubborn as the snow that refused to melt before midsummer at this altitude. And it was only March.

At her throat Lexi clutched her ratty down jacket, the same one she had worn since high school, while she fumbled with the restaurant keys in her other gloveless hand. She'd forced her only pair of gloves into her daughter's coat pockets that morning because Molly had lost hers coming home from school.

Which could only mean she hadn't been wearing them. Chances were, Molly hadn't worn the gloves today either. Well, she was only nine. Lexi smiled at that and thought she might get them back. If only she could be a kid again, oblivious to weather and wet.

Lexi shoved the key into the cheap lock and turned it easily. That hamburger grease coated everything. Above her head, a yellow bug light shone over a cracked concrete slab. Her tired breath formed a cloud in the night air and then a fog on the wire-threaded glass of the door.

It was 2:13 a.m. Thirteen minutes later than Lexi usually locked up, thanks to the frozen computer that she had to reboot twice before she could close out the cash drawer and lock the day's receipts in the safe. Thirteen minutes gone from the precious few she got to spend with Molly, curled up next to her in their one flimsy bed. Between Lexi's two jobs and Molly's school days, she figured they had an average of ninety-four minutes together, awake, per day. It wasn't enough.

Lexi closed the restaurant every Monday, Thursday, and Friday nights. *Restaurant* was too generous a word for the greasy spoon a half mile off the main tourist drag, too far off to draw many out-of-towners. But the staff was family-like enough, and the locals were loyal and tipped fair, and the extra fifty dollars she got for being the last to leave three times a week didn't hurt. Every little bit put her and Molly that much closer to a better situation. A better home in a better part of town. A more reliable car. Warmer clothes.

Molly needed new shoes, and once Lexi got caught up on that past-due utility bill, she thought she'd have enough to buy the pair with sequins stitched onto the sides. Maybe for Molly's birthday. She'd seen her daughter bent over a picture of the shoes in the Sunday circulars left out by their roommate, Gina.

After jiggling the locked kitchen door for good measure, Lexi turned her back on the glare of the naked bulb and headed toward her Volvo. The sturdy old thing was parked on the far side of the sprawling blacktop, fender nosing a swaying field of tall grasses, because that was where the only operating lamp-post stood, and Lexi was no idiot when it came to vacant lots and late-night lockups.

The wind cut through her thin khaki pants, numbing her thighs.

She fingered the can of pepper spray on her key chain as she passed the shadowy Dumpster behind the kitchen. A large man could squeeze between it and the trash can's cinderblock cove easily enough. The dishwasher Jacob did this on his breaks to catch a smoke, because the manager wouldn't tolerate cigarettes, not even outside.

A dark form darted out, leaping over the long shadow of her body cast by the gold light behind. She flinched, then scolded.

"Scat, Felix." The resident alley cat carried something in his mouth. Lexi guessed a chicken bone, but it might have been a mouse. He jumped the wobbly wood-slat fence between the restaurant and the dry cleaner next door.

The grasses in the field, as tall as her shoulders, whispered secrets.

She stepped from the slab onto the asphalt lot. The spotlight over her dull silver Volvo, which tilted to the left due to a weak strut, went out for a second, then hiccupped back to life. It was only a matter of time before the lamp finally died, then weeks or months would probably pass before the property manager would get around to resurrecting it. Each time she locked up, she found herself hoping the light would last one more night. She weighed whether she ought to start parking closer to the kitchen. Just in case.

Just in case what? Tara had been murdered in bright shopping mall, in a bustling crowd. Maybe where a woman parked in the darkness of night didn't matter as much as she hoped.

Lexi's soft-soled shoes made an audible, squishy noise on the cold blacktop as she quickened her step, eyes sweeping the lot like some state-of-the-art scanner. Her keys sang a metallic song as they swung against the can of pepper spray. There was an extra can in the book bag slung over her shoulder. Another one in her glove box. A fourth buried in the planter outside her kitchen window at home, right by the front door. Lexi wondered for the millionth time how old Molly should be before starting to carry some in her backpack.

Glimpsing the dark glass of the car's rear doors, she wished again that she had a key fob that could turn on the interior lights from a cautious distance.

The parking lot light gasped again and this time faded to black. The steady yellow light behind her also flickered once and died, stranding Lexi in black air exactly halfway between the restaurant and car. She stopped. A second later, two at most, the light over the Volvo staggered back to relative brilliance.

She gasped. The thin air knifed her throat. The grasses had fallen silent, and the winds were as still as if God had stepped between them and the earth.

All four doors of her car were flung wide. Two seconds earlier they had been sealed shut, but now they gaped open like Lexi's disbelieving mouth, popped open with the speed of a switchblade, with the flip of an invisible lever, the flick of an illusionist's light.

A heavy hand came down on her shoulder from behind. Lexi yelped and whirled out from under the palm.

"Sexy Lexi."

Her hand was at her throat, her pulse pounding through the layers of the thin jacket, her breathing too shallow for her to speak.

A slim white envelope fluttered between the restless fingers of the man's left hand. A tattoo peeked out from under his T-shirt sleeve on the left, filling most of his upper arm. It was a set of keys, skeleton keys, hanging from a wide round ring.

He was middle aged, sallow skinned, and his dark hair needed a trim. Oily strands flipped up in little curls that stuck out the bottom of a knit cap. The scrappy T-shirt looked thin across his narrow chest and sinewy arms, but he did not shiver in the low temperatures.

He said, "I half expected you'd be out of town after all these years."

Lexi's fright came off its startled high and settled into unease. She took a step back, glancing involuntarily at her car. Years ago, Warden Pavo had taken adolescent delight in pranks. She wondered how many people would have to be involved to pull off one like this.

"Why would I leave Crag's Nest if I thought you'd never set foot here again, Ward?"

"Warden."

"Yeah. I forgot."

He smirked. "How's the family?"

"Fine."

"Your mom's still globetrotting?"

Lexi stared at him, finding his interest in her family new and strange, and perhaps offensive.

"Any improvement in dear old dad?" he asked.

"What do you want, Ward?"

"Warden."

Lexi crossed her arms to hide their quivering.

"What?" he said. "I heard that your old man fell off the deep end, and I've been worried about you."

"You've never worried about anyone but yourself. Besides, that happened years ago."

"After that whole thing with your sister. What a tragedy. Man, I'm really sorry about that, you know."

Ward removed a nylon lanyard from the pocket of his jeans. A small keychain weighted the end of it. Twirling the cord like a propeller blade, he wound it around his wrist, wrapping and unwrapping it.

Lexi looked away. "It's behind us now," she said.

"Is it? Von Ruden's up for parole. I assume you heard."

She hadn't. A shiver shook her shoulders though the wind had not picked up again. Up for parole after only seven years.

Norman Von Ruden had killed Tara, Lexi's older sister. He knifed her in a food court at lunch time during the Christmas rush, when there were so many people that no one noticed she'd been attacked until someone accidentally whacked her crumpled form with a shopping bag. After Tara's funeral, Lexi's father raised the drawbridge of his mind and left her with her mother on the wrong side of the moat.

"Why is it that whenever you show up, I can expect bad news?"

"Aw, that's not fair, Lexi. I'm only here to help you, as always."

"One finger is too many to count the ways you've helped me."

"Be nice."

"I am. You could have helped me years ago by refusing to sell to Norm."

"C'mon now. You know that's not what happened."

Lexi turned away and moved quickly toward her gaping Volvo.

Ward's voice chased her. "Norm was Grant's client, not mine."

Lexi kept walking. Ward followed.

"If you blame anyone, gotta blame Grant." Ward's keys clanked together as they hit the inside of his wrist. "You can blame Grant for a whole lotta your problems."

"I'd appreciate you not bringing Grant up," she said.

It was true that Lexi's husband had not paved the streets of her life with gold. The same year Tara was killed, Grant drove their only car out of town and never came back. Lexi, having no money to pay for a divorce, never received divorce papers from Grant either and sometimes wondered whether abandonment laws alone made their separation official.

Beyond that, she'd managed to prevent her thoughts from chasing Grant too often. Only Molly was worth Lexi's wholehearted concentration. For Molly's sake, Lexi had made a vow to be more clearheaded than Grant ever was.

Lexi reached out and slammed the door behind the driver's seat. The metal frame was warm to the touch, sun-baked without the sun. The unexpected sensation caused her to hesitate before she walked around the back to the other side and slammed the other rear door. It, too, was unnaturally heated. She wiped her palm on the seat of her pants.

"If that's all you came to tell me, good night."

"But it's not."

Ward stopped twirling the lanyard and stood at the driver's door. She glanced at him across the roof of the Volvo and took new notice of the envelope he held and extended toward her.

"Picked up your mail for you."

"How?"

"Intercepted the mailman."

"Why?"

"Save you the trouble."

"Seeing as it's no trouble, please don't do it again."

"You really could be more grateful."

She leaned against the car and lay her arm across the roof, gesturing that he give the envelope to her. He dangled it above her open palm. She snatched it out of his fingers.

"Thank you," she said, hoping he would leave. She lifted the flap of her book bag, intending to cram the letter into the side.

"Open it."

"I will, when I get home."

"Now." Ward's keys cut the air on that whirling cord again. Rather than irritate her, the motion threatened. Those keys were weapons that could inflict serious pain if they hit her between the eyes with any momentum. She thought she saw them striking out at her and jerked back, then felt embarrassed.

"I read my mail without an audience."

"Add a little excitement to your life. Do it differently tonight."

"No."

"It's not a suggestion."

Lexi closed the third door and made her way back around the rear of the car, where Ward was waiting. She focused on getting into the front seat and maintaining a confident voice. "Ward, it's late. I'm going home. My daughter—"

"Molly. She's all grown up and fresh to be picked by now, isn't she?" Heat rose up Lexi's neck. "I saw her at the school today. They're a bit lax over there about security, in my humble opinion."

The tears that rushed to Lexi's eyes were as hot and blinding as her anger. That level of offensiveness didn't deserve a response. In two long strides she reached the open driver's side door and, still holding the mystery letter, placed her left hand on the frame to balance her entry.

Ward's lanyard snaked out and struck her wrist, knocking her hand off the door, which slammed shut. The paper fluttered to the ground. She stared at it stupidly, not comprehending what was happening.

He stooped to pick it up. "Read the letter, Lexi, then I'll let you go home."

Her wrist bone ached where the keys had struck it. She took a step away from Ward, then turned the letter over to read the return address. The envelope was from the office of a neighboring county's district attorney. It quivered in her fingers. She held it under the light of the lamppost for several seconds. The beam flickered.

"The postmark on this is more than a month old," she said.

"Yeah, well, I didn't say I picked up your mail *today*."

Her perspiring fingers were tacky and warped the linen stationery slightly. Lexi tapped the short side of the envelope on the roof of the Volvo, then tore a narrow strip off the opposite side and let the scrap fall to the ground. She withdrew a piece of heavy folded paper, then spread it flat on the hood.

She thought it was a notice of Norman Von Ruden's parole hearing. She saw, at a glance, phrases like *your right to participate* and *verbal or written testimony*. But a red scrawl like a kindergartener gone crazy with a Sharpie obscured much of the text. A balloon poked by half a dozen arrows surrounded the date and time. Stick figures at the bottom of the page depicted a man coming out of an open jail cell, and a happy woman waiting for him.

Ward was breathing across Lexi's ear. She felt his body too close behind her.

"Isn't that nice?" he said, pointing. "That's Norm, and that's you!"

Lexi looked at the backside of the envelope to see if he'd tampered with the letter but it was still securely sealed. He knew. How could he know? She pushed off the car and shoved him away from her, leaving the letter behind. She snapped at him so that he wouldn't hear the fear she felt.

"You're sick, Ward. I'm going home."

"I'm entirely well, though I appreciate your concern. Aren't you going to ask me what it means?"

"It means you haven't changed one bit since the last time I saw you. I don't have time for your pranks."

She pulled the door open and dropped onto the seat without taking the book bag off her shoulder.

Ward picked up the abandoned letter and turned it over, holding it out to her. He propped his forearms on the open door and lowered the sheet, scrawled with another juvenile drawing, to her eye level. A red figure that looked like a child with *x*'s for eyes was visible through the glass door of an oven.

"No prank, Sexy Lexi."

Lexi felt blood rush out of her head. She took a shallow breath and lowered her voice.

"Okay. What does it mean, Ward?"

"War-*den*. *Warden*. Get it right."

There was no sarcasm in her voice now. "Warden. What does it mean?"

"That's my girl. It means—if you love your daughter like I think you do—that you are going to show up at Matthew's hearing next Friday and testify on his behalf."

"What? Why?"

"Because you love your daughter."

"I can't do that."

"You can't love her?"

"No! I can't . . . Norman Von Ruden? He's insane."

"Not clinically."

"Don't do that. They diagnosed him with something."

"Nothing a fine shrink and a few bottles of pills couldn't handle."

"No." She shook her head. "No. I hate him."

"You loved him once. I'll wager there's still whore in you."

Lexi lashed out, clawing the letter out of his hands and scratching the skin of his knuckles. His keys fell onto the blacktop.

"How dare you!"

Ward seized both her wrists easily and shoved her back down onto the seat of the car.

"He killed my sister! He wrecked my family! My parents—"

"Will be mourning the loss of little miss Molly as well if you don't come to the party. So be wise about it, or I'll tell your secrets to everyone you love—and plenty of people you don't."

"Why are you doing this?"

"Because you should have chosen me, Lexi. All those years ago, you chose Von Ruden. But you should have chosen me." He crumpled the letter into a ball and tossed it across Lexi onto the passenger seat.

The light over the car died again. In the blackness, Lexi reached out and slammed the car door, then punched down the manual lock, then contorted her body to hit the three remaining knobs in sequence.

"Save the date," he said through the glass.

She willed the wind to carry his words away, but the air was as still as her dead sister, bleeding on the sticky tiles of the mall floor.